A Promise at Midnight

by

jj Keller

A Promise at Midnight

Contact Information: info@thewildrosepress.com

Cover Art by *Kim Mendoza*

The Wild Rose Press, Inc.
PO Box 708
Adams Basin, NY 14410-0708

Visit us at www.thewildrosepress.com

Publishing History
First Edition, 2023
Trade Paperback ISBN 978-1-5092-4874-2
Digital ISBN 978-1-5092-4875-9

Published in the United States of America

Henry sat at a round, shiny table. A skinny white-haired blonde, with duck feathers fluttering, lifted her green skirt and exposed a garter. She sat on his lap. Her upper body hid his facial expression. He wasn't fighting her off, and he didn't sound like he was in pain. As a matter of fact, he was saying something under his breath.

Emma stood in front of them, her back getting straighter like the arrow clenched in her hand. He couldn't see her, either because of the feathers or the blond hair which was as large as the piano player's bowler hat. He lowered his hand. A cigar was wedged between two fingers. She stuck the arrow straight into the stink stick, piercing and bonding the cigar to the tabletop.

The music stopped. Red dress lady stopped tapping. Henry moved his arm around the blonde's waist. She giggled, and he lifted her from his lap. Emma stared straight into his cheating eyes. How could he carry on with this…this trollop a few hours after kissing her?

"Emma." He lifted an eyebrow, then tugged the arrow out of the cigar, and extinguished the loathsome split stick in a glass of beer. "What a pleasant surprise."

The harlot whispered into his ear. He shook his head. She frowned and said something else.

"No, Lulu. Go entertain the customers." He tapped her bottom, shooing her away, and then lifted his hand to smooth his tousled hair.

Dedication

In memoriam of my father, your story will live forever
in my heart.

Chapter 1

Emma Cody turned the pages until she came to the introduction. *The Wild, Wild West*. *"Blood dripped along the stagecoach window frame. The wind blew crimson dustings onto his leather riding gloves. Bullets whizzed through the stagecoach. They were going to die!"*

"Mac, the mysterious dark character who had joined them at the last way station, drew his six-shooter from its hard leather holster and aimed."

What malarky! Who wrote this nonsense? As if the plot, a catastrophe for sure, would ever really happen in true form.

Front Range Mountains, visible through the coach windows, marked the end of the journey for her. She tucked the dreadful novel into her bag and tried to ignore the windbag sitting beside her.

"This coach travels at a pace between five to twelve miles an hour." Warren repeated the same litany when Mrs. Landers and her companion, Treasure, came on board, at Camp Dunlap, on the northern end of Walnut Creek. The jostling and jolting of the carriage didn't unnerve Emma as much as the boring story. The man hadn't stopped talking since St. Louis...five days ago.

"This here Wells-Fargo Stagecoach is brand-spankin' new." The thin man flipped his hat over in his hands, his glance scanning his captive audience. He shook his bald head as if in disbelief. "Yes, siree, as an employee and quality-check rider for the coach-line they allowed me to put the emblem on this beauty by myself, two weeks ago." He leaned forward and lowered his voice. "Can you believe in this year, eighteen hundred and seventy-seven, a horse-drawn carriage cost around one thousand dollars? Whewee."

Mrs. Ethel Landers, the heavy-set woman seated across from him gasped and covered her mouth with gloved hands. The banana sleeves of her black crape dress rubbed, creating a sound like a cat scratching on the door.

Mr. Warren tugged the bottle green lapel of his jacket, revealing a gold vest underneath. "Yes siree, Mrs. Landers, sure cost a bunch. I'm ridin' all the way to Santa Fe. Why with six good horses, we can outrun any Injuns bold enough to get close."

Mrs. Landers clutched her crushed velvet travel bag tight to her bosom with one arm and grabbed her pale thin traveling companion with the other. "Did you hear that, Treasure? Indians."

"I did, Mrs. Landers. I did." Treasure's high-pitched young voice vibrated off the paneled walls of the coach. Her dark-brown eyes sparkled, and her tiny leather clad feet patted a quick cadence on the floor, whether from nervousness or habit Emma didn't know.

"Mr. Warren, there isn't a reason to get the ladies excited about something which is unlikely to happen," Mr. Courtland stated. He tipped his black cowboy hat, displaying a firm chin and full lips.

Mr. Henry "King" Courtland had appeared asleep, yet an energy exuded from him. He'd jumped on board eight miles back when his horse went lame, told everyone his name, and sat across from her. He stretched his long canvas covered legs and hadn't twitched, until now. He was an enigma, and her curiosity about his nonchalant attitude drew her.

Mr. Courtland's blond chest hairs showed through the opening of his white shirt. Of course, she looked away and detested herself for continually returning her glance to his body. She didn't know why he fascinated her. She'd seen a man's bare chest before, discreetly from the second story window of her home, so why did her heart flutter simply by glancing at this man's bits of fur?

Mr. Warren took her hand into his. "Miss Cody, I didn't mean to frighten you."

His sweaty palm oozed through her thin yellow traveling gloves. She snatched her hand from his grasp. "I'm not afraid, Mr. Warren," she muttered.

Mr. Courtland grunted and shifted in the seat. His coat, made of the finest cloth, and his black and green silk waistcoat were fashionable. The glass buttons, catching the light, winked at her. His untied black string tie hung alongside his shirt. Mortified she'd spent time staring at him, she glanced at her lap, then up and met his stare. Blast, his glimmering eyes sent tingles to her stomach.

Mr. Courtland lifted his hat and grinned, as if he knew her thoughts. Heat rose to her face. She raised her lavender scented handkerchief to dab perspiration, but more to hide her embarrassment at being caught doing the unthinkable. He clearly was not a gentleman.

His coat slid further to the back, revealing a pair of guns. The pliable leather of his gun belt and the scuffed leather of his boots were the only pieces of his attire showing wear, the rest appeared crisp and clean, fresh from the trading post shelves or mail order catalog.

"Miss Emma doesn't appear to be afraid of Indians or any other varmint that's likely to try and take advantage of her." Mr. Courtland's deep husky voice vibrated throughout the carriage. If his facial expression provided any indication of his true opinion, then he was teasing her.

She met his insolent bold stare, nodded in acknowledgement, and the blasted fellow chuckled. Odious man, what right did he have to judge. Now she wasn't embarrassed, but rather annoyed.

"You're going to Fort Collins to see a relative Mrs. Cody, or rather Miss?" Mrs. Landers' lips formed a tight line. The elderly lady believed she should be traveling with a companion, as would most upper class, unmarried ladies.

"I'm going to Pineview, several miles outside of Fort Collins, to help my sister-in-law through her lying-in-period. My traveling companion became ill and could not attend, but I had already given my word to Rachel." Emma would be there to support her during the final stages of pregnancy regardless of how many Indians attacked the coach. Family stuck together.

"Oh well, honey-child, you're safe with us." Mrs. Landers nodded. The peacock feathers, attached to the top of her hat, rapped against the back of the carriage. Her jowls vibrated like a grisly bulldog.

"Thank you, Mrs. Landers. That is a comfort to me," she politely responded.

"Not to worry, Miss Emma, I'll protect you." Mr. Warren sat up straighter on the seat as if a rod had been inserted in his back.

"Umph," grunted Mrs. Landers. Emma struggled to keep from laughing.

"And you and Treasure, too, Mrs. Landers." Mr. Warren's face brightened to a deep red. He reached across her frontside to open the window cover, letting dust and cool wind invade the small space.

She held a half-lace handkerchief across the lower part of her face, trying to prevent the dirt devils from settling in her nose and throat. Disgusting man, this trip would not end soon enough. Suddenly aware of the cloud of soil hovering over the group he lowered the flap, then raised it again with a snap. Curiosity took hold, and a touch of fear of the unknown created goosebumps on her forearms.

"Oh my!" Mr. Warren screeched like a night owl.

Mr. Courtland raised the flap on his window. She leaned forward to peer outside. A band of riders, shotguns and pistols raised, were fast approaching the coach.

"Yee-haw," Tater shouted. The snap of the leather reins spurred the horses into a gallop. Loud blasts, from rifle fire, vibrated throughout the stagecoach. As a sharpshooter, the second driver, Mick, claimed to be better than Wyatt Earp. Emma hoped he hadn't been boasting, and silently prayed the driver could outrun the outlaws.

The coach rocked from side to side. She tightened her grip on the rawhide strap attached near the door frame. *Don't panic.*

Mrs. Landry fainted, falling directly into Mr. Warren's lap, her hat feathers inserted into his peppered chin hair. Treasure sniffled and clung to Mr.

Courtland's arm. Emma took a deep gulp of air. Along with the stagecoach, her stomach rolled and heaved.

"Miss Treasure, release my arm and get down on the floor. I need to help Mick."

"We're going to die." Treasure's lips wobbled.

Mr. Courtland pried her hand from his arm. Physically shaking, she lowered her thin calico clad body to the floor, just in time as a bullet pierced through the coach and embedded itself between Emma and Mr. Warren.

She glanced out the window. The click-bang from Mick's shotgun stopped. True terror gripped her as thundering horse hooves drew closer to the stagecoach. Her life couldn't end here, in the wilderness of the strange state of Colorado.

A bandana covered face appeared in the window frame. Her throat closed off.

Mr. Courtland palmed his pistol. Quick as lightning, he leaned out the window and fired shots.

Her chest tightness pressed deeper. "Mr. Courtland, if I could have your second revolver or the one from inside your jacket pocket, I'll help." She released the leather strap and removed her glove. Mr. Courtland turned a surprised expression to her but reached for his gun.

Mr. Warren disengaged Mrs. Landers, who plopped deeper between his legs. "Miss Emma, a lady does not launch a pistol. Get on the floor with Treasure."

"She does if she doesn't want to be shot or violated." Emma read enough Penny Dreadful novels, and heard enough tales, she understood the consequences of being caught by bandits or Indians.

She'd been taught the mechanics of a pistol and rifle and hoped she'd be able to shoot another human.

"You can call me, King." He smiled, showing rows of perfect teeth, and extended his pistol. She leaned forward to take the gun, and the scent of his bay rum soap rose to her nostrils, tantalizing her as much as his cool demeanor.

She reviewed the piece, then lifted the window shade. She leveled the sight on a bandit, wearing a red and white bandana, and pulled the trigger. He clutched his leather clad chest and fell to the side of his horse. *My God, what have I done?* Hand shaking, she lowered the killing weapon to her lap and took a deep breath. Billows of dust rose, there were so many of them.

Mr. Courtland clicked off shots like it was a duck hunt.

Out of the corner of her eye, a man with a cowboy hat and disfigurement running from his forehead to his cheek pointed a pistol toward Mr. Courtland. She swung her gun toward *scar*face, lined the barrel, and shot. It missed, but the bandit retreated.

An outlaw dressed in linen-looking black shirt and quality black trousers reined his horse outside her window. "Emma," he mouthed the words.

My God! Bile left her stomach and threatened to erupt from her mouth. She lowered the gun and prayed she was wrong. He wouldn't rob a stagecoach.

A bullet flew past, close enough that loose pieces of her hair fluttered in the wind. Mr. Warren fainted, fell forward, and encompassed Mrs. Landers in a strange pose. She didn't have time to think inconsequential things and gripped the wooden pistol handle, pulled the cock, aimed toward a bandit wearing a black Sombrero and pulled the trigger. The recoil of the gun made her arm hurt; however, she'd hit the target. His hat fell to the middle of his back as he slid from his horse.

She lined up the next shot, until she heard the all too familiar voice again.

"Retreat. Fall back." His voice confirmed her suspicions. Her heart pounded, not because of fear, rather because the leader of the bandits was a lying bastard.

The stagecoach slowed to a stop. Her eyes watered, and she coughed as dust and gunfire sulfur remnants settled. The drivers hadn't said anything. Were they dead?

Light from bullet holes lit the interior, making the dreadful incident surreal. "Treasure?" she whispered. Had the sweet girl been hit?

She came out from under Mrs. Landers' skirts and glanced around. "Is it over, Miss Emma?" The whites of her eyes were large in her colorless face. The piece of lace on top of her head slid to the side and tendrils of glossy black hair fell to her thin shaking shoulders.

"I hope so." She exhaled and glanced at Henry, refusing to think of him as King. "Mr. Courtland?"

"I'm going to find out what's happened. I want all of you to remain inside the coach. Emma, here are some shells. Reload. If I don't return in a few minutes, shoot to kill anyone who comes near you."

"Henry," she whispered. A look of surprise crossed his face when she called him by his given name. Her arms shook, small tremors running clear through to her fingertips. "Be careful."

He smiled, exhibiting a dimple on the right side of

his face and crinkles around his eyes. Tipping the bill of his hat, he slid from the coach.

****

"Miss Emma." King wanted to announce he planned to open the door, so she wouldn't shoot him. He'd witnessed her skill at shooting the .45. She was capable of hitting his heart dead-on. Except for that one time she'd hesitated, and the surprised expression changed her face almost as if she recognized the bandit. A crazy thought. She said she was from Fort Wayne. How would she know an outlaw in Colorado? The woman became a mystery he wanted to slowly solve.

"Yes, Mr. Courtland." Her voice cracked.

"I'm going to open the door." He tugged the coach door with the same caution he would use moving around a rattlesnake. The barrel of his gun was pointed directly on his forehead. Her beautiful green eyes, with the brown starburst at the center, glanced behind him before she lowered the pistol.

"Didn't know if they were holding you hostage," she said and coughed delicately as the dust continued to settle around the coach.

"Are they gone, Mr. Courtland?" Treasure asked from her squat position on the floor.

"Yes Miss Treasure, for now they are gone." He locked glances with Emma and held out his hand, expecting her to give him the gun and wanting above all else for her to jump into his arms because she was safe. "The drivers have been shot. Anyone shot in here?"

"No, we're all unharmed. I'm sure the outlaws won't return." She handed him the revolver, straightened her satin bonnet, and gathered her muslin dress.

He extended his hand. She took hold and climbed from the coach. Treasure breathed heavily and crawled to the edge of the opening, then King helped her out. Why was Emma so confident the bandits wouldn't return?

Mr. Warren and Mrs. Landers stirred. The image of the robust woman's face between the skinny man's thighs gave a new meaning to burlesque.

King pushed down the urge to laugh. "Mr. Warren, the bandits fled. You'll help Mrs. Landers?"

Mr. Warren raised his head, looked at King, then glanced at his lap. The Wells-Fargo aficionado jiggled his legs as if ants invaded his breeches. Unable to resist, King chuckled. "Need to check the boot for a necessities kit."

Mr. Warren shoved her large shoulders and shifted on the seat.

King felt the stagecoach rock and looked up. Emma perched on top of the conveyance, turned Mick's head, and put her fingers on his neck. She was something else.

"Miss Emma?"

She leaned across the bloody stagecoach rail. "Mr. Courtland, the reinsman, Mick, is alive but I'm afraid Tater has passed. Will you help me get Mick down?" She tugged the body, not moving him any closer to the edge of the seat.

He climbed up the side, and together they lowered the grizzled and bronzed Mick to the ground. No bullet holes or blood was evident on his leather vest or canvas trousers. The crimson fluid, on the rail, must have been Taters.

Emma beelined for the clean slice of skin through

his hair. "He's lucky to have the bullet graze his head. Another inch and it would have pierced his brain."

"There isn't a medicinal box. We'll have to make do."

She untied her neck scarf. Treasure removed a canteen from the inside of the coach, uncapped it, and handed her the container. She doused the scarf with water and gently patted at the gunshot wound on the side of Mick's head, and King climbed onto the seat to check Tater reposed on the rail.

"He doesn't have a pulse and the bullet went straight into his heart." King glanced at the sun, set low in the sky. Night would provide minimal cover. The bandits might regroup and attack again. From his limited observation, the gang consisted of the eight members. Four littered the road behind them, so they could have four to contend with. He jumped from the coach seat and knelt beside Emma.

She turned her beautiful, heart-shaped face toward him. Her glorious brown locks glinted, as they tumbled out from beneath her bonnet. Emma hadn't lost her cool composure for a moment with the bandits, but when he glanced her way, she blushed and turned her head as if she noticed something of interest on the ground. He admired her courage and how well she conducted herself in a life and death situation. They had a connection—God-given or a tease from the devil, he didn't know—but from one glance she intuitively understood what he wanted to convey.

The other passengers crowded around.

She wiped the driver's forehead. "He's unconscious and needs a doctor. If you could help get him inside the coach, please."

"The nearest station is perhaps twenty miles away. It's a possibility the bandits will return, but we can't outrun them with tired horses. We'll need to bury Tater by the trees over there." He nodded to the west. "We'll settle in for the night. At daybreak, we'll travel to the run, the next station."

"See here, Mr. Courtland, you don't have the authority to determine what will happen. I think we should wait right here until Mick opens his eyes and can take us directly to the station," Mr. Warren sputtered.

"We'll be sitting ducks in the open, Mr. Warren," King drawled. Damn, it had been a long difficult week of him chasing the bandits responsible for stealing his payroll. A mere twenty-eight miles from home, his horse had fallen into a prairie dog hole and broken a leg. Now, he had a load of citified chatterboxes to take care of. The cards weren't dealt in his favor today.

"Treasure, please help me bind Mick's head, then Mr. Courtland can put him on the coach seat," Emma said.

"Yes 'em." Treasure sat near Mick and situated herself beneath his shoulders to hold his head up.

Emma ripped part of her petticoat. King noticed the tiny ankle showing above the low-top brown boot. Her stockings looked like silk strands webbed together encasing sleek legs.

"Miss Cody, a lady does not reveal her undergarments to gentlemen or otherwise," Mrs. Landers huffed out, while cooling herself with a cardboard fan advertising Wells-Fargo.

Clutching the long piece of white cotton in her hand, she snapped, "Mrs. Landers, why don't you get back inside the coach."

"Here now. No reason to be rude." Mr. Warren held out his hand to the obnoxious woman. "Mrs. Landers, I'll help you."

Emma's face grew bright red, but she finished wrapping the cloth around Mick's head. King lifted the injured man and placed him inside the coach.

"Mr. Warren, if you'll help the ladies into the coach, I'll drive." King handed Emma his revolver and climbed on top of the conveyance, secured Tater to the back rest of the wide seat and grabbed the reins, checking to see if the passengers were seated. Looking out over the mass of barren land, with its rare sprinkling of trees, he shook out the reins and tried to outrun the great clouds of dust billowing up behind them. Miss Emma was wrong. The bandits were returning.

Chapter 2

Shoulders aching from pulling on the reins, King guided the horses to a stop at the mouth of a small canyon. He'd evaded the bandits, seemingly as if they didn't want to catch the stagecoach. What about the cashbox which was bolted to the floor? Bandits were known to burn the carriage and take the cashbox. Could it be possible they went to retrieve their wounded or dead?

Regardless, the canyon would provide them coverage from three sides if they were attacked. He unfettered the horses and removed a shovel from the boot.

"Here, Warren, take this shovel and dig a hole the size of a big man."

"You're not..."

King shot him a glare, and Warren grudgingly took the shovel.

King settled Mick on a blanket. Emma and Treasure gathered wood for a small, confined fire. He led the horses to a pool of fresh water at the base of a large rock formation. The horses drank their fill and munched on the few stalks of summer grass and weeds nearby. Exhausted and dirty, he wanted to climb into the pool and let his qualms about bandits float away. *Not possible.*

He fashioned a net from the horse whip and Tater's

hat and plunged the vessel into the murky basin, snagging few squirming rainbow-trout swimming near the rocky edge of the pool, and lifted the catch. The water chilled his hand but washed away the dust. He inhaled the earthy scent of moss and freshwater weeds, as he gazed into the black fluid and relived the events of the last hour. If it hadn't been for Emma, they might not be alive. It was evident Warren would not be an asset in a time of need. Damn the man, how had he become such a coward. Hopefully, the bandits had given up and set their sights on the next coach or as his luck would have it, his next payroll run.

The Relay Gang were a bunch of thieves robbing his payroll delivery every month. The miners and their families were strapped without their income. The women lacked food and clothing for their children, and he wouldn't let the robberies continue. Determined bandits would stop the coach, with or without killing passengers, and take all things valuable. What did the outlaws know that he didn't? Why had they retreated?

Cold air descended from the mountains and mixed with the heat of the rocks, creating a moderate mist around the canyon and added to their cover. He crossed the clearing to check on Mick. The fish laden hat dripped, sprinkling pungent water along his side.

"Ladies, how's Mick doing?"

"He has a fever, Mr. Courtland, but I swear I saw his eyes open." Treasure wrung out a cloth and placed it on Mick's brow. His gray hair gleamed brighter beneath the white material. Would they see his bright brown eyes and happy carefree grin again? He sure didn't want to lose another man.

"Fine, Treasure, keep him comfortable. Emma, I'd

like to talk to you." She glanced at him with a hesitant, tender, smile. She created an urgency he'd never experienced before, a need to get closer, to keep her safe.

"Really, Mr. Courtland, just because we're in the wilderness doesn't mean you should lose all respect for courtesy," Mrs. Landers scolded. Perched on a log near the fire, her hands were clasped on her lap and as far as he could tell she hadn't moved from that position since they'd arrived.

He walked toward the nitpicker and extended the fish filled hat. "Mrs. Landers, please accept my apology. Here is tonight's dinner, please clean and cook them." He dropped the soaking wet cap near her feet. "Thank you, Mrs. Landers."

"Well, I never." She jumped off the log. The net hat expanded, and the silvery fish floundered around on the ground. "Treasure!" Mrs. Landers lifted her skirts and moved farther from the slimy catch.

"Mrs. Landers, while I'm in charge you'll help with the chores." He put enough steel in his voice to slice the air. Damn annoying people, like her, were the reason he always rode alone and not in a coach.

"Comin', Mrs. Landers, I'll help ya." Treasure patted Mick's arm and ran to collect the fish.

Emma, kneeling at the driver's side, removed her hat and jacket and rolled up her shirt sleeves. Her slender arms gleamed pale in the moonlight as she joined him at the fire.

"You may need your jacket. The nights get teeth-chattering cold near the mountains." In spite of what he said he wanted to see more of her body and run his fingers lightly over her skin, untouched by the sun and smelling of wildflowers.

"I'll be fine for now, Mr. Courtland." She sat beside him on the log, situating her skirt to cover her ankles.

He grinned and tilted his hat. "Please, after all we've been through, you can call me King or Henry as you did earlier."

"Henry, then," she murmured, making his given name sound like the finest music he'd ever witnessed. A light breeze blew a curl of her hair into her face. With delicate hands, she tucked the strand into the nest of other unruly curls secured at the nape of her neck.

"Emma, I'm sure what's in the strongbox under the seat. The contents contain something of value, which is why I don't believe the gang will give up." He stood and extended his hand. Her delicate fingers gripped his, and they walked away from the group.

"Gold?" she whispered with wonder in her voice and keen interest in her eyes. She moved closer to him.

He shrugged. "I plan to have Warren take a shift to guard the entrance of our little hide-a-way. I want you to have a gun and be prepared in case they get past us. Are you willing to do this?"

They stopped at the drop off of the pool. The moon moved away from a cloud and cast its bright orb reflection onto the water. In the shimmer, an image appeared of them standing close enough that their breaths mingled.

"Of course, Mr. um…Henry. I'll do whatever I can to help. Do you want me to take guard duty as well?" Her velvety precise voice flowed over him, like the mild breeze blowing dust balls across the plain.

"By providing a back-up in the camp, you'll be

helping. How did you learn to shoot like that?" He wasn't sure what to do with his hands. If she were a paid companion, he'd have her supple body lying beside him on the ground by now, but she was a lady. He chose to slide his hands into his trouser pockets but sidled closer to her.

"My cousins are sharpshooters. As a youngster, I always tagged along. Finally, they gave in and taught me how to shoot pistols, rifles, bows and arrows. I hit the target dead-on most of the time." She lifted an eyebrow. "Have you heard of Buffalo Bill?"

"Of course. You can't live in the west without knowing who Cody is and the number of Indians he's slaughtered." He hadn't gotten to be the most successful businessman in Pineview by sitting idle, and he'd done riskier things than pursue a gentlewoman. "And you're Emma Cody."

"That might be information from a Penny Dreadful. His shooting skills are legendary and his sister, Helen, taught me how to shoot with some accuracy."

Quick defense, he smiled, admiring her loyalty-however misplaced. "Emma."

Her green eyes caught the echo of the moon. "Yes, Henry."

She shouldn't have licked her mouth with her tiny pink tongue. He drew her closer and kissed her gentle-like at first, when she relaxed her lips, he added pressure.

"Mr. Courtland. Miss Emma," Treasure shouted from behind them.

Emma backed away, placing her fingertips to her lips. They were shiny and puffy like they'd been stung, and at another time and place he would have sucked away the sting.

Treasure ran into the clearing huffing out inaudible breaths. "Mr. Mick…"

"Yes, Treasure. What about Mr. Mick?"

She took a deep inhale. "He's awake."

He clasped Emma's hand, and together they ran to the campsite. The driver's shoulders were propped against King's saddle, and he held a tin cup of steaming coffee. He knelt beside him, relieved he woke.

"Mick, how do you feel?"

"Like my head is pinched between two boulders." He rubbed circles on his forehead.

King grinned. "Well, let's just say you're going to have an interesting split in your hair after today."

Mick sputtered a mouth full of coffee, sprinkling his clothing and everything in a twenty-four-inch perimeter. "At least I'm not dead. At least I don't think so. My head smells like lavender, and a body's supposed to smell roses in heaven. Right?"

King sat back on his heels. "I don't know about that, but it's good you're alive. The robbers didn't get the strongbox."

"Good thang." He flapped his hand for him to come closer. "Important documents for the Cap'n in the strongbox. No money though. Your payroll comes in two weeks, and I signed up to ride shotgun." Mick winked at him.

King nodded. "Thank you. Did you recognize any of them? Could you describe them for the sheriff?" Emma stiffened beside him. Her tiny hands fisted at her sides.

"Na, too fer away. When we seen 'em acomin'

Tater told me he couldn't see how many 'cause his eyes jest don't see so good fer distance. How about Tater? Did he git shot up?" Mick lowered the coffee cup to the ground.

King rubbed his jaw line. "Sorry, Mick." He looked away.

"He was my friend." Mick drew his shirt sleeve over his face appearing to wipe his mouth and swiped at the tears.

"He was a good guy."

"Mick, are ya hungry? We've got fish and biscuits." Treasure twisted her hands.

"Tha'd be right nice, Miss Treasure." She ran to the fire, her calico skirts flying at her sides.

Warren came into the clearing, carrying his suit jacket. "Courtland, I need help getting Tater into the hole."

Emma drew a deep breath and knelt beside Mick.

King planned to have private words with Warren; the scoundrel didn't have consideration for others.

"Oh, dear lord." Mrs. Landers fainted, falling flat onto the ground.

Emma rushed to her side. "Mrs. Landers?"

King touched her arm. "If she's breathing, leave her alone. Come with me, I want to reload your gun and give you a holster to wear." Luggage was piled high on top of the coach. His bag was tied on the outside boot at the rear.

She tugged Mrs. Landers' dress to cover her ankles and crossed her hands over her bulging middle, then picked up her full skirt and rushed to his side. He lifted Tater's gun belt off the side of the coach and presented the weapon to her.

"Do you know how to wear a belt? Shoot after drawing from a holster?" He unclenched the hoop from the metal pin, creating a long string of leather instead of a circle.

She frowned. "You are kidding, right? Did you listen to my story about Helen and Buffalo Bill?"

"Right, sorry." He grinned and in two steps was within inches of her. She quickly took two paces back.

"What are you doing?" she whispered.

"I was going to help you put it on." The rapid pulse near her sweat covered collarbone glowed in the moonshine.

"I can fasten a belt. Thank you for the offer." All prim and proper, she took the belt and fastened the heavy leather around her dress. Her small waist made the instrument sag over her hips, emphasizing her curves. The strong contrast of a dainty lady and a sharpshooter struck him. She went from a pampered beautiful girl riding in the stagecoach to become a strong desirable woman ready to defend fellow passengers.

She whipped out the Colt, twirled the metal around her index finger and shoved the pistol back into the holster. Impressed with her agility, he crossed his arms willing her glance to meet his.

"Excuse me." Warren's snarly voice broke the silence.

"I'm coming, Mr. Warren." King hoisted the blanket-wrapped Tater.

****

Emma watched Henry's smooth stride and strong back as he walked away. His hard strength pressed against her body made heat rise fast and throughout.

Stop, I can't contemplate a romance.

Why was her brother robbing a stagecoach? Evident from the precision of the gang, the attempt today wasn't the first time. What desperate reason would permit him to forgo all of his values and adopt the life of a criminal. Did he think because of her father's position in the government he could avoid the hangman's noose? What if he was the one who shot Tater? Shivers cascaded over her at the memory of the bullets hitting the side of the stagecoach. Could she live with the guilt of knowing who the leader of the gang was and not report him? Should she deceive all of these people?

When she got to Pineview, she'd convince him to stop being a thief. She settled the gun more comfortably on her hip and strolled to the campfire. A recovered Mrs. Landers chewed on a fish and biscuit sandwich. Mick, sitting straight up, also gnawed on a biscuit.

"Miss Emma, come eat with us." Treasure placed a small piece of fish and a biscuit on a tin plate.

She grasped the offering and wrinkled her nose at the burnt odor. "Thank you, Treasure."

How could she eat, anything? Her heart raced with the memory of Henry's kiss. Should she let him kiss her again? His lips felt smooth and cool, then hard and determined. She licked her lips, trying to recapture his taste.

The gun clanged against the log as she sat down. Thankfully, Mrs. Landers didn't say anything about the weapon sheltered on Emma's hip as it pulled the green muslin traveling dress tight against her body. Emma teetered at the edge of her patience with the woman. She poked at the fish, charcoal on one side and raw on the other, but hunger drove her to eat the bread.

Regardless of how much experience she had with a gun, shooting cans off of a fence was different from shooting a bullet into someone's flesh. The shocked and pained look on the robber's face as the slug entered his chest and blood seeped between his fingers didn't sit well on her conscience. She'd almost shot her brother directly in the heart. Good heavens, she would need to seek absolution when she found the next church and sent a silent prayer to save the men's souls.

The question hovered in her mind, if they were attacked again, could she shoot someone whom she loved?

Chapter 3

The Wells-Fargo brand spankin' new, slightly shot-up, stagecoach stopped on the main street in Pineview, Colorado. Exhausted from being alert all night, Emma had half-listened to Mrs. Landers' rendition of proper etiquette for the last twenty or so miles. Mr. Warren perched beside Mrs. Landers and encouraged her by saying, "Very important. Being a lady should be simple."

Maybe she could shoot another man. She reached low and released the slim piece of leather, holding the gun in place, and caught Treasure's gaze. Emma grinned, and Treasure smiled in response. The clever girl had pretended to be asleep.

Upon exiting the coach, Emma un-strapped the gun belt and added the weapon to Tater's hat, shotgun and bedroll. The Wells-Fargo authorities would return his personal effects to his closest kin. Henry shouted for assistance. An older man with a tin-badge ran forward, and together they got Mick off the coach seat. He'd refused to ride inside the conveyance, wanting to be the sharp-shooter in the shot-gun seat. Really, a blessing in disguise as he didn't have to listen to the boring dialogue.

A tall, thin, black man ran toward Henry and the sheriff. "Mr. Courtland, welcome home, sir." The man was dressed in a three-piece, dark blue suit and cream-tinted shirt. He kept clutching his neck.

"Thank you, Martin. Please get my saddle while I take Mick to the doctor's office." Henry glanced at Emma and shot her a smile. Her cheeks grew hot. Would he return and talk to her? Ask her for an outing?

"Yes, sir, Mr. Courtland." Martin flashed Emma a brief smile and nodded. Grabbing the saddle, blanket roll, and dark well-used leather bag, he followed.

Mr. Warren stepped out of the vermillion painted coach, puffed out his chest and tightened his tie. He straightened his suit jacket and bowler hat as he directed men to unload the luggage. Finished asserting fanciful authority, he strutted into the sheriff's office. Odious man.

Two men unloaded her bags and set them on the wooden platform. They unpacked the coach and drove it to the blacksmith's workshop at the end of the street, where the horses would be stabled, and the conveyance repaired. She glanced around but didn't see Rachel or Jayden. What was the likelihood of him appearing in front of the coach he tried to rob? Should she find Henry and ask him to take her to Rachel's house? No, he was in the sheriff's office and being an honest and God-fearing person, she wanted to avoid talking to the law at all costs. Someone tugged her dress.

A red-haired child, holding a cap in one hand and a newspaper in the other, stared at her. The bold headlines indicated a woman of ill-repute escaped after killing a local resident and inventor. "Miss?"

Emma withdrew a coin from her purse, dropped it in the lad's hat, and took the newspaper. "Thank you." She opened the paper, reading the headlines and advertisements to find a hotel where she could spend the night.

"Miss." The squeaky child-like voice lifted an octave.

She absently patted the boy's head, concentrating on the room and board section.

"Argh."

She glanced at the child. He'd placed his cap on his crown and stood with his hands on his hips. "Are you Miss Emma Cody?" The snappish lad lifted a shaggy eyebrow, giving him a comical appearance.

"Why, yes. How may I help you?"

She gasped as he tilted his head, exposing chin chairs. He was a full-grown man at four feet. Diminutive lines spread out from around his eyes. His dapper brown tweed suit fitted him perfectly and the jade vest made his green eyes a deeper shade. She guessed his age to be ten years older than her twenty and two days. Hand to her chest, she tried to decide what to say to this little person without offending?

"I'm sorry. I didn't know. I'm Emma." Unsure if she should squat to be eye-level with him, or remain standing nineteen inches above him, she held out her gloved hand to shake his hairy one. Awkward, but her curiosity peaked, and she needed to mend the misunderstanding.

"I'm Sam. Sam McCloud, a friend of Rachel and Jayden Drake. If you're ready, I'll take you to their home around three miles from here." The sharpness of his voice didn't dissipate, nor did his eyebrows relax to a straight position.

Heat rushed through her, closing her throat. What to say? Maybe she should have listened to the endless lecture on etiquette rules.

"Yes, I'm ready. Thank you, Mr. McCloud." She searched for her fellow passengers to say farewell and hoped to see Henry one more time. None to be found, she tucked the hat box under her arm and clutched the two heavy bags. She looked for a carriage, buckboard, or whatever transportation he'd provided, and while pivoting she dropped the hat box.

Mr. Cloud grasped her hat box and meandered forward. "Let's go."

The back of the buckboard was filled with stacks of flour bags, gunny sacks of something, the lettering partially hidden, a tin of lard, and a barrel of pickles. He hurled the hat box into the back, took her two satchels and heaved them over the side. The largest one thumped against a sack of potatoes causing lint to fly. The angry little man held a good deal of strength.

"Please do not abuse my luggage. I have a baby gift for Rachel in that one." She pointed to the tote upside down on top of the lard.

Mr. McCloud bristled around the wagon, pulled a rope at the side of the buckboard and automatically a step lowered.

Not wanting to further aggravate him, she smiled her 'please make a charitable donation smile' and climbed onto the seat. While arranging her skirts, she glanced at him. He nimbly scaled the ladder and settled onto the bench, then retracting the cable the steps collapsed.

He clicked his tongue, making a sound like, "snick, snick," and flapped the reins against the backs of the twin brown horses. However clever, the man was rude.

She'd overcome the first negative interaction and start fresh. "The steps are brilliant, Mr. McCloud. Did you devise them yourself?"

"No, ma'am." His stubby fingers tightened on the reins.

Anxious to hear about her sister-in-law, Emma widened her smile. "How is Rachel faring?"

"You'll see in a due time," he replied shortly.

You'd think he'd be curious about the shot-up stagecoach and blood on her dress, but he didn't ask any questions. An hour later, Mr. McCloud pulled the buckboard into a circular gravel driveway. A few steps away stood a simple three-story house made of hardwood slats with three windows at the front, two down and one up. The home was sparsely surrounded by evergreen trees.

Emma waited until he came around to her side and extended his hand. She awkwardly leaned to grab hold and stepped down. Excited, she rushed toward the veranda steps, opened the solid oak door and ran inside. "Rachel?"

The tomb-like silent interior bore the faint smell of rancid meat. She extracted a handkerchief from her blood-stained and travel worn gown and glanced at Mr. McCloud. Fear clouded his eyes. Panic, in addition to the malodorous scent, made her gag. *Please, don't let my sister-in-law be injured or worse.*

She ran up the winding staircase, which overlooked the octagon shaped foyer. Heart racing, she rushed from room to room. The third and last bedroom exhibited a bouquet of dying flowers on a center table and a baby's bassinet in the corner.

"I've found her." Sam yelled from the foyer.

She leaned over the banister. "Is she…"

"Yes, she's alive." He replaced a kerchief over his

nose and walked away.

She flew down the stairs and into a small parlor. The organic musty smell of dried copper of old blood penetrated the cloth she'd pressed to her nose. She coughed and ran toward Rachel sprawled across a fainting bench. In the center of the room, a pine casket rested on a set of wooden horses. The rancid odor seeped from its crevices. "Rachel!"

Mr. McCloud opened the window, allowing the late afternoon air to flow through the room. She knelt beside her sister-in-law. Her dark locks straggled along the side of her thin face, the braid falling over her shoulder. Emotionless glassy mahogany eyes stared at the casket.

"Emma. I'm sorry I didn't meet you. Welcome." She touched the sleeve of Emma's dress, then entwined their fingers.

"Let's go outside for some fresh air." Emma held the cloth tighter to cover her nose and mouth.

"He's dead. I can't let him go."

"Who's dead?" Emma whispered, her heart racing with a new fear.

"Jayden. Shot dead." Rachel pulled a dainty little cloth from her waistband of her black satin mourning dress and wiped her eyes.

"I'm sorry, but please let's go outside." Emma tugged Rachel's hand, still wrapped in hers. It couldn't be Jayden, she saw him yesterday riding alongside the stagecoach, trying to rob them. Could he have been shot later in the day? The fast undulation in her chest made breathing more difficult.

"I can't leave Jayden."

"Rachel, I'm going to help you up, and we're going

outside," Sam softly, but firmly insisted. He eased his hands under her arms and lifted her to an upright position. She swayed and Emma wrapped her arm around Rachel's thick waist and hugged her close. They appeared to be a stack, Rachel the tallest, then Emma and finally Sam. All joined together, with their arms interlaced, they rambled out the front door and onto the veranda.

Sweet country air never smelled so good. Rachel plopped onto a rocking chair and leaned her head against the wooden slats.

"They brought him home a few hours after you left, Sam. They said they would bury him in the cemetery, at the back of the property, with the Drake family. You know, to the North of the windmill. I told them we would need a showing, and we would take care of the burial. They offered to come back, but I refused. I don't want him to leave me." Her quiet voice held sadness, so miserable and so deep her whispers carried in the wind.

Chills racked Emma's body. The person inside that box was not her half-brother. Should she tell Rachel?

Her sister-in-law held her head in her hands and sobbed. "I'm sorry, Jayden."

Emma knelt and awkwardly rocked her, wishing the motion would ease her heartrending grief. Her throat hurt from restraining her own pain and tears. What if he was dead?

The tears subsided, and she backed away. "We must bury, Jayden. He needs to be put to rest." She wiped away Rachel's tears with her handkerchief and covered her cold clammy hands, trying to transfer her heat. "Mr. McCloud?"

"Sam. Yes, Rachel. He is rotting and needs to be put underground."

"I don't want him to leave. I should have told him; I didn't want him to leave." Rachel let go of Emma's hands and smoothed her dress, over the baby hill, working the wrinkles out of her gown.

"I'm sorry about your loss, but we must bury him," Emma whispered and glanced at Sam. He nodded and walked off the veranda.

Rachel pressed the backside of her hands to her eyes.

"I'm going to help Sam take care of Jayden. You want us to bury him, right?"

Rachel's hands returned to smoothing the wrinkles or soothing the baby. "Yes. Help."

"If I get you something to eat and drink, would you be able to help me unpack?" Emma stood. The best method to distract a person in mourning was to keep him or her busy and entertained.

"I'm sorry, Emma, I'm a bad hostess." She rose from the chair.

"No, you're in mourning." Emma held her arm and led her inside the house and up the stairs. "I assume I get the guest room with the beautiful patchwork quilt?" *Suck back the tears; you need to be strong for her. Don't let your weakness show.*

"Yes. Jayden made a big house, so we could have a large family." Rachel rested her head on Emma's shoulder. "I need you so much."

"And I you." She settled Rachel on an overstuffed green paisley-printed chair by the window. The gold damask curtains were swagged and outside, night had arrived. "I'll be right back, please don't move."

Downstairs, she gathered bread, cheese, and butter from the icebox, made a sandwich and poured a glass of tea. She placed the items on a tray and hauled everything up the stairs. Rachel hadn't moved, barely breathed. "Just a few things, but I insist you eat something and drink tea." She situated the meal on the small table beside the chair.

Rachel picked up a sandwich half. "Thank you, dear. I've missed you."

"I've missed you, too." She fixed a strand of hair behind her ear. "I need to help Sam. Please get some rest."

By the time all three pieces of luggage were carted up the stairs, Rachel had devoured the sandwich and drank the tea. Her head rested against the back of the chair. Emma placed a blanket over her lap and tip-toed from the room. She exhaled. Her arrival had evolved into an emotional mess.

She ran into the master suite and rummaged through the dresser, finding a pair of her brother's canvas trousers, suspenders, shirt, and leather gloves. She stripped off her clothes and slipped on the shirt and pants. The suspender buttons were closer together on one side, so she attached the Y at the backside and pulled the bands around the front. Emma grabbed the gloves, a bandana and gathered her dress.

Downstairs, the air continued to be rancid but less intense. She put the dress and jacket in a little cubbyhole at the side of the kitchen, tied the bandana around her mouth and nose and went to the parlor. Sam moved a large wheelbarrow into the room and set it by the casket. Rope in hand, he stood beside the box.

He cleared his throat. "I'm not sure this will work,

but we'll place the casket on top and secure it with a rope. You hold the tail end. I'll pull, and you'll push the barrel to wheel it out the front door. The buckboard is right outside. We'll drive around to the graveyard, dig a hole and use pulleys to lower him."

Pulleys? She held her breath and bounced her gaze from the wheelbarrow to the crate. Impossible. Get the task done, the litany played through her mind.

"Let's go." Somehow she needed to look inside that casket. When they got him to the gravesite, she'd open the thin container. More than likely the box would fall open, and she'd confirm if her brother was inside.

She pulled on thin leather gloves and went to the end of the casket, closest to the windows.

Sam levered himself near the handle end of the wheelbarrow. "Grab hold of your end, and we'll ease it off the table onto the wheel barrel. Ready?"

She nodded her head, took a deep breath, and grabbed the sharp corner of the coffer.

They moved the case to the edge, the box tilted more to the right than the left. Emma shifted her hands to compensate, letting go for just a second. The casket fell sideways onto the wheelbarrow. The lid flew open.

"Damn," Sam said.

"Blast," Emma hissed. A stranger with the same height and coloring as Jayden was inside the box. Most of the right side of his face was missing; however, the birthmark on the unblemished left side wasn't there. The death wound might have been from a gunshot, probably a rifle. Tears, from learning her brother wasn't inside, or from the exhausting last two days, dribbled along her cheeks. No doubt he was temporarily avoiding death.

The unspeakable grotesqueness of a decomposing corpse made her gag. Not just the overwhelming noxious smell, but the white skin pasted to the skeletal form and the bugs crawling over the exposed muscle and bone. She met Sam's glance and nodded. He flipped the lid closed; however an arm caught between the top and bottom of the wooden sides. They proceeded to maneuver the wheelbarrow out of the parlor, balancing the awkward shape. Despite the appendage dangling outside the casket, they were able to squeeze through the doorway and onto the veranda. He'd arranged a ramp leading to the back of the wagon. They managed to shove the carcass along the ramp and onto the flatbed.

After lowering the metal legs of the wheelbarrow to the wooden floor, they jumped down and pushed the ramp to the side of the buckboard. He placed two shovels behind the wheels to prevent the box from moving backwards. She ran a few feet away, braced her hands on her knees, took a deep breath, and wiped the tears off her cheeks. *Don't think about it. It is a task to help Jayden. He must want to hide. Maybe he wants to stop being an outlaw?*

"We're losing sunlight," he shouted from the wagon seat.

"Alright." She heaved and dragged her feet to the side and pulled herself onto the seat.

"Where should we put him?" She shielded her nose with her hand. The lavender scent of her lotion on her wrist wasn't nearly strong enough to overpower the smell of death. "Two choices: one is beside Rango, his favorite dog, or next to an elm. Which spot do you choose?"

His elfin face whitened. "I didn't know him well enough, but the tree will have roots to cut through."

"Dog it is. Let's get this over with."

Splinters from the old shovel handle pierced her skin and damaged the gloves within the first twenty minutes. Her hands had welts and the clear part of the white blisters was ready to break open. Her sides ached as much as her shoulders. Sam tossed bits of soil high over his head spattering the ground above. The desire to heave the shovel, go back to the house and climb into bed until the last several hours had been forgotten grew stronger.

She wiped the sweat off her forehead with her dirty sleeve. "Is it deep enough? In a few minutes it'll be pitch black."

"Not yet. If it's too shallow, animals will dig him up." The edge to his voice echoed off the cool earthen walls. Aromatic nature odors were a refreshing change from putrid rotting flesh.

"Why are you still angry? I've gone out of my way to be nice to you. I'm helping you dig a grave for heaven's sake." Frustration made her voice sharp, a tone her mother tried to eradicate.

"You treat me like a child. I'm not a child, but a man."

"I didn't see your face. I saw a small person, who I thought was selling newspapers." Exhausted, she set the shovel against the dirt wall, and folded her arms across her chest.

He placed his shovel beside hers. "You patted my head."

"I think it's time to take a break and get a drink." She used angry energy to scramble from the hole.

Sam struggled to climb out. She didn't offer to help him. Certainly not a condition of the Etiquette Rules, but annoyance clouded her view. The man didn't know her. People make mistakes. What a miserable trip so far. Should she grab her bags and return to Indiana?

"Treat me with respect, deserving a man." His tinny voice pierced the night.

Emma found it strange he continued to wear all of his city finery, wool pants, and a green vest over a white cotton shirt. His bright red hair became a beacon in the darkness. She focused on the crimson glow and tried to subdue her bitterness.

He pounded his chest. "I'm a man, with a man's desires. When I see a beautiful woman, don't you think I want her to see me as a man?"

"I didn't see your face when I handed you the coin or patted your head, but now I do think you're acting like a child." She glared at him. "I'm getting a drink."

"I'll bite your knees like a child."

Could he be serious? She glanced at his little twisted face and took off at a run. The flap, flap of his feet in rapid movement forced her to move faster. She glanced back to check his progress and bumped into a human wall.

Her face touched the rough texture of a coat. Hard large hands inappropriately grasped her rear and back. Emma jerked her head and viewed a granite jawline.

"Henry," she said breathlessly, because of the run or seeing him she couldn't decide.

"Emma. Sam, what's going on here?"

Sam drew deep breaths.

"You know each other?" She stepped away, defiantly not remaining within the touching territory.

Using the filigree, from her sleeve, she wiped sweat from her forehead.

"Sam used to work for my family. After my father passed, he went to work for Drake." Henry stared at the casket. "What's going on?"

"We're going to…get a drink of water. We were digging a hole to bury the man," she coughed to cover her mistake, "my half-brother, Jayden Drake." She ducked her head. Had he heard her faux pas?

His questioning glance gave her the impression he'd noticed. "Jayden hasn't been buried, yet? The sheriff said he's been dead for two or three days."

"Rachel had trouble releasing the body." Sam pushed his foot around in the dirt, drawing what appeared to be half circles.

"Get your drink, then meet me at the buckboard," his tone was a mix of wonder and dismay.

She turned to leave, but Henry wrapped his arm around hers. "No, Emma, you come with me. Sam, will you get her a drink of water, please?"

"Of course." He may have mumbled, "Anything for the princess."

"I'm sorry for your loss." They walked toward the buckboard.

She wanted to snuggle into his warmth to feel safe and secure, instead she raised the bandana to cover her nose. Henry gave her a questioning look, until they got closer. He jerked her back, and they went to the downwind side of the partially dug grave.

He removed his jacket and waistcoat, placing each piece on the buckboard seat. A grim expression on his face made her aware of how much he cared for her brother or the gruesome task ahead of him.

Her heart pounded harder as it adjusted to her multiplying unintended lies. "You don't need to do this. Sam and I can finish."

"Go on, take care of Rachel. We'll bury him." He jumped into the hole. "I wouldn't be a good neighbor if I didn't help." The sound of shovel grinding into rocky soil split the air.

"Thank you." Emma took hold of his clothing and ran toward the dimly lit house. She dropped his jacket, waistcoat, and her muddy travel boots in the foyer, and ran up the stairs to the guest room.

Her luggage had been unpacked, but Rachel wasn't in the room. She went into the bathroom, poured cool water from the pitcher into a bowl and washed her hands and face. The tub looked appealing, but first she needed to locate the depressed widow.

The scent of spicy onions flew into her nostrils as she descended and grew stronger as she approached the kitchen. She wrapped an arm around Rachel's shoulders and peered into the pot. "What are you cooking?"

"Potato soup. It's Jayden's favorite." She hummed *Thou God of Love*.

Emma sighed. "Why don't I take over, and you rest. You're carrying a baby, you know."

She touched her rounded belly. "Yes, I'm beneath God's sheltering wings. I'll have a part of Jayden with me, won't I?"

"Yes, dear, you will." Emma went to the ice box and withdrew a pitcher of milk. She poured a glass and set it before Rachel. Pulling out another chair, she lifted the mother-to-be's swollen legs onto the seat. "Where is the cook or housekeeper?"

"The odious witch left when Jayden came home.

38

Said she wasn't staying in the same house with a corpse." She took a long drink of the milk. "I'm glad she's gone."

"What about neighbors? Did they stop by to see you? To pay their respects?"

"I didn't answer the door. I couldn't leave Jayden alone." Rachel leaned against the chair rods and folded her hands over her belly. "I'm glad you're here."

"So am I." She put a teapot on the stove and turned to assess her sister-in-law. "Do you want to come back to Indiana and stay with my parents?"

"No. I want to stay here. I like this house. Jayden had electricity put in." She rubbed a puffy ankle.

"As you wish." She'd revisit the topic after the baby arrived.

"We had a lovely time on our honeymoon. In England, we met a man by the name of Sir Humphrey Davy, who invented the first electrical lamp in 1801. He and Jayden talked for several days. Sir Davy's apprentice returned with us to Colorado, and he installed electricity throughout the house. He didn't promise that it would work, but it does. We use a windmill to provide the power. It also produces current for the lanterns outside and inside." Rachel nervously finger-combed her stringy brown hair and continued to ramble.

"Unbelievable. I'm excited to see how it works." And how Jayden paid for it. Was the expensive house the reason he robbed stagecoaches?

"Let's hope the wind keeps blowing then. We only have two burners on the stove. You'll need to put more wood inside in order to provide enough heat to keep the soup boiling."

"All right." She opened the iron door and heaved a few pieces of wood inside. "Jayden would have wanted his father's pocket watch to be buried with him. Did you put it in his pocket?"

"I..." Her chin hit her chest. "I couldn't look at him. Is that wrong? I made the excuse the baby would want to have his or her father's watch."

"Not at all. In your condition it is probably good you didn't open the coffin." She stirred the soup. "You seem calmer."

"I am. King's here. He'll help us."

"In your letters you didn't mention Mr. Courtland. Were he and Jayden business partners?" She removed bread from the box and proceeded to cut thin slices.

"At one time, Jayden planned to own a mine with King. He came to the house, and they'd talked for hours in the office. Sometimes he stayed overnight, I think because of the whisky. I don't know if they became partners," she whispered, and got up to snatch a piece of bread. She placed a large amount of strawberry jam on the slice of wheat and sat, propping her feet on the chair again.

"Why is he called—"

"Ladies."

"King. We were just talking about you. Thank you for coming." She licked away a smear of red jam.

He took her hand into his. "I'm sorry for your loss."

"What smells so good?" Sam's red hair dripped water onto his shoulders.

"We made potato soup. Sit down, Sam, and I'll get you a bowl." Rachel lowered her feet.

"Sit, I'll do it." Henry went to the cupboards and

pulled out four bowls.

Emma ladled the soup and Henry served. Like an odd family, they sat at the table and shared the meager meal. Silence prevailed, all of them were undoubtedly thinking about what had transpired. She was anxious to find out where the man died, the man people believed to be Jayden Drake.

Chapter 4

Emma evaluated the mourners: Henry and a few neighbors she'd yet to meet. Rachel sobbed, her pale hand shaking the handkerchief. Next to her, Sam's coal black suit jacket fluttered in the wind. A harsh rain mixed with the wind gusts created a spiral of the soil and flowers and sprinkling a multicolored blanket over the earth mound. After a final prayer by the minister, the mourners separated, returning to their homes before the storm became more pronounced.

She swiped empathetic tears and glanced at Rachel, who rubbed her stomach. The minister, a young handsome man with a brown goatee and a flat-billed hat, closed the Bible. He walked forward, with a solemn expression, and took Rachel's hand into his. His low tumbled voice gave words of comfort. "Let me know if I can be of service to you."

Emma kept her head lowered. She could not look a man of the cloth in the eye and admit her lie—the person in the ground was not a loss to her.

Rachel ambled toward Jayden's grave and dropped a couple of early spring hyacinths on top of the pile of rich, black dirt. She swayed. Emma jolted forward, but Henry caught Rachel before she fell. His glance met hers. She nodded and ran ahead then opened the door. He carried the widow into the house and up the stairs. Emma took the servant's stairs to the main bedroom, tugged the covers to the end of the bed, so he could lay Rachel down. He walked out of the room, and Emma removed Rachel's shoes and overcoat. Emma pulled the quilt over her, intending to ease her guilt, and tell Rachel the man in the grave wasn't her husband. Her eyes closed and the moment was lost.

Henry sat at the kitchen table with a cup of coffee in front of him. "Sam took the minister to town and should return soon. I'll have him check to see why the light isn't working. He mentioned the cook quit, and you desperately need one. The ladies from the church sent a week's worth of food, which will give us plenty of time to hire someone."

Us? The glow from a candle and the wood stove provided relief from the gloominess. She placed towels over the meats and potatoes, then stacked them in the ice box. "Thank you. We appreciate your help."

He nodded. "Rachel's acting rather strange, don't you think?" Outside the window, a sharp streak of light followed by loud blasts of thunder rang, validating his comment.

"I haven't been around very many grieving people. Our parents are alive. When my half-brother inherited the Drake homestead and moved, I felt sad, but I became involved in different activities, and I missed him but not as much." She washed the few dishes in the sink and picked up the towel to dry them.

"In my business, death is frequent, and I don't remember someone grieving quite the way she is."

"I'm sure she'll be fine, given time." Emma didn't feel comfortable talking about Rachel and her anguish; however, she agreed with him, she wasn't quite right. She'd made unusual statements about Jayden, and that it was her fault. What was her fault?

"Your parents didn't mind that you traveled out west alone?" He placed his empty cup in the sink.

"No. My father is in politics, and we traveled quite a bit, so they know I'm adept at taking care of myself. He and my mother are traveling overseas right now. What is your trade, Henry?" She washed the cup, dried it with the flour sack towel, and placed it in the cupboard.

"I own and manage a variety of businesses." He stuffed his hands in his black wool coat pockets.

"What kind of —"

Short stepping, heavy feet flapped against the stone floor. "Is there any food left?" Sam's voice held an angry sting as he threw his hat. The bowler landed directly on the coat rack near the door.

Despite how much they'd worked together over the last couple of days, she still hadn't come to some sort of communicative relationship with him. "Yes. You can get it yourself."

Henry's hands went into a stop motion. "What is bloody wrong with you two? The other night I felt the friction and suspected you were not getting along, but what is the problem?"

She looked at Sam. He started it, so he could explain why the anger continued to exist.

Sam removed a casserole dish from the top of the stack. He opened the correct drawer, obtained a large spoon, and shoveled an ample amount of ham and potatoes onto a plate. Fork in hand, he placed the platter onto the scarred oak table.

"It's personal." He took a glass from the shelf and filled the container with water.

The strongest desire to pump the faucet for him, as he stood on tiptoe to reach the knob, became unbearable. Instead, she strolled toward the door, leading to the main part of the house, ready to exit if warranted.

"Emma?" Henry growled.

She sent a glower toward Sam. "I've apologized for the misunderstanding, so I'm not sure why the animosity continues."

Sam placed his water glass on the table, sat, and gave a great amount of attention to the food.

"Emma, would you please leave us alone?"

"Certainly, I'll be on the front porch if anyone wants to apologize for his rude behavior."

Sam murmured something under his breath.

****

King got a second cup and filled it with coffee and scooted the offering toward Sam. He needed to resolve this little situation, arrange an outing with Emma, and get back to Pineview. He'd been away from the saloon business too long, and he needed to get control over the rampant disagreements between his bartenders, the piano player, and the dance-hall girls. The natives believe when a full moon is waxing, tempers, human and animal, seem to be disjointed-wildly chaotic. This belief was proving to be true.

"Out with it, Sam. You just met her a few days ago? What could possibly have happened to get your tail in a bind?" He leaned back, snug to the chair rungs, and took a sip of the strong, hot coffee.

"She's a beautiful woman. Her skin has a pearl essence and looks so smooth. Her eyes hold intelligence and a compassion I haven't seen in a while. Those perfect pink lips on her heart-shaped face threw my heart into a stutter. And do you know what she did?"

His friend's poetry brought forth laughter, which was difficult to restrain. He shook his head, then coughed.

"She gave me a dime, took my newspaper, and patted my head like a child. I think she may have called me a child. I was furious." Sam pushed the plate away and lifted the glass of water.

"No surprise, remember the Alpine incident? People make assumptions, and you are unique."

"Height requirements be damned," he growled. "I wanted her to see me as a man. The more I thought about it the angrier I became, and before I knew it, I'd buried myself six feet under." He rubbed his hands over his face.

King wasn't sure how to respond. He was also interested in her but telling Sam at this moment would be like throwing fat into the fire. She might not be interested in being courted by him, a simple businessman, who didn't have any experience with a big city lady. "I can't leave here and wonder if you two are acting like children and plotting tricks to play against each other. The way I see it, you have two choices. One, you can go out and talk to her. Tell her about your feelings and that you want to start fresh or come to an agreement to keep conversation limited to management of the Drake estate."

The lack of response didn't bother him. Sam, typically, was quiet a thoughtful man. "If you want, I'll go with you."

"Maybe it would be best if you paved the way?" He stood, straightened his satin vest, and knotted his string tie.

"Not at any time do you call her the spawn of the devil." He pressed his finger into Sam's chest.

"Not the way to win the lady?" Sam scrunched his face, creating wrinkles.

"No. Ladies like to be complimented. Tell her how nice her hair is arranged. That her dress is pretty." King understood why his friend continued to be unmarried. At least the girls in his saloon, King's Court, liked Sam and didn't mind his shortcomings. Of course, they make money entertaining men, regardless of limitations.

King walked onto the porch. He inhaled, taking in her beauty. A faint lamplight cast shadows on her face and figure as she stopped the to and fro motion of the wicker rocker. Sam shut the door drawing her gaze from the patch of trees. She met King's stare. He smiled, a small hope-you-understand-smile, and shifted his glance to Sam and his bandy-legged arrogance.

"Emma. Sam would like to talk to you about the, ah, clash you have…er communication problem." A crack of thunder sounded inches away.

Her eyes grew cold, and her mouth went from the pink smile to a thin white line. He sat on the side table in front of the bench and motioned for Sam to take the seat closest to Emma.

"Please, continue." She folded her hands modestly on her lap.

He cleared his throat, stalling for time. How to approach the delicate subject. "Sam feels he made a bad first impression and wants to start over."

She lifted an eyebrow and faced Sam. "I would like to be your friend, Sam."

"Miss Emma, I thank you for that." He finger-combed his hair. "Your dress doesn't make you look like a matron at all."

King groaned. "He meant that you look very pretty in the dark blue dress you're wearing. It makes your eyes a brighter green and brings out the wonderful color of your skin."

A red flush appeared on her face at his compliment. She met his gaze and looked away.

"You know he's a teacher. He built bookshelves all along the walls of the bunkhouse and has books covering every square inch."

"I didn't know. We finally have something in common, other than gravedigging."

"I'd like to know if I have permission to court you, Miss Emma?" Sam rushed the statement. A fine sheen of sweat appeared on his forehead. He rubbed his palms against his trousers.

Her attention went from King to Sam. "I'm honored that you want to court me, but I'm in mourning at this time." A streak of lightning lit the dark sky.

"How long?"

"Excuse me?" she whispered.

"How long will you be in mourning?" Sam shifted. Impatience evident in the way he swung his dangling feet. The man was tenacious, even if he did lack common sense.

"I hope we can become friends, but I'm not interested in being courted. I hope this doesn't upset you. It isn't because of your, um, size." Her face flushed a deeper red.

"Right." Sam scooted to the edge of the bench, lowered his feet to the floor and stomped away.

Emma gave a slight smile, stood, and sashayed into

the house. Her lavender scent wafted in her trail. Her delicate heels thumped on the floor as she ascended the stairs.

Well, hell, courting Miss Emma was going to be a challenge.

Chapter 5

A brilliant yellow blast of early morning sunlight greeted Emma as she went to the garden to evaluate the status of the spring plants. They were almost out of the church-donated food, and she wanted to take stock of edible food before determining what needed to be purchased and planted. When she went into Pineview later, she'd place an advertisement in the newspaper to find a cook and maybe a gardener. The previous greenskeeper left for the Doric Mine in Clear Creek County last winter, because of a gold rush. From what she understood, people in this area, desperate for money, tried their luck at gold mining or...joined bandit gangs.

She hadn't talked to Rachel about Jayden, simply by saying his name she left the room sobbing, then reentered her dark place of silence. The subject of the dead stranger buried in the graveyard could wait.

The feeling of being watched unnerved her. Sam was tinkering with a lawn mowing device, so it wasn't him. His courting declaration threw her off guard. Although she didn't want a romantic relationship with him, they'd reached a common ground and were becoming friends. She folded her shivering arms at her waist and walked through the half-acre of tilled soil. The plot of ground had been well-cared for, but now weeds popped out proud and strong. She pulled a couple of the interlopers and piled them in the middle of the row. Now the lettuce could sprout from underneath. The sage, thyme, and tarragon looked fresh and presented new vibrant green shoots. The basil was in a protected spot between rows and covered by a vented jar, or it would not have regenerated. She inhaled the fresh earthy scents of nature.

Near the end of the garden, a forest of evergreens, red oak, and walnut trees created a flush wonderland of plant life as an entry. A white-tailed deer, majestic in its simplicity, munched on wild grass. A doe, ready to produce an offspring, stood near the buck. Emma spied green shoots of carrot tops. With a gloved hand she wiped away the top layer of dirt. A large stone stood between her and the start of a stew. She pried the rock and tossed it onto the weed pile in the center of the row. The hardened blisters, tender despite the gloves, stung.

A few steps to the south, the chives looked ready to be harvested. She grabbed a large stick and knelt down. A pop sound echoed through the woods, she looked up and a whizzing noise passed by her head. Emma jumped and scoured the area. The deer took off at a lope going deeper into the forest. The rear end of a chestnut-colored horse weaved through the trees. She lifted her skirts and ran toward the carriage house.

"Gunfire. Woods." She rushed the words between heaving gasps of air.

Sam wiped his hands on an old flour sack. "What are you blubbering about?"

"I was in the garden. A gunshot. Bullet buzzed by my head. A chestnut-coated horse galloped away." She held her hand to her throat, feeling her pulse rapidly vibrate. The urgency to flee or to get a gun and chase the attacker warred inside her.

"Didn't you fight off bandits from a coach?" He walked outside and glanced in the direction of the ambush.

"Bandits were visible, today's shooter was not." Curiosity drew her forward. She gained control of her breathing. "Why would someone shoot at me?"

"I can guess," he muttered.

She wasn't opposed to sharing some of her irritation with him. "What?"

"More than likely it's a hunter. The woods are filled with deer." Sam took a saddle and gear from the tack room, climbed onto a stool and threw a blanket over a black stallion. "I'll go take a look."

"Please be careful. Do you have a gun?" The horse leaned back and nipped at the trim on Sam's leather jacket. Saddle in place, the horse moved to the side hitting Sam. He lost his balance and hit the stall wall. She rushed forward, attempting to catch him. He bristled and brushed her hands away. She tucked her hands into the bulging pockets of her day gown. "Sure about this horse?"

"I don't need a gun. Black Bart is the only riding horse, a champion. He belonged to Jayden." He pulled the cinch tight. The equine expanded his stomach. Sam put his foot in a stirrup and tugged on the strap. Black Bart blew out a puff of air, and he finished the task. The man was stronger than he appeared.

Jayden must have put his money into the modernization of the house instead of farmstock. Other than the two work horses, a single cow, and a flock of chickens, no other livestock existed on the ranch.

"I see, please be careful."

"Are you startin' to care for me, Miss Emma?" He finished saddling the horse and backed him out of the stall.

He didn't wait for her response, but stepped to the mounting block, settled onto the saddle, and galloped away. She glanced across the grounds. All clear, she walked briskly to the house. The carrots and chives made her pockets heavy, they flapped against her legs. The hunter was probably an incompetent shooter. She hoped he hadn't killed the beautiful doe.

She shut the kitchen door and leaned against the panel. Rachel, dressed in a white cotton night gown and fat housecoat, which appeared as if it jumped directly off the sheep and onto her body, stood in front of a teapot.

"Emma, where have you been?"

Keep the gunfire to yourself. There has been enough misery and a hunter shooting toward the house would make her anxious. "I went to the garden to see what vegetables and herbs are available. We're almost out of food from the church. We should probably talk about finances." She placed the limited produce on the countertop.

"I don't know about any of that. Mable always went to the market and bought food. If I wanted something special, Jayden and I would go into Fort Collins, and he'd buy it for me." Rachel frowned, then a surprised expression changed her features, and finally a solemn look held firm.

Emma's heart broke, watching the realization of her sister-in-law's future become a reality. Mable must have been the cook. All of the staff took off and left Rachel forsaken and alone. "Please have a seat, and I'll

53

fix you some breakfast. Do you want eggs? I can prepare eggs."

"Yes, sounds fine. What will I do?" Rachel whispered, pulled out a chair and lowered her bulk onto it.

"What do you want to do?" She broke eggs into a skillet, then uncovered yesterday's biscuits. *Now would be a good time to mention Indiana again.*

"How will I survive?" She lowered her head and mumbled. "I should have thought about this sooner."

"Don't worry. We'll go into Jayden's office and sort through his finances."

Rachel lifted her head and smiled. "The room next to the drawing room is his office."

"Good. Later today, if you are feeling up to it, we'll take the carriage into town and talk to a bank representative. It'll be fine. I'm sure you're not destitute." She scooped eggs onto a plate, added a stale biscuit to the side and placed the meal on the table. Black around the edges and clear glossy centers, they stood out like eyeballs.

Rachel was destitute. They filtered through desk drawers, sorted papers, threw away malodorous half-smoked cigars and previously opened nonsense letters. Finally, they uncovered the ledgers. Excited about going to Pineview, Rachel went upstairs to change into a traveling gown. Emma reviewed the numbers again. Her finishing school didn't cover budgets, but her mother oversaw the accounts in the Cody household. Like sewing a precise stitch house management and finances were mixed into her lessons.

She put the ledgers into an oversize bag and placed it on the marble table in the foyer. After a quick bath, she assessed the two-day dresses she'd packed for her trip. Which one would make a good impression on a banker?

"I'm getting too big for my dresses. We'll have to let out the seams." Rachel stood behind her and twisted to look at her side view in the mirror. "I hope the baby is a girl."

"I hope the baby is healthy, doesn't matter whether it is a boy or girl. Which one do you think I should wear? The blue or the green?" Emma held one in front of her and then the other.

"The green." She sat at the edge of the bed and rubbed the satin of the corset between her fingers. Emma dreaded putting it on. Perhaps in the west, she could forego the corset and simply wear a chemise, draws, and of course the crinolette.

"I brought a new gestation stay for you to wear during your pregnancy. It'll allow room for the baby to grow. I didn't know how easy they are to get out here in the West. I'd planned to give it to you when I arrived." She tugged a drawer open and removed a wrapped package.

"How do you know about this stay thing?"

"When I was preparing to come help you, I went to classes with my friend, Dr. Matthew Bambridge."

Rachel tore open the package and lifted the silky stay. She held the fabric up to her face and smiled. "It looks so easy to put on with the buttons in the front and no boning."

"I agree. The cream color and the softness of the fabric makes me wish I'd purchased one of my own for everyday wear."

"I miss the variety of merchandize Fort Wayne has

to offer. Do you think I should go back and live with his parents?"

Rachel had a lost little girl expression. How could Emma give advice about something she knew nothing of? She'd been in Colorado for a short time and met very few people. So far, her experiences have dealt with death and attacks. She guessed the decision would be made following the discussion with the banker today.

"Do you want to move back?"

"Well, not really. I love living out here in the country. The house is so new, and I don't think I could tolerate the smell of kerosene lanterns." She wrinkled her nose.

"There is that. Why don't you think on it for a while? You shouldn't travel a great distance until after the baby has arrived anyway. You have two months left?"

"Six weeks." She used the hook to unfasten her dress.

Emma took the device. "Here let me help you, and then you can help me fasten this torture garment by the name of corset."

An hour later, dressed in their finest garments, including hats and gloves, they strolled to the carriage. Sam, waiting for them with the step lowered, gave a long slow whistle.

Rachel smiled coquettishly. Emma curtsied, feeling a rush of warmth for the man making a widow smile. Life was so much better with friends.

"I'll be escorting the two loveliest ladies in all of the state." He assisted them into the open carriage. Rachel, with her ivory skin, instantly placed an umbrella over their heads for shade. She'd rather enjoy the warmth of the sun, but societal rules and decorum prevailed…sometimes.

"Miss Emma, I believe the shot was a stray bullet meant for a deer, as I didn't find evidence to contradict," Sam announced.

"Thank you, for checking." She sighed, knowing deep down the bullet was intended for her. Either the shooter missed the target, or they only wanted to frighten her.

"What is Sam talking about?"

"A hunter was in the woods today and had a poor aim. A bullet went past my head. Not to worry."

Rachel frowned. "Sam, will you post a no hunting sign, please. I don't want stray bullets to hit one of us."

Chapter 6

King stood near the front window of the saloon. Very few people walked along the boardwalks, and King's Court was practically empty. He'll need to find another rider to accompany the payroll delivery next week. Maybe two. He didn't want the money to be stolen again. The thieves were emptying his coffers. Provision of the payroll came from his personal bank account, at least until Wells Fargo got reimbursed from the insurance company.

Cassidy tickled the keys on the piano creating a fast-paced song. Miss Cat enclosed in the office was currently interviewing a new upstairs girl. Two wranglers were playing cards with Sam Shade, a card-shark if he'd ever seen one. He expected a fight to break out, so he hovered in the main room.

He removed a cigar from inside his pocket and glanced at the bank across the street and caddy-corner from Courtland-Carter Land Development office. To his surprise Mrs. Drake and Emma walked into the bank. *What are they doing?* Five minutes later, Widow Drake walked out, with a spring in her step and headed toward the mercantile.

Behind him, Sam McCloud and Miss Cat discussed the exchange of money for comfort. Soon the chatter of a woman's voice and the thump of booted footsteps went up the stairs. He smiled. Sam needed a little tender loving care after being turned down by Emma. Cat provided him with Desire; a busy lass and good at building a man's ego.

King smoked the entire cigar before Emma strolled from the bank. The ebony of her dress gleamed in the sunlight. No, it was a dark green. The short jacket clung tightly to her breasts and loose around her small waist. Even in the high heeled boots her step was surefooted. An aura of determination surrounded her, with her head held high and her shoulders straight. He grinned and rubbed his jaw. He intended to get closer to the little tight-laced sharpshooter. She would feel pillow soft and taste as sweet as a summer apple.

She stilled and turned. He glanced in the same direction. Morgan Palinurus flew out of the bank. The long tails of his black suit coat flying behind him, making him look like a blackbird. Palinurus slowed to a dignified walk when he got closer to Emma. To avoid a dust storm, from a herd of cattle being run through town to the stock yard, Palinurus took her arm and escorted her into the alley between the mercantile and Pineview Bank.

King moved outside to stand on the boardwalk. The dust settled, giving him the visual of Palinurus' hand on her arm. He was talking adamantly. She nodded. He pointed toward the hotel next to King's land-development business. With a bright smile, she lowered his hand from her arm, gave it a sharp jerky shake and strode into the mercantile. Palinurus stood on the boardwalk, focused on the sway of her skirts. With a shit-eating grin, he pulled his pocket-watch out and sauntered back into the bank. King tossed his extinguished cigar onto the dirt road. He went into his

jj Keller

office, grabbed his coat off the rack, and walked into the hallway.

"Mr. King, I'm going to be working in yer place." A high squeaky voice declared.

He turned. Treasure outfitted in a short full red skirt, black stockings, and a white lacy camisole which bared most of her small breasts. Due to his recent review of operating costs, he had a new and firm understanding of women's apparel.

"Miss Treasure, what a surprise. Where is Mrs. Landers?" He glanced over her head, out the window, and then at the woman.

"Mr. King, she was mean. Mean to da bone. I couldn't work for her n' more. She don't own me. I kin do what I want." Treasure tugged the tightly laced top.

"Have you done this type of work before?"

"No, sir. I'm sure it is easier than takin' care of Mrs. Landers." She twisted to pull a red high heel snug onto her foot and pushed her rising skirt down.

A dusty cowboy, with a battered hat and a long scraggly beard, came up to the bar and glanced at Treasure. She spread a hesitant smile and edged closer to the wall. The cowboy tipped his hat and grinned at her. She placed both hands on the sides of her head, patting her braided hair.

"Howdy, Miss."

"Howdy, I'm Treasure." She moved closer to King, until her hip bumped against his leg.

Her tiny bones shook. He didn't have time for this. He wanted to find out what Palinurus was doing with Emma. More importantly, he wanted to ask her to step out with him.

"Yes, you are and how many pieces of gold to

60

spend time with you?" The cowboy dipped his chin toward King and sneered. "Or are you busy with this dandy?"

When did a simple dark blue suit make him a dandy? He wrapped his arm around Treasure. "Did Miss Cat explain about what happens when you took this job? That you'd be relieving men of their needs?"

She sniffled and shook her head.

"Are you for sale or what?" The cowboy lifted his beer mug, drank all the brew, and slammed the empty glass onto the counter. His gaze roamed from Treasure's dark head to her tiny feet, scoping in all of her four-foot-seven frame.

Her entire body began to convulse. "I don't have nothin' else to do."

Damn. "Would you like to be a cook for Miss Emma, and her sister-in-law, Mrs. Drake?"

Treasure's eyes widened to the size of silver dollars. "For sure, Mr. King?"

He smiled at her. "For sure, Miss Treasure."

Miss Cat, in her low-cut red dress, with billows of lace surrounding her Rubenesque body, descended the stairs and headed toward them.

"Treasure, there is a customer waiting for you. Go upstairs now, darlin'." Her quiet voice held a hint of irritation. She placed her hand low on Treasure's back, pushing her forward.

"Treasure is going to work for the widow Drake. You'll need to find another girl." He pointed toward the rear staircase. "Treasure, go get changed, gather your things, and I'll take you to Mrs. Drake."

"Yes 'um, Mr. King." She scurried along the hallway with Miss Cat on her heels.

The cowboy stood red faced. "What's goin' on here? She was mine." He threw a punch.

King blocked the blow with his right hand and twisted the man's arm behind his back. "Now, I'm going to forgive you, 'cause you just came off a cattle drive. I'm sure you're hungry, thirsty, and needing the softness of a woman. The little lady wasn't for sale. We'll find you another." He gritted out the dictate and applied pressure to the struggling man's arm. "My treat."

The cowboy stopped thrashing. King released him and waved to Lulu. The gal had been trying to get him upstairs for months. Although he didn't care to be entertained by her, she would go for the range rider. Her bright blond locks bounced as she put her hand on his forearm and gushed, "Yes, King."

"Miss Lulu, I'd like you to meet…"

"Dewey, Dewey Lake." The cowboy ran his glance up and down Lulu.

"Mr. Lake would like to have some of your time, Lulu. I'd appreciate if you'd make him comfortable here at King's Court. I'll take care of the costs."

A pout formed on her lined face. "Of course. Come Dewey. Would you like another drink before we go upstairs?" She released his arm and entwined her hand with Dewey's.

"King, we agreed you wouldn't interfere with my business, and I wouldn't interfere with yours. Now, I'm going to be a girl short. We have two herds of cattle arriving today, which means a whole passel of cowboys lookin' for entertainment." Miss Cat's flour pasted face and bright red cheeks didn't give him an indication if she was angry or not. It didn't matter; he wanted to protect Treasure. This was not the life for her.

"I'll make it up to you. Treasure is an innocent who's had some recent bad luck. You'll get another girl." He patted her backside and kissed her cheek. "Umm, you smell good, Cat."

"Don't start with me. You'll owe me, and you'll have to pay for the dress."

He frowned. "What are you talking about?"

"Your Treasure just walked out the door, wearing one of my custom-made French designs." Her infamous feline smile broadened.

He doubted the dress was custom-made, as it looked like every other dancehall outfit. He went out the back door to find Treasure, all the while his mind was on the red glints of Emma's hair as she strolled toward the hotel twenty minutes ago, arm-in-arm with Rachel. They were laughing, and he'd never seen her laugh. If possible, she was even more beautiful.

"Treasure?"

"Yes 'um, Mr. King."

"Where are you?"

"I'm over here, behind the water barrels."

He peered behind the large containers. There she was, kneeling behind one of the oak barrels, her skinny knees shaking. She was hugging a carpet bag to her chest.

"Why are you hiding behind the barrels in the back alley?"

"Mr. King. I don't have no clothes to wear. One of the girls musta' throwed my dress away."

Big fat tears dripped down her face. He kicked himself for getting involved and the ensuing bundle of money needed to resolve the situation. His life of desirable solitude was quickly disintegrating.

"Treasure, I want you to come into my office. I'll go to the mercantile and get you a dress. Is there anything else you might need? Do you have shoes?" He sighed, keeping it low, so she wouldn't hear him.

"I got shoes, Mr. King. I don't want to owe ya. I'll pay ya back." She wiped tears from her cheeks.

"My gift to you, Treasure. You'll be helping me." He held out his hand. She grasped hold, like a lifeline. He led her to his office and walked across the street to purchase women's clothing. God help him.

A short time later, he held the bundled items snug under his arm and headed toward his office. Sam came running down the saloon stairs. "Sam."

"Hi ya, King. How are ya doing? I need to get back to the carriage. Rachel's waiting."

"I've hired a cook for you all. She's in my office. Take this package to her, introduce yourself, and wait while she changes her clothes. I'll tell the ladies about her and escort them to the carriage."

Sam danced around in place. "A cook? Yes. Whatever you want. A cook. I can't wait. Do we need to stop and get food? Might need to, since we ran out of the church-ladies food a few days ago."

"Was the cooking that bad?"

His smile downturned, and he glanced around. "Yes. All of the meals were burnt or undercooked.

"Well, since you have the buggy, I'll get staples and bring them out later today or tomorrow."

"What's the cook's name, again?" He tucked his shirt into place and settled the hat on his head.

"Treasure."

Sam smiled. "The Irish in me rejoices. I'll have a

treasure to guard." He took the package and strutted along the hallway.

King grinned. *Yep, Miss Cat gave Sam, Desire*. He took off at a lope to find the beautiful Miss Emma.

Chapter 7

Paintings of snow-capped mountains, buffalo roaming the plains, and Indians decorated the pine walls of the hotel dining room. Lace window curtains softened the overwhelming amount of wood. Various men, from miners to sodbusters, and businessmen in suits, sat the tables.

Emma smothered a laugh. Morgan Palinurus was charming, holding the door for her and pulling out her chair at the table. He asked about her food likes and dislikes. He smiled at her and gave a flirtatious side nod in agreement when she discussed the railroad.

Blast! It didn't matter how attractive he was or how sweet, her mind kept returning to Henry. The desire to see him, during their time in Pineview, was strong and pulled at her. Ignoring the conversations in the background, she kept sliding a glance out the window hoping to catch a glimpse of him. Rachel mentioned he owned a land development business near the hotel. He had other businesses as well, but she hadn't elaborated.

"Miss Emma, I know we've only met a few hours ago, but there is a dance Friday night at the town hall, and I'd like to escort you. And of course, Mrs. Drake as well."

Rachel's face lit up, like a lightening bug on a June night, then faded. She straightened her shroud and focused on the tablecloth.

Emma must refuse, their heavy mourning period just started. However, she wanted to see Rachel's light come again, more than a small flash. "Mr. Palinurus, we'd love to go to the dance with you. However—"

"Ladies, Palinurus." Henry pulled out the fourth chair across from her. "What dance?"

"Mr. Palinurus has invited us to go with him to a town hall dance. What is the celebration Mr. Palinurus?" Rachel's excitement was catching. Emma's heart pounded as she embraced the joy of the occasion or perhaps due to Henry's foot bumping against hers under the table.

She hated to be the one to take Rachel's smile away, although odd for her to be celebrating while in mourning. Perhaps societal rules were more relaxed in the west. She glanced at Henry. He pulled at the white cuffs of his sleeves. Had he rushed to pull on his blue jacket? His blond hair fell from a split in the middle and tiny pieces fell forward on each side above his eyebrows. She held her hands tight in her lap to keep from reaching over to move those silky strands, so they wouldn't hide his eyes.

"The warm weather has made the townspeople want to forget the dreary winter and celebrate. Miss Emma, as you're new to the area, this doesn't mean the snow has ended. We'll get another snowstorm before Mid-West type spring weather arrives." Palinurus touched the top of her hand, as she reached for her cup of tea. "It will be an honor to escort such beautiful women."

Henry coughed.

"I'll have two lovely ladies, one on each arm, and the envy of all the single men of Pineview," Palinurus continued.

She slid her hand from beneath his and picked up her cup. Before taking a sip, she smiled. "It will be a pleasure to be escorted by you to the dance, right Rachel?"

Rachel picked at the tablecloth. "Oh, yes. King, are you going to join us?"

Palinurus scooted to the edge of his seat. Over the top of the teacup, Emma slid her glance from his gaze to meet Henry's beautiful, blue-green eyed stare.

He grinned, enough his dimples winked at her. "I wouldn't miss it."

Palinurus stood. "I need to get back to the bank. Ladies, thank you for sharing lunch with me. I'll be out to your house at six o'clock on Friday."

He'd paid the bill for lunch a few minutes earlier. A good thing as she didn't have much of her traveling cash left. She dreaded telling Rachel about her lack of funds. Either the Widow Drake would be forced to go to Indiana and live with the Cody's, or Emma would need to come up with a plan to make fluid funds.

The plain-faced waitress, with mousey-brown hair coming loose from her cap, set a cup of steaming coffee in front of Henry. "Thank you."

"You're welcome, Mr. Courtland." She widened her smile, patted her apron, and skipped away.

He lifted the white ceramic cup to his perfect lips and sipped the brew.

"Oh, Emma, I'm so excited. I haven't been to a dance, since, well, my wedding. I need to go look at fabric for a new dress." She stood and gathered her bag and shawl. "Oh, you still have half of your pie to eat."

"I'm finished."

"Please stay, and I'll go to the mercantile to browse." Rachel's foot tapped a quick tune as she glanced out the window.

Emma dragged her fork through the blueberry pie. "That's fine. I'll join you in a few minutes. I saw a bolt of blue satin that would look lovely on you."

Rachel gave a quick wave and waddled toward the door.

Alone with Henry in a group of chattering diners, the clanking dish noise faded. Her stomach fluttered. He moved his foot away from hers and leaned forward. She felt the loss, wanting him to remain close.

"I thought you weren't interested in being courted?"

She shrugged. "I'm not, but Rachel seemed so excited about the dance. It might be a temporary method to mask her grief and socialize with locals."

"You could have refused Palinurus." He lifted a fork and took a bite of her slice of pie. "Are you interested in being courted by him?"

"Would you care if I said yes?"

"You're your own woman. We've only known each other a few weeks."

"Oh, well, then." She'd made a wrong assumption that he was attracted to her. Despite her sudden breathlessness, she tried to keep her voice uninflected. "Since there's no reason why I shouldn't, if Morgan Palinurus wishes to court me, I might accept." Lowering her eyelids, she watched him.

He laid the fork down on the empty pie plate and lifted his coffee cup. The blue of his eyes contained a dangerous glint, and his mouth formed a straight line. Maybe he would care if she was courted by Morgan. "I hired a cook for you today, so you don't need to put an ad in the paper."

"Who gave you the authority to hire a cook? I don't recall Rachel saying, Henry please hire a cook for us." God they couldn't afford a cook. They couldn't even buy food.

"No, she didn't. Why do you have a burr up your...? I'm trying to help you." He touched her hand, as Morgan had earlier. This time she didn't want to pull away, but societal rules prevailed.

She crossed her hands on her lap. "I'm sorry. It has been a trying day. I should go. Rachel is waiting, and she'll need to rest."

"Emma, I hired Treasure. I'll be responsible for paying her, until Jayden's estate is settled. She's in the buggy now with Sam. I told him I would buy food and bring it out later." He rubbed his fingers back and forth over the top of the table.

Her first instinct was to tell him they didn't need his handouts, but they did. Her last few coins would go toward the material for Rachel's dress. Would the woman continue to lack a grasp on reality? She rose from the chair and tucked her purse under her arm.

"Thank you, Henry. I'm sure Rachel and Sam will be relieved to have decent meals. Have a good day." She lifted her chin and strolled toward the door.

****

King jumped up, dug a quarter out of his pocket, dropped it on the table, and ran after her. He bumped into the waitress on the way to the door. A step to the left, and she moved in the same direction.

"I left the money on the table."

"Thanks, King."

70

Two steps and he'd be outside. She reached out and grabbed his arm. "There's a dance Friday night, and I was wondering if you were going to be there."

"Yes, Miss Mabel, I might be." He lifted her hand from his arm and rushed out the door. The Drakes were passing the Stock Yard. The cowboys whistling and carrying on must have encouraged her, the blue striped umbrella twisted faster.

He'd never met a woman who scared him more. However, she didn't seem the least bit interested in him. The heart chooses who to reach out to, and his heart wanted Miss Emma Cody. If he played his cards right, it wouldn't take long to convince her to see only him.

****

A few hours had passed since Emma talked with Henry, and she admitted she was a coward. Through the open bedroom window came the whisper of wagon wheels pulling to a stop in front of the barn. She didn't believe it possible, but right now if asked, she'd claim weakness due to her monthly trial and supposed grief. She'd remain in her room, a cool cloth on her forehead, and avoid seeing the western Don Juan.

A knock sounded on her door. "Come in, Rachel."

"Heard you were ill. How are you doing?" Henry's voice was very close.

She lifted the cloth from her head and pulled the covers up to her neck. His smooth-shaven face, a mere inch away, caused heat to rush to her face. "A gentleman shouldn't be in a lady's room, with her in bed." She clutched the damp cloth in her hand.

"I know you don't cater to rules of etiquette, Emma." He held one hand behind his back.

She narrowed her eyes. The blanket grew moist from the damp cloth. She loosened her fingers. "Of course, I do. I've standards."

His delicious well-shaped mouth turned into a grin. She covered her eyes, the once cool cloth now warm. He didn't get the hint to leave.

"Do you think you'll be able to go to the dance with Palinurus on Friday?"

Blasted man. She moved the edge of her mask and glanced into his eyes. They were clear blue, full of questions, with a tint of hardness. *Ah, shouldn't have done that.* "Yes, I'm honorable and always keep my promises."

His grin turned into a frown. "Even if you continue to be ill?"

"I'll be fine on Friday. It's a minor inconvenience." She broke contact with his sincere gaze. "What is wrong with your arm?"

He whipped his appendage from behind his back, exposing three purple hyacinths. "I brought you flowers."

The sweet spring scent perfumed the air as he extended them. She took the bouquet and held the blooms to her nose. "Thank you, Henry. What a nice surprise and very refreshing."

"Emma, I'd like to ask you…"

"King, what are you doing in here? This is an unmarried woman, in her bedclothes. You should not be in her bed chamber." Rachel fluttered her hands in the air.

He bowed. "I was just leaving. Good day, Emma." He grinned and strut from the room.

She ignored Rachel's questioning look, placed the

flowers in her glass of water on the bedside table and settled the damp cloth over her eyes. Shortly after, the door clicked shut.

Two days later, Emma sat in the rocker on the veranda in front of the house. A true sign of spring, birds musical voices filled the air and fresh pine aroma scented the breeze. The bit of warm weather made her feel invigorated and anxious at the same time. Jayden was the source of her anxiety, and Rachel's financial future drove her to consider asking for help.

Henry rode up the drive on a buff-colored horse. He tipped his hat back when he got closer to the veranda. A simple wink from him, and her heart fluttered. Inevitably she'd return to Fort Wayne, so she shouldn't be courted by him. Her goal was to help Rachel through this childbirth and return home. Although, she did enjoy his kiss. Perhaps she could get a few more kisses before returning home.

He dismounted, tied his horse to the railing, and opened a saddlebag. Withdrawing a gold square tin, he sauntered toward her. The man swaggered like no other, broad shoulders, trim waist, and a disarming cocky grin. He leaned against the railing across from her seat, set his hat on the bench, and widened that damn smile. "Good afternoon, Emma, and how are you today?"

"I'm well, and how are you, Henry?" She folded her hands in her lap and stopped the motion of the rocker. He tilted forward, cupped her chin into his rough hand, and stared.

"You're not as pale today." He smiled, exposing the dimples.

"I'm feeling much better, thank you." Her heart started that quick pounding again. She turned her head.

"What is that you have in your hand?"

"A box of chocolates. For you. Whenever my mother didn't feel well, my father brought her a box of chocolates, and she felt much better." He extended a gold tin.

"Thank you, Henry." She opened the lid and smelled the sweet scent of the cocoa wrapped confections. "Yum. I'm sure we'll all enjoy this fine treat."

He returned to lean against the rail, but his shirt pulled apart in the process and those blasted chest hairs poked through the opening at his neck. She closed her eyes and took a deep breath. *Think of something other than his fine appearance. Think of shooting the bandit. That was abhorrent. Think of the dead body. That was repulsive.* Gunfire, frightening and fresh, clouded her mind.

"Bad memories, Emma?" he whispered.

She opened her eyes. "Yes. I'm fine. It was very nice of you to come all this way to bring a box of candy."

He nodded.

"Henry, we'll pay you for the goods and services."

"Consider them a gift. Are you still going to the dance tomorrow night with Palinurus?"

"Yes, I honor my obligations." She considered the upcoming evening with Banker Morgan an obligation instead of a pleasure. He'd mentioned foreclosure. She needed details. "And Rachel needs to be around people and experience a bit of joy."

"I see. How is Treasure doing?" His voice rumbled, then his lips were tight.

"Treasure is as her name implies."

"Is she around? I need to retrieve a dress she borrowed from one of my friends."

"Ah, the bawdy French design dress." The garment certainly didn't look French, but it didn't stop Emma from holding the dress in front of her, making the flounces flip up and the skirt came just to the top of her knees. Treasure giggled and described Miss Cat from the town saloon.

"Yes." He moved his hands to his very muscular thighs.

This is insane. Move. Take him inside, around other people, and for god's sake stop wishing he'd take you into his arms and kiss you. "Come along. We'll take this special gift in and share with the others." She rose. He tucked his hand under her arm, and together they went inside. Her body hummed.

He stayed for supper, then returned to town. She spent the remainder of the evening in her room, reviewing ledgers, papers, and looking for possible financial solutions. For now, she would avoid talking with the fragile mother-to-be about finances.

A simple plan would be for Rachel to live in Fort Wayne. Emma understood why she was reluctant to leave. Colorado's scenery was breathtakingly beautiful. The bristlecone pine trees in front of the white capped mountain ranges, and the plains dotted with sage brush, wildflowers, and ponderosa pine trees adding yet another color of green called out, and she fell in love. This land quickly became a loveable haven.

Rachel carried fresh spring flowers to Jayden's grave each day and spent time talking to the entombed. She wouldn't be able to visit his shrine if she moved. Emma needed to find her brother and get an explanation about the path he'd chosen, and if he wanted to remain dead in the public eye. First, she had to acquire financial stability.

Friday arrived sooner than she desired. She bathed, washed her hair, and while it dried, rubbed lavender scented lotion onto her dry skin. Gardening equaled hands chafed to rough sandpaper texture. She threw a robe over her underclothing and stockings, trying not to mess the hairstyle. A strong cup of tea would strengthen her resolve to have a good time at the dance and above all else, weasel information out of Banker Morgan.

She pushed open the kitchen door and overheard Sam say something in a lowered voice to Treasure, who giggled in response. Thankfully, he'd found a romantic interest besides her. Tea could wait. She pivoted and headed toward the staircase giving the couple privacy.

"Rachel?" Emma eased the door open a couple of inches and noticed her pinched face in the reflection of the mirror. She walked into the room.

"Why aren't you ready? Morgan Palinurus is supposed to be here in fifteen minutes." Rachel's sharp, clipped voice made her wince. "I want to talk to him about buying a new buggy."

"It'll only take a moment to remove this robe and slide into the dress. You'll need to fasten it." Emma plopped onto the coverlet and stretched out. *You need to tell her she doesn't have any money to buy things.*

"You'll muss your hair, and I worked thirty minutes on it to make it look presentable."

"Sorry. I'll be careful." To prove it, she leaned on her side and propped her head with the palm of her hand. "Rachel, I need to tell you about your finances."

"They're bad, aren't they? I didn't want to ask

because I think I knew the answer."

"You have some choices to make. A solution," Emma made figure eight patterns on the cover with her index finger, "might be to create a boarding house, although we're so far out from town, maybe a bed and breakfast inn."

"I don't want strangers in my home." She sighed. "Get dressed, and you can tell me why I should open this inn, while I fasten you."

She removed her only formal dress from the hanger. The gown was a beautiful blue gray with a light brownish-gray piping. Cut very low in front, the sleeves tapered from the shoulders to the wrist, emphasizing her waist.

She removed the robe and dragged the mountain of material over her head. Rachel turned her around and buttoned the row of tiny cloth covered buttons.

"Did Jayden have friends that he visited?"

"He went to see King in town. Sit and I'll fix your hair."

"When I was younger, I'd go to a wooded area near our house, you know at the edge of Spy Run?" She removed a small box of silver hairpins from her robe pocket.

"Yes, I know where. Jay took me there one day."

"Did Jayden have a special place he'd go to get away?"

"Oh my, no. He spent all his free time inventing." Rachel patted a curl into place. "He did see someone special though."

"Who did he see?"

"Mr. Morgan's here, Miss Emma." Treasure announced from the doorway. She had one foot inside the room and one foot out, while straightening her dress and touching her hair. Impatient to get back to her liaison with Sam?

"Treasure, please ask him to wait in the parlor and offer him tea or coffee."

"Yes 'am."

She'd make the best of the evening, even if she didn't want to be in a crowded room full of strangers. The dress was fastened, she turned to evaluate her sister-in-law. *Pale face, change the subject.*

"I overheard Treasure and Sam talking and giggling in the kitchen." She got a pair of slippers from the closet. "Black or brown?"

"Black. I've seen them walk hand in hand in the garden. Good fit since she's only a few inches taller than him." Rachel smothered a giggle with her hand.

"Yes." She chuckled. "Come on, let's go down and see Mr. Morgan."

Rachel grimaced. "You go ahead. I need to use the facilities."

"Are you alright?" She looked as white as her elbow length gloves.

"Maybe I should stay at home. Suddenly, I don't feel so well." Rachel sat down on the dark green fireside chair and rubbed her stomach.

"I'll explain to Mr. Morgan we're not going to the dance." Emma cleared the threshold.

"Emma," Rachel's raspy pain-filled voice cried.

Chapter 8

Jealousy, eating away at his insides, became a lasso tightening a knot in his gut. King stayed in his office reviewing accounts, while stealing glances at the clock. He didn't want to go to the dance and see Emma in another man's arms. His goal was to catch the payroll thieves and search into Jayden's murder. He talked to the sheriff and most of the people in the saloon. The most valuable person who could provide answers was Cat, and she'd mysteriously disappeared. The girls said she'd be gone for a few days.

He snatched a cigar from the humidor and walked through the nearly empty saloon. Damn. Was everyone at the dance? Ah, Ben Fireman leaned against the bar, nursing a beer. His black cotton trousers had a hole in the rear pocket and his chambray shirt was frayed at the cuffs.

When King was looking for someone to take care of his homestead, Ben came into the saloon asking for work and farming was his only skill. King hired him two months ago and hadn't regretted the decision. His innovative improvements increased the value of the farm. "Evening, Ben, how's the farm?"

"Good. Thanks for asking, King. I'll brin' a barrel of the wheat to you next time I'm in town." His smile broadened.

"That'd be a fine thing." God knew he didn't want

to farm it, nor did he want to sell the Courtland homestead because of family traditions. Maybe one day, he'd want to settle down. "Let me know if you need anything."

"Will do, boss."

Clean crisp air assaulted his nostrils as he flung open the saloon door. Danny, the kid he hired to take out the trash and clean the place, had recently swept off the boardwalk. The boy was loyal and did an honest day's work.

King leaned against the support post and pulled out a match to light the cigar. He could hear the musicians playing his favorite song, *Oh, Shenandoah!* He tapped his foot a quick beat on the wood floor adding to the instrumentals. The image of her dancing in Palinurus' arms made his gut clench. The man's hands would touch her while they danced. Her laughter and green-eyed, half-shuttered glances entered his head causing him to regret not insisting she go with him to the dance.

Damn. He threw the cigar onto the dusty road and marched toward the celebration. A couple of feet away from the building he stopped. His black wool pants and white cotton shirt were not party clothes, pivoting to return to the saloon he peered through a window. Couples danced in the brightly lit hall. The musicians strummed a folk song, *Oh My Darling Clementine*. The band was comprised of a fiddler, pianist chiming the church's piano, and a flutist. The flute player was a new addition. He continued to follow the rustic clapboard lines of the townhall. A tall man with a derby hat escorted a shapely woman in a white dress out the back door.

King took off at a jog toward the backside of the

building. A lantern, hanging at the edge of the backdoor, illuminated the red glints of her hair as they walked arm in arm into the grove of spruce trees. The moonlight hid some of the shadowed areas, so he stopped and listened, separating the noise. A hoot owl's call screeched through the wind. Tree branches rubbed against each other, creaking and groaning like a barn door loose on its hinges. Soft feminine laughter came from a path leading through the park.

When Johnny Comes Marching Home Again provided him with a steady rhythm as he approached his quarry. Her back was against the rough bark of an oak tree, her head bowed, she didn't appear to be struggling. It didn't matter. She was his and had become the day he kissed her by the pond. He grabbed the man's arm and swung him around, ready to plow his fist into the sidewinder's square face.

"What the hell? King is that you?" Aubrey Carter, his land development partner, shouted. His hand stopped King's fist from connecting with his left cheek.

"Sorry, Aubrey, I thought you were someone else." He dipped his head into a nod. "Mrs. Bullington, it's a nice evening. How's Captain Bullington?"

Aubrey looked abash, ducked his head onto his chest. Mrs. Bullington drew her white, almost transparent, dress together in the front. Her overflowing orbs of flesh confined, she winked at him.

Outrageous!

He tugged Aubrey a short distance from the viper. "As your friend, I can tell you, this can only get as tangled as a cat's tail. The woman is married to a very powerful, angry man."

For the first time in the five years, he'd known

Aubrey, the man was at a loss for words. He frowned. "Well, have a nice night. Don't forget married women are trouble."

The music stopped, indicating the band was on a break. He marched toward the front of the building, greeting friends along the way. Torn between taking a look inside and going back to the saloon before he made more of a fool of himself, he pulled out his pocket watch and noted the time.

"Howdy, King."

"Hi ya, Cliff. Havin' fun at the dance?"

"You betcha. I shut down the mercantile early, so I could dance with a few of the ladies." He grinned, showing crooked front teeth that jetted out over the bottom ivories.

"The men sound good tonight. A couple of new songs and the flute's a nice addition. Did you see Morgan Palinurus inside?" He nodded toward the hall.

Cliff scratched his gray beard. "Can't say that I did."

"Did you see Rachel Drake and her sister-in-law, Emma Cody?"

"No, they haven't been here. I'd hoped they would, 'cause I'd like to spin the beautiful Miss Cody." Cliff glanced along the street. "Nice talkin' to ya, King. I need to get on home."

"Night, Cliff."

Had something happened? King strode toward the bank, which was dark inside, and then past Mrs. Butter's rooming house. Palinurus' window showed only darkness. With each step, his heart pounded harder in his chest. At the stables, he asked Jimmy to saddle his horse, Maverick. Back in his office he strapped on a gun and threw on a duster.

"Nick, I'll be out at the Drake's if anyone is looking for me."

Nick drew a beer from the keg and waved. "Right, boss."

No broken-down carriage on the road, and no sign of foul play. Where were they? Had Rachel gone into early labor. No. He remembered seeing Dr. Grayson at the dance, catching a breath of fresh air. At the sight of house lights, his heart settled to a regular beat.

His horse slid to a stop. Clouds of dust blew up and covered his boots as he jumped from the steed. He loosely tied Maverick's reins onto the hitching post and stopped dead in his tracks. Through the parlor window, he spied Emma dancing with Palinurus. Rachel sat at the piano playing an engaging melody, by Bach if he remembered correctly.

As fast as the owl's blink, his fear turned into unreasonable anger. He knocked on the door and waited. All right, so their bodies were not touching, that was one thing. Rachel was in the room, so they were not alone. Pleasant feminine laughter filtered through the slowly opening door.

He smelled her lavender scent, before she came into view. At first glance, she made his heart flutter. The shiny blue gown was cut low in the front, tapering at the waist, and then flaring into a full skirt. It was trimmed in a light brown, almost like a deer skin color. He couldn't keep his gaze off the deep cleavage she exposed.

"You were going to wear that dress, a dress showing your," he pointed toward her chest, "and parade in a town full of randy men?" Crimson color crept up to her cheeks, and her upturned pink lips became a straight line. *Shit.*

"I believe, Mr. Courtland, that my dress choice is mine and not yours. You do not have the right to judge what I wear." Her chin tilted up, and her shoulders straightened into a stiff line, making said breasts more prominent. Granted, he should have kept his focus on her face instead of the beautiful white orbs begging to be released from the constraints of the gown.

"Mr. Courtland, if you would look at my face, please."

He grinned at her schoolmarm voice, but quickly lost all humor as his glance met hers. "I beg your forgiveness, Miss Emma."

"Yes. Well, what is it you wish—"

"King, what a wonderful surprise! We have four to dance, which will complete the quadrant. I'll see if Sam is around. He can play the piano, and we can all dance. Mr. Palinurus, will you stay for one more song?" Rachel tucked her hand between his arm and side and tugged him forward.

"Yes, of course, Mrs. Drake," Palinurus replied.

Emma blew out a harsh breath and shut the door, hard.

"Here, let's get this coat off of you." Rachel pulled on his sleeve. "Oh Sam, great, you happened to arrive at the perfect time. Would you be a dear and put King's horse in the barn? It's late and since we have a meeting in the morning, he'll stay the night."

Sam nodded. "Sure will."

"As you wish." King smiled and strode into the room.

"Where's Treasure? We could make this a party,"

Rachel said in a singsong voice.

"I'll get Treasure, and then put King's horse in the barn."

"Lovely, thank you." She widened her smile.

He flushed a red color, to match his hair. "Anything for you, Miss Rachel."

King hung his duster on the coatrack, untied the belt pull holding the gun holster to his leg and unfastened the gun belt. The leather on leather made a slithering sound as it was removed. He placed the gun belt next to his coat, and within easy access, then glanced at Emma. Her skirts swirled as she sashayed into the parlor.

He brushed at dust on his shirt and pants. "I'm sorry for my appearance. I rushed out of town after I had a vision, a fear really, that you were delivering." Part truth. His thoughts dealt with Emma kissing another man, but he was concerned for Rachel.

"Oh, nonsense, although I did have an upset stomach earlier tonight. Emma wanted to cancel our evening with Mr. Palinurus. Of course, he wouldn't have anything to do with that. We created our own little dance right here." She led him into the parlor.

"What would you like to drink, King?"

Palinurus and Emma were standing near the window, her head bowed and his mouth close to her ear. Jealously roared throughout him, but he stifled the urge to physically break them apart. He was not a jealous man, what the hell was happening to him?

"Whisky, if you have it." He kept his glance on Emma. She looked upset. Her frown created worry lines. What could Palinurus possibly be saying to her that would agitate her?

"Here you go." Rachel handed him the drink and picked up her cup of tea. "To new beginnings."

He clicked his short glass to her teacup and repeated, "To new beginnings."

Treasure came in carrying a tray of cheese and seasonal fruit made up of fragrant strawberries and lightly grilled rhubarb coated with sugar and arranged in a half circle on the platter. A few minutes later, Sam arrived, having recently brushed his hair and rolled his sleeves down.

"Sam, what would you like to drink?" Rachel bubbled, as she arranged a serving tray of beverages.

"Is there any of the juice-drink Treasure made?" He glanced at the decanters.

"I don't know. Treasure, do you know what he's talking about?"

"Yes, mam. I'm not sure you folks would like it though. It's a mix of berries and other fruits mashed together, with a little soda water. My pappy used to add moonshine, but I don't cotton to that." She straightened the already aligned glasses on the tray.

"It sounds delicious, Treasure. I would like to try it, without the moonshine of course," Emma said.

"Thank you, Miss Emma. I'll get the jug." She smiled brightly, pivoted, and scurried toward the kitchen.

"Sam, what new experiments are you working on?" Palinurus asked.

Sam sat at the piano and ran his fingers lightly over the keyboard. "I'm trying to figure out a way to run electricity to Rachel's sewing machine. She likes to sew, but its tiring on her legs. The chain-stitch sewing machine works well, and if I could connect it to be power-driven, she could shoot out dresses, curtains, tablecloths quick-like."

"You like to sew?" Emma's voice held a hint of surprise.

Rachel bustled to the piano, grabbed the sheet music, and flipped through the onion-skin paper. "Yes. I have been so bored sitting here every day. I don't have an interest in herb gardening like you do. Couldn't walk to the neighbors, and I'm not good at guiding a buggy, so I started drawing sketches of dresses, which led to sewing the dresses." Her face took on an embarrassed look, like women do when they are privately proud of something they've done but were taught not to brag about the accomplishment.

King stared at Emma. Her glance latched onto Palinurus', and they both smiled at the same time. A secret was passed between the two, and he resented being left out.

"Here, please play this song. It has a nice rhythm for our little party." Rachel handed Sam a couple sheets of music, then grasped King's hand and tugged him to the center of the room. King could not imagine what had gotten into her. When was the last time he saw her crack more than a polite smile? Ah, yes, when he'd ended his friendship with Jayden. Drake tried to cheat him out ownership of Blair's Mine.

"Rachel, you seem to be exceedingly happy." He made a turn.

She gasped. "Oh, King, I feel free for the first time in two years."

The song ended. He escorted her to the settee. She sat, lifted a cardboard fan, and flashed it back and forth. Sam handed a glass of juice to Treasure.

"Treasure, how is the new job going?" King grasped his glass of whisky, picturing the fish burnt on one side and raw on the other.

"Treasure is an excellent cook. Her fried fish is my favorite," Sam announced.

Treasure lowered her head, but not before King caught her broad smile. *Drink to Me Only with Thine Eyes* filled the room with its pleasurable musical notes. Sam took Treasure into his arms and swayed to the music. Rachel, sitting at the piano, was lost in her mystical world of music and dreams.

He placed his glass on the tray and extended his hand to Emma. She met his glance and quirked her lips. Oh, yes, she might feel the bond-pull as much as he did. "Emma, may I have this dance."

****

Like magnet to steel they drew together. Henry's arms hauled her close, entirely too close as his thighs collided with her hips.

"Mr. Courtland, this is not the proper space between a couple dancing," she whispered, and glanced at Morgan. The frown smeared across his face needed to be erased. They may need him for funding to start a dress shop. Her mind was working fast and furious to create a plan to get funds for Rachel, so that she could remain in Pineview. Emma brushed off the notion that she would be staying as well.

His lips touched her ear, causing the blue-diamond earbob to swing. "When you say my given name, I'll put space between us."

She shoved his hand. "King." Immature, yes, and especially when unconstrained laughter flew from her lips.

He danced her out the open door to the veranda. The stars gleamed brighter in Colorado, the scents of the spring night fresher. The men more romantic.

"You little vixen. There will come a time when I will extract just rewards." He brushed his face against her hair and sniffed. His lips caressed the side of her face. The body hum returned.

His manhood briefly brushed her frontside, creating a tingle, an itch, a feeling she couldn't describe. Her breath caught and her breasts ached. A cough from the doorway alerted her to the fact the music stopped.

"Thank you, Henry, for a lovely dance." With a pivot, she rushed through the entryway stopping just inside, safe from her wanton thoughts.

Morgan appeared beside her. Rachel fingered the keys, creating a ballad. Sam and Treasure danced, circling around them. A whirlwind of confused emotions smashed together, warmth for Henry and a desire to slap Morgan's hands. Could she run away, get lost in the darkness?

"I believe this is our dance," Morgan stated loudly, rising above the piano tunes.

"I thought you needed to return to town?" She couldn't take her focus off Henry. He crossed to the brick half-wall surrounding the veranda and leaned against the baluster. The moon highlighted his hair, the layers clearly defined on a perfectly shaped head.

Morgan pulled her into a waltz. "I have time for one more dance and to talk to you and Rachel about her financial future."

He pinched her waist. His mouth was moving. She tried to decipher what he was saying.

"Yes, of course, we'll talk."

"A woman made an anonymous payment today at the bank, on the Drake mortgage." He leaned closer to her ear. "Rachel has another month before the bank forecloses."

The dance ended. Emma stepped away and clapped for Rachel's performance. How could her body react in such different ways with two very attractive men? Heat rose from her knees up when Henry touched her, and chills racked her body when Morgan placed a hand on hers.

Sam and Treasure continued to move in dance steps. Rachel slowed down the beat with *Greensleeves.*

Henry took her into his arms. She was constantly aware of where his hands were located; on her hand, at her waist, higher on her back, then they returned to her waist. "I didn't know about your meeting tomorrow. What is the topic of discussion?"

"Hum, if Rachel didn't tell you, then maybe I should keep her confidence."

The song ended. Rachel slumped, clanging the keyboard.

Emma touched her earlobe. "I believe it's late, and I need to make certain our little mother gets her rest."

A contemplating stare came from Rachel. Emma, knees wobbly, walked to the piano. "Come along, I'll help you settle in for the night."

"Thank you, Emma. Sam and Treasure, thank you for joining us tonight and for the delicious drink. King, you'll take the room at the end of the hall. Morgan, it was a pleasure dancing with you, and I so enjoyed your company. I hope that you'll join us for Sunday brunch."

Morgan, being a gentleman, kissed Rachel's

outstretched hand. "It will be my pleasure Mrs., uh, Rachel."

"Come along then, we'll show you to the door. Good night, everyone." Like the princess she could be, Rachel, leaning heavily on her, paraded the way to the foyer.

"Good night, all."

Morgan slid into his overcoat and with a quick stride moved closer to Emma. "I'd like to have a house exactly like this someday soon. Thank you for inviting me to stay and dance." His glance scanned the foyer. "Miss Emma, I'd like to talk with you about the arrangement. Perhaps we can find some time alone on Sunday."

Emma forced her mouth to form a smile. "Of course on Sunday. Thank you for dancing with us."

"Emma, I'm suddenly very tired. Could you help me upstairs?" Rachel's voice cracked. She'd spent too much time on her feet today.

"Good night, Morgan."

"Good night, ladies."

She climbed into bed a solid hour later. A bit of coaxing and reassurance to get the mother-to-be to quiet down. She asked questions regarding Henry, and why Morgan wanted a private discussion. Emma reassured her she didn't know but explained about the possibility of starting a dress-making business. Rachel enthusiastically agreed to create gowns.

Emma snuggled under the quilt. She'd ask Sam if he could craft unique toys. Mothers would shop for dresses and children could play. If they were successful, they would branch out to Fort Collins and Boulder. Visions of flying dollars jumped across her mind, soothing her to sleep. Wait, what woman made a mortgage payment? She'd ask Morgan if he knew who'd made the anonymous payment.

"Emma." She didn't want to wake and moved her head back and forth on the pillow, ignoring the annoying voice.

A nudge to her shoulder, and she pushed her head further into the feathers. "Emma."

She slowly peeled her eyelids open, resenting the intrusion.

He knelt beside her bed.

Chapter 9

"What are you doing in my room?" Emma gave an unladylike yawn and rolled to her side. She peeked over the edge of the bed. He was kneeling on the step leading up to the feather mattress, which brought his upper thighs directly in line with her face. She raised her head bypassing Henry's lovely chest, vibrant beneath the unbuttoned shirt. A look of pain flashed across his face.

"What's wrong? Why are you here?" She tried to sit upright in bed. Her white cotton nightgown, caught underneath her, separated between her breasts. Blast. The tie came undone again.

"Lordy," he whispered.

His voice held a rasp that added a new dimension to her already strong attraction. Emma pulled the two pieces of gown together, lowered her voice. "Why are you in my bedroom?"

Her heart raced with the excitement of having a man in her room. A man she desired. Etiquette wise, very wrong to continue a conversation. She touched his arm. He inhaled.

"Are you ill?" She moved her legs over to the side of the bed, bracing the cloth against her thighs, and put a palm on his forehead.

"Someone is downstairs. I want you to go to Rachel's room and lock the door."

If possible, his face took on an even greater degree of pain. The man must be dying or at least he'd lost his senses. His hands were in tight fists beside his body. She rubbed her hand across his whiskered face. The tiny hairs pricked her fingers. "It's just Sam and Treasure."

"Sam told me about the shooter. Emma, please go to Rachel's room while I check downstairs." He stood.

She crunched her fingers into his shirttail and pulled herself to her knees. His kiss stopped her movement, the sweet tender embrace of a man who sought solace from his plight. She wrapped her arms around his neck and returned his kiss. The scent and taste of the spearmint toothpowder he used earlier was still present on his mouth. The man was a good kisser. Not that she had a lot of experience, but she had pecked Parker Carlton in the sixth grade, and Matthew Bambridge stole a few kisses in the walking park before she left for Colorado. But none of those kisses compared to this man's lips on hers.

His hand slid along her arm, to her waist, across her thigh and trailed upward again. She held her breath. No male had ever touched her so intimately. Would he caress her breasts? She hoped he would as they ached something fierce, as if they operated on their own and sought relief. The pounding, the tingling, caused her to shove her chest against his. Instant multiplication of the ache occurred. Her lower region came into contact with the hardness of his body.

He moved his lips from hers, kissed her ear, and the side of her neck. She lowered one hand from around his neck and separated his shirt to expose his skin.

He groaned louder. She resisted the need to touch

and explore. His free hand went to the front of her gown; pulled the material away and eased the throbbing of her breasts.

She pressed against his rough palm gaining instant relief, wanting to experience all of the unknown fantasies she'd dreamt.

"Emma, are you awake?" Rachel whispered through the door. "I can't sleep, will you make hot chocolate for me?"

"Yes, I'll meet you downstairs." Her glance went from his face to the doorknob and returned to meet his gaze. He held his finger up to her swollen hot lips, shifted his hand to cup her cheek. He kissed her gently on the lips, then backed away. He turned and walked into the chifforobe.

The hallway door opened, and Rachel entered.

Emma moved the covers down and rubbed her eyes.

"I'm awake. Come in." She yawned and patted the top of the mattress. "Come."

Rachel climbed into the bed from the opposite side and snuggled close. "Why, you're breathing fast, and your body is hot. Are you ill?"

"No, I'm worried about the noise," Emma whispered.

"I've been having dreams since Jayden left me. I can't seem to sleep through the night. Sometimes I wake to find him sitting beside me on the bed with that horrible surprised look on his face."

She clasped Rachel's hand. "It'll be all right. Jayden has only been…gone a few weeks. Give it some time. The dreams will stop."

"I know they will because I did what I had to do.

But I'm afraid of the future. What will I do?" Rachel laid her head on the pillow.

"What do you mean? You did what you had to do?"

Rachel coughed and mumbled, "Why I kept him in the parlor for days."

"We'll survive," she murmured. The widow was hiding something, but she could never process guilt and would reveal the secret in good time.

"Yes, but I don't feel like I know you very well."

Sadness rushed through Emma, she knew Rachel very well, her thoughts, her actions, but she didn't have the courage to face the truth. "Do you think you'll be able to sew dresses?"

"Yes, I'm so excited about doing something useful. I've some great ideas." She placed her hands behind her head.

"In a couple of hours, I'll take Black Bart into Pineview and send Mother and Father a telegram asking for funds."

Loud snoring came from Rachel. Emma lifted the covers and stepped down the stairs to the floor, and then covered her sister-in-law. She opened the drapes a tiny bit to allow the sun to enter. She reached deep into the chifforobe drew out a riding habit and while searching for boots pressed her fingers near the frame, a piece of wood insert shifted. The door swung inward, into the next room.

She climbed through to find the space empty. Had Henry entered her room through the secret passage? What right did he have to come into her chamber without permission? Who did he think he was? She touched her swollen lips. Her mind battled with her body because she liked his embraces.

Reentering her room, she quietly gathered clothing and shoes and went into the bathroom. She bathed using tepid water, dressed, and whipped her hair into a braid then jogged down the stairs. Treasure hummed in the kitchen, and decadent pastry scents spread through the hallway.

"Good morning, Treasure." She glanced around. Henry wasn't present.

"Mornin', Miss Emma. Did you sleep good or well?"

"Well, and you?" Sam had been teaching Treasure how to speak without dropping letters and the proper use of words. She was proving to be a quick learner.

"Like a baby. Would you like pancakes for breakfast? If you would look in the basket on the table, there might be some berries to go on top." She slowly enunciated the words.

"Thank you." She nibbled on an edge of a pancake. "Did you see Mr. Courtland this morning?"

"Yes, he thought he heard an intruder." Treasure flipped another cake, the butter sizzled in the skillet.

Emma glanced out the window. "Where is he now?"

"Got onto his horse and galloped into the woods."

She lifted the basket. There were a few tiny raspberries, which she dumped into a bowl. "It's nearly empty. I'll go collect more."

"All right. Hurry back, it'll only take me a short time to get a stack of pancakes cooked."

Emma grabbed a shawl off the hook by the door and stepped into the glowing sun. She loved spring and inhaled the sweet scents of reawakening earth. The songbirds chirped merry tunes. Berries fell from the brush branches in sparse clusters. She grabbed a few choice morsels and quick-stepped further into a grouping of oak, fir, and spruce trees. The buds on the oak were the slightest slivers of green. In a couple of weeks, they would bloom into full leaves.

She spied a wild raspberry bush lush with fruit and pulled the delectable bits from the branches squishing a few to test the ripeness, creating reddish-purple stains on her fingers. Her basket was full, but the quiet of the morning made her aware of how busy the house was and how much responsibility it would be to take on the large task of having dependents, if she agreed to stay and help Rachel.

Could she leave her easy free life to safeguard other people's welfare? What if she failed? Sam, Treasure, and Rachel would be disappointed, and the downfall would be her fault. She couldn't bungle because she always succeeded in whatever endeavor she chose. However, if her decision was to stay, she'd remain closer to Henry. What about Matthew's proposal? Her shawl slid from her shoulder. She bent to retrieve the material when a whizzing noise went overhead.

An arrow was embedded in the tree behind her. The gallop of hooves went in the opposite direction. She dropped to her knees, left the basket, and crawled behind the tree. If she hadn't ducked, she would have been pierced. A note was attached to the arrow. She stood and pulled the arrow, tugging the shaft and wiggling the point until the head released from the wooden bed. She read the message. *We will get you.*

She tucked the note into her pocket, gripped the

arrow, grabbed her basket of berries, and ran to the house. "Where's Rachel?"

"Upstairs. I heard her humming a few minutes ago." Treasure moved a stack of pancakes piled on a warming platter and waved the spatula back and forth. "What is that you have in your hand?"

Emma put the basket on the tabletop and ran up the stairs. Treasure's footsteps thumped behind her. She threw open the door.

Rachel turned with a frightened expression. "What's wrong?"

Emma took a deep breath, placed the arrow on the table and fastened the buttons on the backside of the dress.

"What's with the arrow?" Rachel smoothed the wrinkles.

"Shot at me. It had this note attached." She removed the paper from her pocket.

"What does it say, Miss Rachel?" Treasure wrung her hands.

"It's a threat, saying they're going to get Emma." Rachel turned around. "Did you see the person?"

Emma sat on the bed. "No. Just saw the back end of a chestnut horse. Who could possibly want to harm me? I'm not even from Colorado." Her breathing relaxed and steadied to a regular rhythm. She held her hands together, resisting the urge to twist them. Now, she not only had the fear of failure, but someone wanted her dead.

Rachel sat beside her. "I don't know."

"When I ride into town, to send a telegram to Father and Mother, I'll talk to the sheriff about the attacks. Maybe he'll have some ideas." She wasn't going to let an unknown threaten her.

"Do you think it's safe to ride alone?" Rachel's mouth was drawn tight in anger, and her eyes held a smidgen of fear.

"I don't have a choice. Sam went to the Barn's, to borrow a tool. You have a meeting with Mr. Courtland. Treasure must stay here to be with you. I'll take my gun and ride like the wind."

"King cancelled. He had to check on the mine. If you're going to ride Black Bart, I have the perfect outfit for you." She pressed her hands to the bed, lifted, then went into her closet. She returned with a white blouse, a shirt-waist vest and a split skirt. "Here try it on. It should fit perfect, as it was short on me, and you're smaller than I am."

"It'll be easier to ride on a horse with a split skirt." She undid the clasps on the front of her habit and let it drop to the floor. She drew on the white linen blouse and fastened the tiny buttons from her chest to the neck. The dark blue satin skirt, with a row of buttons on the inside of each leg, was heavenly to touch. She crossed to the full-length mirror and looked at her reflection.

"It's beautiful, Miss Emma," Treasure murmured.

"If the buttons are unfastened, they can be attached at the front and back to create a skirt. If you want it split, fasten the two sides together on the inside of each leg." Rachel fussed with the lines of the garment.

"The freedom of movement, because of the split, is amazing. You're brilliant." She reaffirmed the idea of a dress shop.

"Here, top it off with this belt. Oh, here's the vest." Rachel grabbed the matching vest. Two tiny pockets were sewn near the points at the bottom.

Emma slid into it and fastened the hooks and eyes. "I love this garment. You designed this?"

"Yes, but it needs something."

"I've got just da thang," Treasure announced.

They turned toward her. Red spots appeared on her cheeks. "If you all don't mind."

"Show us, Treasure."

"Yes, 'em." Her light footsteps beat a quick rhythm on the stairs.

A few seconds later, she arrived with a small cloth flower in her hand. "Will you wear the flower, Miss Emma?"

She nodded. Treasure pinned the accessory to the left shoulder of the vest.

"It's beautiful. The cloth tapestry is old fashion, supple, with a touch of silver woven in the three different blue colors and the shapes look like..." Emma quirked an eyebrow.

"Like fleur-de-lis," she proudly announced. "It's French, meaning flower. Do you really like it?"

"I love it." Rachel stepped closer to the pin. "This looks handmade."

"It is. I made it."

The woman-child could not have shocked her more. The tiny jewel, a delicate bit of a cloth sparkling in its blue and silver glory became a life saver. Emma met Rachel's gaze.

"Treasure, have a seat."

A look of skepticism crossed her features as she sat on the straight high-backed chair. Emma knelt to see her eye to eye, and Rachel hovered as near as possible, considering the baby mound.

"Do you have more of the fleur-de-lis?" Rachel

asked.

"Maybe five." Treasure's glance bounced between them. "Why?"

"We're going to be honest with you, Treasure. You like working with us, right?"

"Yes, um." She drew the words out.

"We like having you as a part of our family," Emma added.

Rachel nodded her head in agreement.

"Thank you." Treasure pushed her black curly hair into the tight bun. "Am I bein' let go? I didn't steal it. I made it."

Rachel crossed her hands in front. "We believe you. It's, we don't have any money, so I may have to sell the house. You'll be without a position again. You don't want that to happen, do you?"

"No. What can I do?" Treasure's glance shot to her hands, twisting in front of her.

Emma touched the spongy pin. "You can make the rose pins for vest or dresses, maybe hats? Do you think you could create more?"

"Yes, I can." Treasure nodded.

Rachel clapped her hands. "We should have a partnership. The three of us. We'll make dresses and hats and sell them."

"Rachel, you know I don't sew." Emma walked to the mirror and turned to look at the front and back of the garb, noting the little details of pleats and tucks.

"You can sell them. You are very good at talking with people. You can sell our dresses."

Treasure jumped to a stand. "That's right, Miss Emma. You could talk people into buying the clothes. I want to stay with you all, and if that means I make fleur-de-lis, I'm willing to make them. I can make hats, too."

"I'm only here until after the baby is born, and then I must return home." Emma glanced at the clock on the dresser.

"Why can't you stay forever?" Tears pooled in Rachel eyes.

Blast, she shouldn't have brought it up. "You know I don't belong here. I came to help you during childbirth, but when you're settled, with the baby, I'll return to what I know. I've obligations back in Fort Wayne." She laid her arm on Rachel's shoulder. "We'll talk about this later. We've plenty of time to discuss the future."

Treasure grasped Rachel's hand and Emma held out hers, they formed a circle.

"In the meantime, we'll do whatever we can to make this endeavor a success and keep us together," Emma vowed.

"I promise to help in any way I can," Treasure added.

"I vow to design and sew women's clothing in order to remain independent of men and become successful." Rachel nodded her head. "Alright, we remain together and keep the house."

"Remain together and keep the house," Treasure whispered.

"Even if we have to forego personal pleasures," Rachel added at the last minute.

An instant image of Henry and the early morning wake up flooded Emma's thoughts. He wasn't a personal pleasure, rather he constantly made her mind work faster to think up clever answers. "Now, how am I going to get money to send a telegram? I don't think they'll take a voucher." She gathered her dress from the floor.

Rachel gasped. "Egg money."

"What?" Emma blinked.

"You'll take the egg money. Ride Black Bart into town, send your telegram, buy some material, and we'll make dresses with beautiful ornamentation." Rachel preened. "Put the dress down and come with me."

"I'll get my bag and the address in London for my parents. I'll meet you downstairs." Emma tucked the note into her pocket and grabbed the arrow.

"In the kitchen." Rachel took Treasure's hand and led her out of the room. "Will you show me the other pretties you've made?"

"Sure 'nuf, Miss Rachel."

"We're partners now, Treasure, just call me, Rachel."

A few minutes later Emma mounted on Black Bart, the fifty dollars of egg money snug in a bag strapped across her shoulder. She glanced at the small flock of hens. How could Rachel get fifty dollars from those little squatters? Could she have acquired the money through other venues? No, why did she contemplate conspiracy theories?

"I think we should concentrate on trying to sell this outfit. It's magnifique and everyone will want one. Rachel, do you know of a shop in town that might put one on display and sell it on commission? Do you have any material left over to make another?"

"Just the mercantile." Rachel bit her lip. "You shouldn't ask because they order from a catalogue."

Emma met Treasure's glance. Rachel was hiding

something.

"Until my parents send funds, we'll have to use the resources we have, and they won't last long." She adjusted the saddle cinch and tried to control Black Bart as he pranced. The sun beamed off the saddle's silver adornments then sparked off Rachel's gold necklace.

"While you're in town, Treasure and I'll go into the attic and see if we can find material to use." Rachel held her hand over her eyes above the brow. "Be careful, we couldn't sell Bart, because he's mean."

Emma climbed onto the block and settled onto the saddle. "I'd be an embarrassment to the Cody name if I loss control over this fella." She stroked the horse's fragrant neck. "I'll be back before dark falls."

****

King knelt beside the dead body. Dried rusty brown blood created a beacon for the scavengers circling overhead. The canvas bag open flap lay out against the dry rocky ground, so the bold print Courtland-Carter Mining Ltd. gleamed in the early morning sun. Damn, an insider was giving the robbers information. The change of date and delivery location, Blair's Mine, hadn't detoured the Relay Gang. Not only did they get the money, but they killed one of his riders. Who kept the thieves informed?

He removed the blanket from the saddle and wrapped the body. Maverick shied away as he brought the corpse close. The scent of blood, fresh or old, caused him to strain against his reins. "Whoa boy, settle. Settle." He hoisted the man onto the back of Maverick, tied the stiff body to the saddle and mounted. Patting his hand against the side of steed's neck, he steered him toward Pineview.

King glanced at the Front Range Mountains, toward Blair's Mine. Once again, he'd have to empty his safe to provide funds for the miners. The next delivery would be on time and the information shared with the usual people. However, he would be the courier. *One month and it'll all be over.*

Chapter 10

Emma, constantly checking her surroundings, galloped into Pineview. She contemplated a logical explanation for the unskilled hunters. A gunshot gone astray, an arrow missing her by a pinch along with the note, the attacks weren't a coincidence and most certainly were executed for her benefit.

Black Bart shied to the side as a group of wranglers rode beside them. She rubbed his neck. "Easy sweet fellow. You're the best."

The horse's ears perked up, and he moaned like he was in heaven. Rachel was mistaken, he wasn't mean. Like most males in the west, he needed the right motivation and a gentle caress now and then.

The Sheriff's office, a square box made of rough-hewn, white-washed wood was her first stop. A large stove pipe jetted into the sky behind the building. Handbills of scraggly looking bandits and one woman wanted for bank robbery, decorated a bulletin board outside the door. She reviewed the posters, hoping to get a glimpse of what a supposed murderer resembled. Not seeing anything of value, she peered in the window, and then lightly knocked. Black Bart snorted. She turned. He nodded and pulled the reins taut against the hitching post.

"Okay, I'm going." She opened the door and walked in, without being granted permission.

A robust man, sporting long greasy hair and beady eyes, sat behind a nicked and scared red oak desk. She marched forward, wishing for a cloth to cover her nose. He glanced at her but didn't bother to rise or offer a greeting.

"Sheriff, I'm Emma Cody. I'm staying with my sister-in-law, Rachel Drake."

"I know who you are. How is Mrs. Drake faring?" He rubbed his hand through his hair, separating the oily strands even more.

"As expected, thank you for asking, Sheriff—"

"Jones, ma'am, Theodore Jones."

"Sheriff Jones, I'm here because someone shot an arrow at me this morning. Still hot from being imbedded in a tree with a note attached." She handed him the arrow and note.

"It's a Cheyenne arrow." He laid the arrow on the desk and opened the note. "Looks like an Injun's trying to scare you away." He rubbed a large, scarred hand over his whiskered face. "They've been persnickety, lately."

"Are you going to investigate?"

"Nothin' to 'vestigate. Did you see anyone?" He lowered his hand to his belt and hoisted it higher on his stomach.

"Chestnut colored horse."

"Half the men in Pineview own a chestnut. If'n you didn't see a person then you're wasting my time with this, missy." He shifted the arrow and note to the front of his desk and picked up his coffee cup.

Emma grabbed the arrow and note, hoping the sticky coffee residue wouldn't tear the paper. "Thank you, Sheriff Jones." By the smile on his face, he'd missed her sarcastic intonation.

"My pleasure to help." He leaned back in his chair, the rungs squeaking as his heavy weight pressed against them.

Next door was the mercantile, a two-story bramble-roofed building and not a single customer. "Hello, I'm Miss Emma Cody."

"Mr. Clifton. How may I help you?" He grabbed a brass hair comb. "Just got these in today."

"No, thank you. I'm here to discuss my sister-in-law's account. Mrs. Rachel Drake—"

"I can't extend credit to Mrs. Drake. There is still an outstanding debt, and until the balance is paid, no more credit." He hurried to a stack of calico gowns and refolded them.

"Then I'd like to open an account."

He glanced at her, giving her the up and down evaluation. "Do you have something of value for me to hold as a collateral?"

The selection of materials was limited, which made Emma suspicious if his business flourished. "Mr. Clifton, how many women live in Pineview?"

"Twenty. Half of which are married, and the other half work over at King's Court." He pointed toward the saloon across the street. She could guess at what other business adventures Henry was involved in and explained Miss Cat's French designed dress.

"Do you take merchandise on commission?"

He focused on refolding the dresses again. "I don't understand."

"I would provide a model dress, and you'd sell pre-orders for it."

He lifted an eyebrow. "Do you sew?"

"No, Mrs. Drake does." She glanced at the street. No activity, so she'd have privacy. "I'm wearing the outfit we would be interested in providing as a model." Emma pivoted to show him all sides. "And it is a riding—"

"I'm not interested. If you could provide something of value gold or silver jewelry is always acceptable, I'll consider opening a credit account for you."

"I'll consider your offer. Thank you." She exited the mercantile, turned right into the false-fronted telegraph office and mail room. A façade exterior with a square top hid the roof and gave the impression of a larger structure. Inside the building was a tiny square, no bigger than a railroad car. A narrow workstation and crate holding various sized envelopes took up most of the space.

The pock-marked face of a young, brown-haired, thin man stood behind the counter. "May I help you?"

"Good day, sir." She smiled and tucked a tendril of wayward hair underneath the floppy hat Rachel forced on her at the last minute.

He cleared his voice. "How may I help you, ma'am?" He rubbed his long beak of a nose.

"I need to send a telegram to my parents."

A red tint crept up his neck. "Where do you need to send the telegram?"

"Oh, silly me, to London, England."

"Fill out this form, the maximum is twenty words including the address." With shaking hands, he handed her a sheet of parchment.

She removed the slip of paper with her parents' London address from her purse.

Pen in hand she wrote:

Frank Cody
21 Kinsington
London England
Help. Send Money. Pineview, Colorado. Love,
Emma

She handed the form to the clerk. As he was reading the missive, she glanced across the counter and viewed an open book of Western Tales, featuring Buffalo Bill, Sitting Bull, and Colonel Custer. He brought out charts and graphs and calculated the units from one telegraph station to another—the scribbles on the paper being the only sound in the small space.

"There isn't a guarantee the telegraph will reach London. We've had two successful messages from the Queen to our President, but there are not any guarantees the telegram will transmit. They continue to lay the wire hoping to get a connection, so chances are fifty-fifty. Do you still want to send?"

"Yes. It's very important."

"That will be sixty dollars, Miss." He held out his hand, waiting.

"Why such a large amount? It's only five dollars to send a telegram to Fort Wayne?"

"The distance. You see it's so much money for each ten units, from station to station. Your message route will go across the states to the eastern seaboard and overseas is still being perfected. Miss?"

"Cody. Miss Cody, and you are?" She blinked at him and crossed her hands together in front of her.

"I'm uh, Otis, ma'am. Otis Sue." The red flush had reached the top of his head.

"Otis, I'm a little short of cash. Could I pay you half now and half when my funds arrive?" She rested her hands on the counter.

"No, ma'am, I'm sorry. That isn't our policy." His face grew redder.

"I see you like to read about Buffalo Bill Cody." She smiled.

"Yes, Miss Cody." He shook his head and glanced at the dime novel.

"What do you say I give you fifty dollars to send the telegram and promise you within six months, my cousin, Buffalo Bill, will come meet you and autograph your favorite book?"

Otis's Adam's apple lifted and lowered as fast the second hand on the clock directly behind his slim body. "You can do that ma'am? Get Buffalo Bill himself to come see me personally?"

"Yes, Otis, I promise you, I will try." She smiled, the knowing smile of victory.

"If you wait a minute, I'll send this over directly, and I'll provide the extra ten dollars. Six months you say?"

"Yes, Otis, within six months." Bill would come to help her, they were family.

"Thank you, Miss Cody." He flipped the form. "Please write your offer on this paper and sign."

"I will. Thank you, Otis." Blast, she was out of funds again.

She marched across the dirt street and along the wooden boardwalk to one of the sleekest more elaborate buildings in town, King's Court. Instead of a false front, the second story presented a walk and a wooden railing. No one was outside, taking in the fresh sunshine and air.

Curious, she walked around the building, finding

an alley in the back. Two horses were tied to a hitching post. The alley was large enough for wagons and carriages to get through and for unloading supplies though the backdoor. At the rear of the structure, a staircase led to the highest level with a smaller staircase at the front.

She completed the circle, bypassing water barrels on the sides of the boardwalk, and stood in front of the half doors. Taking a deep breath of courage, she opened the right side and entered the saloon. The odors of fermented fruit, unwashed bodies, and cloying perfume overwhelmed her. A piano man, with a bowler hat and stripped vest, complete with a bow string tie, played Brown's *The Yellow Rose of Texas*. A woman in a short red dress with most of her upper body expanding out from the lace top tapped a high heeled black shoe in rhythm.

"I'm looking for Henry Courtland." Emma raised her voice above the tune.

"Back table." Without missing a beat, the piano player nodded toward the rear of the saloon.

Henry sat at a round, shiny table. A skinny white-haired blonde, with duck feathers fluttering, lifted her green skirt and exposed a garter. She sat on his lap. Her upper body hid his facial expression. He wasn't fighting her off, and he didn't sound like he was in pain. As a matter of fact, he was saying something under his breath.

Emma stood in front of them, her back getting straighter like the arrow clenched in her hand. He couldn't see her, either because of the feathers or the blonde hair which was as large as the piano player's bowler hat. He lowered his hand. A cigar was wedged between two fingers. She stuck the arrow straight into the stink stick, piercing and bonding the cigar to the tabletop.

The music stopped. Red dress lady stopped tapping. Henry moved his arm around the blonde's waist. She giggled, and he lifted her from his lap. Emma stared straight into his cheating eyes. How could he carry on with this…this trollop a few hours after kissing her?

"Emma." He lifted an eyebrow, then tugged the arrow out of the cigar, and extinguished the loathsome split stick in a glass of beer. "What a pleasant surprise."

The harlot whispered into his ear. He shook his head. She frowned and said something else.

"No, Lulu. Go entertain the customers." He tapped her bottom, shooing her away, and then lifted his hand to smooth his tousled hair.

"Later tonight, I'll come to you." She swished her rear and climbed the stairs to the next level.

At least he managed to keep his attention on her, instead of the whore's whizzing exit. Well, giving up personal pleasures wasn't going to be so difficult after all.

"Come with me to my office and tell me what brings you into Pineview." His voice, although flat and monotone, contradicted the look of interest on his face. He stood, snatched the arrow off the table and led her, with his nice muscular backside and smooth gait, through a dark hallway.

Her eyes adjusted to the dingy interior. A child held a cat, on closer inspection a rodent, an enormous squealing rat. The vermin squirmed and clawed the air as the boy shook the prehistoric beast by its tail.

"Look boss, I got 'em," the boy said.

Henry grinned, withdrew a silver coin out of his pocket, and handed the money to the child. "Good job, Danny. Get rid of him, and I'll give you another."

"Thanks, King." The dark-haired, dirty-faced boy ran down the hallway. A few seconds later a door slammed shut.

Chills racked her body. Could there be other bizarre rats the size of cats in this building? A disgusting place, but she needed to talk to Henry. He held open the office door. His gaze created an uneasy fluttering in her stomach. The nerve of the man, having a trollop straddling his lap one moment and looking at her as if she were dessert the next. She swallowed the bile lodged in her throat and sashayed into the room.

"Fetching outfit, Emma."

"Thank you, Henry." Her voice became her mother's, all prim and proper.

The door closed and so did her heart.

He sighed. "Tell me, what brings you and your arrow into Pineview today." His voice was husky and quiet as he crossed to the window, the one overlooking the alley. He shut the drapes, enclosing them into a temporary semi-darkness. She squirmed a bit, wondering why he didn't leave the window drapes open and allow the light to enter. Before she could examine the thought further, the strike of a match buzzed, and a soft yellow glow warmed the room. He shook out the match, and sulfur and wax candle odors filtered up her nostrils.

"Please have a seat." He flipped his hand over and back to indicate an upholstered leather chair, the color of doe skin, opposite the large walnut desk. The workspace had an odd resemblance to a horse tank, wide with rounded corners instead of sharp edges.

"Not necessary. As much as it pains me, I need to ask a favor." The man unnerved her. Instead of walking around and sitting in the monstrous, high-backed chair, he leaned against the front of the desk, spread his long legs out in front of him, crossed his ankles, and tucked his hands into his trouser pockets.

"I assume it has to do with the arrow." He reached around and snatched the dart off his desk. "The one you severed my cigar with?" He bent his head and turned the shaft over.

Unleashed emotion should never rule over your mind. Well blast, her father was right, and now she regretted spearing the blackguard's cigar. Damnable heat rushed to her face. She crossed her hands behind her back. "Yes, that is the reason."

"It looks like a Cheyenne arrow. Where did you get it?"

"This morning, after you left, I went outside, and it pierced a birch tree four inches from my head. This note was attached." She reached into the vest pocket and withdrew the crinkled warning. His legs uncrossed, and his body tightened. He took the paper from her trembling fingers but continued to hold her hand in his large one. His touch calmed her. *Let go!* She released her hand and sat on the chair.

"Since the gold and silver rushes, miners by the thousands have taken up residence in the Cheyenne and Arapaho territory. The Cheyenne have been angry, and after the Pike's Peak Gold Rush, they have become very active. Typically, they attack wagon trains, mining camps, and stagecoach lines. I've never heard that they attacked a woman, especially one alone in her garden near her home."

How did he know where she was at the time?

He opened the note and quickly scanned the message. His brows furrowed, and his lips tightened.

"It wasn't an Indian who wrote this note. The spelling is perfect." He handed her the paper. "We'll take it to Sheriff Jones."

"Already did that. He said it was an Indian trying to frighten me."

He crossed the room, took his gun belt from a peg on the wall and strapped it on, then he drew on his duster. "We'll go see Bullington at the military garrison."

She jumped from the chair. "I appreciate the offer, Henry, but…"

"But?" He pivoted and stood beside her.

"I don't want the military, which has very few soldiers available, involved in this." She moved from foot to foot. *Don't look into those gorgeous cyan eyes. Don't look. Keep your gaze focused on his boot tips.*

"Because?"

She glanced into his face. "They will alert my father, and I don't want him to interfere" She refocused on the floor, anywhere but into his eyes. "I need to travel to Boulder tomorrow, and I was hoping you could go with me, as an escort."

"Why won't you look at me?"

Blast! She popped her head up, faster than a gopher sticking its head out of the hole on the first spring day and met his glance. He smiled, exhibiting those deeply grooved dimples. For a moment, she forgot about Lulu and the squirming.

"That's better." He took a step and lifted her chin. "I'll protect you with my life. Will it be simply the two of us, Emma?" He reached for a lock of her hair and rubbed the strand between two fingers.

"Yes, Sam will need to stay with Rachel in case she needs a doctor. She'll want Treasure by her if she goes into labor. If it wasn't necessary, I'd postpone the trip until after the baby arrives. It can't wait." She glanced at the door and took a few steps. The man was overwhelming with his presence, his scent outdoorsy with a touch of cherry. Was it from the tobacco? Her head came in line with his shoulders. If needed, she could hide behind the great hunk of a tree named Courtland. Hide from Jayden, her parents and Matthew Bambridge. Yes, hiding sounded very good.

Henry dropped the thin slice of curls and drew his hand along her shoulder. Her disloyal breath started coming out in short pants instead of normal breathing. With her heart beating as fast as native drums, she took a step back. He took a step forward. She took another step back, bumped into the closed door, and crossed her arms at her waist.

"What is the reason you can't wait, my dear?" He whispered into her ear, holding the arrow in his hand.

She pulled the arrow from his light grasp, crossed the shaft diagonally over his chest and pushed with all her might. "Are you taking this seriously? I'm only here to ask for help, not to get a…a kiss. I need someone skilled with guns to travel with me for business reasons. Business, Henry. I suggest you go whisper in Lulu's ear, as mine is off limits to you."

She pivoted, opened the door until it butted against his boot, then she sailed through the slim wedge of space. "I'll see you at Rachel's house six in the morning, and I'm not your dear."

She didn't look back but contemplated how she could get an iron chastity belt in Fort Collins. Head down, she didn't see the miner shuffling down the boardwalk and bumped into him. The grubby miner stumbled forward, and Emma catapulted onto the wall of the mail office. Her hand grasped onto the first solid bit and pulled a flyer from the bulletin board, before clinging to the edge of the frame.

"Sorry, wasn't watching where I was walking." On two solid feet again, she held the paper in her left hand and touched the miner with her free one. "Are you injured?"

"Not to worry. Not injured." A toothless smile spread across his face, and then he continued along the walkway.

She glanced into the storefront window. Was that Henry's reflection in the glass? She shrugged aside the idea and looked at the wrinkled handbill. *Attention MEN. Contest for sharp shooting, test your shooting skills. Meet Sir Reginald Hayworth, creator of the hexangular bore, bullets to match, telescopic sight. Fort Collins, Colorado, April twenty-second, nine o'clock in the morning. Prizes: first place one hundred dollars plus a Hayworth rifle; second place, fifty dollars; third place, twenty-five dollars. Entry fee, two dollars.*

How was she going to make two dollars in one day and enter the contest?

Chapter 11

"Do you think I'll pass muster?" Emma glanced in the mirror at the sides then pivoted so the reflection would show her behind. "It looks a little feminine, don't you think? Should I also pad the stomach?"

"No. In this outfit you could pass for a boy, but not if you have a big stomach." Rachel patted the thin pad on the backside of the outfit. "Is that too tight? I can release it if you can't breathe. In order to shoot and win, you can't faint. We must have that money."

"It's fine. Sam's okay with loaning us the funds for the entry fee and an overnight stay in a hotel, right? Although he found something with Treasure, I still think he hates me. It's only because of you, he gave us the money." She tugged at the binding. Her breasts weren't massive, but she could fill out a chemise. As a result of Rachel's manipulation, they were flattened to her chest. Uncomfortably snug she gasped for breath. A couple of tugs and the cloth loosened.

"Nonsense. He knows it's simply a loan." Rachel perched on the fainting couch, stuffing socks into a pair of Jayden's shoes.

She sat beside her and glanced around the lavish bedroom, tastefully decorated in muted tones of green and gold. Simply beautiful. Rachel had more than sewing talents. "You know what to ask Morgan Palinurus, from the bank, right?" She stuffed a bandana

120

in the travel bag, resting on the stripped overstuffed Georgian style fireside chair. Her foot bumped against the claw leg, shooting sharp agonizing pain ripped through her great toe.

"Yes, hear his proposal. If he suggests we start a business to sell women's clothing in Pineview, don't question the lack of women, but do ask about the financial values. How much to rent a building, remodel, buy stock, etc. Do you use the house as collateral? Don't ever let him know we're aware of his possible deceit." Rachel dropped the boots onto the floor.

Emma put one on her non-aching foot and tied the ties. "It looks like a jester's shoe. Do you think I could get away with wearing my own boots? Do men really look at each other's feet? You might show him around the entire house, find out if he wants you to foreclose, so he can buy the homestead for himself."

Rachel gasped. "Emma, when did you become so mistrusting?"

Since I walked into a saloon and saw a woman grinding her rear onto a man who I thought cared for me. "Not mistrusting, just cautious."

"Yes. I think you can wear your own riding boots. The trousers are long enough that most of the tips will be covered. The banker isn't going to get my house. I'll make sure of that." Rachel's determined look, like a mother bear guarding her cub, did not change. "My child will walk through these halls, play in the yard, and plant a garden. No one is going to take my house."

She awkwardly hugged Rachel. In the last couple of days, she'd appeared more like her old-spirited self. "You won't have the baby until I get back, right?"

"Goodness no, she'll wait until her auntie returns."

Rachel smoothed her hand over her stomach.

"Think it's a girl?"

"I know it's a girl, and we'll call her Margaret Mae Drake, Margaret, for my favorite grandmother, and May, the month of her birth."

"I like it. Maggie Mae." Emma smiled broadly. "It has a nice ring to it."

Rachel's serene expression faltered. "What will I tell King when he comes tomorrow? He'll be angry. You wanted him as a bodyguard, and then you traveled alone."

"Explain that I needed some things in Fort Collins, and he is to meet me at the Gold Nugget Hotel dining room at eight o'clock. Does it have a dining room? I know it's a new building."

"I think so. What if he asks questions?" Rachel stood at the mirror looking at her side view. The black dress made her hair a mousy light brown, and her pale skin almost ghostly.

"Don't lie. It'll be easier to tell him the truth."

"Even that you're in love with him?" Rachel grinned into the mirror.

Aghast, she noted the wicked gleam in her sister-in-law's eyes. "Why would you make such a statement?"

"I've known you most of your adult life. You don't think I see what is going on between you two? He would make a very good partner for you. You know what? I suggest you have a nice round of sex and be done with it. Marriage isn't all the poetry and dreams that we stuff in our hope chests. It's misery, dishonesty, and unfaithfulness." Anger changed Rachel's docile features.

"What happened between you and Jayden? I thought you were happy. You wouldn't bury him for God's sake, and now that I have to leave, you're inferring he was dishonest and unfaithful?"

"How do you know it wasn't me, who was unfaithful?" Rachel put her hands on her hips, elbows jutting out at the sides.

"Because I know you as well as myself." She placed the strap of her bag to cross over her chest. "The Fort Collins newspaper stated a local inventor was killed by a prostitute. The paper disappeared, before I could read the article. Jayden was the man that was killed, wasn't he?"

Emma anticipated huge racking tears to fall, instead Rachel had the stubborn look of a woman at a bargain bin fighting for the best cloak at the least price.

"Yes, he was."

"You're keeping something else from me." Emma pierced her with a questioning look.

Rachel hugged her. "Time to leave, or you'll not make it to the competition."

Patience. Words could not be forced from Rachel. She'd tell all in her own time. "Alright, but we'll talk about this later. Keep Maggie Mae safe until I return."

****

"Name?" The man wore a three-piece suit in the middle of unseasonably hot and humid day, in a nearly treeless field. What could he possibly be thinking?

"Emmet Cody, sir." Emma tried to lower her voice to sound less feminine. Apparently not well done, he jerked his head shifting the stiff collar of his shirt as fast as a turtle ducking his head back inside his shell. His glance roamed from the top of her head to her knees.

"Are you over sixteen, Emmet Cody?" he snarled.

"Yes, sir," she replied, as baritone as she could produce. The man didn't look at her again.

"Sign this release form. It states if any accidents occur the town of Fort Collins, Colorado or the Hayworth Rife Company will not be held responsible."

"Yes, sir." She scribbled her real name across the paper. If discovered, she'd claim she'd signed her real name on the release form, and they misunderstood her sex.

He flung the paper on top of the stack and replaced the rock to hold them in place. "You need to join the others, over yonder, for the first elimination round."

She looked in the direction he'd pointed. Fifty men of a variety of sizes, ages, and backgrounds were in line. Evaluating the competition as she walked toward the rear of the line, she determined there were two true challenging contestants. A gunslinger with his pistol strapped to his thigh. He didn't have a rifle in hand, so that could be his weakness. Another contestant, a cowboy, held a rifle and a dual set of pistols. A rugged, two-day-old, dark-brown beard and long mustache covered his hard sundried face. His cowboy hat had been pulled low over his eyebrows, but his eyes glittered when he met her glance. She tugged her bandana, just under her nose to cover most of her hairless chin. Her skin crawled at his piercing assessment. Did he suspect that she wasn't a "male" as required for the competition? Would he get her eliminated before the first round?

While waiting, she extracted the old copy of the press she'd obtained from the newspaper office. An article declared a local inventor Jayden Drake was found dead, shot by his mistress and soiled dove Bell Grind. The fallen angel was last seen wearing a brown dress running toward the livery. A description followed: five-foot-five, long brown hair, brown eyes, and a mole on the lower right side of her lip. The stable hand overheard her saying she was going to Boulder or Denver.

Two hours later, Emma stood at the shooting line. The target was a good thirty feet away.

"You must use the newest Hayworth rifle, make the one shot your best." An attendant handed her the shiny weapon.

She tipped her hat farther on her forehead, shifted the rifle in her grasp and tried to remember everything Helen and Bill taught her about targets, rifles, and setting the site.

"Do not go beyond the red line, or you'll be disqualified." The judge pointed to the ground and the crimson painted indentation in the dirt.

"Yes, sir." She placed the Hayworth against her shoulder, lowered the bandana and repositioned the gun. With the cloth away from her face and less of a distraction, she lined the site and sent the bullet straight, aiming for the center of the circle.

A miner ran to the paper. "Dead center."

She tugged the cloth over her chin and handed the gun to the attendant.

A short time later, after a break to drink free beer and eat a bowl of beans, the final three were announced: Tom Corm, Jason Black, and Emmet Cody. After two more challenges she'd, at least, place third, and the winnings would enough to repay Sam.

For this challenge, they placed a target with the bull's-eye fifty feet away. Not a problem for her. Crisp dollars may as well be stuffed in her pocket.

"How old are you, son?" Jason Black coughed hard enough to rack his body with shakes. He withdrew a handkerchief and wiped spital from his face.

She opened her mouth to answer and promptly shut it.

"Ol' 'nugh to know yer goin' to hit the ground before you win this contest old man," Corm growled.

"First man up is Jason Black. Step forward, please." The three-piece suited man announced.

Black walked forward and instead of being handed a rifle or even a pistol, he was given a bow and arrow. Emma could have wet herself. How lucky could she get today?

"What has this to do with sharp shooting?" Black whined like a child.

"Sharp shooting isn't just about your skills with a pistol or a rifle, but how good you are at hitting the target. Do you want to drop out of the competition?" Suit man tucked his thumbs into his trouser pockets.

"No. I'd like to lodge a complaint though." Black grasped the bow, top down. He missed the target completely.

She smiled and glanced at Corm to see how he was taking the news. His eyes beamed, and his smile broadened.

"What are you doing here, dressed like a boy?"

Her smile died. Blast! Must not be her lucky day after all. "Rachel must have told you why I was here?" She refused to lose her concentration by looking at Henry.

"I want to hear your version." His clear enunciated words carried, and many of the onlookers glanced at them. She stepped away from his closeness.

"Tom Corm," the announcer yelled.

Corm stepped to the line and faced the bull's-eye.

Henry edged closer to her. Emma sidled to the right. "My version will have to wait until I'm finished here today. Go get a beer or coffee. I need to focus."

He grabbed her arm.

"Bull's-eye. Wait a moment folks. It seems we have a mistake. John, will you repeat that?" The man in the suit turned toward the crowd and in his deep snake-oil salesman's voice shouted, "It's not a bull's-eye, but it is on the line."

"Emmet Cody." She shrugged off Henry's hand and moved forward.

Corm whispered into her ear. "Is he bothering you? Some fellers like boys. I'll get rid of him if'n he is."

She'd fooled him after all and looked into his youngish face, more than likely he was her age, and smiled. No, she hadn't, Corm looked at her with the same pained expression Henry exhibited the morning he came into her room. Blast, he could give her deception away.

She exaggerated reaching and scratching between her legs, moving one out slightly as she did. Collecting saliva in her mouth, she spat the goop on the ground. "I can handle myself. Is it really you, who likes boys?"

He sneered at her and retreated a few paces. That comment certainly ruffled his feathers. "Places." The announcement drew people tighter to the start.

Emma worked her shoulders back and forth, at an attempt to release the tension. She bent her knees and bounced. Henry coughed, one of his intentional-stop-it-now-coughs. Blast, she'd forgotten she'd removed the rear pad. Standing straight, she jerked her coat to cover her bottom.

There was a selection of arrows to choose from, and she picked two. She held each arrow in her site line, placed the middle edge on her index finger and chose the perfectly straight and balanced one. She ignored the murmurs coming from behind her and pulled the string of the bow. Tight.

She placed the arrow on the notch, pulled back, lined the head, and let it fly. With a *spling* and a *whoosh*, the point hit the target.

"Bull's-eye, dead center." The joy clear in John's voice, he wanted a close competition.

The crowd clapped loudly. Even Sir Hayworth himself came and slapped her on the back, throwing her forward. When she steadied, the dapper man shook her hand. She raised her glance to connect with Henry. He smiled and the tightness of her chest eased. She released a long sigh and paid attention to the announcer.

"The last challenge is between Tom Corm and Emmet Cody. Gentlemen, you'll ride, bend to the side, and shoot a strawman using one of Hayworth's rifles. The target is drawn on the pumpkin's forehead."

She felt his presence and smelled the cherry from his cigar smoke before he said anything. "Can you do that?"

"Of course, I can. Remember my story about Helen and Buffalo Bill?" She bit her lip hard enough it bled. The boast was just that, bravado. She didn't have any experience shooting from the side of a horse. Hit a small target? Her stomach muscles clinched. She had a

128

new worry. Her immediate goal was to win this money in order to buy cloth for the dresses and to keep her vow to help Rachel. Would she break her neck at the attempt?

Emma released Black Bart from his temporary hitching post, a rope strung between two poles. She pulled on his saddle, jerked the leather straps—checking for tightness and security—and examined the reins for any breaks.

"Come on, Black Bart, you'll need to help me out, and I promise I'll get you a little mare when we have money."

"Emma...et, wait a minute," Henry said.

"Can't, Tom is at the starting line, and I need to watch him ride."

Henry resituated his Stetson and walked beside her. Corm, mounted on his horse, shot her a cocky grin. He kicked his horse's flanks, and the Appaloosa took off at a jump start.

"You have three minutes to complete the mile and the one that hits the target or closest to the center of the straw man's pumpkin head wins the contest," a rusty male voice said. Emma glanced beside her to see a miner clothed in dark brown clothes. "They announced it while you were getting your horse."

Corm slid to the side, his rifle posed and ready to fire. He got off a round, and as he straightened the horse hit a dip in the dirt. Tom slipped and tried to regain control but fell to the side of his mount. His boot caught where the stirrup was, preventing him from falling free.

The rifle bounced across the ground, making puffs of loose soil fly into the air. Corm recoiled from the ground, tried to grab the reins to stop his mount and pull up. The split reins went underneath the horse and the rider followed. His boot finally free of the shackle, allowed him to slide under the horse. He rolled over, until a sagebrush stopped his spin.

The audience was eerily quiet as the dust settled. A few murmurs occurred. Men ran out to help him. With assistance, he limped toward her. The right side of his face was already swelling, with bits of rocks and dirt mixed with blood inside the open wounds.

"Good luck, boy," he said as he passed.

She nodded and mounted Black Bart. Her breath caught in her throat. She couldn't do it. Her heart raced as fast as the Appaloosa running free across the field. John straightened the wrinkled scarecrow and placed a new mold-ridden pumpkin head on top. Black Bart pranced, ready to run and get away from the boisterous crowd. A hand grabbed the edge of her coat.

"You can't do this. Whatever bauble you feel you need I'll buy it for you." Henry tipped his hat upward, daggers shot from his eyes.

"I don't want to buy a..." She noticed people watching them, and she nudged her horse forward. Henry's hand fell to his side, but he continued to walk beside her. "It's not for me. It's for Rachel. Jayden left her in debt. She doesn't have any money, and Palinurus wants her house."

"I have money. I'll take care of it." He extended his hand. "Get off the horse."

She glared at him. "Men just don't get it. Women don't want to be hand-fed. They want to be an active part of life." Anger made her braver. She could and would do this. Not only that, she may just be intimate with Henry and leave him in the dust.

He must have noticed the change from fear to determination. "You'll be hurt or killed," he rasped.

"Emmet Cody, get to the start." The announcer's shout rang through the crowd.

"If you insist on this foolish act, tell them you want to warm up the horse. I assume you're…" his glance dropped to her chest, and then lifted to her eyes, "…wrapped."

Without looking down she gave a light nod and waved to the announcer.

"Walk your horse toward the trees, pull down a piece of the cloth and wrap it around the saddle horn. Bring your coat up to hide the knot. After you shoot and start to sit up, make sure you weave to the right, there's a rut on the left side."

Her empty stomach rebelled by pitching and rolling. She breathed in deeply and out slowly. She could do this. "Thank you."

He took her cold hand into his, and she leaned into his loveable maleness. "Emma, I care about you, do not get yourself killed."

****

King's heart literally stopped as Emma straightened her overly large hat, nudged her horse toward the announcer. She pointed toward the trees. He nodded, and she prodded Black Bart into a canter. Within a couple of minutes, she was back at the starting line. She took the rifle handed to her, checked to see if it was loaded, and cocked the hammer by pulling back the slide. A quick nod to the announcer, and he set his time clock.

A simple poke to Black Bart's sides, and he took

off like a Roman candle on the fourth of July. She apparently double tied her hat because it barely moved in the wind. Ride like the wind she did. King's gut felt like he'd been punched by a sledgehammer, as she leaned to the side. She remained hanging onto the horn and lowered the rifle.

He waited. Murmurs went around beside him, guessing if she would fall. He released a breath when a shot exploded. She lifted upright onto the saddle. Either she pulled on the reins or Black Bart unintentionally missed the rut, but she didn't lose control over her horse.

His muscles relaxed as she galloped to the starting line. Black Bart stopped on the other side of the line, and Emma jumped down. She rubbed the horse's neck in soothing motions and whispered into his ear. King joined her and took the reins from her shaking hands. "Don't lose it now, you're too close."

She let out a deep breath and relaxed. They turned around as John ran forward with two pumpkin heads in his hands. "Tom Corm's bullet is outside the circle, on the chin."

He held aloft the second pumpkin. The circle etched in the center showed one clear bullet hole, slightly to the left inside the ring. "This is Emmet Cody's score."

"You are the clear winner, especially because you were able to stay on your horse," King stated with pride.

The judges gathered around the pumpkins and talked adamantly.

"Might as well take your fifty bucks and go home, little boy," Corm insisted.

"I say, you take your second-place payout and get a bath. You tasted dirt, and I didn't." Emma's chew-on-that-fat type grin drew King closer.

"Why you little bugger, I'll…" he reached out to grab her.

King slid between them. The crowd parted and Hayworth, from the Hayworth Rifle Company, stood on top of the sign-in table. More than seventy people, assembled to participate or watch the event, grew silent.

"We've decided a winner of the Hayworth Rifle Contest. Although, Tom Corm's bullet hit the pumpkin, the shot did not hit inside the target, and he did not remain on his horse. The best sharpshooter in Fort Collins and the great state of Colorado is Emmet Cody. Emmet, come here to claim your Hayworth Rife and the one-hundred-dollar grand prize."

"Told you." King nudged her. "Go, it's what you wanted."

She strutted to the table and extended her gloved hand. Mr. Hayworth jumped from the board, handed her the rifle and an envelope stuffed with bills.

King, beside her, clapped for the second and third place winners. He held Black Bart's reins while they took him to the livery, removed the saddle, and the stable boy took the horse to a stall.

"Congratulations, I'll meet you back here at six tomorrow morning," he said and left her standing in front of the Gold Nugget Hotel holding her saddle, cash prize, and Hayworth Rifle.

"You're assuming a lot. What makes you think I'm staying at this hotel?" She shouted, "Where are you going?"

Chapter 12

Beads of sweat clustered on Emma's forehead. The binding had been arranged, so by a flick of the hand the cloth should come free. To secure her body to the saddle, she tugged and twisted the material. She was trapped in a straitjacket and some misbegotten fool was knocking at her hotel room. She jerked on the shirt, threw on the jacket, buttoned one center button, and flung the door open.

"Because of the contest, there aren't any rooms left." Henry tried to pass by her. His saddle bumped into the doorframe.

She shoved her shoulder against the door. "Sleep in the stables."

He lowered the saddle to wedge against the frame, preventing the entryway from closing. "I'm not into boys, so it shouldn't be an issue." His loud voice carried through the hallway, creating laughter from fellow contestants.

"You're sleeping on the floor," she hissed and stepped back. The sudden movement rubbed her saddle sores, painful burning agony enveloped her.

"What's wrong with you?"

"I can't get the binding off, it's constricting my chest."

He placed his saddle in the corner with hers, shut and locked the door. "Take off your coat and shirt, and

I'll help you."

"I'm desperate. People know I rented the room as a boy, so I can't suddenly walk out as a flat-chest woman and go to the bathhouse. I am confined to this room and to the binds." She tapped her finger against her chin. "I'm sure you're safe."

He crossed his arms and with half-lidded eyes watched her.

"Fine. Don't look at my body. Just cut the blasted cloth off."

"You want me to use a knife near your skin and not look?" He had the audacity to smile. She narrowed her eyes, and he chuckled. Idiot. If she could maneuver her arms without feeling the pain of the bindings, she'd use his knife and cut the material.

He went to his saddlebags and extracted a large Bowie knife. He threw his hat and coat on top of his gear. His boot heels hit the wooden floor and for some reason irritated her more.

"Take them off." He placed the knife on the washstand and rolled the sleeves of his chambray shirt.

Emma removed the jacket and threw it onto the bed. She lowered one shoulder, presented her back to him, then removed the shirt completely. She kept the cloth clutched to her frontside. He didn't say anything. What was he waiting on? "Mr. Courtland?"

"I want to find the best place to cut." His tone changed, as if someone stabbed him with the Bowie. "Don't want to nick the velvety, white, unblemished skin," he whispered in a deep whisky-hued voice.

She put one of her arms back in the sleeve. He halted her action and the shirt fell forward. "Don't. Sorry, lost control for a moment."

His fingers inched between her back and the binding. Her breath caught as the cold blade touched her hot skin. The constraints loosened, freeing her. "Umm, sweet release."

He inhaled, like the breath of a dying man. The binding fell to the floor, and she spread the shirt covering her breasts. She bent, picked up the sweat-stained lavender scented cloth and observed their reflections in the mirror. From where they stood, he could see the entire side of her upper body.

"Since, I cannot go out of the room tonight. I want you to leave, so I can take a quick sponge bath."

"Emma, it's late. I'll crawl into my designated corner and close my eyes."

"Fine. Keep them shut. I'm a virgin and plan to stay that way until my wedding day. Got that Mr. Courtland?" Her empty words were sharp, while the area between her thighs and her stomach tingled with desire.

"Yes, indeed, Emma."

"Hum." She grabbed her satchel and pulled out a nightshirt and a bar of lavender soap. She took a quick glance at Henry. His long legs were sprawled out on the floor, and his head rested against his saddle. His eyelids were shut, and his mouth relaxed.

She'd dreamed of soaking in a tub of hot water and bubbles clear to her neck. Instead, she poured tepid water from the red rose glazed pitcher into the matching bowl. Picking up a washcloth, she checked to make sure his hat covered his forehead. A flick of the wrist the material went into the water, she squeezed off the excess liquid and soaped the cloth with a large amount of herbal heaven. She inhaled the relaxing lavender scent and rubbed the washrag over and under her breasts and down her arm. Something that sounded like a wounded animal stirred from behind her. She held the dripping rectangle to her chest and turned. Did he moan? His hat hadn't moved. Maybe the noise was her imagination.

Next, she removed her trousers and evaluated her legs to see the burns on her thighs. Thank goodness Rachel packed a small bottle of salve. She slipped on a nightshirt, retrieved her lotion from the satchel and climbed on the bed.

"I have to go out for a while," he croaked. He'd tipped his hat higher on his forehead, exhibiting a pained facial expression.

"Okay, take the key." She tossed the quilt from the bed to the floor. The door slammed shut. She scooped a handful of lotion from the container and warmed the wax-based lubricant in her hands. The application instantly eased the painful burn.

Hot, she raised the window an inch. Piano music and laughter filtered from the saloon next door. She crawled into bed, raised the sheet to her neck, leaned over and lowered the wick of the oil lamp. A billow of black smoke rose to the ceiling. A golden hue clouded the room, while the high-stepping *Camp Town Girls,* sung by a talented soprano, filled the space.

The sheet smelled like fresh spring air. She snuggled deeper into the bed and listened to the music, the laughter, and dreamt.

****

Emma snored and not the whistling light rhythmic snore, but one a bear would make. King found the noise adorable but dropped his boots to the floor to try and get her to roll over. The snoring continued. He removed his shirt, spread out on the quilt covering the hard floor and rested his neck on the saddle.

"Emmet, are you in there? Come out and buy me a drink. The true winner of ta' day's contest." The door vibrated with each fist pound on the wood. "Emmet, you little weasel." Pound. Pound.

He jumped to a stand, snapped on the belt and holster, then touched the comforting wooden gun handle.

"Who is it?" she whispered from under the covers.

Now she wakes up. "Second place winner. I'll get rid of him. Do not show your face. If he sees your hair, he'll think I have a woman in the bed." He paused, waiting for her to agree. "Emma?"

"Alright. Be careful, his name is Tom Horm, and he's a gunslinger."

"Emmet. Come and buy me a drink." The door bounced on its hinges.

"Why didn't you tell people at the contest? He could have been eliminated, and you wouldn't have ridden the horse sideways." Frustration and anger splintered the air. She'd taken needless risks.

"I think he suspected I was a woman," she hissed, "and I didn't want to be a winner because of default."

"Shit." He threw the bolt and opened the door a fraction of an inch. "Go away."

"Where is the boy?" Tom Horm tried to push the door. "Are you, his father?"

Emma giggled. He halted Horm's step from moving past the threshold and glanced at the bed. She was smart enough to keep her face turned away from the hallway light, but her long silky light brown hair spread across the pillow.

"A woman. Where's the boy?" Horm kept his drunken gaze pinned on her. King hated drunks. They were the worse.

"He's probably down at Mi-ling's." He shoved the man farther into the hallway.

"Are you done with her? She looks—"

He slammed the door, threw the bolt home, and withdrew a bottle of whisky from his saddlebag. He hoped to God dawn was close because sleep would elude him.

"Thank you," she whispered into the darkness. "Goodnight, father."

"Goodnight, Emmet." King settled on the planks and tucked the pistol near his hand. He'd shoot himself before he let her know the gibe bothered him.

Chapter 13

Emma glanced upward in amazement at the buildings, seven stores tall. The city was so massive compared to Pineview, it seemed oppressive. She'd been in the countryside far too long. She had always loved traveling to big cities, seeing the people and shopping. Boulder was the perfect metropolitan to buy dressmaking supplies. Ladies strolled along cobblestone sidewalks and twirled umbrellas over their shoulders, probably discussing the current style of dress, politics, or social functions.

On display in her man's attire, she swiped the dust off the sleeves of her dirty jacket. She glanced at Henry, who was oblivious to the people staring at them. His perpetual frown warned friendly folk to stay away. *Grump.*

He guided his horse to the first hotel. "Wait here, and I'll get us a couple of rooms, and then we'll stable the horses."

A few seconds later he returned. "No rooms. A famous piano player, Madame Ernestine something is in town for the next two days."

She grimaced. "How many hotels are there?"

"Three and one widow lady on Eighteenth Street has rooms for rent. Don't worry, we'll get a room."

"Two rooms." She put her feet in the stirrups and lifted off the saddle. Her raw sores were healing, but she wanted to settle into a nice hot bath and dress in women's finery.

He grinned and mounted his horse. All the hotels were central to the Boulder Auditorium, which was where Madame Ernestine Schumann-Heink, a contralto, was going to perform. No rooms at the inns, but Mrs. McCullagh's Boarding House had a single room located on the top floor.

The attic was one floor above the bathroom, so Emma took her necessities to the second floor. Mrs. McCullagh filled the tub with steaming hot water, and Emma soaked until her skin pinked and puckered. She threw on her shirt and trousers, gathered the rest of her belongings, and trotted to the third floor.

"At least, at the top, we're not surrounded by the symphony enthusiasts we've seen all over Boulder." A smile flashed across his face. He was lounging on the bed, his back against the black metal headboard, his boots hanging off the edge.

"You need to leave, allowing me privacy. We'll take shifts with the bed. This afternoon, I'll go find dress making materials, so you might consider making use of the comfort."

"I thought the bath would help your bad-temperedness. Still not very sociable, are you?" He threw his hat onto the chair near the bed, arranged the pillows behind his head supporting his back and crossed his ankles.

"Henry, you were supposed to assist me on this trip. So far, you've interrupted my attempt to get money to buy material, you insisted on putting me in an awkward position, and take a tepid bath out of a finger bowl in front of you, and now you're getting your dusty boots all over the cover. Do you think I have reason to be grumpy?" She removed her dress from the satchel and shook it, two strong thrusts and loud pops sounded as the cloth blew a blast of air mussing his fair hair.

"Not really. I'm doing a banner job of keeping miscreants like Tom Horm away from you." He smoothed his hair, eliminating the hat ring where the band rested. His blue-green eyes sparkled with annoying amusement.

"Leave," she growled, and rubbed the light brown velvet piping on the sleek, dark blue dress. He jumped off the bed, grabbed his satchel and left the room.

Within minutes she'd dressed, then dragged the chair to the bureau and tossed her hat on top. She stepped onto the chair and turned, checking the dress in the mirror. A wrinkled mess, the bustle was lopsided, but hopefully the shopkeepers would notice the drawing and sample more than her backside. The jacket had one large button at the waist and drew the eye from her stand-up collar around her neck, down the lacy blouse to her waist. She'd lost weight over the last few weeks, which made her waist a tiny seventeen inches. The west has a way of changing a person.

She stepped off the chair, leaned closer to the mirror, and wound her still damp hair into a tight coiffure. Henry entered the room and dropped his satchel on the bed. The mint scent drew her gaze to his clean-shaven face and new clothing. "You look nice. The vest is very attractive."

She picked up the matching sailor's hat and attached it by hat pins to her hair.

"Thank you." He rubbed his hands along the front of the dark blue paisley vest.

She sucked in air as he rolled his shirt sleeves, covering those beautiful muscular arms. *Deflect*. "Will you please knock before you enter next time?"

"Why? It's my room." He snatched a belt from the satchel, then faced her. His lips twisted into a grin. "To be polite?"

"You're right, it is your room. I'll just make sure I'm always dressed." She lifted the portfolio with the hand-drawn images and business cards from the table, then walked to the wall of clothes hooks, and removed the sample bag. The model of the split skirt bulged in the center. "See you in a couple of hours."

"Where do you think you're going? Do not walk out that door." He didn't shout, however, his calm low tone stopped her in her tracks.

She narrowed her eyes. He slid a belt through the loops, drawing attention to his triangle shape. She glanced away. "I'm going to the dress shops. I have four on my list to see today, and one tomorrow before we return to Pineview."

He didn't say anything. She sighed and took a quick peek. He sorted through his satchel, exhibiting a well-rounded tight rear. She pivoted and twisted the handle. The door hinges squeaked as the bolts grinded open.

"Stop, you're dressed like a woman."

"Thank you. Glad you noticed. Now, I'm in a bit of a rush." At the sound of his jacket sliding into place, the image of his muscles in play created a heat inside her. She decided there were different levels of losing one's virginity. She'd attended enough medical lectures with Matthew to understand about the mechanics of passing into womanhood. This intimacy, a man dressing in front of a female and glimpsing male body parts, must be a prelude.

The illustrations of a man and woman joining didn't bother her in the least. However, having Henry near, often semi-dressed, did strange things to her nether region. She closed the door but continued to face the light oak wood. She transferred the dress tote to her arm with the purse and portfolio and fluffed the crushed bustle.

"Whoever wrote the note may still be out there, ready to attack. While we're in Boulder, you do not go outside without me. I'm your bodyguard." His commanding voice, stronger and louder than the tone which made her tingle. "That is why you wanted me to travel with you."

She pivoted. Her bustle swished against the wood. "We are in the middle of a cosmopolitan city. No one would dare shoot me here." She stared at him. Thankfully, he'd fastened his belt, hid his chest behind a completely buttoned shirt, and pulled on a coat. Temptation was out of sight.

"Maybe not, but they could corner you in an alley, or shove you into a coach." He sat on the bed, tugged off a boot, turned it upside down and replaced the footwear.

"Hum, I see your point. Well, hurry up and get that wild mass of hair ruled, and let's get out there and make some contacts." Excited, she rubbed her hands together.

During the ride to Boulder, she'd explained the details of Jayden's finances. Henry questioned the debt and promised to look into the matter. She anticipated he'd insist they turn around and head back to Pineview, instead he supported the dress making idea.

If the telegram didn't get through to her parents, she'd contact her solicitor and have him provide the trust funds left to her by her maternal grandmother. They should be able to survive on that money for at least a year or until the dress making business provided a profit.

"Ready."

She inhaled. He looked amazing, dressed in an elegant black suit, cardboard collar and bow tie. "You look quite handsome."

"Why, thank you Miss Emma." He slid his arm around her waist. "Are you still serious about the virginity-marriage notion?"

She tilted her head to the side, trying to decide if he was teasing. "Yes, Henry. Celebrate, you've a couch to sleep on tonight instead of the hard floor."

"Will you marry me?"

"Very funny." She sighed in exasperation and tapped his cheek. "I find you adorable at times and very appealing. But, when I marry, it'll be for love and for life. No affairs for my husband, or he'll be one big bull's-eye." She pried his fingers from around her waist and handed him the dress bag. "Still want to marry me?"

The door opened and a man staggered inside. Henry shoved her behind him and drew out a little pistol from inside his jacket pocket. She raised on her toes to see over his shoulder.

The drunken reveler glanced at the revolver. "Sorry, mate, wrong room." He turned and stumbled down the stairs to the second floor.

Henry never answered her question.

The next five hours went slow and fast at the same

time. The proprietors were willing to listen and made favorable comments about the innovative garment but were hesitant to place an order. Their skepticism revolved around the futuristic design not being accepted by the general public. One shop, The French Clothier, agreed to take ten outfits and gave a deposit, the remainder due upon arrival. Two stores prepaid for one garment to be put on display and took a business card. If orders were made, they would agree to purchase in bulk.

"After looking at the drawings and your product I think we should go to the courthouse and get a patent, just in case the other dressmakers use yours as a pattern," Henry said as they strolled along First Street.

She nodded, and they walked into the courthouse office as the clerk was locking the drawers. "I need to get a patent for a dress design I'm selling."

"We're closed." The pudgy bald-headed man didn't look at her and kept locking office doors.

"The sign on the door indicates you're open until four. If I give you five-dollars for ten minutes will you give her the form?" Henry removed five silver coins from his vest pocket.

The man took a form from under the cabinet.

"I need two, please." She completed one form, signed her and Rachel's name on the drawing of the riding outfit. Treasure had created a handmade business card, *Three Maids Dress Creations*, which Emma submitted with the drawing. He paid the processing fee, and they registered the riding outfit. "Thank you for your assistance." She gave him a broad smile.

The clerk nodded. His already red cheeks grew brighter.

Henry held her arm as they walked from the office. "Who is the second form for?"

"Treasure, she is making accessories. I didn't feel right signing her name. Thank you, Henry. Good business sense." She smiled at him and licked her lips.

"Grateful enough to let me sleep with...er in the bed?" He winked.

She laughed. Sexually aroused, she wished they could copulate.

They meandered along the sidewalks. He took her arm into his when they were going to cross an intersection. She felt comfortable, like a couple in love, out for a stroll on a warm spring evening.

"Do you want to stop and eat, or go out later?" Close to the boarding house, they'd passed several restaurants. Decadent aromas of yeasty bread, barbequed steaks, and sweet cakes and chocolates scented the air. Her mouth salivated, and her stomach growled.

"Maybe later. I want to see if a family friend is in town." He acted a little twitchy like he was planning something. Maybe he needed to smoke a cigar? She'd overheard her father's friends talk about needing to smoke. Matthew claimed smoking was a deadly addiction.

"I'm going to the corral and check on Black Bart. He was acting a little morose when we arrived in Boulder." Emma hung the dress bag on the hall tree and placed the portfolio on a table in the foyer of the boarding house.

"You'll go to the room, after checking on the horse?"

"Of course."

147

"Maybe I should go with you."

"Nonsense. I'll only be a moment. As a matter of fact, why don't you do whatever you want tonight? I'll stay here, maybe take in the meal Mrs. McCullagh provides and call it an early night." She smiled and nodded her head.

His eyes narrowed. "Is that what you want, Emma? To be relieved of me tonight?"

"Of course. I'll even fix your couch bed. Besides, I need to add some totals, calculate how much cloth to buy tomorrow before we head back. You'll be bored watching me add figures." She rested her hand on his sleeve, felt the hard muscles bunch beneath her fingertips. The man was as tightly wound as a grandfather clock.

"Fine," he murmured. Henry hurried from the boarding house without a good-bye or see you soon. She wouldn't let his bad attitude bother her. A man had urges. *He's probably on his way to a brothel now.* If he returned with the scent of a trollop all over his body and stone-cold drunk, she'd kick him out of the room. He could sleep in the hall. And if he didn't... Could she spend another night alone with him and not ask him to kiss her, hold her, and touch her? The tingling, itchy feeling in-between the junction of her thighs returned. Blast. She'd consider Rachel's idea to have an experience with intimacy before returning to Fort Wayne.

She walked to the corral. Black Bart shared the pen, a split-rail wooden fence, with a white shiny-coated mare. Henry's Palomino, Maverick's head was sticking out from the open barn slider. Black Bart kept neck-to-neck with the mare running along the edges of the fence row. Maverick ignored both of them and chewed on the wood doorframe. The mare threw back her head, teasing Black Bart. He shook his head in agreement, then nipped her rear. The mare took off at a run. The tease stopped and chewed on a few stalks of glossy grass, presenting her rear to him.

Emma chuckled and whistled. The mare ran toward her, and the steed followed. She removed the sugar cubes she'd snatched off the dining table at lunch from her pocket and extended one to the mare, and then one to her horse. He swallowed the treat without chewing. She rubbed his sweaty neck. He shoved his head, pushing against her arm and hand. He blew his sweetened breath into her empty hand. Not finding more treats, he nuzzled her palm. His rubbery black nose moistened her fingers. "Aw Black Bart, I know I promised you a little lady of your own. I don't know if she's for sale, and it's a really bad time to spend money on a mate for you."

She caught the movement of the white horse from her peripheral vision. The mare nosed her way to Emma's hand, nudging Black Bart out of the way. "Well, aren't you a prima donna?" She rubbed the velvety muzzle of the horse. Black Bart edged his head against the white. Together they took off at a gallop. The white flipped her tail into Black Bart's face. He neighed.

"They are beautiful together, don't you think?"

She turned toward the dulcet voice. "Yes, I do."

"She's for sale, if you're interested." The melodious lyrical Irish words flowed over Emma.

She met the woman's dark-brown glance. The simple straight lines made the designer black dress elegant. A lady owned the beautiful equine. "If you are anything like me, parting with such an exquisite beast will be an agonizing challenge."

"Yes, selling her is painful."

"I think Black Bart's very interested." He attempted to mount the mare, and she didn't appear to be reluctant. "She has the look of an Arabian."

"Yes, Brandy with her soulful brown eyes, is a thoroughbred." The woman rested her hands on top of the railing.

"Why are you selling her?"

"Thieves murdered my husband last month. I'm leaving tomorrow to return to my homeland, Ireland. A long voyage for her. Needless travel." The sadness of her heartfelt love for the horse seeped through her voice.

"Have you had any offers?" Brandy avoided being mounted by Black Bart and was running along the fence line, tossing her silky flowing mane in the wind.

"Yes, a man inside the boarding house is willin' to give me one hundred dollars. But I sense he is a cruel man, and I would not rest easy knowin' Brandy was in his hands."

"Mrs.?"

"McGregor, call me Aliana." She continued to watch the equines; a tender smile appeared as Black Bart nipped Brandy's neck.

"I'll give you a brand-new, special made Hayworth rifle with a high retail value and twenty-five dollars in cash for her. Also, the promise Brandy will be well cared for and loved by Black Bart and me." She hoped the offer was enough, but considering women are excellent deal makers and breakers, she anticipated a refusal.

"I'm sorry, I've no desire to own a rifle." Her response matched her down-turned lips.

"If you change your mind, my name is Emma Cody, and I'm on the top floor. Please don't sell her to anyone, especially not the mean man, without allowing me to find a way to provide more cash."

"Yes, I'll consider it." Her heartrending sigh carried in the wind. Brandy's ears picked up, and she ran toward Aliana.

"Good-night, Aliana." Emma fought back the tears. She trapped herself into a corner by making so many promises. A drop of rain plopped onto her face, merging with her tears. By the time she entered the foyer the damn burst and tears poured down in a steady stream of water.

She gathered her items from the entry of the boarding house and noticed the time on the grandfather clock. Blast! Nine o'clock at night, she wouldn't be able to talk to the people at the stagecoach office or the train station. Her one opportunity to check into the location of Bell Grind, and she'd lost the chance.

She went into the kitchen to find a piece of bread, instead she found Mrs. McCullagh washing dishes. The older lady pivoted and smiled, showing tea-stained teeth. "Good evening, dearie. Where's your young man?"

"Henry went out. I missed dinner, do you have a slice of bread and cheese I could nibble on?" The aroma of cinnamon and apples of a pie, fresh from the oven, was tantalizing.

"Nonsense. I can't let you waste away. Sit. Put your garments on the chair. I'll get you something to eat." Mrs. McCullagh dried her hands and opened a cupboard to remove a plate.

Soon a veritable feast was in front of her. She couldn't decide what to eat first, maybe the pie, and if there was room, the main course. She took a sip of water and spooned the sweet-smelling ham and fried potatoes onto her plate. On the side, she added green beans and a slice of bread. Unable to stop eating, she didn't talk.

Finished, she pushed away from the table and sighed. "Mrs. McCullagh you're a divine cook. If you should ever grow tired of keeping house for strangers, you'll always be welcome in my kitchen."

"Thank ye, dearie. What a nice thing to say." The rails of the wooden chair squeaked as she sat across from Emma.

"Do you think you could pack a lunch for us when we leave tomorrow?"

"Yes, I would enjoy creating a little picnic for newlyweds." She grinned and her brown eyes glittered with joy. "Young lovers are so special."

In order to rent the only room available, she'd fibbed to the landlady, claiming they were newly married. "Our marriage is one of necessity." She drew circles on the rough texture of the oak table. "Why, do you think he loves me?"

"The way ye look at each other." Mrs. McCullagh tapped her hand. "My Peter was the same way. He would look at me with a longing. The protective way Henry acts around ye. The way he watches ye walk. His eyes are always on yer face when ye talk. The man is in love with ye. And don't ye be denying ye don't love him back because I know ye do."

She looked out the window. A silent rain cascaded along the glass. "Aye, Mrs. McCullagh, I do love the man, but he agreed to sign marriage papers as an act of Galahad honor. My brother, the reason I'm in Colorado, died recently, and I found out that he was cheating on his wife. She is pregnant with their first child."

"Not to disrespect yer brother, but she got a bad one. Don't mean yer man will treat ye the same way." Mrs. McCullagh stood and gathered the dishes.

"He's not my man, and I plan to return to Indiana after I help her." She slid off the chair, grabbed a dish cloth and cleaned the dishes. "Thank you, Mrs. McCullagh. I'm going to bed. Have a restful sleep."

"Thank ye, dearie." She halted and turned. "Don't worry, yer man loves ye, and I'm sure he'll show ye in many ways."

Emma nodded, wearily gathered her items, and climbed to the third floor.

Teeth brushed, face washed, hair in a long braid, and nightgown in place, she opened the window a couple of inches. Spring rain scented breeze entered. She glanced at the cloud covered sky and wished for...*not going to happen, the earlier conversation made me have romantic longing*. She climbed into bed with her back against the headboard, lifted her knees to use as a hard surface and made two columns on a piece of paper; amount of cash on hand; amount of cloth necessary and approximate costs. Rachel had written out the values of cloth needed per outfit. Simply multiply the cloth value times the number of orders and approximate the costs of thread, buttons, pins, and accessories for the broaches. All said and done, she would have fifty dollars left after the purchase of the material.

She could take the rifle to a gun shop and sell it outright. The rifle money added to the fifty, might give her enough to buy the mare from Aliana. The decision made, she laid the pen and paper aside. Unable to sleep, she tucked a blanket on the sofa and tossed an extra quilt on top. With his bed made, she settled onto the mattress and her eyelids shuttered closed.

The door flew open, wind whooshed through the room, banging the portal against the wall. She jerked and catapulted upright in bed. Her gown fell to the side, exposing the top of her chest. A chill brushed over her. She hadn't locked the bedroom door. Had the drunk reveler returned? She reached under the pillow for her gun.

Chapter 14

"Reverend, I thank you for coming with me under such short notice." King herded the couple up the twisting flights of stairs, stopping on the landing outside his rented room. The robust Mrs. Fitzgerald huffed, trying to catch her breath. "The air's thinner, and warmer on the third floor."

An elegantly dressed woman with hair as shiny as a crow's wing was placing a note under the door.

"May I help you?"

"Perhaps," she answered with a sweet melodic Irish accent. "Emma didn't answer my knock, so I thought to leave a note. Are ye her husband?"

"I'm her fiancé, Henry Courtland, most people call me King. May I help you?" His voice was unintentionally harsh as he knew the minister and his wife were adamantly listening to the conversation. He didn't want them to think various women appeared at his door all hours of the night.

"She wanted to buy my horse. I have a cash offer of one hundred dollars, if she could provide a like amount, in cash and not with a rifle. I'll sell her the mare."

Mrs. Fitzgerald gasped.

"A rather high dollar amount for a horse." Did Emma plan to create a breeding stable? Is that why she continued to talk about returning to her hometown, she has a business venture started with someone else?

The woman nodded, and her glance focused on the couple behind him.

"This is Reverend and Mrs. Theodore Fitzgerald." He nodded toward the minister who clutched the Bible close to his chest. Mrs. Fitzgerald scraped water from her overcoat.

"Pleasure to meet ye, I'm Aliana McGregor." Her attention returned to him. "The mare is first quality blood-line Arabian." Her voice was firm.

"I assume you have papers to prove it?"

"Yes."

"I'll buy the horse as a gift for my bride. When do you need the money?"

"My ship sails at ten o'clock tomorrow."

"I'll meet you in the foyer at seven then."

Alaina held out her thin white hand. "We have a deal, Mr. Courtland. You'll tell Emma the good news?"

He nodded. "Yes, I'll tell her, sometime after the wedding."

"Good night, then." Mrs. McGregor walked down the stairs.

King wondered where his vision of beauty was, if she hadn't answered the knock. He inserted the key and turned the bolt. The door was unlocked. His heart palpitated a hundred-wheel turns. The wind caught the mighty oak and flung the door into the wall. "Emma."

She shot straight-up in bed and grabbed a gun from under her pillow. Her gown separated, allowing her beautiful breasts to glimmer in the hallway light. He glanced behind him. Reverend and the Mrs. remained in the hallway but were trying to peek around the corner.

"Cover up. I've got some people who want to meet

you."

In one minute, her sleep-induced daze shifted to be a wide-eyed wonder. Emma replaced the pearl-handled pistol under her pillow and pulled the gown closed, then whipped the strings into a bow.

"You were right, Mr. Courtland. The little lamb has gone astray," Mrs. Fitzgerald whispered as she removed her rain-soaked bonnet.

Emma tugged the sheet to her chin.

He'd probably go to hell for his actions this evening, but she was worth the possibility. "Emma, I'd like you to meet the Reverend and Mrs. Fitzgerald. Reverend and Mrs. Fitzgerald, please meet my wife-to-be, Emma Cody."

Mrs. Fitzgerald's gray head bobbed as she scooted forward and rested a fat hand on his lady love's white knuckled fingers gripping the covers. "There, there little one, we'll help you. The lord forgives those who go astray. At least Mr. Courtland wants to make it right."

Emma's keen green eyes met his stare. He dared her to contradict him. "What have you told them?"

"Darling, the Reverend is from Central Presbyterian Church, on the corner." He pointed toward the window. "I went there tonight to confess my sins and ask forgiveness." He drew the Reverend closer. The minister kept his head bent and hands folded at his belt buckle.

"The Reverend..." He smiled at Mrs. Fitzgerald. "And Mrs. Fitzgerald...have agreed to help me right my wrong and marry us post haste."

"What the hell? What are you talking about?" Emma's face grew crimson, darker than the quilted bedcover.

Mrs. Fitzgerald shifted, sitting on the edge of the bed. A small room with four people, one who was breathing hot air, created a moist environment. The wetness from their wool overcoats created a dank stinky sock smell. King removed his coat and hung it on the wall hook near the door. He offered to help Mrs. Fitzgerald with hers, placing the garment on a second hook.

"Why, we're getting married, dear. I explained how I've been sharing sleeping quarters with you for the last two nights, and I wanted to rectify the situation." King tried to look ashamed.

"Whatever are you blubbering about? We've never slept together. I'm still a virgin and will submit to any test by a doctor or mid-wife to prove it." In addition to her red face, her words were sharp and short. The marriage ceremony wasn't going to be as easy as he'd thought.

"Is this true, Mr. Courtland?" Mrs. Fitzgerald pierced him with her watery blue gaze.

He whispered into the Reverend's ear. "She took off all of her clothes and bathed in front of me, what do you think?"

The Reverend turned his hell and damnation demeanor onto Emma. She shot King a glare. He shrugged his shoulders. *The end justifies the means.*

"Miss Cody, did you take your clothes off in front of this man?" Reverend Fitzgerald pointed an accusatory finger at her, and then at him.

Her eyes narrowed. "Yes, but—"

"Jezebel!" Spittle flew from the minister's mouth.

Mrs. Fitzgerald raised her hand to rest on Emma's

shoulder. "Poor little lamb."

The reverend lectured for the next twenty minutes about fornication and forsaking God. King assumed a devout expression while stealing a glance at Emma. She shoved the dark gray dress over her nightgown and stood rigid beside him. He anticipated an elbow dig to his side.

"We'll witness the exchange of vows," Reverend Fitzgerald declared.

King took her cold hand into his and rubbed his thumb across her palm.

"This couldn't wait until the morning?" Emma hissed.

He squeezed her hand.

"Do you, Emma Cody, take this man, Henry Courtland, to be your husband, in sickness and health, richer, poorer, better, worse, faithfully for the rest of your life?" Reverend Fitzgerald extended the Bible as if he wanted her to place her hand on top and vow.

"Do I have a choice?" she spat.

"Emma," he cajoled.

"You need to say yes, or I do." Mrs. Fitzgerald nodded her head.

"Yes," she croaked between clinched teeth.

"Henry, do you take Emma to be your wife?"

"What? Where is the sick, health, rich, poor, faithful decree you gave to me?" she shouted.

He squeezed her hand.

The Reverend squinted. "You could say, no, and let her go to the devil as his handmaiden."

Instead of fuming, she smiled. Her hand relaxed beneath his, and her small body leaned against him. He understood her fear about promiscuity, with the information about Jayden's betrayal so fresh in her mind.

"I do take Emma Cody to be my wife, faithfully and forever."

"I believe you have a ring?" Reverend Fitzgerald whispered.

Emma's head snapped, as she turned and stared at him.

Yes siree, he'd be sleeping on the floor tonight. He pulled a gold band from his coat pocket.

The good Reverend took the ring, said a Latin blessing or a spell over it, and returned the sparkler to him.

"With this ring, I thee wed." He lifted her fragile left hand and slid the simple circle onto her third finger. A perfect fit.

"You may kiss, Mrs. Courtland." The man of cloth announced.

"Oh, sweet little lambs." Mrs. Fitzgerald wiped tears from her eyes.

King lifted Mrs. Courtland's chin and cringed at the sight of the tears. He didn't know if they were from anger, or dare he think, happiness? He inhaled her lavender scent, lowered his mouth, and kissed her gently on the lips, sealing the vow.

"If you'd sign the ledger and your own marriage decree, we'll be on our way. Martha, the decree." Reverend Fitzgerald, having saved another lamb, was impatient to leave.

Mrs. Fitzgerald pulled out a tome of a book from inside her bag and handed a fountain pen to her husband. She also withdrew a cream vellum paper completely filled out except for the signatures. Martha handed the crisp paper to King. He took the document, signed above his name and dropped the pen, splattering his boots with black dots. He retrieved it, handed the writing instrument and the legally binding document to Emma. Her glance met his. She heaved a sigh and scribbled a signature on the line and handed the paper to the Reverend. King handed the pen to Mrs. Fitzgerald, then withdrew an envelope from his coat pocket and handed the thick pouch to the Reverend. "Thank you. Goodnight and God Bless."

The door shut as loud as the thunder outside the boarding house, leaving him alone with his wife. She stood in the middle of the room, her nightgown overlapping the gray formal dress. Left hand extended, she stared at the ring. King couldn't decide if she was happy, sad, or frightened. He'd give her time to adjust to the fact they were married. A wooing would begin tomorrow.

"Good night, dear wife." He took the marriage license from her, tucked it in his satchel and extinguished the flame in the lantern. As promised, she'd made the couch into a bed. He undressed in the dark and tried to find a comfortable position, given his calves hung off the end.

"Ugh." She removed the dress, then the hanger rattled against the wall hook. A few seconds later, the mattress springs creaked and moaned. Mrs. Courtland flopped from side to side.

He went to sleep with a sense of contentment and a satisfied smile.

****

Emma was beyond being angry. When she woke, her husband of a few hours was missing. She decided during the ceremony to relax, go through the charade, and have sex. A win-win. Henry wanted her, and she wanted to experience intimacy. She'd enjoy her husband and all of his attributes. First thing she'd do, dig her fingers into those chest hairs, then touch every part of his anatomy. The idiot of a man crawled, like a sneaky snake, onto the couch and snored within seconds.

The bell tower in the town square rang seven bells. Where could he have gotten to? She stomped to the second floor to relieve herself and wash off the lack of sleep. Cosmetic items gathered, she walked into the hallway. Mrs. McCullagh came out of a guestroom, carrying soiled linens.

"Good morning, Mrs. Courtland. It's a fine day. I saw your sweet husband earlier." The elderly woman winked. "He has a wonderful surprise for you."

"And what would that be Mrs. McCullagh?"

"Why I can't tell ye that, dearie. What a wonderful man. A romantic. He was certainly all smiles this morning."

"Yes, he is one of a kind. Mrs. McCullagh, we need to go to a couple of stores this morning, to meet check-out could I put our bags downstairs until we come back."

"Yes, dearie. That would be fine." The landlady hummed and descended the stairs.

Emma was conflicted. Henry hadn't asked her to marry him. He assumed she'd be content, even docile. Like a fool, she went along with the quick bogus marriage ceremony and waited, excited about the consummation act. Why didn't he make love to her? He married her, what he deemed as forever, why not share coitus?

Eight bells rang when he arrived, toting a large silver tray set with breakfast for two. Since a dining table wasn't available, they sat on the edge of the bed and shared an egg and bacon casserole, toast, strawberries, coffee for him and tea for her. Why not eat? She'd need the energy to get through the day. Limited conversation made the lovely meal uncomfortable. Was this the destiny of her probable short marriage? He acted like he wanted to say something, opened his mouth, then shoved a fork of egg inside. Maybe they needed to battle bandits to get their communication to return.

They took their baggage to the desk in the lobby. Mrs. McCullagh shooed them away, "Have fun, you two." She winked. "I'll see you in a couple of hours."

Elegant Designs, the last dress shop to visit, was two blocks east of the boarding house. The owner, Mrs. Flanders, ordered ten of the outfits, which landed her budget back into the zero balance after she purchased material. Unable to purchase Brandy, she mentally apologized to Black Bart for disappointing him. A mean, crusty, old man would acquire the prized white horse.

Henry continued to be polite and agreeable as they traveled from store to store purchasing the materials. He was able to get a better price on a satin, and as a result she bought a large satchel to carry the material home. Poor Black Bart, she hoped he was able to get his needs met last night because he was going to be a packhorse as well as her mount.

"Mrs. McCullagh packed a lunch, so we could get on the road straight-away." Emma hoisted a wrapped package under her arm.

He shifted the bundles around in his arms. "Thank you for arranging the lunch. It'll be good to get home."

Maybe he feels like he made a mistake taking her on as a wife. Fine. She recalled how his body looked yesterday, after his bath, water beaded on his firm chest. His tight rear muscles bunched as he walked across the room. He kissed her with such luscious passion. Maybe she could entice him into making love with her.

Well, if the lovemaking was good, she might try to tempt him into it twice. According to Rachel, the first time wasn't very pleasant and the other times questionable. Since Emma didn't have personal knowledge, she couldn't ask why they were paradoxical. Painful because of size?

"I'll get the horses and meet you out front."

"Thank you, Henry." She smiled. When he winked, her heart lifted, and joy encompassed her. *Mrs. Henry Courtland, you are going to tease him into desiring you.*

"Thank you, Mrs. McCullagh for the use of the room to change clothing. We had a lovely stay. And thank you very much for lunch. I dislike hard tack and jerky. Now, I won't starve." She tapped the leather satchel packed with decadent smelling breads.

"Ye're welcome, Mrs. Courtland. "'Tis a pleasure ta 'ave ya, now." Mrs. McCullagh hugged her close. "Ye take care of that handsome young man now, ya hear?"

"Yes, ma'am, I will." Emma grabbed the saddlebags, and the satchels. "I'll put these on the porch and come back for the other."

"I'll take 'em out for ye, now." The elderly lady smiled broadly, lifted the lunch satchel and followed.

Henry stood at the edge of the porch, holding the reins of three horses, Maverick, Black Bart, and Brandy. Emma dropped the bags and jumped, landing flat against his chest. He stepped backward trying to regain his balance, and the horses side-stepped.

She kissed him, full on his lips. Yes, she was angry he married her without properly proposing or letting her plan a ceremony. He didn't claim to love her, but he sure as heck showed he cared. She was falling in love with Henry Courtland, and her heart would break when she had to let him go.

"Henry, thank you so very much." She released him and lowered her feet to the ground, then grabbed Brandy around the neck. "Brandy, welcome to the family." The mare lifted her head, nodding in agreement. "How did you know, about Brandy?"

Mrs. McCullagh sniffed and blew her nose into her hanky. He loaded the bags onto the back of Black Bart and helped Emma onto the sugar white horse. "I met Mrs. McGregor last night."

She nodded. "Good-bye, Mrs. McCullagh." They turned away from the boarding house.

"Good-bye, children, stay here the next time ye're in Boulder."

"We will," she shouted.

She waited until they left the sky-high buildings behind and were immersed in the plains. "Thank you, for Brandy."

He tilted his head. "Sure, last night Mrs. McGregor was trying to slip a note under the door. She explained about the horse, and I wanted to get you a wedding gift."

"It's the nicest gift I've ever received, and Black Bart is very happy, too." She rubbed Brandy's neck. The horse blew out a hay scented breath and nodded.

They rode in silence until the sky grew dark and the uneven road became risky to travel.

"The prairie dog holes are large." Her inane conversation skills wouldn't spark romance.

"Yup."

"It's only a couple of miles to Fort Collins, but could we stop for the night?" She lifted off the seat. Her saddle sores burned. Feeling unattractive, she glanced at her men's garb. No wonder he seemed disinterested in her.

****

King knew of a secluded area he and a friend stayed at one time after a night of entertainment in Fort Collins. She hadn't mentioned taking a break for lunch, so when she asked to stop for the night, he agreed. He didn't make promises without the intent to keep them.

He hobbled the horses, removed the saddles and packages, while contemplating what to say. He'd forced marriage on her. Maybe he was arrogant and vain. Other people find him attractive, but she might not.

He washed his face and hands at the bubbling stream and made a vow, the marriage would be ''til death do they part', so she might as well get used to the notion.

She'd placed a blanket on the ground and set the picnic lunch out. "Mrs. McCullagh sent a bottle of wine, but we don't have glasses. If you don't mind, we'll share."

"Sure." He widened his stance and hooked his

thumbs in front of his gun belt. "Emma, we need to talk."

"I agree. Let's eat first. I'm starved." She patted the blanket.

Though cold, the meat pies, and the fresh baked bread had his stomach growling. He sat across from her, removed his hat and fluffed his hair. She seemed different in some way. Her face lightened as she told humorous stories about growing up in Fort Wayne. Like a cowboy at the end of a drive, she drank the alcohol directly from the bottle, and too soon the charming dinner ended. They packed the remaining food in a bag and hung the fare from a tree branch.

She lowered the bottle and tipped the glass onto the ground. "Well, that didn't last long." She hiccupped and rummaged around in her saddlebags and withdrew her bathing supplies and turned toward him. "It's dark with a wavering moon, and I'd love to wash off some of this travel dust. Would you mind assisting me, please?"

The woman batted her eyelashes at him. The little vixen was up to something, or could her pleasantness be a result of the wine? He pictured her naked in the water and could not breathe. His heart pounded a quick cadence like galloping horse hooves. He rubbed his ear lobe, considered replacing the hat on his head and saying he needed to keep watch for bandits or something. Instead, he looked into her green eyes, smelled the lavender scented soap ready to fall out of her hand and nodded. He'd get a paper and pen and write out his last will and testament, because he would be dead after watching her run a cloth over those perfectly shaped breasts, taunt abdomen, and rounded bottom, again.

"Are you all right, you're walking like you've been in the saddle for days?"

"Yes, I'm fine." His hoarse answer sounded as deep as Maverick's snort.

She had to be finished. He unbuttoned his pants, unleashing the beast within, but it didn't relieve the pressure. Was this his hell, his punishment for their arranged marriage? Would this version of hell end soon?

The moon beamed rays came from behind a cloud and like the lady of the lake, she walked toward him. He buttoned the top button of his canvas pants, jumped up, and reached out to her. She clasped his hand, handed him her soap, toothpowder, and stopped his heart by bending over. She picked up her discarded clothing. Her rear was a tight heart shaped glowing mirage.

Buck naked, his wife walked into their camp site. To cap off his heart failure, she bent her knees to spread her clothing over a fallen tree. She reclined on the picnic blanket. "I think I'll let the air dry my skin." Her hand reached toward him. "Come lie beside me, tell me about yourself. What other businesses do you manage?"

"I have to go…" He pointed in the direction of the stream.

"I'll be here when you get back." She placed her hands behind her head, lifting her chin. Her pearl buds rose.

He practically ran to the stream, threw off his boots, clothes, and slid into the freezing water. Mistake, it wasn't deep enough to soak, and the rocks hurt his feet. What game was she playing? He left the stream, pulled on his pants, gathered the rest of his clothing and boots and marched back to the campsite. Her games were over. Either she committed to him and agreed to be his wife, fully, or…what?

"What took you so long? I'm cold, and I'd like to have you right here beside me." She rolled to her side, patted the blanket and watched him with those witchy eyes. He spread his clothing beside hers.

He stood in front of her, the flaps of his pants bent over and his hands on his hips. She must have seen his mutinous expression because she jumped up and placed her cold arms around his neck.

"Please make love to me, Henry." She pressed her mouth hard against his and outlined his lips with her tongue.

"There's no going back, Emma."

Her hands physically moved his hands to her waist, then she lowered his trousers past his hips. "I understand," she said, the raspy tone coming from deep in her throat.

"Love, it's going to be so hard to take it slow." Kicking off his trousers, he lowered his body to press against hers. His tongue flicked inside her mouth, and she returned the action. She lifted her upper body to connect with his. Her hands roamed over his back, his waist, down his hips and back to his chest.

His kissed her neck and down to those pale nubs, which begged to be caressed. She moaned and moved her hips back and forth. "Don't move, I want to make it good for you, and I want you so much I won't be able to wait."

He inserted his finger into her moistness. She stilled. "That feels so good. Is there a hard and fast rule that says you have to take your time?"

"No, but the first time for a woman, it's painful, unless you're prepared," he whispered into her ear, then wrapped his lips around her lobe. He gripped the tender skin with his teeth, gently pulled, and sucked.

"How do we speed up the prepared part, I want to stop the itch, the tingle that occurs where your fingers are right now."

He withdrew his fingers, kissed her breasts, promising to spend more time with them in the future.

"More, please."

He inhaled the scent of her excitement, mixed with his musk aroma, his desire awakened sharp and forever. He eased into the beckoning heat, slow until he reached the breach and stopped.

"Why are you stopping? Is it over? No more? I still feel the need, an indescribable desire. I want to feel you deeper inside me." She spread her thighs, quickly adapting to his full pulsating muscle, edging toward something indescribable. Could only Henry make her feel this way?

"I don't want to hurt you." He kissed her, then gently thrust.

Her fingernails gripped his back. "Ow! Blast. That does hurt."

"Sorry, the pain will ease." He kissed her with all the pent-up passion of a man in love, and held still, willing her to adjust to the newness of him.

"Yes, feels much better." Her fingers stopped the skin extraction from his back, and she lifted her hips, pushing her thighs against his hips.

He thrust, found a rhythm, complementing and satisfying.

Her spasms sucked him in deeper. She clenched

him tight. His hardness burst into her welcoming warmth. "Love, our marriage will be—"

Don't let him talk about the marriage, or this lovely interlude would end, and she wanted to experience more, get to know him as a person and lover. She tightened her arms around his neck. "My God, that was so much better than I thought it was going to be. Can we do it again?"

"Please be quiet for a while. I've never made love with someone who talked non-stop." He kissed her gently, halting her words, momentarily.

"I think we're good together." She whispered, "If I'm quiet, could we do it again?"

He laughed. She giggled. He grew hard.

Chapter 15

His hand covered her mouth. Emma had closed her eyes, what seemed like moments before, and now her stomach muscles clenched in anxiety. Had the bandits returned? The men who were trying to kill her?

"The horses are making noise. Someone or something is out there. Get dressed, quietly and quickly," he whispered. His glance traveled from the horses to the edge of the mountain, where the sun was beginning to peak. He released her mouth, pulled on his trousers and boots. Gun belt in place, he grabbed the rifle and made his way toward the horses.

Emma didn't waste time. She tugged on her trousers, jerked on her blouse, and tied the ends instead of buttoning. She slid on her boots and glanced around. Where was her rifle? Blast, she'd left the weapon on her saddle. She threw a blanket over a small log, making it look like a sleeping body, and crept toward their baggage and saddles. Her rifle, within eyesight, peeked from its red cloth bag. Only a few more steps...

The report of a gunshot came from nearby, followed by a second bang. She ran forward, snatched the gun, a box of shells, and bolted toward the horses. She ducked behind the horses, stopping on the other side. Her man walked toward her. Her heart did happy flip flops, beating faster than when she'd slid to the side of Black Bart and shot the pumpkin head. He meant something to her, he mattered. She took a deep breath, admitting she'd fallen in love with him. Her heart ached at the thought he didn't love her. A moment of regret made her weak-kneed.

"Henry? Are you?" she whispered but couldn't enunciate the words of the question she really wanted to voice.

"Yes. I'm fine. A mountain lion, female, hunting for food. I shot over her head to scare it away."

She let the tightness leave her shoulders and threw herself into his arms. She wasn't naïve, realizing the marriage would end when they got back to civilization, and he found out the truth. But, right now, she rejoiced for his safety and the love she felt for her hero.

"Whoa, there. I'm fine. What's this all about?" He stepped back, regaining his balance.

"I heard two gunshots. I was afraid the shots were for you and not by you."

He kissed her hard and quick. She leaned into the kiss, wrapped her arm around his neck, letting the bullets and gun dangle. She wanted more and regretted that she couldn't get more. Soon the honeymoon would end.

"What do you say we don't stop? With dawn peaking, we could make it to Pineview today." He kissed her brow and backed away. "I believe a spring snow is coming, and we need to get ahead of the blast."

"Has to be the shortest honeymoon in the history of marriage," she muttered.

"What did you say?"

"Maybe we can manage to keep on the road and avoid the storm."

Within minutes the horses were saddled, and they

were on their way home.

They didn't stop. The winds blew down from the mountain, inching under her clothing creating a deep chill. At a signal from Henry, they stopped. He removed white blankets, with arm holes, from his saddlebag. "It's called a poncho."

The poncho was like a woman's shawl that draped over her shoulders with a built-in head covering. At the foothills, the winds blew at sixty miles per hour bringing snow and sleet. She led Brandy close to Maverick, and he blocked some of the gusts.

"Are you warmer?" The snowfall pounded the side of Henry's face.

"Yes, now that I have a cover." Her lips quivered, and her eyes watered.

"Do you want to stop?"

"No, thank you." She pulled the hood closer around her face and clutched the reins.

The house windows gleamed with light, and billows of smoke rose from its chimneys. The roof frosted by a coat of snow made it appear *fairytailish*, like a figment of her imagination. A smattering of fir, spruce, and oak trees in an otherwise treeless plains environment. She nudged Brandy to a faster pace.

Emma vowed to talk to Rachel and make sure she was checked by a physician. If Jayden had been unfaithful, especially with a prostitute, then she needed to make sure she didn't have a venereal disease. Rumors told of syphilis being at epidemic proportions for married women throughout the west.

Henry led, with Black Bart trailing behind, and Emma at the back of the line. Single file they trotted into the stables. Sam was inside hitching the carriage to the brown horse. She navigated Brandy beside the mounting block and dismounted.

"Where are you going this early and with a spring snowstorm hitting us hard?" Henry helped her remove the bags from Black Bart.

"To get Dr. Grayson, Rachel's been in labor for hours. There's a problem." Sam's face was whiter than usual and dark blue-gray circles formed under his eyes.

"The roads aren't safe for carriages. Put this saddle on Black Bart, he's still fresh, and I'll ride into Pineview to get the doctor." Henry gave Sam the saddle and blanket.

She grabbed her satchel and started toward the house. "I need to go to Rachel. Please be careful and hurry."

He mounted Black Bart and edged beside her. She put her hand on his leg and glanced into his face.

"I'll hurry, and I'll be careful." He kissed her, warming her cold lips. "Tell Rachel, I'll bring back the doc." With a wink and a smile, he nudged Black Bart into a gallop.

"So, you're not courting, but you'll let King kiss you?" Sam shouted.

She stopped at the open door, turned, and gave him a gamine smile. "Yes, I let my husband kiss me."

Inside the house, she dropped her bag onto the kitchen floor and hung the poncho on a hook beside the door.

Treasure rushed into the room. "Visitors. Parlor. Rachel, needs a drink." She held a hand to her chest and took a deep breath.

"Whoa, calm down. Is Rachel," she swallowed, "alright?"

Treasure nodded.

"Who is in the parlor?"

"Don't know the dark man, but the rich white scoundrel has been here for two days." Treasure poured hot water into a cup and added the tea diffuser.

"I'll check on Rachel, and then I'll go to the foyer and see who has the audacity to make a social call during a snowstorm." Emma put the teacup on a tray with sugar and a spoon. "Will you see if they need tea or anything, please?"

"Yes, ma'am, but the dark one scares me." Treasure twisted her hands, keeping them close to her stomach.

"I'll return after seeing Rachel." She used the back staircase, carefully balancing the tray.

Elbowing the door to Rachel's room, she placed the tray on the bureau and walked to the bed. Rachel lay on her side and moaned. Her normally glowing pink features had been replaced with parchment white and shades of blue.

"Rachel." Emma pushed sweaty strands of hair from her forehead. "You're sweating." She lifted the bedclothes and found them wet. "I need you to move to the chair, so I can change the linens. You're wet and could become ill."

"Emma. I can't have this baby. I'm going to die. Please don't let the banker take my house," she whispered.

"No, honey, you're not going to die. Come on, let me help you up." Emma shifted the fragile woman's shaking legs to the edge of the bed. Watered down blood was on the sheets. *Please God, don't let her die.* In a sitting position, she wavered. Emma moved

Rachel's hand to the mattress edge. "Hold on."

She jerked the top blanket off the bed and ran to the rocking chair. She threw the cover over the chair and dragged the seat to the bed. "Now, I'm going to help you move to this chair. I'll make the bed, and then we'll get you cleaned up a bit."

"Why do I need to clean up?"

"Your water broke, and it's soaked everything. Don't worry, this is normal." She helped her to stand, pivot and sit in the chair. "Remember I told you about my friend, Matthew Bambridge, who's going to be a doctor. I went to all the lectures about enceinte, birth, and aftercare. As your handmaiden, I was going to be prepared."

She glanced at Rachel, who appeared to be asleep. Emma ran to the linen closet and gathered as many sheets as possible. After changing the bedclothes, she folded two sheets into squares and placed them on the bed. She got a fresh gown from the bureau and placed the soft garment on the bed.

"Emma, Jayden had a disease."

"We'll have the doctor make sure you're healthy. Don't worry."

"I did something unforgivable." Rachel moaned.

"We'll talk about your confession later. There isn't much time. I need to get hot water. Will you please stay in the chair?" She held Rachel's cold hand. Blue veins were pronounced beneath the skin.

"Yes. Will you take care of Margaret Mae when I die?"

Emma turned away and used the back of her hands to swipe tears from her eyes. "You will not die. Do you hear me, Rachel? I want you to tell me that you will not die."

Rachel sucked in a deep breath. "I should die because of what I've done, but I won't since you're ordering me not to."

She offered a shaky smile, bundled the sheets, and rushed out of the room. Dumping the soiled items in the washroom, she went into the kitchen. Treasure had the foresight to start several pots of water to boil.

"Treasure, Rachel is sitting in a rocker. Would you be kind enough to help her get bathed and changed? If she feels all right sitting up, the bath can wait." Fear took all of the energy from her legs. She grabbed onto the edge of the table. What if Henry didn't make it back in time with the doctor, and Rachel and the baby died?

"I'll help her. I helped my sisters, so I know about birthin' babies." She filled a pitcher with hot water. "You better go see those men in the parlor."

Emma grimaced. Blast, forgot about the visitors. What next? She straightened her belt, which had twisted around, and tucked in the shirt. Her satchel was still on the kitchen floor, she could change into a dress. No, she didn't want to take the time. She'd see what they wanted and send them away. Low murmurs came from the parlor as she entered.

"Matthew." She threw herself into his outstretched arms and hugged him, then glanced at the dark man.

Matthew pressed his face close to hers, and she adroitly backed away.

"Please forgive my lack of manners. My name is Emma Cody, and you are?"

The man had an understated sophisticated charm. Slightly under six foot, he looked taller because of his apparent thinness or as a result of his monochromatic garments. He was totally dressed in white from his cap, pointed in the front with a wide band, to the tip of his trousers peeking out from under his robe. A touch of black hair, dark like ebony piano keys, escaped from under his hat.

"My name is Raja Sekhar. I am an emissary sent to you from your parents." His stare was direct, unflinching, his dark brown eyes showed keen intelligence and sincerity. Raja's skin was the color of a ripe walnut, which had fallen to the ground and weathered to a burnished brown.

"Welcome, Mr. Sekhar."

He bowed. "May I speak with you in private?" His voice had a soothing rhythm.

"Yes, except my sister-in-law, Rachel needs a doctor." She pivoted and grabbed Matthew's arm. "You can help her."

"Em, I'm not a doctor yet." Matthew blustered. Frills flounced from his necktie as he talked. The white caveat on white shirt contrasted against the dark suit jacket. His formal apparel was a distinct contradiction to the flowing garments Raja wore and her trousers and cotton shirt.

She wiped the sweat from her forehead. "It's an emergency. Rachel," her voice cracked, "she's having difficulty delivering her baby. With the storm, I don't know if the doctor will make it here in time."

"Miss E-ma, I will be able to assist you in this." Raja removed his cap to reveal the expected shiny coal black hair. He placed the hat on the baggage near the entrance of the drawing room.

"Come." She ran toward the stairs. The one thing she'd learned since being in the west was to rely on the

179

help of strangers.

"Emma, wouldn't you rather have one of your own help?" Matthew shouted. She pivoted. He'd placed his suit jacket on the chair.

"Who has experience in delivering a baby?" she asked.

"I have done this before," Raja said.

"I don't have actual experience, but I have read multiple books, and listened to the lectures." Matthew gave her the, I know better than you expression.

She pierced each of them with a narrow-eyed look. "East meets west because I don't want to lose my sister-in-law or her baby. Mr. Sekhar, since you've had actual experience, I want you to lead. Matthew, you can assist."

"But, Emma, you can't possibly let this stranger—"

"If you'd rather stay here, do, but Rachel and her baby might be dying, and whoever has an ounce of decency will come with me to save their lives." She hiked up her trousers and ran up the stairs, etiquette be damned.

Rachel was in bed, on her side, clutching her stomach and moaning. The peony soap aroma didn't cover the smell of tainted water and metallic odor of blood. She scooted against the headboard, fear flashing in her bloodshot eyes.

Emma held her hand. "I'd like you to meet Raja Sekhar and Matthew Bambridge. Both are doctors, of a sort, and are here to help you. Now, I'm going to lower the covers, so they might take a look and get Maggie out here to join us."

A spasm overtook her, and she clutched Emma's hand hard enough her fingers turned white. Rachel released a breath and Emma's hand.

"Rachel, the next time you have a contraction, the pain in your belly, exhale quick, shallow breaths." Raja blew three times. "Do not hold your breath. Do you understand?"

She glanced at Raja. He'd removed his outer tunic and stood in a white form fitting shirt and pants. His accented voice sounded confident and reassuring.

"Yes, I'll try," Rachel whispered and relaxed her grip on the sheet.

"I'm going to take my hands and place them on your stomach to check the position of the baby." Raja felt around the top, bottom, sides, and middle. "I must check to see if the head is crowning, the progress of the birth. I'm going to lift your legs, look and examine."

Rachel held the expression of a doomed person. Judgement determined and the only thing to do was adjust to the verdict. She nodded.

"E-ma, I'd like to cleanse my hands first. Do you have disinfectant soap?" Raja asked.

Emma glanced at her. Between clinched teeth Rachel said, "get the clothes' soap. The lye will take the skin off his hands."

"I'll get it, Miss Rachel," Treasure said. She must have been in the shadows when they entered.

"Thank you, Treasure."

Raja sniffed the soap, then added some to fresh water. He rolled his sleeves and washed from his fingernails to his elbows. "Rachel, lift your legs please."

She locked her legs, keeping her knees together. Raja placed the sheet on her knees, then put the edge of the gown on top. Fresh thick red blood pooled on the cloth pad. Eyes closed, Rachel's breathing became shallow.

"Dr. Bambridge, would you come here?"

Matthew edged closer to the bed.

"The head isn't crowning. I believe the position of the baby is turned," Raja explained.

"Um, hum." Matthew glanced at her, but she couldn't read his facial expression.

"May I speak to you both outside please? Miss Treasure, please bring more hot water and clean cloths." Raja strode through the open door.

In the hallway Raja paced. "The baby is positioned in such a way it is necessary to perform surgery."

My God! The earth rocked beneath her feet. She reached out to grab onto the stair railing.

"Emma, are you alright?" Matthew dashed toward her.

"Fine, I'm worried." She licked her lips. "Matthew, the lecture we attended about mother's giving birth, if surgery was necessary, the majority of the women do not survive."

"Not always, but we'll have to do a Cesarean Section," Matthew said, with a touch of joy in his voice. They both knew the high mortality rate of a patient prevents the surgery from being performed. He would have the rare opportunity and barely hid his enthusiasm.

She plopped onto the floor and placed her head between her knees. "Please, don't let my sister-in-law die."

"Why are you dressed like a boy?" Matthew asked.

"Long story." She pressed her fists against her eye sockets and rocked back and forth.

"Get up, E-ma. You need to find datura, for anesthesia. We will get the baby out." Raja acted like the birthing procedure was equivalent to removing a splinter.

A few minutes later they hovered around the kitchen table.

"Mr. Sekhar, draw a picture. We need to know exactly what it looks like because it's snowing outside," she growled.

"Raja, please."

Raja scribbled on the paper. Matthew paced. Sam sat beside Raja trying to understand what he needed. She brewed tea which would be used to transfer the drug. Treasure remained upstairs by Rachel's side. Sam and Emma were the only two among them who walked the grounds and might be able to recognize the plant.

Raja handed her the drawing.

"No, I don't recognize the plant." She handed the paper to Sam.

"I've seen this, in the open field before the trees. It looks like a thistle. I think we call it jimson weed." Sam, excited and ready to hunt, slid off the chair.

"In my country we call the plant thorn-apple." Raja was drawing the shape of a pregnant woman, in different poses.

Emma grabbed the poncho off the hook. "Well, Sam, I guess we're digging together, again."

"Lucky, me," he muttered.

"Bring back the leaves, probably this early in the spring, you're not going to get the fruit," Raja announced as they walked out the door.

One hour later they'd administered the drugged tea to Rachel. Emma paced beside the bed. "How long does it take the tea to work?"

"Not very long, E-ma."

"The knives are sharp enough? The whisky will sterilize everything, right? Even the thread?"

"Yes, Emma. We'll do everything possible to save them both." Matthew pulled the rocker closer to the bed. "Sit."

"Did you actually see the drawings Dr. Max Sanger created after he did a uterine suturing?" Emma asked. "She's very quiet, will she ramble odd comments? She did earlier."

"The drug may make her hallucinate. E-ma, drink this." Raja handed her a laced cup of tea.

She extended her palm, facing outward. "I get the message. I'll be pacing downstairs, if you need me. If you want anything, give me a shout, and I'll take care of it." First, she'd look outside for Henry.

Where was he? She'd estimated the trip would take almost an hour to get to Pineview, locate the doctor, and return. He should have been here at the latest six hours ago. Had something happened? He rode Black Bart and wore a poncho exactly like hers, what if the people who tried to shoot her, attacked him? No, she refused to think negative thoughts. She could not endure the possibility of losing two people she loved on the same day.

She stood alone in front of the paned-glass front parlor window, surrounded by oppressive cherry furniture. If she were to ever have a house, it would have lighter wood. Oak or maple. The darker woods made the room dreary and closed in. God, why was she thinking about furniture when there were so many more important worries: Rachel, Maggie Mae, and most of all…Henry. Was he safe?

Hands grasped her arms and turned her around. By the strong cedar-based cologne, she knew it was Matthew, and she was afraid to know the truth. He lifted her chin, and she met his intelligent, brown-eyed gaze.

"She did very well. Raja is amazing at suturing."

"And the baby?"

"She survived," Matthew paused, "blueish at first, but she got pink."

She! Tears flowed along her cheeks. He jerked her close and rubbed her shoulder blade. She took deep gulps of air and relief exploded from her parched lips. Rachel and Maggie lived. Emotionally drained, she needed to sit. Matthew supported her back with one hand and lifted her chin with his other.

"Emma, I don't want to wait any longer, will you marry me?"

"No. Thank you for asking, I'm not getting married," she wearily responded.

"Why not? We were meant to be together." Matthew's voice held a strong smattering of annoyance.

"Because she's married to me," Henry said. He stood in the doorway, his jaw taunt, and his eyes glittering with anger.

"Who the hell are you?" Matthew released her and started toward him.

For the first time in her life, she collapsed into a swoon. Henry caught her before she fell to the floor.

"Love, what's wrong?" He carried her to the divan.

"I was worried about you. Problems with baby being turned. I'm so glad you're home."

"Emma, who is this man? What does he mean,

you're married to him?" Matthew pushed beside her, ready to pull Henry away.

"Matthew, meet Henry Courtland. Henry, this is a friend from Fort Wayne, soon to be doctor Bambridge." She shifted her legs to the edge of the green and gold striped divan, leaned her elbows on her knees, with a palm cupping her chin.

"Are you telling me after courting you for a year and struggling to get a kiss, two months in no-where Colorado you married this cowboy?" His face heated to a bright crimson. The twitch on his jaw appeared.

"Yes. Henry, could you help me upstairs?" She placed her hand into his.

Matthew stomped to a table and poured a cup full of whisky. "Congratulations."

"Thank you, Matthew. I'll talk with you tomorrow. I assume you're staying in the room at the end of the hallway."

"For the past two nights, while I waited for you," he snarled.

"Yes, well, goodnight." She forced her legs to move. Her head weighed two tons.

Henry held her arm as they ascended the stairs. They went into Rachel's bedroom. The soiled clothes had been removed and fresh towels were stacked on a chair. A slight mewling came from the cradle near the fireplace. Dr. Grayson leaned over Rachel, checking her heart rate.

"Mrs. Courtland, congratulations on your recent nuptials."

"Thank you, Dr. Grayson. How is Rachel?"

"She was very lucky to have such an excellent surgeon here, during her time of need. He did a superior job. I'm going to leave an herb remedy to help fight off any infection that might occur. If she develops a fever, send for me right away." Dr. Grayson put his stethoscope into the bag and closed it tight.

On silent feet, Raja entered the room. "Dr. Grayson, this is Mr. Raja Sekhar, the man who delivered Rachel's baby and saved her life." She glanced at Raja. "Raja, please meet Dr. Grayson and my husband, Henry Courtland."

Thankfully, Henry held her close, because in her weakness she'd have dropped to the floor.

"Since everything seems to be under control here, I'll go and see the next patient. Why does a spring snowstorm seem to bring babies into the world?" Dr. Grayson shook Raja's hand, then Henry's. "I'll see myself out." He rushed from the room.

"Good evening, sir." Raja closed the distance between them and held out his hand. "You are E-ma's husband?" He slid a sideways glance at her. She squirmed.

Henry removed his hat and extended a hand. "Yes, I am. Most people call me, King. And who are you to Emma?" He squeezed her waist, and she stopped fidgeting.

"My name is Raja Vaishnav Dushyanth Sekhar. I am an emissary from Calcutta, India. Also, I am a friend of Ambassador Cody and Mrs. Cody." Raja shook his hand, took a step back, and stood with his hands behind his back. "As a favor to them, I have traveled to America to protect their E-ma, until they are able to return."

Henry finger combed his hair and glanced at her. "It appears as if I've missed quite a lot in the few hours

I was gone."

"Yes," she whispered. Her heart shattered into tiny pieces. Rachel could die from infection as a result of the surgery. Had the added stress of financial worries induced an early labor and caused the difficulties?

"Mr. Sekhar, I would like to talk to you in detail about the events. Right now, I want to get my wife into bed before she collapses onto the floor."

"Raja, if you please." The baby mewled again. Raja wrapped her snug in a blanket and held her close.

As if in a trance, Emma went to the infant. The baby was the size of a child's doll. "May I hold her?"

Raja placed the baby in her arms. Maggie Mae probably only weighed six pounds at the most. She lifted the covers from the side of the baby's face, the pure innocent blue eyes opened, and so did her little mouth. A tiny screech pierced the air.

"She's hungry. I'll go down and get a sugar tit."

"No need, Miss Treasure is getting one."

Henry took the baby and gently laid her in the cradle. "No. You need to rest. She'll be well cared for."

"Don't worry, E-ma, I'll take care of Rachel and the baby." Raja lifted the squalling newborn.

"Thank you." Henry helped her across the hall to her bedroom. She removed a fresh nightgown from the bureau and gathered her bathing items.

"What are you doing?"

"I have to bathe. I've travel dust, and snow, and blood all over me. I must be clean." She went to the end of the hall and into the washroom. She'd rejoice in the newness of her niece and the fact that Rachel survived the surgery, after she removed the ugliness of the last few hours.

"I'll help you. Undress and I'll prepare your bath." From his travel-worn face, he was as tired as she.

Henry filled the hip bath, and she lowered, as much as possible, savoring the soothing warmth of the water.

"Were you engaged to Bambridge?" He handed her a bar of soap.

"He asked. I came west." She sighed, ducked under the water to get her hair wet, then handed him a washcloth and scrubbed her head. "I'm so tired. Aren't you?"

"Are you in love with him?" He wouldn't let it pass. Soap slid along her neck. She'd made a verbal vow. Why couldn't he see that she was only in love with Henry Courtland?

"No, we're friends. He helped me prepare to come help Rachel." She guided his hand to her breast, and he circled the washcloth over them. "However, tonight I found out I'm not good if blood is involved in childbirth."

The bath ended too soon. He tucked her into their bed and with a quick kiss he started to leave. "Henry, next time, could you bathe me a little slower and pay more attention to certain areas?" She yawned and snuggled into the covers.

He stilled, went back to her side, and kissed her, gentle and luscious. "You bet, Mrs. Courtland. Now, I need to stable Black Bart."

"You don't have syphilis, do you?"

He jerked as if she'd struck him. "No. Why do you ask?"

"Because Jayden was with a woman of ill repute, Bell something, and he contracted the disease." She waited for his reaction. "Miss Cat was known, according to the newspaper article, to be the whore with a heart of gold in a gold-mining town. Would she really turn one of her soiled doves out because of a little rash? Colorado has thirty-two thousand men, looking for gold or providing supplies. With only two thousand women, the odds were twenty to one." From what Treasure said about the infamous Miss Cat, the woman would never release a high-income commodity, diseased or not.

"The girls are always checked by Miss Cat and Dr. Grayson. If something suspicious is spotted, it is treated. Jayden was not with one of Cat's girls."

"But the article—"

"He never came to visit Cat's girls." His expression was the version that said, 'Don't contest this, Emma.'

"Before we make love again, could you have Dr. Grayson check you for any diseases?" Did he condone Jayden's infidelity or applaud it?

"It's not necessary."

"I love you, Henry, but—"

The door slammed shut, only the walls received the declaration.

Chapter 16

The whoosh of air indicated the door opened. Boot heels clacking on the floorboards made her stomach quiver. Emma smelled his outdoorsy aroma, a mixture of soap, cigar, and pine trees. If she were blindfolded in a room filled with men, she was confident she could go directly to him by scent and that needle-in-the-haystack connection existing between them.

"You didn't sleep," Henry whispered.

She finally forced her eyes to open and set the rocker into motion. "I couldn't. I do feel rested, though."

"Is she still…?" He peered inside the crib.

"Maggie Mae has been up twice in the past two hours. We might need to get a wet nurse. Rachel hasn't come around." She gripped the arms of the rocker. "Do you think I made a mistake? Letting a stranger perform surgery on her?"

"At a time of emergency, people do what is necessary."

"For some odd reason, I instinctively trust Raja. Not only because of his calm demeanor, but he gives the impression of honesty and piety." Lately, she'd been trusting her gut instinct more than ever.

"I don't know him, but I'll look for those attributes. The sun will be up soon. I'll ride into town to tie up some loose ends. I need to put Martin in charge of the

191

saloon and let Aubrey know I'll be in and out for a couple of days. Do you want me to bring back anything when I return?"

"Thank you for asking. I don't need anything, but please ask Treasure."

"I'll take Bambridge with me and put him on a stagecoach to Indiana."

"I don't know if he wants to leave."

"I imagine he doesn't want to leave. He wants you, but you *are* mine," he whispered.

She jerked upward, barely missing hitting his chin. "What are you talking about? I'm not a mare on the docket to be bid upon and owned." Anger caused her voice to rise. She glanced at Rachel, undisturbed in her healing sleep.

"Do you have feelings for Bambridge?" He crossed to the French doors opening onto a widow's walk. The sun peaked over the horizon, providing bright rays in the room.

"No, I don't." Her heart hurt. *I love you, Henry.* "He's just a friend."

He shifted his hands behind him and continued to stare through the glass. "What do you want from this marriage, Emma?"

What was he thinking? What did he want from her? Should she tell him what she'd done in Boulder? *Confess; get it out in the open?* Maybe he did just want to make love one time, and now their brief affair was over. He told her to be quiet during the intercourse. She might be very bad at lovemaking. "For better or worse, regardless of what the future holds I'll always be faithfully yours. If you want out of the marriage, fine, it's simple enough to do."

As fast as a petty thief upon hearing the law approached, he pivoted and marched to her. He lifted her out of the rocker. "Listen to me, Emma, as I will only say this once. I'm sorry because I tricked you into marriage. However, the church sanctioned documents were signed by us. You may believe our marriage should end, but I intend this union to be forever."

She nodded, guilt weighing on her heart. Her breath came out in shallow puffs of air. He bent his head and kissed her lips, hard and sure. She returned the kiss and added the passion that she always seemed to have for him.

"Emma?" Rachel's pain-filled voice was barely above a whisper.

Emma broke away and knelt beside the bed, taking Rachel's cold, dry hand into hers. "I'm right here."

"Is she al…"

"Yes, she is healthy." Emma helped her sit upright, against the pillows. Quivers of pain rushed across her face. Emma admired Rachel's undeniable willpower and tucked the covers around her. "Here, drink."

She guzzled the cold tea.

Henry lowered the whimpering baby into the mother's arms.

"Oh, she's beautiful," Rachel crooned.

Henry's hand rested on Emma's back as they'd watched the mother and baby. The warmth of his hand reassured her of his presence, his commitment to the relationship, and dare she think…his love? A believer in words, she wanted to hear him say them.

"Yes, she is beautiful." The little wonder rooted around for her meal.

He stepped back. "I'll be in the hall."

Emma smiled. Men were always so bashful around the basics of life.

"Good day, King." Rachel's voice had a new strength, a mother protecting its cub strength. A strength that even if she was at death's door, she would not relinquish the life and wellbeing of her offspring.

"Henry's going into Pineview to manage some of his business. I'm going to step out a moment. Raja is right outside the door. If you need him, call out." She glanced at the doorway. Raja nodded, then shuffled toward Rachel's bedside.

"Thank you, Raja." Emma nodded. "I'll bring up a breakfast tray."

"I'm pleased to help." He lifted the baby.

She walked to the staircase and glanced around. "Henry?"

He grabbed her around the waist, tugged her close, and placed his hand at the back of her head. Her heart clicked fast, pounding hard against her chest, and she lifted her chin. He nuzzled her neck.

The door at the end of the hallway opened. Embarrassed, Emma moved sideways, breaking the contact as the thud of heavy footsteps approached.

"I hope you're able to conclude your business in Pineview and check everything out. Please ask Dr. Grayson, when you see him, if Rachel can get up and move around." Emma lifted a brow, and Henry nodded in acknowledgement.

"Good morning, Emma. Mr. Courtland. I couldn't help but overhear, and I can answer any questions you might have about Rachel." Matthew placed his hands on his hips. "Actually, you went with me to most of the lectures about childbirth and should remember the answer to that."

"My wife has experienced a few traumatic days, and I'm sure you can understand why she might not remember a lecture from several months ago." Henry wrapped his arm around her shoulders.

"Henry, do you want to have breakfast before you leave?" She led the way down the stairs.

Matthew jumped in front of him and was side by side with her as they descended. He tucked his arm underneath hers. "I'd like to talk with you about your metropolitan city of Pineview. I believe it might need an additional physician, and I would consider moving here after I pass my medical boards."

"Pineview is provincial, Matthew, not a metropolis and you would probably be bored after the first week." She stepped into the foyer.

Henry claimed her hand. "Mr. Bambridge, in the future I'd appreciate you keeping your hands off my wife."

"How close is Denver to Emma, er, Pineview?"

Henry frowned. "Not far enough." His hand tightened on hers. They walked into the cinnamon and spice scented kitchen. Treasure placed a stack of pancakes on a gold-rimmed platter in the center of the table.

"Good morning, Treasure. How are you this morning?"

"Fine, Emma, and how are you?"

"Well. Thank you. I'll take a breakfast tray to Rachel."

Treasure gave a whoop. "Thank the Lord, she's going to be fine. I'll be up later to check on her."

"Great. When she takes a nap, I'll help with the

laundry. It looks like it's going to be a sunny day." She set a cup of steaming tea on the tray and turned toward Henry. "How long do you think it'll take until the dusting of snow melts?"

"Three or four hours of warm weather." He drank a hot cup of coffee. "Mrs. Courtland, I'll see you in a few hours." He kissed her cheek. "Treasure, do you need anything from town?"

"I've a list." She handed him a slip of paper.

"Bye, dear husband." Emma gripped the tray. She needed to do the right thing and tell him.

****

"I've called you in here to let you know I plan to sell the saloon. My goals have changed, and I want to focus on different business ventures. Miss Cat, you have a vested interest, since your girls operate here. Martin, you have wanted to own this saloon since it was built by my father." King watched his two friends, questioning if Cat did keep diseased girls on service.

Miss Cat glanced at Martin. He hoped Martin would be able to come to an agreement with Cat, and they could be partners. One way or another, he was going to sell the saloon.

"King, I'm kind of surprised about this sudden decision to sell. The saloon's been in your family for what, fifty years now?" Cat's moue smeared her bright red lips.

"Time to move on, forget the past, and take on new adventures." He absently wrote numbers on two pieces of paper.

"Is this because of the Relay Gang stealing your payroll? Going to focus on that?"

"What do you know about the Relay Gang, Cat?"

His gut clenched.

"Just what I overhear in the saloon. You said you'd never let a woman convince you to tie the knot. What makes you think this city girl will be happy in the west?" Cat leaned forward and put her thick fingers on the edge of the desk.

King glanced into her cold-hearted eyes, suspecting she wasn't what she presented. "If you'd each like to consider the purchase, I've given you the lowest amount I'll accept. You can each make a bid or perhaps form a partnership." He stood, his knee hit the desk casing, where his hidden revolver was stored. He gave them the pieces of paper.

"One more thing, Miss Cat, do you know what happened to Bell?"

"She never worked here."

"Bell Grind?" Martin asked.

"Yes, do you know her?"

"No, but she was here once, met with some guy and they went upstairs."

"She wasn't one of my girls, King. I think she musta' taken to the hills, maybe one of the mining camps." She didn't meet his stare but focused on the paper. She's avoiding the topic. Cat knew exactly where to find Bell. Did she know where the Relay Gang was also located?

"I see. If you'll excuse me, I need to go to the development office." He gave Martin a nod and walked out of the office. They could decide between themselves who would buy the saloon. Or if needed, he'd advertise. Despite what Cat inferred, he wasn't selling the saloon because of Emma, rather, she'd given him incentive to change course. He recaptured the image of her this morning with shadows under her eyes. What about Bambridge? He'd encourage him to leave.

King opened the door to Courtland-Carter Land Development. Mrs. Bullington slammed shut a file drawer and twisted around so fast her skirt billowed.

"Why King, what a surprise." She opened her handbag, withdrew a handkerchief and wiped her upper lip. The light brown mustache matched the color of her piled-high hair.

"That's obvious. Where is Aubrey?"

Aubrey Carter entered from the back door, hung his duster on a hook and faced his partner. "Henry, you have a way of blowing in with the winds."

"I need to get back to the fort. King, have a good day. Dar—Mr. Carter, I'll continue our discussion later." She resituated her purse higher on her forearm and strutted from the office.

"Good day, Mrs. Bullington." King emphasized the Mrs.

Aubrey leaned against the desk and tucked his hands into his pockets. "Thank goodness this is the last snow of the season. Now we can settle into a nice spring. I hear you tied the knot."

"How did you find out?"

"Dr. Grayson. At the saloon, he shared with everyone. Be prepared to have disappointed ladies flocking around you, wishing you well, I'm sure." Aubrey smirked, whether from his reference to the upstairs girls as ladies or maybe he was a tad bit envious.

"Aubrey, I didn't realize you had such a mean streak in you. What about the Captain's prize?" He nodded toward the door.

"Still his prize, I'm currently available. If your lovely wife has a sister, I'll be more than happy to entertain her when she visits." Aubrey finger combed his curly nutmeg hair, then settled into a chair behind his desk.

"How do you know my wife is lovely? You haven't met her."

"Dr. Grayson. Cliff added his thoughts on the matter. How come I miss out on opportunities to meet fine young women who wander into town?"

"Because you're spending time with the married ones." He crossed to the file cabinet and pulled papers concerning a tract of land. The company just purchased the perfect piece of ground to build a house, one where he could start roots and begin a family. He scanned the files to see if one had been misplaced or taken. "Why were Mrs. Bullington bony fingers in my documents?"

"I found that unusual too. I'll find out. Want me to get a lock from the General Store?"

"I might have one in my other office." He tilted his head, evaluating his friend. "Let me know what she was looking for."

Aubrey stood and looked at his pocket watch. "I'm sure it was nothing." His voice was sharp as a Bowie knife.

"Sorry, bad form. A lot on my mind. I want to purchase this tract of land. I'll buy your half. Will you decide what you consider fair?" He placed the deed on the desk and the map of the layout of the boundaries.

"Nesting, are you?" Aubrey smiled. "You've known the lovely Emma for a month or two. Did you have a shotgun wedding?"

"Certainly not. I had to be clever in order to get her

to marry me. I don't think my wife would be happy living at the back of a saloon is all."

"Probably not the place for a lady of quality. Did you know she's related to Buffalo Bill?"

"Yes, and she's a damn fine shot." King flashed back to the image of her sliding to the side of the horse and shooting a rifle. She was a handful, and he looked forward to trying to rope her in and tame her. By God, he'd woo her into loving him.

"Well, I want to be invited to the reception and meet Buffalo Bill." Aubrey grinned.

"Sure. Which would you prefer, William Duck or Camden Presario as an architect?"

"Camden Presario. Duck is too simplistic. I imagine you want something grand for the Mrs. Courtland." Aubrey's grin spread wider.

King shot him a frown. "I know you're having a good time with this."

"It's so rare for you to spend that hoard of money you've stashed away. I'm going to enjoy it very much." He laughed even harder after King threw on his hat and coat and headed toward the door.

"I plan to be the courier for the next payroll. Do you want to run shotgun?" King asked.

"Yes, partner, it'll be fun. You haven't gotten rusty with the gun, have you? I don't want to have my life end before I find the lady of my dreams."

"My skills haven't changed. Glad to see yours have." He grinned as he shut the door and glanced at the gray clouds. They weren't clouds, but night approached. He hadn't been to see Grayson, and he wasn't going to spend another night in bed with his wife without touching her. He also wanted to connect with the architect. Danny was coming out of the saloon front doors with a bucket and broom in hand. The lad should be in a school and certainly not working in a saloon, but he couldn't save all of the orphans in Pineview. Well, damn if he wasn't going to try to help in some way.

"Danny, come here lad."

He removed his cap, releasing long brown hair. "Yes, Mr. Courtland." The boy wiped his runny nose using his shirt sleeve.

"How is your mother faring?"

"She's feeling poorly, sir. Dr. Grayson said it won't be long until she'll join my pa in heaven." Danny lowered the bucket and placed the broom at the edge of his boot.

"I just married, and I'll be building a home. I want you to become a member of my staff. Would you like to work at my house instead of the saloon?"

He wiped his nose again. "Do I 'ave to wear fancy clothes?"

"We can talk about details, clean clothes certainly."

"All right, boss. What about my mum?"

"We'll work something out. I'd like you to be a messenger between Jayden Drake's house and here. Since, it's going to be dark in an hour or two. I want you to ride Maverick out to the Drakes and give a message to Mrs. Courtland. Stay the night and then come back tomorrow, with a return message if needed. I'll ask one of the girls to take dinner to your mother."

"What about my job here?"

"You're done. You'll only work at my house, and it'll be the same pay, maybe more, depending on how well you do in school."

"School. You didn't say nothin' about school," Danny squealed.

"A tutor, then."

"Don't know what that means, but I ain't goin' ta school." He kicked the bottom of the broom with his boots. Holes at the toes showed gray socks with brown smudges.

"Go get, Maverick, and I'll meet you here in a few minutes."

"Okay, boss. Not goin' ta school." He handed him the broom and bucket and sprinted toward the livery.

Chapter 17

Emma kept her nose pressed close to the glass. Unintentional, at least that is what she told herself. She'd stopped the circular cleaning motion of the vinegar scented cloth a few seconds earlier and verbally flogged herself for giving into the temptation of being a voyeur.

"He does this every day?" Rachel asked from the fireside chair a few feet away. She gently patted Maggie Mae's back.

"Consecutively for the past three days. Today it's warm, and we should be praising the deities for the cold air to have migrated back to the mountains, because he's not wearing a shirt."

"And you've cleaned the windows every day?" A smirk tightened her pale face.

"Don't you judge me? You've been down here the past two days."

The smug look left Rachel's face. "I'm not interested in men, and you certainly should not be if you've been married for less than a week. Here you are watching another man, doing, whatever it is he is doing. Maggie's stomach is full and all I need is a burp." Rachel touched the top button of her dress. When choosing a gown, she'd made it clear her dress would be up to her neck, and her breasts hidden from sight.

"My husband has been absent for the past four

days. Besides, where is it written we cannot watch and learn an ancient exercise from another human being?" She dropped the pretense of washing the glass and simply sat on the window ledge, alternating her glance from a perfectly formed male human being and Rachel.

"Did you tell Henry that I was in the sharpshooting contest?"

"No. He never came the next day. I assumed he met up with you on your way to Fort Collins, and you told him." Rachel lifted a well-manicured eyebrow. "Why?"

"He must have been following me. I thought I saw him in the window after I left his saloon, but quickly forgot about it when I read the contest notice. He protected me."

"Not unusual. That's the way King is, always thinking of others. We should assume Raja knows we're watching him." Bright red spots appeared on her cheeks.

"Probably, but he goes to his place of tranquility. He told me of his religious beliefs, but I couldn't take my eyes off, you know."

"Yes, I know," Rachel whispered. Her eyes widened as her focus went toward the subject at hand.

"Do you think he shaves his chest hair, or he simply doesn't grow chest hair? We'll ask, again, about the exercise and his religion. I don't think it would be a bad idea to listen to what he has to say about his culture. Possibly convince him to let us exercise with him."

"Emma."

Laughter bellowed from deep within her chest at the censure of her tight lipped, strait-laced voice.

"When did you become such a prude?" Emma asked between giggles.

"Prude? My recently married sister-in-law ogles a half-naked Indian man from the windows of the parlor, and you're calling me a prude." Rachel swiped at her hair but didn't take her eyes off of his spread-eagle pose.

His trim waist and well-defined muscles drew her attention. He was wearing a thin pair of tight white breeches, period. His quite large bare feet were planted firmly on the conservatory floor. Arms stretched overhead, then he leveled them to the side at shoulder level. Currently, his chest glowed with rivulets of sweat and with each arm movement his nipples would shift slightly, contracting the muscles above and below the firm peaked nubs.

Short black hair stood up in spikes on his head as the heat radiated off of his body. Almond shaped eyes held dark brown mysteries. Rachel claimed his lips were the same pink color as Maggie Mae's and had a similar bow shape. They were not very masculine, but the widow hinted at wanting to touch them.

Yes, Raja was gorgeous, and Emma did enjoy watching him commune with his higher-level consciousness, but he wasn't Henry. She wanted her husband. It must have been bad news at Grayson's, or he would have been back with her. The tingling started in her lower region, as she remembered the night by the stream. Lordy, she desired that release again.

"Looks like we're done, cleaning, for the day." Rachel nodded toward the window, where Raja gathered his discarded clothing.

"Yes. I'm glad we're keeping the place spotless."

Emma smiled.

Rachel chuckled. Oh, so good for her to laugh.

"Do you want me to help you back upstairs?"

"Yes, I'm rather tired after all this work."

Emma hee-hawed, and the baby twitched as if frightened. "I'll get you settled and check on the plants in the garden. I've a thought for a new hand cream and soap recipe with lemon balm. I read somewhere that it is a healthy scent with intensely beneficial healing properties. After you rest, maybe you'd like to sit outside and get some fresh air?"

"That would be lovely." Rachel stood, a little unsteady, but she was moving and healing, which was a good sign.

Emma reached into the cradle and lifted Maggie Mae. She nuzzled her neck, briefly, and inhaled the newborn scent, then supported her sister-in-law as they shuffled up the stairs. Rachel sat on the bed, and she laid Maggie in her crib. The infant smiled, then shut her eyes and her tiny mouth made sucking movements. She pivoted, wanting to share the joy. Rachel, cuddling a pillow, was fast asleep. She covered her and quietly left the room.

****

"What are you doing?" King must have frightened her, because she jumped to a stand at the sound of his voice.

"What does it look like I'm doing?" With a shaking hand, she pushed a strand of hair under her hat. Dressed in white shirt and canvas trousers, her tight heart-shaped rear was exposed to any onlooker. At an appropriate time, he'd tell her not to wear those revealing garments.

"I'm preparing soil for an herbal garden." Her expression told him she thought him dull witted.

"I can smell the preparation part." He wrinkled his nose as the wind caught the earthy horse manure odor and twirled fragrant fragments into the air. "What are you doing out here alone? The tree line would be an excellent hiding place for the attacker. You apparently have forgotten that you are a target?"

"Raja is on the veranda, making notes in a journal."

He glanced toward the house. Sekhar held up a hand in acknowledgement. The man's white apparel blended in with the white trim of the veranda. Well done, as a disguise. "Good day, Raja."

"Henry." He smiled, then returned to his journal.

Emma was converting everyone into calling him Henry and for some reason it gave him joy. "How's Rachel?"

A bright smile spread across her face. "They are doing well. Rachel's napping, but later she'll get some fresh air. Sweet little Maggie's growing like a weed."

Needing to touch her, he brushed a bit of dirt from her face. Five long days and nights since he'd stroked her silky skin and celebrated their union. He tugged her close, wanting to share her warmth. She placed the rake in front of his chest and pushed.

"What did you find out?" She squinted. Her green eyes flashed through the narrowed slits.

"Find out about?" He couldn't focus. The only thing he wanted to do was relieve the ache that was growing in his breeches.

"Grayson and..." She looked around as if to check who might overhear.

"Clean. Disease free. I'll quote him, you can safely

go at it like rabbits." He smiled, longing to go at it like rabbits, horses, dogs, any breed that could breed.

"And the girls in the…your place of business? Did he check them to make sure they're not spreading anything?"

"Yes, Miss Cat takes very good care of her girls. They're clean."

"If they were clean, how did Jayden get it? What happened to the girl who shot him and ran away? Did they find her and bring her to justice?"

"I've been looking into the murder. I've a lead, but I didn't want to travel without seeing you first."

"I feel honored that you chose to see me at all." She tucked the rake under an arm and clapped her hands, getting soil off her gloves.

Was that a hint of sarcasm in her voice? "Ah, love, did you miss me?"

She snorted and put the rake in front of her again.

He'd hardly slept the last few days, between trying to get a house plan initiated and contractors to start building. Martin and Miss Cat were battling between themselves about who would buy King's Court. And Aubrey seemed to have caught a mental illness that made him continually laugh. All the while, Morgan Palinurus at the bank avoided him. He insisted King didn't have the right to investigate the Drake's financial records.

"Emma, I've missed you so much." He lowered the rake, dropping it to the ground. "Aren't you happy to see me, my wife, my heart?"

She leaped back. "I hardly remember you. I think I stood in front of a preacher with a man similar to your stature. He smelled of cigars like you do."

The little vixen. He plucked her hat from her head and the curls, glowing bits of red in the sunlight, came tumbling down. He reached out, and she backed away. Her feet slipped in the newly turned earth. She caught onto the nearest thing for support, his jacket, and yanked him off his feet. Twisted, they fell to the ground. The mud sloshed and sprayed manure-scented dirt drops through the air to land on their faces and in their hair. Dung odors rose up around them. Finally, his body connected with her soft curves.

"Blast."

"I've been meaning to talk to you about your language. Really, a lady shouldn't use foul words." Her body tensed under him, exciting him more.

"Damn." She gripped the soggy earth at her sides. "Move off of me...you large oaf," she hissed between her mud splattered lips.

"Not until you tell me that you're happy to see me, and you've missed me." He smiled, pressing his hips firmly on top of hers.

"Is everything all right down there?" Rachel shouted from behind them.

He glanced around. Raja held Rachel's arm as they leaned over the railing of the widow's walk.

His delicate little wife said, "No, my idiot—"

He kissed her. Not the sweet tender kiss he'd envisioned in his head, but a passionate kiss. Moving from one side of her nose to the other, back and forth creating little mud balls. He planned to be locked together until the spring rains started or the cold drove them inside the house and immediately onto a mattress.

His cheek to hers, he sniffed her hair. He leaned away and peered into her eyes. "You smell like manure."

She levered her hands against his shoulders, moved her knee up to his juncture and pushed with all her might. He fell to the side. She possessed the strength of an ox. She'd made it half-way to the house before he maneuvered out of the muck and caught her.

She dropped her gloves to the ground. "Blast. Blast. Blast."

"That's enough." He picked her up and carried her to the horse tank a few feet away. "Despite your foul language, I'm very happy to see you, my dear wife. However, I'm afraid you've mud on your face, and I can't rightly see how beautiful you are." He dropped her flat into the horse tank.

Water splashed, she came up sputtering, mad as a hornet. A couple of shakes of her head, and she gripped the sides of the bin.

"Good God, man, what are you doing?" Matthew ran forward and gripped her under her arms. "Emma, darling, are you alright?"

The irritating voice was his undoing. He clutched the dandy's coat lapel and yanked him away from his wife. "I've told you before, do not put your hands on my wife."

She plopped into the basin and water shot up like a geyser. He was at a loss about what to do, help his love out of the container or smash the annoying rejected suitor in the face.

"Get your bags packed. You're leaving today." He turned and gathered Emma in his arms. Her blue tinted fingertips clasped his jacket.

Sam stood outside the barn. "And you told me not to insult a woman. Is this the way to a woman's heart,

Henry?"

Treasure met them at the kitchen doorway, holding a blanket. He took the cloth, wrapped it around Emma, and carried her into the washroom. The tub, filled with water, had steam filtering into the air. He lowered her legs to the floor, then toe to heel removed his mud-caked boots.

She stood shaking, the tremors moving the blanket in waves.

"Love, I'm sorry. You make me so…"

"Do-n-'t taaalk tooooo mee."

He rubbed her back. "What was that?"

She raised on her toes and shouted, "Don't taaaaalk toooo meee."

She did sound angry, but he was foolish enough to think she would get past the minor annoyance. "Here darlin', I'll help you get undressed, and you'll be right as rain again."

"Henry, if you value your manhood, you will leave this room." She stated it quite clearly, but the shroud surrounding her face hid her expression.

"I've decided to sell King's Court." He stripped off the blanket. "And I've purchased land about three miles from here." He removed her shoes and the suspenders had fallen over her arms. The thin white shirt was torn, so he split it into two pieces and dropped the rag to the floor. "I've met with an architect, and he has started the rendering of a house." Without her blouse, her cold hard nipples jutted up at him. He made the mistake of glancing into her face. The cold wasn't just affecting her perky breasts, but her eyes as well.

He shrugged off his dirty coat and went about removing her camisole. The trousers were sticky and more difficult to remove. He lifted her inside the tub, and she sank into the water. When she came up, he asked, "Why aren't you saying anything?"

She lowered further down into the water, getting her hair wet. When she resurfaced, he held out the shampoo bar soap. "Shall I do the honors?"

A nod of her head didn't loosen the tautness of her jaws. He wasn't out of the woods, yet. Bits of leaves, twigs, and one squiggling worm came from the soothing scrubbing. Adding cold water to hot, he rinsed her hair. Anger radiated from her body. A fact verified when she rushed through the soaping process instead of leisurely taking her time and teasing him the way she had in the past. None of his self-berating stopped his cock from responding to her allurement.

She stood upright. He handed her a towel, and she wrapped it around herself with a jerky motion. Wet footprints marked the hall and up the stairs. He managed to keep his moans in his throat and followed. Their bedroom door slammed and the click of the lock turning echoed, shutting him out.

Treasure and Sam stood at the top of the staircase, Raja and Rachel perched at her bedroom entryway. All of them had the same expression, the look of doom, of ending, of no-happy-ever-after.

There would be a blissful future, by damn. King marched into Raja's room and climbed through the chifforobe. She stood at the window, with the towel wrapped around her, crying into her hands. Silently, he hastened to her side and rubbed his hand on her back in small round, hopefully soothing, movements. Sobs racked her body and stopped his heart. He'd seen women cry on numerous occasions, but none affected him the way her tears did. With each drop that drizzled along her cheeks, he felt a part of himself die.

"Emma, what's wrong?" He lifted her into his arms and settled onto the bed with her seated on his lap.

She wiped her tears with the edge of the towel. "You've yet to tell me where you've been for the past few days. You've made decisions about my life without consulting me and purchased land without requesting my opinion. A designer is creating a house that you expect me to live in without any input from me. It is all about you. We do not have a marriage. We don't even have a partnership." She shoved his arm and stood. "It's over, please leave now."

He strode from the room, smiled at the foursome and took the stairs, holding his breath until he was outside.

"Guess you don't know a lot about women, eh, Henry." Sam chuckled.

"Guess not. She is so…"

"Come on, I think we need a drink, and I'll share some wisdom about the ladies."

King glanced around the bunk house. "You've made some changes. Looks like a home. I'm glad you were able to keep all the books." A whole wall of bookshelves was loaded with leather bound hardcovers.

"I've made it livable." Sam handed him a cigar. "Here, I only have one left. Treasure made me destroy them after Emma told her they would kill me." He uncapped Irish whisky. "Maybe you should consider stopping as well. You know, with a wife and all."

King lit the cigar and took two puffs. Damnation. His life was going to totally change. "Okay, but I'm not giving up whisky."

Sam nodded. "I hear you." He poured two glasses. "Let's go to the porch and watch the evening sun set."

"Sure, Cyrano, I'm willing to learn from you." King sauntered outside. "Put your college education to work and help me save my marriage."

The chair was cold against his wet back, but he needed advice, and his father wasn't alive. Sam had always been more than an employee.

"First, and I would think this is obvious, you don't drop your wife into a horse tank."

"The woman is so frustrating."

"Second, all women are frustrating, you just need to learn how to train them." He took a swig of his drink. "Like a horse, gentle touch, soft words, build a trust."

King rolled the glass in his palm. He'd been dictatorial. "She might want to decide where the kitchen stove should be located."

"Yep." Sam snickered. "And to be asked to be involved in the decision making."

"I had to make quick decisions about the land and an architect needs to be enlisted early on in the building process."

"Yep, still need to ask her what her thoughts are regarding the home she's going to be living in most of her life."

"Right. He's still in town. I'll take Emma to Pineview tomorrow and let her talk to the architect."

"Now, you're getting somewhere." Sam laughed. "You should have seen her face when you fell on top of her in the shit pile."

"Accidental fall." He swallowed the rest of the whisky and put his cigar out in the glass.

Sam put his tumbler on the floor. "Yep, but the

water tank was not accidental." He tucked his hands into his coat pockets. "You've a long way to go to make her feel better about the dunking."

Chapter 18

Emma stood at the parlor room window, without a care about incorporating cleaning or even fake cleaning. She toyed absently with the feather duster she'd left behind yesterday. "He seems to have jerky motions today. Is he upset about something?"

Rachel flushed cranberry red. "Why would I know?"

"Yes, why would you know?"

"You should stop giving Henry's clothes to Treasure to be made into rosettes." Rachel smoothed loose hair strands to the back of her head.

"The blue striped vest was torn, couldn't be repaired."

"Because you shredded it. Matthew left first thing this morning. He wanted to see you before he left, but you weren't answering the door. Tell me what happened with your husband last night." Rachel sat on the edge of the desk. They'd fashioned a bunting for the baby. The cloth, wrapped around her front and back, was tied at her shoulder. Nestled inside the cocoon, Maggie Mae slept.

"He made decisions about my future, my life, without asking me. I was upset, told him it was over. He left, and I found him beside me this morning smelling of cigars and whisky."

Raja moved on to the upper body movements,

which was usually her favorite part of the exercise. Today, it didn't do anything for her. His body glistened with sweat. His movements, usually graceful, grew sharper and faster.

"I'd like to talk to you." Henry's gravelly and barbed voice came from the doorway.

They both jumped, then forged a wall between him and the window.

"Move away from there. You think I don't know what you're doing?" His frown added credence to his calm controlled voice.

"Cleaning the drawing room?" Behind her back, she groped searching for the feather duster.

"Danny told me you come here each day and watch…that." He pointed toward Raja who resumed the mat reclining positions.

"Where is that little tattletale? Shouldn't he be in school?" A sudden rustling of clothing and little feet scurried away.

"Emma, please come with me?" He extended his hand.

She sighed and put the feather duster on the cabinet. "Rachel, do you want me to help you climb the stairs?"

"No, I think I'll clean in here a little more." Her eyes glittered with humor.

He placed his hand low on Emma's back and escorted her from the house. Sam held Black Bart by the reins. His little gnome smile flashed as brilliantly as the morning sun.

"Aren't you supposed to be putting a lock on my chifforobe?" she asked.

"Henry advised me not to, Mrs. Courtland." He

winked at the co-conspirator.

The man would find his shorts in a bind later. She was in charge of laundry today.

Henry lifted her onto the saddle and swung up behind her. With a subtle touch to Black Bart's sides, they cantered.

"Where are we going?" She hadn't put on a hat, so her head fit beneath his chin.

He placed his hand on the side of her head and nudged her to rest against his chest. "We'll be there in a minute."

Black Bart wanted to run but with her sitting sidesaddle on a western saddle she wouldn't remain seated. She'd take the horse out later and let him run wild. Horse and mistress had been cooped up too long and needed to blow off some stream. A no-restraint gallop would be perfect.

A few minutes later, he led Black Bart up the side of a hill and stopped. He dismounted and lifted his arms. She held her body taunt, so she wouldn't come into contact with his muscular deliciousness. The odious man chuckled.

"Why are we here? Shouldn't you be in town, doing business or Lulu?" Her feet sunk into the moist spongy ground.

He laughed outright, grabbed her hand, and pulled her to the edge of the overlook.

The panoramic view was beautiful. The valley below would be a bright green, mixed with brown brush in a few weeks. Snow-capped mountains towered in the background. To the left was Pineview, resembling a little village the size of a child's train track accessory. At Rachel's house the windows glistened, and smoke billowed from the chimney. Sam and Treasure were hanging clothes on a rope line.

Henry drew her in front of him, her back to his front, and whispered. She didn't hear a word he said. Her mind was on the contact of his body to hers and the scent of his woodsy aftershave. She loved that he shaved his face close instead of growing a beard or goatee. A kiss. A light kiss on the side of her face fractured the ice, which had formed around her heart. "I'm sorry, what did you say?"

"I bought this tract of land because I knew it would sell fast. Beautiful isn't it?" he whispered.

"Yes," she answered hoarsely, fighting the urge to give into temptation.

"You can understand why I didn't wait to ask you, before I purchased it?" He nuzzled her neck, and she let him.

"Yes." The ice was dripping from her heart now. *Fight it!*

"I'm sorry about the house plans. Tomorrow, we'll make a day of it and go into Fort Collins to meet with the architect. You can see what he has done so far with the drawing. You can make changes or suggestions until you're blue in the face. If you don't like it, we'll start fresh. Will that make you happy?"

He shifted his hands, from her shoulders, and rested them on her lower abdomen. He tugged her closer. Her heart pounded. She admitted to herself, regardless of what issues would arise in this odd, possibly short-term fake marriage, she would always love him.

She turned into his arms and kissed him, lightly, on the lips. The heat intensified and the tingling multiplied.

He lifted her chin. "One thing, we must get straight, sometimes I'll make decisions without consulting you because I'm the head of the family. You'll need to adhere to some rules as well."

She stiffened. Blast him. He was making rules, like she was going to do whatever little thing he said. "What rules?" she gritted out between clinched teeth and shoved his hand from her chin.

"You do not run off by yourself, even after we catch the man or men looking for you. There are still Indians, miners, miscreants out there who would take advantage of a beautiful woman."

She nodded her head in agreement. Okay, she liked the beautiful woman comment, and she could live with having her wings clipped a little bit. "Other rules?"

"I don't want a repeat of the rifle contest. Talk to me before you make impulsive decisions."

"Blast, that wasn't a rash decision. We needed money, and I could get it for us. I'll not discuss every little recipe or detail of my life with you."

"Don't exaggerate. Also, I'm tired of you flirting with men, Palinurus, Bambridge, and Raja. You are my wife. You'll stay my wife, and I don't want men to see you as anything but my wife."

"I don't flirt with men. I'm a friendly person. Your jealously is unfounded." She turned to stalk away, avoiding the dishonesty, not revealing the truth and slipped on a toad stool. Her arms flailed through thin air. She screamed, a high-pitched wail, which certainly scared all the small animals within hearing range.

He grabbed her, jerked her close, and they both fell to the ground. He rolled, holding her off the sod and preventing his weight from pressing into her. A bramble bush and rock stopped their plummet down the hill.

"Henry, are you alright?" She shook him. His hat had flown off during the tumble, and his blond hair was peppered with sticks and pieces of thistle.

"Yes." He moaned.

"I guess I do act rashly, sometimes." She picked thistles from his hair. The blue shirt made the color of his eyes appear bluer, larger, and softer. "And clearly, I've a problem with balance when I'm around you."

"You're right, I'm jealous. You act differently around them." He touched the side of her face.

She turned and kissed his hand. "That is because I love you."

He lowered his hand to her neck. Their glances met.

"What did you say?" His voice was gravelly again. She adored the sound of his deep voice, especially when the hoarse intonation was present.

"I love you."

"Say it again." He moved his hand to her waist.

She leaned onto her side, her elbow propping her head and kissed the line on his cheek. "I love you, Henry Gray Courtland. Do you seriously think I would have let that clergyman say the words if I didn't love you?"

He smiled at that.

"Do you really think I would prance around naked in thirty-degree weather if I wasn't insanely in love with you?"

His smile broadened, deepening his dimples.

Maybe it'll work. I can't tell him the truth. I've fallen in love. She climbed onto his lap and kissed him with the passion, which had been stewing for the past several days. Breaking away, she leaned back. "But if you think, for one minute, I'm ever going to let another woman sit on your lap and move about, then you're dead wrong, mister."

To get the point across she shifted. "Oh my."

She closed her eyes getting to know his contours. "I'd rather no other woman sit on your lap, but me." She increased the pace, appreciating the sensations.

"Emma, you're killing me. Please unbutton my pants, and let the king enter his queen."

She opened her eyes and grinned. "I never liked that nickname, until now." Reaching down, she unfastened his breeches and withdrew the king. She lifted, and he shifted her dress and pantalets out of the way. The king found its way into the queen. She planted her hands beside his head, groaned and rocked up and down, forward and backward and in little circles.

He placed his hands on her hips helping her to get the rhythm. Too soon the dance came to a climatic conclusion. Still connected, she dropped on top of his chest. He kissed her forehead and rested his head against the ground, his hands encircling her waist. "I now know how to keep you quiet during lovemaking."

"How is that?" She rolled off of him and lay flat to the ground.

He wrapped his arm around her shoulder and tugged her close. "If you're on top, you don't say a word. Your facial expressions do say a lot though."

She shoved his chest and stood up. He chuckled.

Heat infiltrated her neck. "Let's go. I think we need a bed, so we can prove or disprove this theory of yours." She grabbed his hat and ran up the hill.

Chapter 19

The kitchen door slammed shut, drawing Emma away from hallway-dancing with Maggie. She laid the baby in her cradle and walked into the kitchen. Danny, sweat coating his shirt, got a glass of water from the faucet. His shoulders were bent forward. What in tarnation? He was two hours late for his lessons.

"Why aren't you helping Sam?" Helping was code for lessons on the sly, she'd learned a few weeks ago not to say the word "school". Sam believed the boy could be eased into a proper educational environment, given time.

He shrugged and put the glass on the countertop. With each shoulder lift, she heard barely discernable sniffling. She went to his side. "Danny, what is wrong? Are you hurt?"

He turned into her, burying his face into her stomach. She wrapped her arms around him and glanced at Sam who entered through the back door. He lifted his palms upward in an I-don't-know manner.

"My mum," Danny paused, "she's dead."

Emma hugged him, wishing she could say something to help ease the child's pain of losing his only parent. "I'm so sorry, Danny. Was it an accident?"

"No," he sniffed, "she's been sick fer a long time. Dr. Grayson said it was fer the best, as she was ailing and in pain."

"Oh dear, I didn't know." She glanced at Sam.

"Danny, I'm sorry for your loss. I know you tried to do right by your mother." Sam placed his hand on the boy's shoulder. "Is there anything I can do to help you?"

"The landlord said I had to git our stuff from the room today and pay him rent for the week. He said I was going to be put on the orphan train." Danny used his shirt sleeve to wipe his nose. "The undertaker said my mum would have to be buried in the poor cemetery, 'cause I don't have money for a casket or funeral."

"We'll go help you get your personal items, and I'll pay the rent money." Emma smoothed his hair.

Sam nodded. "Yes. We have some crates in the barn."

"We'll talk to Rachel, maybe your mother could be buried outside." She glanced at Sam. He shrugged, but by the glimmer in his eyes he wanted the same thing.

"By Mr. Drake?" Danny's voice held a lift, a promise of hope.

"Yes. Why don't you and Sam get the wagon hitched and crates put in the back. I'll talk to Rachel."

Danny nodded, and they left the house.

Emma rushed into the parlor.

Rachel was nursing the baby. "Did Danny finally get here?"

"Yes. His mother died. He can't afford to bury her. Would you be willing to let his mother be buried in the back, by—"

"Yes." She switched the baby to her other breast. "We'll have a funeral. It'll be a celebration of life."

"Thank you. We're going into Pineview to get his personal items from his rental room. Could he use the maid's room?"

Rachel lifted an eyebrow. "What about Treasure?"

"She could use the guest bedroom."

"Short term." Rachel smoothed the front of her dress. "Do you believe Sam will marry her?" The have/have not conversation came up a couple of times as they watched the couple strolling in the moonlight.

"Maybe. Sam and Danny are out front. We might be a while getting everything arranged. Will you talk to Treasure and see if she's okay with the change? If she is, please get the room ready for the boy. Sam's going to teach him math and reading. Perhaps Raja could move a desk and lamp into the room for him?"

"Yes. We'll get it all taken care of, Emma. Go on. Help the boy." Rachel placed Maggie Mae in her cradle.

Emma crawled onto the wagon seat, on the other side of Danny, and tied her bonnet. "Ready."

"Giddy up." Sam shook the reins, and the horses pulled the wagon with a jerking start.

She put her arm around the boy's shoulders. "Danny, I want you to know you'll not be put on an orphan train. I don't know what the process is, but Henry and I will adopt you into our family. If you want to be adopted." She glanced into his dark brown eyes. "Do you want to become a part of our family and live with us?"

"Yes, Miss Emma. I would like to stay with you and King." He swallowed. "I mean, Henry."

A tear slid along his cheek. Sam was indeed a kindhearted soul.

****

As time passed Danny cemented their small family,

and Emma's love grew stronger for the boy. Despite Henry's dictate Rachel and Emma met in the drawing room each morning until Raja insisted, they quit being observers and join him in the exercise.

In the courtyard outside Jayden's office, Emma sat crossed legged on the cloth mat and watched Raja move Rachel's limbs into the proper position for the ritual sequence. She lifted her face to the sun.

Raja instructed them to sit on the floor with their ankles crossed under their legs. "Chuan Fa is an ancient art of training used to strengthen, stabilize, and create stamina. The three are ruled by the earth element and should be practiced each day at sunrise. Physical fluidity and adaptability are ruled by water, the exercise should not be harsh, fast movements, but slow smooth ones. Power and speed are ruled by fire and tactics by air." He removed his outer tunic, shirt, and sandals. He stood before them in his blousy trousers only. Rachel inhaled a breath. Emma pictured Henry, shirtless, in the widespread stance. *Oh my, stop daydreaming.*

"Ladies, please stand. Earth governs the stances." He braced his legs, rolled his neck, and shoulders.

They stood with legs apart and mimicked his actions.

"Water is the blocking technique. I want you to picture in your mind a brook, or stream of water and how fluid it is. Brace your feet on the floor and with easygoing flowing motions, like water coursing down the stream, push your right leg forward, extend your right arm, raise the left arm fisted in front of your face at neck level. Fist your right hand and punch it out, your target will be the center neck of the opponent. One direct hit and the person will be on his knees. With your left arm, protect your weak area."

They practiced this routine several times.

"The last element is air. Breathing is very important to the physical sequences and rhythms. You need to integrate breathing patterns with the movements. When you push your arm out, exhale and when you pull it back, inhale. You will need to practice and concentrate in order to get the air, fire and earth exercises perfected. Associate each practice, principle with another, and you will see their place with the great Mandala of existence."

"What about the," she waved her hands about in precise slow movement, "that you do at the beginning and end?"

"Many different levels and principles, E-ma. Today I have taught you self-defense techniques. Other levels include different body and mental healing practices together with mystical studies. Those are the rituals you have seen while you watched me through the window."

Rachel's face flushed cherry red. Emma rolled her eyes. "Wear more clothes. Otherwise, women will want to reach your inner temple."

That earned her a narrow-eyed-look from Raja. Rachel snorted or laughed. It was difficult to tell.

Every morning they dressed in loose garments that Rachel threw together and exercised with Raja. Maggie Mae would lie in her cradle cooing and gurgling. She was a picture of health, resembling Jayden with light brown hair and green eyes.

Custom design orders for clothing continued to come in, and Rachel sewed an original design and registered their patents. She sent the clothing samples to the stores in Boulder. Treasure added her little touches with the woven flowers and hats.

The house Emma and Henry designed together was under construction and should be completed in six or seven months. In the meantime, Emma dabbled in the garden and concocted new scents for soaps and lotions made with lemon balm. After the morning ritual, she and Raja walked along the garden. "In the new recipe, I've used verbena for revitalization, chamomile to soothe, an antiseptic calendula and rosemary to protect the fresh citrus smell of the balm. Mixed with shea butter, the lotion should be perfect. What's missing?"

Raja silently followed her. Henry's rule, never be alone. "E-ma, perhaps mimosa is what you are seeking?"

She halted on the path and stared at him. "What is mimosa, and why do I want it?"

"Mimosa is a plant, shrub, or tree belonging to the genus *Mimosa*. It is native to warmer climates and has small flowers in globular heads or spikes. You might want to use the plant because it is a restorative. The properties will rejuvenate you if you place the essence in your lotion and soap." His hands were clasped behind his back. He seemed to be in a thoughtful mood lately.

"Rejuvenate. Sounds like it would be worth a try. Colorado isn't a warm climate. Do you think we could find the shrub or bush?"

"Near the edge of the woods. The plant likes to have full sun to part shade in a rich moist soil. Those conditions are right over there, in the clearing." Raja pointed to a section which gets a significant amount of noonday sun. "Not likely we will find one, but stranger things have happened."

They walked toward the south side of the woods. "Tell me what it looks like again."

"It has leaves similar to this pine tree. Green with little shoots out the sides and one-inch purple feathery globe flowers, spikes shooting out."

She approached a plant and touched the leaves. "Like this one?"

Raja knelt and touched the plant. "No, E-ma. It is a very sensitive plant, much like Rachel. If it is touched, a simple flick of a finger, the leaf will close. Add some heat to the leaflets, a slower response will occur, and the stimulus of the leaf can be seen."

"Heat source huh, gentle touch. What is going on between you and Rachel?"

"I do not understand." He turned his head. "I am talking about the mimosa plant."

"Right, suddenly you have a language block." She faced him, put her hands on her hips and clearly enunciated. "Why is it, Raja, when you say Rachel's name is sounds like a calm wind blowing the leaves of a pine tree, and when you say my name is sounds like a goat bleating, eeema, eeema?"

Raja sprang to his feet. "You are—" The sound of a hiss, resembling a snake, passed by her ear. A light thud in conjunction with snapping twigs followed. An arrow went straight into his shoulder, pinning him to the ground. Emma scrambled to his side. Strong man hands gripped her arms, hoisting her.

"I've been waiting for months to finally touch you, little missy."

His breath smelled like beans, then slime-coated lips sucked her cheek. Unable to see the foe, she stared at her friend, hoping he lived. Raja jerked his shoulder free and jumped to a stand, then nodded. She bit the attacker on his hand and ducked. Raja kicked the assailant with such force a crack sounded, and his neck vibrated against her shoulder. He crumbled to the ground. Her defender lost his balance and grabbed a tree limb to remain upright.

"Raja," she screamed.

A chestnut-colored horse appeared beside her, and a thin arm lifted her, using the back of her dress. He plopped her face down on the saddle in front of him. Like a puppet on a string, she clung to the edge of the saddle with one hand and used her free hand to claw at the rider. A second horse galloped beside them. Raja. Her captor used his gun and butted her friend. Raja fell, crying out as the head of the arrow thrust deeper in his shoulder.

She screamed like the hounds of hell were attacking. Her voice echoed through the woods. The attacker pulled her upright onto the saddle and stuffed a dank putrid bandana into her mouth. She gagged and spat out the tainted cloth. Her dress prevented her from using her legs to kick. She lifted her arm, brought the elements together and punched him in his bearded throat. He fell to the side of the horse, clutching the hem of her dress the material tore. His weight dragged her down. She held onto the saddle horn. Water splashed, making the sides of the horse slick. Her legs dangled, precariously close to the brook.

"Emma."

Henry. She relaxed every muscle in her body and tumbled into the water. He rode past her and fired off two shots. The attacker wrenched upright onto the saddle, and the horse galloped into the forest.

She lugged her feet over the slippery rocks, carrying the bottom of her water laden underskirt. Henry circled around and stopped beside her. He jumped off his horse, yanked her close, then set her at arm's length, ran his gaze along her body, and gathered her even tighter to his chest.

"Ah, love, are you hurt?"

"No, just my ego for getting captured in the first place." Stinky muck water dripped from her face and onto his duster.

****

King paced in the parlor, hoping the angry energy would release with each step. "How many were there? I saw two men. Were there any others?" He struggled to keep his tone calm.

"Three riders, one had a large straw hat," Raja repeated.

"A sombrero."

"Not a word I know, but a large hat yes. The man had a dark complexion, not like Treasure, nor like my light brown, a different color of brown."

"So, they were Mexican, Indian, and white man."

"Perhaps." Raja nodded.

"I see the arrow went through your shoulder, fortunate for you." Sam frowned. "Another inch or two and your heart would have been pierced."

King walked to the window, debating what action to take. "I don't want to lose their trail. I'm going out now."

"Are you, insane man? It's almost dark. In the night, there isn't any way you could pick up a trail. They'll have to stop as well. We'll start in the morning." Sam paced opposite of King, their paths crossing in the middle.

Treasure sat in a chair, holding Maggie.

"Rachel, get the yarrow from E-ma's herb garden, it will stop the flow of blood. Crush and use honey wax to make a paste." Raja's voice changed from impatience to softness, and his accent thickened.

Rachel placed a basket of clean strips of linen on the floor beside him. Her skirts swished as she left and returned several minutes later carrying a jar with honey and a few yellow flowers. She took a cloth soaked it with whisky and cleaned the wound. He didn't flinch. "I think we should pour alcohol through the hole, to wash out any bits of wood."

He nodded and bent at the waist. She handed him a towel, then dripped spirits into the hole.

"Good, sit up please." She smashed flower buds into the honey and applied the pungent tart smelling salve to his injury. Maggie began to fuss. "Treasure, please wrap his arm."

Rachel tended the baby.

"Someone is at the door." Raja took the end of the bandage.

Sam shot King a curious look. He hadn't heard the knock.

"I'll go." Sam glanced at the pistol, in the holster at King's side. "Ready?"

"It's not likely they would come to the door." Regardless, he slid the gun from its sheath and followed.

"Howdy, I'm looking for my cousin, Emma Cody. I heard tell she's staying at the Drake's house." A booming voice pierced the quietness of the entry. The man glanced around the surroundings, while rubbing the dark goatee on his chin.

Sam propped his hands on his hips. "Yes, she is here. Who may I say is calling?"

"You're a might short to be using such formal words. Tell her that her favorite cousin in the whole wide world is here to steal her away."

"And you are?" Sam persisted.

"Why, William Cody." He removed his cowboy hat and bowed his head.

Everyone collected in the foyer, as the forceful theatrical voice of Buffalo Bill Cody thundered against the walls. The man stood straight and tall, the embodiment of the legend. From head to toe he wore supple buckskin that moved and clung to his body. The leather had been worn with such frequency that the elbows, knees, and backside were translucent thin. His tan boots matched the rest of his attire.

"Bill." Rachel, holding the baby, gave him a brush to his cheek and stepped away. "It's so good to see you."

"Why, little Rachel, I haven't seen you, since you were married to that no-account Drake."

"Yes, it's been a while. How are Louisa and the family?"

"The kids are growin' like weeds. Whatcha got there, a little 'un?" Bill peeked at the baby, then bent to chuck her chin. His medallion, on a turquoise beaded necklace, swung outward, and her gaze followed the shiny metal.

"My daughter, Margaret Mae." She pointed toward the group surrounding them. "I'd like you to meet Raja Sekhar, Sam McCloud, Treasure, and Emma's husband, Henry Courtland."

"Husband? We'll talk about that later. Nice to meet you all. Sorry about the late hour, I loaded a skittish horse on a Pacific Railroad Car in Cheyenne, Wyoming. I had to bribe the conductor in order to have the train stop in Ft. Lupton, and after CB, that's my horse, got his land legs back, I finally got on the trail to Pineview. Pardon me if I'm a might cranky, but I'd like to see Emma."

"Bill, rather Mr. Cody."

"Naw, you can call me, Bill. Ever 'body does." He took off his gloves and tucked them in his hat, then scratched his head. "Looks like you're bleedin' man. Might want to stop the flow, before it leaks all over this pretty floor."

Rachel handed Maggie to Treasure and led Raja into the parlor.

King felt her presence, before he glanced at the staircase. Emma's glorious brown hair hung in a braid and dropped over one shoulder. Dressed in a dark blue, split skirt and matching waistcoat she was a picture of serene beauty, surprising considering hours earlier she'd been kidnapped and dropped into a stream.

"Cousin," she whispered.

"Darlin'." Bill threw his hat onto the entryway table and met her as she ran down the stairs. She jumped into his open arms, and he spun her around.

King glanced at her. "Why don't all of us go into the parlor, and we'll explain what's going on."

Buffalo Bill set her feet on the floor and walked into the room. Emma flipped the control switch to turn on the lights. Raja and Rachel stood by the windows, getting the last bit of sunlight.

Bill patted Emma's hand, resting in the bend of his

arm. "Well, don't that beat all. I imagine you like to play with this gadget, since you like to learn new things. That sure is amazin'. Now that I've seen your fancy lights, I'd like to talk to Emma alone." He rubbed his hands over his eyes. "If someone could feed and water my horse, I'd be much obliged."

"I'll take care of him, Bill." Sam rushed from the house.

"I'll go get some coffee and tea. Rachel, do you need more cloth to wrap Raja's arm?" Treasure settled Maggie in the cradle near the fireplace.

"No, thank you. I think it has stopped for now." She gathered the dirty bandages and left the room.

King turned to Bill. "How did you come to be here?"

"A man by the name of Otis sent a telegram to Wyoming. I was there helping the government out. Said Emma needed me, and I was to auto-graph a book for him." He combed his fingers through his hair. "I ain't never written no book, so I was confused. Didn't matter, Emma needed me. A pack of renegades couldn't keep me away."

A guilty frown crossed Emma's face. "Oh, yes, I didn't have enough cash to send a telegram to my parents, so I promised within six months you'd autograph a dime novel for Otis Sue, at the telegraph office. He's a fan of yours."

"Don't mind that atall." Bill rubbed his blond goatee. "You say you're her husband?"

"Yes. A copy of the marriage license is on file in Boulder," King declared firmly. He proceeded to tell him about the rifle contest, which garnered a smile from the legend. Though reconstituting the marriage by

236

Reverend Fitzgerald presented a scowl, even with him omitting parts of the story.

"Don't that beat all, I never thought Emma would leave Fort Wayne. Here she is in Colorado and married to a gun totin' man." Bill shook his head.

Treasure carried a tray with coffee and a bottle of whisky. "Here we are." She poured coffee into cups.

"I think I'll pass on the coffee and have a sip of whisky," Bill said.

"How did you know where to find me?" She sat on the settee.

Bill stood at the fireplace, warming his hands and the whisky. "A man at the bar said you were staying at the Drake homestead." He stared at the hallway. "How'd the Injun get pierced by an arrow?"

Emma proceeded to explain the attempts on her life.

He nodded. "First, I want to help Henry track down the scallywags who are trying to kill you. I say we hit the sack for a couple of hours, until the dawn barely lightens the sky. Load your weapons well, and get grub, cause I ain't going ta come back until we find those polecats." Bill walked toward the front door.

King stood. "Where are you going?"

"To unsaddle my horse and get some shut eye."

"Sam took care of your horse. By now he's tucked into a stall chewing on hay. There's a room upstairs for you."

Bill Cody pivoted. "A soft bed and maybe a bath. I'd say that would be darn close to heaven."

"I'll show you to your room and get the water started." Emma stood.

Bill tipped his head. "I'll see ya'll in the mornin'.

I'll leave without you, if 'in yer late." He ambled toward the stairs with Emma on his arm.

Raja came into the room; no doubt having heard the entire conversation. Treasure lifted the beverage tray.

"Treasure, if you wouldn't mind getting some trail food and water ready for our journey, I'd greatly appreciate it." King stood before the fire, legs braced apart, hands behind his back. After she left, he stared at Raja. "I let my emotions rule over common sense, let my guard down, and I regret that. Now, you'll tell me why you were sent to guard her. There wasn't time for her telegram to get to London, even if it did arrive. So, her parents must be the reason she is a target."

"My loyalty is to Minister Cody." Raja flinched as he sat on the settee. The white strips binding his shoulder sported a half dollar size red spot where he continued to bleed.

"Damn it, her life is in danger, and I'd truly like to put a bullet through your heart for being aware of the circumstances and not telling us." King fisted his hands at his sides. "Who took her, Raja? It'll help us to determine the reason."

"You are right. I must break my vow. E-ma's father is influential in Mexico. President Hayes wants to keep him in place and continue to monitor and prevent Mexican uprisings."

King crossed his arms. "I thought Emma's father was a governor."

"After we met, he was advanced and became the Envoy Extraordinary and Minister Plenipotentiary to Mexico, as appointed by your President. Mr. and Mrs. Cody were on holiday in Europe when he received a message stating if he didn't retire from his position, then E-ma would suffer." Raja stood and pulled on his shirt and tunic. The blood stains were a dark brown against the white of the cloth.

"Before the message arrived, Minister Cody extended his visit to include India. We sought his intelligence about strategies. It was important to my country for him to visit. They honored me, by allowing me to come to America as E-ma Cody's guard and protector. I have failed in my duty." Determination marked his face. "I'll be ready to ride at dawn." Raja rolled his shoulder and stilled. "The man who took E-ma is more-than-likely John B. Eller, Mr. Cody's former assistant. He is in the pocket of the rebels."

"But Rachel hasn't been threatened."

Raja heaved a sigh. "I do not know the man's logic."

King nodded and went into Jayden's study. The key to the gun cabinet should have been in the lap drawer, but a thorough search revealed it was missing. He removed the letter opener and went to the steel cabinet. The key was in the lock, and a revolver had been removed. The sheriff delivered Jayden's belongings without a gun or holster. The gun could have been used by the woman who killed him, and she kept the weapon. Neither Treasure nor Sam would have a reason for taking a pistol. Raja? Unlikely, as guns were not part of his religion. Emma prized her own engraved set of pistols, which left Rachel.

King removed a Colt .45, Peacemaker, a Yellowboy Lever Action Rifle, handcrafted by Winchester himself, and a Bowie knife. He stuffed shells in a cloth bag and jogged upstairs. The room smelled like Emma, a mixture of lavender and the new lemon scent she'd been mixing. He dropped the bag near the door. He wanted a cigar, instead he stepped to the window.

A discarded pair of britches were haphazardly spread across a cherry tea table. He picked up the white cotton and held the material to his face. Danny described how the women wore men's breeches like long john's and formed odd positions with their arms and legs. The boy fell onto the floor, rolling in laughter as he imitated them.

Emma entered the room, but he hadn't realized she was so close until she spoke.

"I'm thinking of wearing trousers tomorrow." She slid an arm through his.

"You're not going." *No way.*

She wrapped her arms around his waist, catching her fingers on his watch fob. He unclasped the chain and laid it on the table. She unbuttoned the ivory buttons on his vest, the shirt, then inserted her small cold hands between the undershirt and his skin. He sucked in much needed air. "Cold."

"You'll warm them soon enough or maybe I should lower them and see if a little friction will make them heat."

He stilled her hand. "Emma, I'll make love to you, but it won't change my mind. You aren't going with us. I'm not putting you at risk. You mean too much to me."

She surprised him when she didn't bounce off in an angry storm. "You're a logical businessman. If you all leave, Rachel, Maggie Mae, Treasure, and I will be unguarded and subject to an attack. Innocents could be killed because the men want me. If I go with you, and they see me, they'll attack a group of people who are prepared."

"No. I'll not put your life in danger." He took a deep breath.

Her hand traveled downward. "We'll negotiate."

He lifted her hand and kissed the backside. "I'm willing to listen."

"You should leave Sam and Raja here to guard the others. Because of honor, Raja will refuse. Sam could take them into town and stay at the inn for a few days."

"I'll consider it." He whirled around, held her snug to his fire driven body. "Thank God you're not wearing anything under that robe." He hoisted her onto the tabletop, making his pocket watch fall and clang on the floor. She placed her hands on his shoulders and wrapped her legs around his waist.

He kissed her neck, the sensitive spot under her ear, her neck, and shoulder.

She lowered her mouth to his chest, touching his pink skin, then lifted her beautiful sultry-laden eyes to meet his gaze. Her braid fell to her back. The light from the fireplace made the red glints brighter. "I need you."

"You drive me mad."

Chapter 20

Emma wanted to shout her frustration at the mountains. The motley group traveled single file through a narrow trail. Bill led. Raja, unsteady on his mount, was next and unfortunately for her, she followed with Henry bringing up the rear.

Raja's face scrunched, and by his jerky movements, anger continued to rule his state of mind. "Make him stop," she whispered, while considering they should take a break so he could find his Zen place.

Henry sighed. "There is a clearing up ahead. I'll ride beside him and make a suggestion."

He nudged Maverick into a trot, until he fell in beside Raja's mount. "No other solution. She can hit a shriveled pumpkin from thirty feet while riding on the side of her saddle. She'll be a benefit."

Obvious by his rigid back and tight hold on the reins, Raja wasn't comfortable on the horse or in the situation. Although, his white garments blended nicely with Brandy's coat. "You do not understand the determination of the people we are pursuing."

She continued past them and steered Black Bart beside her cousin.

"Just like the old days, Emma, you dressed in boy's apparel and followed me around." A grin split Bill's face before he snickered. His roan, CB, shot forward, as they rode single file through a cramped pass. The sprinkling of gray and white merged nicely with the horse's chestnut base color, making CB look like he had bits of snow and soot splattered on his brown trunk.

"There wasn't another who could lead, or who had the patience to teach me about weapons and life. Until…"

"Until?" Bill glanced behind her.

"Until Henry." The pass opened and she rode beside him.

"You're happy then?" He rubbed his goatee. Helen's recent letter mentioned Bill and Louisa were experiencing a rough patch in their marriage.

"Yes, very happy. Not happy about the three pesky men who continue to attempt to end my life."

Bill smiled. She knew he loved a good challenge, especially if he could showcase his skills. "They won't be a problem for much longer."

Near the end of the trail, they exited the mountain pass and came upon a river. Bill slid from his horse and knelt on the ground, evaluating animal and human tracks. "It appears they got on a boat or barge at this point."

Bill glanced across the waterway. "Henry, I'm crossing. Guard Emma."

Henry drew alongside her, and they waited. A few minutes later, Bill returned and the frown on his face said it all. "I didn't see the same indentations. Taking a barge downstream would lead to Denver, where they could catch a Pacific Rail all the way to the edge of Mexico."

Henry looked westward. "Probably not a barge. One sunk a while back, and they stopped the transport."

"Don't you find it odd they gave up and

skedaddled?" she asked.

"Not really. You saw their faces and would identify them. They could tell Eller they killed you and planted your body in the mountains. A note to your parents would convince your father to give up his position, before he could find out the truth." Henry settled onto Maverick's back, nudging him away from Bill. The stallion stretched his neck, trying to chew on the man's fringed leather. He gave the Palomino extra attention by patting his neck.

"Let's ride." Bill pressed a knee into CB's side.

Emma glanced at Henry. "What are you going to do now that you sold the saloon to Martin?"

He tipped his hat. "I've a couple of business ventures lined up."

She lifted an eyebrow. "Do you think Cat and Martin will form an odd partnership?"

"Probably. Why are you asking?"

"'Cause I think he seems like a good guy, and she should be tarred and feathered."

He lifted and lowered his hat. "Emma."

She twisted around in her saddle. "Bill, how much farther by horse? Do you think we should use a boat? Are there Boat Stations, like Stagecoach Stations?"

Bill glanced in her direction and whistled. "Gawd, I forgot what a talker you are."

"She does tend to talk, sometimes at inconvenient times." Henry winked at her.

Red faced, she air-kissed him. "How am I supposed to learn if I don't ask questions?"

The brackish, freshwater scent and slap of waves against the rocks on the shore didn't bother her, but the glow of the afternoon sun bouncing off the red landscape blinded her. Lack of sleep began to take its toll on her body.

Bill led the group along the river's rocky edge until a fork required a turn. "The outlaws will need to stop in Boulder, for fresh horses and supplies. Let's take the main road."

The travel weary group urged their horses into a gallop and arrived in Boulder a few hours later. Separated into two groups, they went to the docks to inquire about the arrival of three banditos.

"Wait here." Henry handed her Maverick's reins. "I'll talk to the dock workers."

She nodded, considering water carries voices she'd hear the conversation. Henry stepped onto the gangway leading to a disreputable looking tugboat. One of the two scruffy men, likely bootleggers, peered at him, then stared at her.

"I'm looking for three men wanting to take a boat to Denver."

"Many men travel this way." Scruffy One picked his teeth, using the middle digit of his four fingers. "Why should we tell you anything?"

He extracted silver coins. "One was British, other two were brown."

The pirate took the coins between his thumb and third finger. "They were here about three hours ago and headed toward the train station."

Henry sauntered towards her. He removed his Stetson and replaced it again. Her glance met his. His frown became a smile and the devilish glints of his eyes sparkled with life. She loved the man. He'd become an essential part of her life. She now understood why Rachel couldn't release Jayden.

"Well?"

"So far Bill and Raja have been exact, on the outlaw's destinations. Curious." He wrapped his arm around her waist and took the horses' reins. "We'll find the other two and see what trouble we can stir up at the train station."

"Henry," she hesitated. One of her guys, family, could be hurt. She couldn't accept one of them being injured or worse, killed, because of a vendetta against her father involving politics. Why hadn't she read about an unrest in Mexico?

"Yes, darlin'."

"Let's go home and forget all of this. We'll let my father handle the problem."

He stilled and turned her toward him. "Do you want to remain a bird-in-a-cage? I won't put your life at risk, which means you do not leave the house unless I'm with you." He hugged her, resting his chin on top of her head.

"No, I wouldn't want to be caged. I need to tell you…" she whispered.

"Oh, love, have more faith in me."

They found the three outlaws hovered around a fire a few feet from Pacific Railroad tracks. A large boned man, his rear flowing over the edge of a railroad rail, was smoking something cloyingly sweet. Another man, a Mexican by his accent and dark skin, passed a glass bottle of clear liquid to the hombre next to him. The third man's beak nose and narrow shaped eyes made him appear native. Emma sent a silent prayer to her guardian angel.

"Pedro, it is your turn to deal the cards."

"Taco, you haven't put in your anti," Pedro

declared.

"I've told you that my name is Tahmelapachme, call me Knife."

"Right, literal translation is dull knife. And since you've missed the woman as a target twice, I'd have to add dull shot as well." The large boned man was British. What an odd twist. Why would a British be involved with attempted murder?

"You were part of the attacks. You're as guilty as any of the rest of us. Is Beller meeting us here?" Taco asked.

"I am going to meet the boss at his train car, and you two are waiting at the livery." The Englishman took a swig from the bottle.

Night descended and the crickets rubbed their wings together, the chirp competed with the sound of rail cars that vibrated on the tracks nearby, adding an odd musical background.

A touch on her shoulder brought her head around and her large floppy hat bounced against Henry's chest. He held his finger up to his lips, took her hand into his. Behind the boulders, they were shielded from the outlaws.

Bill and Raja joined them. She leaned against one of the enormous rocks, the sun-warmed stone took away a little of the chill, but the hardness matched the firm determination in Henry's eyes.

"I'll create a diversion," Bill said.

"Raja, go to the right, and I'll go in through the center." He grabbed his rifle from its sheath on the saddle. "Bill, give a sharp whistle, when you're ready. We'll enter their campsite and tell them to surrender but expect them to be the cowards they are and attack."

"What about me?" Torn between two thoughts. One, she wanted to be a part of the action and protect her loved ones. Second, she wasn't confident she could kill another person. The men, she'd shot during the stagecoach robbery kept playing through her mind. Would she be able to pull the trigger and send someone to heaven or hell? More than likely, hell.

"You stay with the horses. If someone should break through our defenses, you'll be back up." Henry focused on his pistol, rolling the cylinder. He added bullets, then holstered the gun. She hobbled the horses behind the five story boulders. Low to the ground, she crept until the camp came into view.

A sharp whistle pierced the air, Bill approached the group from the left and hurled his powder horn into the fire. Sparks flew. Raja and Henry ran into the clearing. "Drop your weapons. You're surrounded."

The Indian threw a bottle of liquid, then dived behind the stack of railroad ties. The Mexican drew his gun from the ammunition belt strapped across his chest. Thwack. The Englishman toppled onto his side.

Bill shot the Mexican dead-on. The Indian threw a knife at Raja, who fluidly moved to the side. He withdrew an oddly shaped silver object and flung the gadget toward the man, which embedded between the renegade's eyes.

Henry approached the Englishman who continued to rest on the ground. He jostled the man. No response. He knelt beside him.

"He's had loco weed. When combined with Mescal the man's not going to be awake for several hours." Bill stooped and evaluated the shiny metal object in the Indian's forehead. "What is this?"

"Star." Raja sat on the stool, holding his injured arm.

Henry patted the Englishman's chest and sides. He removed a small derringer from the man's waistcoat and threw the gun to Bill who caught it in one hand. He lifted the Englishman by his coat and shook him like Danny waggled the rat in the saloon.

The Englishman's head bobbed from side to side. He released him, and the drunk crumbled onto the ground. She holstered her revolver and searched the campsite for water. No canteens were visible, so she swooped up the clear liquid bottle and handed it to Henry.

"I thought I told you to stay with the horses."

She shrugged. The man snorted then farted, creating a malodorous stink.

Henry poured liquid over the Englishman's face. He came upright sputtered, laughed, and tumbled to the ground again.

"Tie 'em to their horses, and we'll take 'em to the sheriff. Tomorrow we'll get answers." Bill grabbed a circle of rope. They worked together, then mounted their own horses and silently traveled into Boulder.

Except for the saloons, the stores were dark and the streets empty. They rode through an older section of Boulder, which presented false fronts and broken boardwalks. A gentleman in a dark suit and long coat rode past the group. "If you're lookin' for the sheriff, you need to go over another street, turn left."

"Thanks," Henry replied.

At the next alley, they turned and found a small flickering light in the window with *Sheriff, Boulder City*, written across the front in gold letters.

"I'll go in and get the sheriff. Emma—"

"I'll wait here."

Bill tied his horse to the railing and joined him. He turned the doorknob. "Raja, do you have more of those shiny things in case the scoundrel comes around?"

"Yes. I will guard them." Raja climbed off his horse, handed the reins to her and stood on the wooden boardwalk waiting and watching.

"Those little star-shaped things are deadly. You'll teach me how to use them?"

"Yes, E-ma, after we have resolved the threat to you."

"In the meantime, can I see one up close?"

Before Raja could respond, Henry, Bill, the sheriff, and a deputy came out of the building. The deputy was completely dressed in black. His hawk-like features, a sharp long nose, small black eyes, and his broad forehead, made him appear to be a force. The outlaws were face down across the horses. The deputy lifted a head, letting the noggin fall. Next, the native.

"Dead," he declared.

He moved onto the chestnut horse. The blackguard's big rump stood straight up in the air. His head hung down, the queue had come undone, and his hair shielded his features. Reaching over, the deputy turned the man's head. "Well, lookee here, we got ourselves a wanted man and alive at that." The deputy dropped the Englishman's head, and his face smashed against the stirrup with a thump and a clang. The action renewed the pungent scent of the loco weed.

"Who is he?" she asked.

The deputy swept his gaze from the top of her floppy hat to her booted feet, then a grin appeared on his narrow face. It was obvious he hadn't known her feminine status until she opened her mouth. She glanced at Henry.

"Little lady, this here is Reginald Coldham, wanted by the Texas Rangers, and the New York port authorities for smuggling, and I'm guessing wanted by you all."

The sheriff spit a wad of tobacco into the dirt street. "Excuse Deputy Moutain, he's our puzzle solver. He has a good-eye and keeps track of all the wanted men."

The brown goo pooled in the dirt, and the pungent tobacco odor filtered through the air. She wanted to vomit. "Raja, do you think you could draw a picture of Eller, on the off-chance Deputy Moutain could have seen him?"

"Yes, I could do this likeness as you describe the man," Raja answered.

Deputy Moutain took Coldham off the horse, and the sheriff helped carry the dead weight inside the building. With Henry's help, she dismounted and tied her horse to the post. They followed the group inside the office.

She removed her hat and stood near the desk. The Sheriff handed Raja a piece of paper and a pencil. He took his boot and shoved a chair away from the desk. Raja sat, placed the cardstock on the tabletop and sketched a man's face according to her directive.

"Ma'am, I'm Sheriff Marcus Weatherby." He nodded to her.

She removed her glove, added it to the hat and smoothed a bit of hair behind her ear. "I'm Emma Cody Courtland." This was the first time she'd said her new name out loud. Deep-seeded on her tongue, it sounded nice. Henry winked, and her heart filled. Her breath caught in her throat.

"Oh, so you're hitched to this Courtland?" He nodded toward him.

She nodded.

"Here you are, Deputy Moutain." Raja handed him the sketch of Eller.

"Yesterday this man arrived in a private railcar. He left the car briefly to go to Joe's mercantile. I remember because he caused a ruckus. He wanted his railcar to be hitched to the back, behind the caboose. The Union Pacific Rail train engineer refused. There were fisticuffs and an overnight stay for the coal man, but the railcar was tacked onto the end. He said he was a diplomat, which got him a handshake from the mayor and the ability to leave at sundown." Moutain set the outline of her adversary on top of the desk.

"Where were they headed?" Bill asked.

"Albuquerque, New Mexico," Moutain replied. "Are you the real McCoy? The Buffalo Bill Cody?"

"Yes, sir, I am." Bill puffed out his chest and moved his arms to rest on the handles of his pistols. The fringe of his buckskin waved back and forth.

"It's an honor to meet you, Mr. Cody. I have here an ad for a Pony Express Rider, would you be kind enough to autograph it for me." Moutain rifled through the pile of wanted handbills.

Bill smiled broadly and took the pen and paper. "There's one condition attached to this autograph."

Moutain's spine became as straight as the black bars on the cage holding the Englishman. "Yes?"

"We're fixin' to stop that train and have a little talk

with Mr. Eller. I figure we'll still be in Colorado when we do. I'm hoping you will contact the sheriff's office and get us released from jail, if needed."

Deputy Moutain's lips split into a wide smile. "It'll be my honor, Mr. Cody."

Bill held out his hand. "I'm Bill, to my friends."

Emma waited for Moutain to wet his drawers' right there in front of them.

He shook Bill's hand. "You might want to hurry. They have a thirty-minute start."

Chapter 21

King knew they approached the correct train as a private rail car trailed behind the caboose. His wife's thrill of excitement when they caught up with the Union Pacific was hardly contained. She wiggled on her saddle and hooted. Bill urged his well-trained horse into a gallop.

"Bill's going to climb to one side of the saddle as the horse gets closer to the train engine. The risk involves him jumping from the side of the horse onto the locomotive platform." She smiled like she approved of the dangerous move.

Bill grabbed ahold of the ladder and landed on the stairs leading to the doorway of the engine room. Soon, thereafter, the train slowed and stopped.

"You're never going to do that." He glanced at her. "Please, stay with the horses. We'll get Eller and then, only then, you'll bring the mounts to us."

She nodded, took the reins, and led the horses to the backside of the train car. Due to the warm weather, many windows were lowered and the soot from the coal-engine was settling inside the railcars.

King glanced at Raja. "Ready? If possible, we snatch Eller and take him back to Boulder."

"Right. I do not believe he will make the experience a pleasant one." Raja withdrew a silver disk from one of his apparently endless pockets.

King threw open the door. Two men were inside, one who looked exactly like Raja's drawing and a Mexican. Eller ran behind the only other door in the car, and the Mexican lifted a double-barrel shotgun. The cinders floated to the floor and the ash smell dissipated. King shot both hands into the air. "We're only after Eller. If you lower your weapon, and let us take him, no injuries."

"Ye're not takin' him, nowhere," the man said. His overall brown appearance, brown hair, trousers, coat, vest, and cream tinted shirt matched his short stocky stature. He pointed his gun at King, pulled the cock. Raja threw the silver star hitting the man directly on his gun holding hand. The weapon fell to the floor, discharging a round.

Somewhere nearby a woman screamed. Had the bullet gone through Eller's car and into the caboose? Eller peered from behind the ajar door. A dandy, he was wearing a dark blue suit with a bright purple vest, highlighting his pale skin with purple veins popping out of his forehead. His watery brown eyes pierced King with a death-to-you stare.

King kicked open the door, gripped Eller's vest with both hands and jerked him into the main cabin. The Mexican was wrapping a cloth around his hand. Raja stood beside him, holding the rifle pointed directly at the man's lap. Eller withdrew a yellow handkerchief from his jacket pocket and wiped sweat and soot from his face.

"Is there anyone else in the car?" King didn't receive an answer. He walked the length of the railcar, opened the lavatory door to find it empty. An unmade bed at the end of the car was separated from the main area of the car by a curtain.

He pointed the barrel of his Colt toward Eller. "We're going to tie up your friend here, and then take you to the sheriff in Boulder." He drew a small circled length of rope from his coat pocket and threw it to Raja.

"I don't understand," Eller stated.

"You've had people try to kill my wife, and I won't have it. You're going to jail, or if I'm lucky, you'll be hung." He waved his gun and within minutes the Mexican was tied to a chair. Raja checked the tautness of the line and stuffed a cloth napkin in the man's mouth. Satisfied with the knots, he took another circle of rope and dragged Eller's arms behind him and bound his wrists.

"First off, I have international immunity, so no jail or hangman's noose." He smiled. "Secondly, who is your wife?"

"Emma Cody." King glanced at Raja. "Is what he said true?"

Raja nodded. "He will be sent back to England, only."

The train jolted forward, and a billow of soot laden smoke filled the confines of the railcar. Eller laughed. "Wouldn't it be ironic if Emma Cody was killed because of something you did instead of me? I guess I should have hired you instead of the incompetent men I did hire."

King centered his pistol on the man's forehead. "One more word, and you're a dead man."

Eller blinked and closed his mouth.

Raja peered out the window. "Surprisingly, she is still there."

King nodded and hauled Eller to a stand. "Let's

go."

Bill, mounted on CB, waited beside Emma. She led Maverick forward, and King took hold of the reins. "Any trouble?"

"None. Waited like a good little soldier."

King stared at her. "Where did the scream come from?"

Bill smoothed his goatee. "Clumsy me, accidently looked into a window, lady on the shitter."

King shook his head, then threw Eller onto Maverick's saddle and tied his hands to the horn.

"I'm thirsty." Eller whined.

King held a canteen to his lips and tipped. Water slid along the sides of his mouth, and he sputtered. "I have civil rights, and one of them is to be treated fairly."

Raja handed King a bandana. "We have the right to not listen to you." He wedged the cloth across Eller's mouth and secured a knot.

Raja mounted Brandy, and King climbed behind Emma.

Bill tipped his hat. "Is this weasel the one you've been looking for?"

"Yes. The blackguard worked for my father, apparently plotting the entire time." Emma glared at Eller. "Hopefully, he won't have a fall from his horse and break his neck on the way to the sheriff's."

Bill laughed and kicked his horse into a canter.

Raja shook his head. "Very dark thought, E-ma."

Chapter 22

Emma's stomach growled, and it was not a dainty grumble, but a loud grinding objection. "I'm so hungry. How much longer until we reach Boulder?"

Henry squeezed his arms tighter around her body. "What about the jerky I gave you? Want more?"

"I don't like it. The smell is rancid and unappealing. It's hard to chew and hurts going into my stomach. Soup sounds good. Oh, Sam's flapjacks are so delicious. No, chocolate would be fantastic. A truffle sounds nice."

"What did you do with the jerky? I never saw you throw it away." Henry rubbed her arm.

"I gave the dried bark to your horse. That Palomino will eat anything." Her right leg had fallen asleep a mile back, and the muscles began to twitch.

"My horse does not eat anything. He's very discerning about what he nibbles on." He glanced at her leg and met her gaze, again. On a full stomach, his bland expression would have made her laugh.

"Your horse nibbled on Mrs. McCullough's barn door." She tried to twist her leg.

"What's going on?"

"Due to hunger, I feel faint, and my leg's fallen asleep." She punched her thigh. "The sun's burning my face." She gripped his hand. "At the campsite, I was frightened. I didn't know if I could shoot another man, even a bad one." She gave a nervous snicker. "It is so easy to hit a target, but when it comes to putting a bullet through a person, very difficult to do."

"You're a brave woman, Emma Courtland, and I admire you for your courage. I'm not worried if faced with a life and death situation, you'd do what is best."

She leaned her head against his chest. "Thank you, Henry. I appreciate your validation."

"Validation? You sound like Sam."

"I like to read, and words are fun to use."

He snorted, then snicked, and Black Bart shot forward.

They carefully made their way to the sheriff's office. Bill helped Eller dismount and removed the gag from his mouth. Bill and Henry dragged the criminal into the sheriff's office, while Raja and Emma waited outside.

"There's a general store across the street. Do you think I could buy a snack and return before they get finished inside?"

Raja glanced at her and then at the false storefront. "Yes. I will tell Henry where you are."

"Want anything?"

"Not unless they have a good English tea."

"Raja, are you well?" she asked.

"Yes, E-ma. Headache only."

She ran across the dusty road and into the store. Removing a few coins from her pocket, she bought a box of crackers and a tin of tea, made in Ceylon. Raja had relocated to a patch of prairie grass directly in the sunlight.

She sat on a barrel, on the boardwalk in front of the office, opened the crackers and satisfied her ravenous hunger. The squeak of a door opening brought her around. "How did it go?"

"Still waiting on the sheriff. The deputy wanted to keep the man, here," Bill pointed toward Raja, who appeared to be lost in his own contentment. "They thought he was responsible for a stagecoach robbery a month ago."

She swallowed cracker dust. "Because?"

"The robber was brown and wore all white." Henry helped her from the barrel. "Will you take Emma down to the diner and get her something to eat? She's feeling faint." He kissed her on the cheek. "I'll join you, after I'm done here."

"Raja!" Bill shouted. Her protector unfolded his legs, focused, and joined them. The threesome walked past three buildings, until they found a diner.

No sooner had they ordered a family style meal when Henry arrived. "As it happens, the circuit judge is a good friend of mine. I gave the sheriff an accounting of the shootings, and I'm confident Eller will be transported to the county seat for a trial."

"What about international immunity?" She hoped he'd somehow bypassed that tidbit.

"The Sheriff sent a telegram when we left a few days ago and discovered Eller was fired, so no bogus protection. He'll be put in jail." He piled potatoes on a plate. "This food smells delicious. Did you order ham?"

Steam rose from the pungent cabbage. She shook her head. "Only meatloaf and potatoes." They ate in silence until the bowls were empty. Then as if synchronized they all sat back in their seats and sighed.

"It has been rewardin' to see you again, my favorite cousin, but I need to head back up to Wyoming and wrangle some buffalo for the army. I've been away too long. I'll spend the night here, in a soft bed and head out tomorrow." He sat back in his seat picking his teeth with the pinpoint of his knife.

"Bill, we've had so little time together. Can't you stay a few more days?" She lowered her fork, savoring the last bite of chocolate cake.

"Sorry, lil' darlin'. I need to return to scout for the Army, and the workers on the Kansas Pacific need their buffalo meat. I'll come back in a few months to check and make sure you're out of trouble."

"Oh, what about Otis Sue, from the telegraph office? I promised him you'd meet him and sign a book." She glanced at Henry. "Could we search for a book here in Boulder? Would you sign a copy before you leave, Bill?"

"Maybe you could meet him when you return? If not for the telegraph, we wouldn't have caught the men trying to get Emma." Henry clasped her cold hand, providing that bit of warmth she needed.

Bill nodded. "Sure, I can do that."

"Do you think Black Bart would like a train ride?" She squinted her eyes, trying to keep a headache at bay.

"Probably as well as CB did. Of course, Maverick and Black Bart will have the cute white mare to keep them warm." Bill grinned.

"Would it be possible to use a private railcar to travel back to Fort Collins?" Raja asked.

She understood. He was probably thinking of how everyone stared, which seemed to happen every time they encountered new people. "I think it's a good idea. We can plan what to do when my father arrives."

"Your father?" Henry's face paled, as if the

meatloaf didn't sit right in his stomach.

When she said, "Yes. Raja, didn't you say my parents would be arriving in June?" Henry's face got a little whiter.

Chapter 23

"Naw, Henry's thinking about meeting your parents. They are bad'uns." Bill smiled, and his top of his mustache almost touched his eyelashes. Emma frowned at him. He teased, but the others didn't know him as well.

Henry rubbed his face. "I'm not worried. I didn't rest well last night."

Bill made a deal with a bookseller, obtained a book titled *Buffalo Bill, the King of the Border Men* by Ned Buntline. In addition to a photo outside the bookstore, he signed several copies, then continued his travel to Wyoming. Raja, Henry, and Emma took a railcar then rode nonstop and arrived in Pineview in record time.

Rachel's house came into view and Emma experienced a sense of homecoming. She glanced at Henry who tilted his hat back, pulled off a buff-colored leather glove, and rubbed his face. He looked nervous. Could it be possible he was apprehensive about meeting her parents? They stopped the horses in front of the house. With agile grace, he dismounted and helped her. Raja took a little more care getting off his mount. She chuckled as he walked bow-legged up the stairs.

Raja entered the house, leaving the door open. "Rachel? Treasure?"

Henry placed his arm at her backside and escorted her to the entry. "I'll put the horses in the barn. They've had a long journey. Will you be able to manage?"

"Yes, I'll be fine. Don't fuss over me." She smiled and pushed him toward the barn, then pivoted. Her parents stood in the foyer, arms entwined, and with expressions of equal amounts of excitement and concern on their aging faces. Ignoring the throb in her leg, she ran forward and hugged them. The house was like a virtual circus. Every time she left and returned newcomers were present. This time, it was a good homecoming. She didn't realize how much she'd missed them for the last eleven months. They remained the same, but she'd gone through a metamorphosis. By their changing expressions, they'd observed the evolution as well.

"Why are you limping?" Of course, her father would notice. He looked handsome in his dapper black suit with the long jacket ending mid-thigh. His white shirt contrasted with his sun-tanned skin to make him look darker, more imposing. His bowtie hung crooked. With the recent events and knowing life was precious, her heart swelled with the knowledge he was alive and well. Could she postpone dealing with the questions?

Frank Cody cuddled her, and she smelled his peppermint scented breath, which gave her a familiar comfort. She tugged at the silver-gray hair resting on his shoulder.

"Legs are numb from riding for so long. Did you see Rachel and your granddaughter?" Emma hugged her mother, sliding her fingers along the black satin gown. Her mother's light brown hair had become peppered gray and white. She'd lost weight, and on her five-foot-seven frame she needed the extra padding.

"Yes, they're taking a nap," her mother responded

with a wide teeth-revealing-smile.

"If you'll make yourselves comfortable in the parlor, I'll freshen up and change out of these dusty clothes." She jerked her soiled garments.

"Of course, dear."

"What happened?" her father demanded.

"We caught Eller, and there was a small incident. Could we talk about this later? I'd like to remove some of this road dust. Then you can tell me about your travels." She smiled like she didn't have any worries and hoped the topic would be delayed until she could sort out how to explain the unimaginable chain of events.

"Yes, of course." Her father waved his hand, indicating she could go.

Emma pulled herself up the stairs, took a quick bath, soaking her head in the warm water. The trick didn't relieve her headache. She threw on a green dress, braided her wet hair, and rejoined her parents in the parlor.

"We talked to Matthew Bambridge." With an obvious agenda, her father didn't hesitate.

Her mother nodded. "He's worried about you. He asked for your hand in marriage?"

It didn't take long for them to jump into the heart of the issue. "Yes, I declined."

Frank Cody stood in front of the massive marble fireplace, with his hands tucked behind his back. She glanced at her mother who perched on a maroon fireside chair.

"How is Matthew?" Emma prayed, *please don't let them know about Henry tossing me into the horse tank and ordering Matthew to leave.*

"Mr. Bambridge told us that you'd married, Emma, and he seemed quite upset about it. The future doctor said you were going to answer his proposal when you got back from Colorado. I didn't believe the impromptu marriage to be true until we arrived, and Rachel confirmed it." Her mother's statement sounded more like carping. Her intelligent, soul-searching, green eyes made Emma squirm in her seat. Blast, she couldn't deny the dismay visible in her gaze.

"I love Henry, Mother. I didn't plan to love him, and sometimes his stubbornness makes me as angry as a raging bull, but he has a tender heart. He's handsome, humorous, and intelligent with idiot tendencies." She sighed. "He's also a savvy businessman."

"Can he keep you in hats and shoes? Will he be able to afford a cook and a housekeeper, both, which you'll certainly need?" Her father demanded as he rubbed his jaw. Always practical and taking a global view, he wouldn't let sleeping dogs lie.

"You'll need to ask him about his financial status. I've been helping to keep house here. Ask Sam, Rachel, and Treasure. They'll confirm I cleaned the drawing room every day. Also, I washed clothes, created a fantastic kitchen garden, and cooked." Feet firmly planted on the floor, she absorbed the pain and shuffled in front of her father. "The chicken was edible, not very flavorful, but it filled our stomachs."

"All well and good."

"Believe it Papa, I've changed." She maintained her stance and lifted her hands into the air. "I'm happy."

"Emma," Her father ran a hand through his coarse hair.

"We know you have, baby. I just want to make sure…"

"What, Mother? Make sure, what?" Docile didn't last very long, her forced calmness hinted at the anger she barely kept controlled.

"Emma, it's just the difference in your history. You're from the city, he's from the country. You've a fabulous education. He owns a saloon. The differences go on and on. Because of the diverse backgrounds, I wonder if you'll continue to be happy." Her mother fluttered her hands, and then clasped them in her lap.

She knelt in front of her. "Do you recall my favorite bedtime story? Why I always followed Bill around? Learned about childbirth to help Rachel? This is my destiny. It's almost as if Henry waited for me to arrive. I'm sure he is my present and my future." Her voice rose with excitement. It meant a great deal to have her parents' approval. If they didn't accept the union, she'd remain in Pineview by Henry's side. She'd tell him the truth about Jayden and the other thing. Her heart pounded so fast she could feel the pressure down through her tender, saddle-sore limbs.

"Honey, we're happy you've found someone to care about, but you've always been impetuous." Frank took out his pocket watch.

Emma stood, leaning on her right leg, assured she'd won their approval.

He sighed. "What does the man do for a living? Other than a slinging beer and a peddler of flesh?"

Her brief moment of joy flew up the fireplace. "Henry has several businesses, including land-development. He owned the saloon, passed down to him from his father, but recently sold the business. He never peddled flesh. There is a madame, who rents space, and provides services." She clamped her jaws tight. Her explanation wouldn't make the situation better.

Frank replaced his timepiece and glanced at the door. "We'll be able to get the marriage annulled, and you'll return with us to Fort Wayne." His voice had an edge, a sarcasm she hadn't experienced before today. Why? In the past, he'd always been supportive of her endeavors.

"It's not necessary. We were never legally married. I signed my name on the documents as Emmet Cody." She forced her legs to march forward. Reaching him, she threaded her shaking arm around his. "Father, I'll do what is right and tell Henry the truth about Jayden leading the gang that robbed him. If you'll repay him for the stolen money, I'll reconsider my future."

"What? Jayden's alive?" her father shouted. Her mother held her hands to her mouth. The horror of the statement clearly shocked them. She'd had months to reconcile his lack of departure. Her mother's eyes glossed over with unshed tears. She wished she could take back the ugly truth.

Henry walked into the room. A tick twitched in his jaw.

Her timing was deplorable. Now, her parents didn't trust her, and he became aware of her secrets. "Henry, meet my parents."

He approached her father and held out his hand. "Mr. Cody."

He crossed the room and clasped her mother's hand. "Mrs. Cody."

Emma smoothed down her green dress and tucked

in a piece of wet hair that tickled her neck. If fear smelled salty and a little like vinegar, she'd been baptized.

"I couldn't help but overhear some of your conversation. If I may speak openly?" Henry had washed off the travel dust and changed into a pair of black cotton trousers, a starched white shirt, topped off by a black silk vest with thin blue lines running vertical. He left off the pocket watch, a good decision if he wanted to insinuate time was not of consequence. But he hadn't made eye contact with her. As far as she knew, he hadn't caught her declaration about the name on the marriage license. She bit her lip. *Maybe he didn't know.* A private secret she shouldn't have shared with anyone but him.

Her father nodded. "We'd prefer honest speaking."

****

King was thankful Sam gave him the warning that Emma's parents were indeed visiting, and their very vocal opinion regarding the marriage. He'd had time to prepare, wash off the travel dust, and plan his strategy to convince them she was meant to remain with him. He'd even shaved the several days of beard growth.

Their marriage would be forever, 'til death do they part. He envisioned a small replica of Emma running around their house. He'd almost convinced himself that he loved her until he overheard her comment, the faithless conniving woman. When he entered the room, Mr. Cody sent him a stern frown, but her mother graced him with a smile.

King cleared his suddenly dry throat and walked to the side table and poured a glass of water from the decanter. He refused to let his hands tremble. "I have enjoyed your daughter's company these past few weeks. We've had a nice marriage arrangement. I'm sorry, Emma." He turned to look at her and their glances met, hers were glassy but he ignored the unshed tears. "That you didn't want to be married."

King placed the glass on the table, extended his hand to her. "Excuse us, I'd like to have a private word with Emma." She stood, and they walked into the office.

"You deceived me and signed Emmet instead of Emma. You said you loved me, and I believed you. Guess I was wrong. I let my feelings for you rule over good sense." He paced to the window and looked through the glass. "You'll have your freedom. I hope your journey back to Fort Wayne will be uneventful, and that you'll be happy with Bambridge."

He didn't give her time to explain the lie. He left the house, anger motivating his quick stride, and entered the barn. He jerked a saddle onto Maverick, leaned his head against the horse's faithful neck, and breathed in the scent of security. A man could always trust his horse.

He rode at break-neck speed, until he arrived at the monster of a house he'd created for his loving wife. At the edge of the clearing, he dismounted and sat on a boulder, placed his hands against the rough stone, and screamed out his anger and pain. Birds scattered from the trees. The howl of a nearby lone wolf replicated his disappointment. For the first time in his adult life, he'd considered letting his heart find and accept love, and she'd deceived him. His stomach muscles clenched. He forced the disappointment and the pain to recede.

She'd never loved him and only said the words to

keep the ruse viable. At least he didn't need a divorce. They'd never been legally married in the first place, only in his heart and soul.

Mounting Maverick, he'd returned to Pineview and resume the life he knew... No! He'd find the apparently "living" Jayden Drake, the very scoundrel who'd been robbing him for the past eight months and hang him high.

Chapter 24

The next day, Emma tied her bonnet low over her forehead to hide the puffiness making her face red and blotchy. She'd imagined Henry crawling into bed with her, kissing her, accepting her apology then they'd make love. His side of the bed remained empty. He'd never forgive her—all due to her stupidity.

The acute pain continued to invade her heart and brought fresh tears. She should have signed her real name. Henry hadn't asked her to marry him, but in retrospect the gesture of an impromptu marriage was sweet and romantic. She pulled on her travel gloves and gritted her teeth, preparing for a day of proving to him that she did love him. He never once said he loved her. Not during the vows, not afterwards, not anytime during the following weeks did he indicate he loved her. He called her "love" but in terms of endearment, not in the same way as saying *Emma, I love you.*

She would marry him again though if he would have her. She'd become a true wife, a forever wife. She glanced at her parents as they sat in the carriage taking in the scenery and asking questions about Courtland Overlook. A rough road, really two ruts which precariously tilted the carriage, led to their newly finished home on the hill.

"We'll just take a moment, so you can meet Danny," Emma said.

The three-story house, nestled in a group of blue spruce pine trees, was delightful and charming. The red brick front presented two main pillars showcasing the set of five concrete steps leading to the portico. Massive paned windows with half-moon arches at the top graced the sides of a maple door. A combination of oak leaves and fleur-de-lis scroll carpentry work detailed the wood panel.

Frank applied the brake and helped her mother from the carriage. Emma slid off the seat and glanced at the pen. Maverick snapped off pieces of wood as if ears of corn. Two feet away from the fence was fresh hay piled as tall as the water trough.

"I say, is that horse chewing on the rail of the corral?" her father asked, with a hint of disbelief.

"That horse will eat anything." She whistled. Maverick looked up, snorted, and resumed his snack. She laughed, and her parents chuckled.

Danny ran from the back of the house. "Howdy, Emma." He grinned and shoved his hands into the pockets of his new trousers.

"Danny, meet my parents, Mr. and Mrs. Cody, this is Danny Tuitt, who has recently become my son." She smiled and patted his shoulder.

"Hiya." He bowed and kicked a clod of dirt with his leather boot.

"Danny, would you mind taking Maverick out to the pasture?"

"Sure." He looked relieved and skipped toward the barn. "Nice to meet y'all."

"I'm going to see this horse that eats wood." Frank walked toward the corral.

Danny ran from the rear entrance of the barn,

carrying a horse lead.

Emma gazed at the house. She would never live in the beautiful home she and Henry had created.

"Are we going inside?"

"Yes," she hesitantly answered. What if he was there? She wanted to glance into his face, see his calmness. Some of her trepidation would be eliminated if she could have a little alone time with him. If he smiled and winked at her, everything would be all right.

"Danny's mother recently passed away. We've adopted him. He's already close to my heart." She climbed the stairs and walked into the house.

"That's a lot of responsibility, raising a child, especially as a single parent," her mother primly stated.

"I think I'll be a good mother." Emma didn't spout the thought lightly, she enjoyed being with Danny as he was so very easy to love. She recalled Henry hugging her to his side and saying, *I think you'll be a terrific mother.* "Besides, Henry and I will soon be remarried."

Emma gasped when they entered the foyer. "I cannot believe how much has been completed. It looks fabulous." She inhaled, taking in the new wood scent and the stringent paint fumes. The wood floor gleamed with fresh varnish. Thankfully, she'd made very few changes to the original design. Henry had exceptional taste in structure and details.

"Sam has been working night and day for the past month to install electricity. The eight-story windmill sitting at the precipice of the overlook should provide enough energy to run several electrical devices at once," she explained.

Her mother ran a hand over the maple banister. The stairs curved upward for the three stories. "Matthew

Bambridge can give you a house better than this one. He still wants you and asked us to persuade you to return with us."

"I'm not in love with Matthew, Mother." She held her hand to her waist to keep the jumping stomach nerves from exposing themselves.

"I like the entrance, Emma." Her father glanced at the twenty-foot ceilings.

"Thank you." She used her nervous energy to lead them through the house, pointing out the use of space. The French doors in the master suite lead out to a terrace, which provided a panoramic view of the evergreens, the valley below and in the distance, Pineview. Emma would have been able to look out from the bedroom or the parlor one flight below and see her husband returning home each night. Late summer aromas of wildflowers blossoming, freshly turned soil, and whispering winds blowing tree limbs added to the beauty.

She stared at the picturesque view of the valley, envisioning holding a baby of her own one day and rocking him or her, here, on the balcony.

"It's a beautiful view," her father said from beside her.

"Yes. Henry designed the house with a local architect."

Seconds later, they were in the guest bedrooms. She murmured to herself, "Is there a hidden door worked into the chifforobe?"

"What did you say?" Her father's concerned expression led her to shrug off the melancholy.

"Nothing, just thinking about the past. Ready to go?" Emma touched the wardrobe door on her way out.

In Pineview, she didn't see Henry at the saloon nor the Courtland-Carter Mine Office. At the hotel dining room, she chose a table by the window. No sign of him.

Later that night, she composed a letter, explaining she didn't want a marriage unless she was in love. She loved him and wanted to be married to him. His presence beside her at night was as necessary as breathing. To tell him she loved him each morning, to carry his baby under her breasts, these were all things she desired. She admitted she should have told him about Jayden's nefarious deeds but was afraid of what he would do, and then time passed, and the fact was more difficult to reveal. The truth came from her heart and translated easily onto the paper.

Emma pinched her cheeks to add color. The trauma of the last couple of months and the stress of her parents' fortnight-long visit exhausted her. Her parents puttered around the house, learned about electricity from Sam, and played with Maggie Mae.

The baby had grown tenfold in the past few weeks. Her eyes twinkled when someone talked to her. She smiled and held onto fingers as if they were lifelines. The doctor's test revealed Rachel didn't have syphilis and soon after her hair regained its luster and a natural pink appeared on the apples of her cheeks. She stopped visiting Jayden's burial site every day but continued to periodically put flowers on his and Danny's mother's graves.

Sam manipulated the power to the sewing machine, and the electricity flowed through the mechanism, allowing the sewing needle to work more often than not. Sam and Treasure's relationship blossomed into a full-fledged courtship. They were a sight to view in town, walking along the boardwalk, hand-in-hand. They'd even been caught kissing behind a tree at a church picnic.

Issues she thought were insurmountable weeks ago had been resolved. Two new designs went to the proprietors providing them a steady business. Treasure gained more confidence in her talents creating hats and fleur-de-lis cloth ornamentation. The outlaws, Eller's men, were either dead or in jail, and the leader, Eller, was in the government protective custody. Information about Mexico and politics would be extracted, before sticking him in the stockade. Why then, did she have astute and profound sadness.

Two weeks had passed since Danny delivered the letter to Henry, and the wait became unbearable. What if he didn't forgive her? Could she be a sedate housewife, or did she need constant chaos in order to be happy? No, she enjoyed a peaceful life before she came to Colorado, something unresolved troubled her, clouding her thoughts.

Emma meandered into the office and withdrew the account books from the desk. Typically, once a week she balanced the totals. She encouraged Rachel to manage her own accounts, but she claimed other responsibilities took priority, Maggie Mae being number one.

She opened to the last account entry and glanced out the window. Raja walked beside Rachel, with Maggie Mae snug in the sling carrier. Emma opened the window a pinch, intending to shout out for her to come inside and help with the books when the couple stopped in center of the path.

Raja lifted his large hand to Rachel's face and

caressed from the apple of her cheek to her jaw. His features softened, and his eyes held a lovelorn look. Rachel pressed her mouth into his palm. Emma felt like a voyeur and wanted to retreat but could not. When she was with Henry...did he look at her with a similar expression?

Emma turned away from the intimate scene. Her heart pounded, choking off her throat. Her friends were in love, but the differences in their backgrounds, religions, and countries would be problematic. She strode into the kitchen, made a cup of tea, and added one of Treasure's fresh blueberry scones on a tray. She returned to the library and peeked out the window. Thankfully, the couple had moved on and were circling the garden.

Snuggled into the desk chair, Emma processed and balanced the accounts. One item confused her. Had Millie's Fine Fashions overpaid for the dresses? She searched through the lower desk drawer for the contract. The document wasn't in the file. Huffing a frustrated breath, she ran upstairs to check her saddlebags for the paper. One side of the leather saddlebag was empty. The other pocket held the newspaper she'd obtained in the Boulder Newspaper office, containing the article about Jayden. Her heart thudded as loud as the blades on the windmill. A niggling thought crept forward, regarding Jayden's faux murder. Memories replayed: the trollop, sharp shooting, Boulder, her marriage, the outlaws, her parents, and Henry. Good and negative vibrations. Most of all Henry. Her body changed into a nervous mess of edginess. She pulled out the newspaper and dropped the saddlebags to straddle the railing.

The day she'd read the article, she'd been worried and anxious she'd be-discovered-to-be-a-female, so she hadn't grasped the details. She re-read the newsprint. Many bits of information formed a picture—one she didn't want to believe.

She dropped to the edge of a chair and listened to the sounds around her. The warblers singing, the laughter coming from her parents below on the terrace and the clunk, clunk, as Treasure cleared dishes from the barbeque lunch. The pleasant outdoor musical sounds didn't override the perception. In the Bible it was written all people have a sixth sense, an ability to see beyond the normal. Most individuals do not tune into this gift, and now she wished that she hadn't.

She needed to prove that the perception she'd gotten was wrong, that her mind was playing tricks on her. It couldn't be true. Regardless of how much she'd come to mistrust people in the past, now more than ever, she wanted to have faith in the goodness of her family and friends.

She grabbed the bag off the rail and headed for her room. She changed into her split light blue riding skirt and matching vest, with a personalized fleur-de-lis. The tiny bit of the blue and black waist coat, that Henry unknowingly donated to their cloth-drive, was special to her. She looked at herself in the mirror, touched the bit of cloth, and remembered the day she'd met him. God, he'd made her feel a yearning.

She placed the book for Otis Sue into the saddlebag. As she stuffed the newspaper back inside the pocket, the original contract from Millie's fell to the floor. She picked up the parchment and saddlebag and jogged down the stairs. Her parents were on the porch saying their farewells to Rachel and Maggie Mae. Sam waited patiently in the buggy. Emma laid the invoice on the desk and walked onto the veranda.

"Emma, we were looking for you. Come along and give me a hug," her mother said. Obediently, she went forward. "You can change your mind. We'll wait for you to pack."

"No, I'm going to try and make it right. He'll hear me out." Emma glanced toward her house, their home.

"It's been two weeks." Her mother frowned.

"If it's really over, I'll consider returning." She amended.

"Fool heartedness. I didn't raise my girl to take risks and chances like this," her father bellowed. He must have realized how he sounded and lowered his voice. "I love you, Emma. If either of you need anything, we'll be here for you. Consider the great divide between you and this man. Whatever you do, don't beg. It's unbecoming." His gruff voice held a hint of acceptance. He understood she'd do whatever she was inclined to do.

"Raja, it has been a pleasure being protected by you. I hope your journey home proves to be uneventful. Godspeed to you." She kissed him on each cheek and sidled beside Rachel who sniffed into her handkerchief. They stood, together, on the porch until the carriage wasn't visible.

She flipped the saddlebag over. "I'm going into town. Do you need anything?"

Rachel nodded. "Actually, yes, I'd like some white cotton to make a baby gown. Don't frown at me. I just need two yards. It'll fit into your saddlebag."

"Will do. It'll be a quick trip there and back." She

went into the barn, flung a blanket over Black Bart, threw the saddle on top and tightened the cinch. Before she put the bridle on, she handed him a sweet red apple. As he munched on the fruit, she placed the saddlebag on him and looked around for Danny. Black Bart finished the apple and snorted for more. She rubbed his cheek. "Later buddy. We need to ride like the wind in order to get into Pineview and back before dark."

The bridle in place, she climbed onto the mounting block and settled onto the saddle.

"Hello, Sam." Danny called out. His eyes must not have had time to adjust from the outdoor light into the interior's darkness.

"It's me, Danny. I'm going to ride into Pineview for a few minutes, and then I'll be back in case anyone is looking for me."

"Yer not 'pose to travel alone, Emma." He shoved his little chin into the air and placed his hands on his hips. Since he'd been living with them, Treasure made sure he was clean. His hair was a light brown, not the black she originally thought, and right now a wayward strand fell across his forehead.

"Fine, come with me then, and I'll buy you a sarsaparilla stick at the mercantile."

He tilted his head and half-closed an eyelid. "A sarsaparilla and cinnamon stick."

"Deal. Climb on, pronto. We're running out of time."

She nudged Black Bart with her knee. His nervous energy was as strong as hers. They trotted, slowing as they approached the road leading to her house. Maverick stood in the middle of the corral. Was Henry at the house? She kept on going, and when she was safely past Courtland Overlook, she let Black Bart gallop as he longed to do. Danny whooped in delight.

Emma approached Pineview from the southside and meandered through the alley to King's Court. Danny slid to the ground, and after she dismounted and tied Black Bart's reins to the hitching post, she tugged the saddlebag. Withdrawing the newspaper, she folded it so the article about Jayden was in front.

"Danny, look at the name in this article. Do you know who this man is?"

He squinted his eyes, and then shook his head. "Nah, I don't think so."

"The newspaper states Raymond Long spends all day playing cards at King's Court. You've never seen him?" She focused on the lad. The additional information made his face brighten.

"Yeah, I've seen him. He's there all the time."

"Could you point him out to me?"

"Why?" He placed his hands on his hips, elbows jutted to the sides. A flash of sadness overcame her, he exactly mimicked Henry.

"I have a couple of questions to ask him. Now, let's move."

She withdrew two silver coins from her skirt pocket. "We'll walk in, and you'll point him out. Then you can take this money down to the mercantile and buy whatever you want. Wait for me there. Do not leave that store, got it?"

"It'll only take me a minute to buy the candy. Why do I have to wait?"

"Because I'd worry about you. I wouldn't know where to find you, and we've only a short amount of time."

"I want to go see my friend, Wyatt."

"Oh, Danny, I'm sorry. Perhaps next time you could visit or go invite him to come to our house tomorrow, and you can show him your new room. How about doing that first, and then go to the mercantile?" She hugged him close and didn't let go until he fidgeted.

"All right. You won't yammer forever. You'll only stay talkin' to ole man Long a minute, right?"

"Yes, I promise. I'll ask him a couple of questions, then go to the store." She drew a cross on her chest.

"Come on then." He tugged her hand and led her through the rat-infested hallway. "There he is." Danny whispered and took off through the hallway, slamming the exit door. Ole man Long sat at the bar with an empty beer mug in front of him.

She drew a deep breath, dug a dollar out of her pocket, and hoped the bribe would be enough. The man had ragged clothing on his thin body. His overcoat hung along his side, nearly touching the sticky floor. His grey and white beard rested on his chest. Emma could swear she heard a ping as a flea jumped from his head to the back of his coat and onto the floor.

She shook off the cold chills and vowed to take a long soak in the tub when she got home. Most of all, her clothes would need to be decontaminated. Regardless of how disgusting the man was, she needed to put her suspicions to rest.

"Mr. Long?"

He turned his brown leather eyes toward her. "Ya, that's me."

His breath smelled like goat cheese and musty socks. She lowered her head, so her nose would be downwind.

"I'd like to ask you about the women you saw running away after Jayden Drake was shot."

"I ain't tellin' nothin'. No one believes me no how." He turned about and lifted his empty mug.

"Looks like you need another drink."

He sat up straighter in the chair. "Hey, Martin, I need a beer."

"No credit for you, Raymond." Martin turned around. A surprised expression lit his features. "Mrs. Courtland. Howdy. Is King with you? We haven't seen him since he sold the place." He shouted the end of the sentence.

This sent her mind spinning. "No, Martin, I'm sorry he's not."

He frowned. "Oh, well, what can I get you?"

"I want to buy Mr. Long a beer." She gave him a casual, good-to-be-neighborly smile.

Martin gave her another frown, deeper, but drew the beer from the tap. He sat the mug on the wood counter with a thunk, and a few foamy bubbles flowed over the side. She climbed onto the stool next to the man and laid the silver dollar on the bar. "You can probably get another beer or two out of this dollar, if you answer my questions."

He took a long drink. She could envision a flea leaping off his beard as his throat moved. Finally, he set the mug down. "What do you want to know?"

"In the newspaper you stated you saw the woman in a brown dress leave twice."

"That's right. I heard the gun shot. A few minutes later the whore came running down the stairs. I went back to drinking my beer and several minutes later, when I stood to leave, she tripped as she rounded the corner, headed toward the back door."

"Are you sure it was the same woman?"

He squished his face and ran a hand through his beard. She shuddered and wiped her hands over her sleeves.

"Brown dress, brown hair, 'bout the size of Lulu over thar." He nodded toward the stairs.

She glanced at Lulu, who stood near the piano flipping through sheets of music. She was slightly shorter than five foot seven. "The newspaper indicated a mole was near her mouth. Did both women have a mole?"

"Don't rightly know. The first time I saw her, she wore a large brown hat, and carried a bag with clothes comin' out on one end. The next time, she was wearin' a fish net over her face. Caused her to trip I bet ya."

"Did you notice her shoes?"

Raymond looked like he enjoyed the attention, and the words flew out. "Nah. The Swede who stays at the boarding house came in for a drink. He buys me one or two beers when he gets one."

She raised a brow, and he looked away. "Thank you, Mr. Long."

"Any time, Mrs. Courtland." He picked up the silver dollar and spun it in the beer residue.

She stood. "Good-bye, Martin."

"Good-bye, Mrs. Courtland." Martin swiped a cloth across a mug.

Her heart stopped beating. Hopefully, she could right the relationship, and she would be Mrs. Courtland. Emma walked through the door and into the alley. She instantly removed the vest, shook the material, and hung it on the saddle horn. She rubbed her hands up and down her arms and along her skirt.

"What the hell are you doin'?" Danny stood in front of her, holding a stick of candy.

"We need to talk about your language and also about schooling. Don't think I missed the fact that you couldn't read the name Long in the paper." She removed a boot and held it upside down.

"I ain't goin' ta school." His lips tightened. She didn't think his little jaw could twitch any harder.

Little did he know he'd already started learning. She replaced her boot, threw on the vest and knelt in front of him. "What if Sam teaches you? At home. You couldn't ask for a more knowledgeable person. He'll help you read and do math."

His jaw relaxed. He tilted his head. "So, no one will know I'm goin' ta school?"

"No, because it'll be our little secret. Do you know Mr. Mark Twain?" She began to swipe her clothes again. Her head itched.

"Is he the new feller at the livery?" He put the end of a candy stick between his lips.

"No, he is a man who writes stories about a little boy like you. Twelve-year old Tom has great adventures. Frog races, and he and his friend Huck Finn took a homemade raft on the Mississippi River pretending to be pirates and hunting for treasure."

"What happens to this boy? Did he find the treasure?" He straddled the rail, with one hand on the candy stick and the other one pushing Black Bart away. Her horse did love sugar.

"Mark Twain said, 'A man who does not read good books has no advantage over the man who can't read them.' I'm certain, as a man, you'd want to read good books. When I order supplies, do you want me to get a couple of stories about Tom Sawyer, and you can discover if he finds a treasure?"

"I guess."

She touched the tip of his nose, then untied Black Bart from the hitching rail. Sam was right, given a little time, the boy was ready for proper learning.

"Come on buddy, we need to deliver a book to Otis at the telegraph office and get cloth for Rachel and items for learning." He skipped along beside her. What a change from a few months ago when he held up a rat, hoping for a coin. She tousled his hair. "We have to take a bath when we get home."

"Nun na. I took one this mornin'."

"I sat beside Long. He had bugs, which means by the time we get home we could have bugs. I can't let you sleep in a nice clean bed with bugs crawling all over you."

"Hel…" She glared at him. "Heck," he amended.

"I know, buddy." She tied Black Bart to the hitching post in front of the telegraph office. Otis moved around inside. She removed the saddlebag and took a deep breath.

Danny wiped his sticky fingers on his trousers, and they entered the building. The interior smelled musty and despite the large window the interior was dark.

"Hi ya, Otis," Danny rushed up to the counter. His chin barely reached the edge.

"Hi ya, Danny. Miss Emma, or rather Mrs. Courtland."

"Good-afternoon, Otis. I have something for you." She unfastened the latch on the saddlebag and withdrew the dime novel and handed the book to her cousin's biggest fan.

"You said I would meet him in person." Otis's voice had an edge.

"You might, the next time he visits. The government called him to duty."

Otis grabbed the book, turned it over, then handed her a stack of envelopes. "Here's your mail."

Was he trying to make her feel better about his sharp retort? While Otis reviewed the contents of the book, she opened a package from Boulder, Colorado and evaluated the picture. Danny leaned over her arm.

"How do I know this is actually his signature and not yours?" Otis whined.

"By looking at this photograph." She turned the photo around. In front of a bookstore, Bill held the book in one hand, with his arm draped over her shoulder. Raja stood on the other side of Bill. Henry held onto her hand.

"I'll be damned." Otis whistled. "I have Buffalo Bill's autograph."

Emma turned the photograph around again and gave a final look at Henry.

Chapter 25

Black Bart pranced along the street, and King caught sight of Emma's overlarge hat before the rest of the party came into view. He pivoted, stood his back pressed against the wood of the saloon door preventing it from swinging back and forth. He lifted the whisky bottle and drank. He couldn't watch her ride through town and out of his life.

"King, come upstairs with me. I'll make you forget her," Lulu whispered and nipped at his ear.

He turned into her bony body and imagined kissing her rouged lips. She gripped his cock. He closed his eyelids and inhaled. Damn, nearly three-fourths of a bottle of Tennessee's best whisky, and he still couldn't get Emma Cody out of his mind.

"I need to get some shut eye." He shoved her clinging sweat scented body and staggered to his office. A large poster, nailed to the door, proclaimed, *King, you need to leave. Get out within four hours. It's no longer your office. Signed, the management.* He chuckled, wadded the paper, and tossed it down the hallway. He opened the door, fell forward, and stubbed his toe on the stacked furniture two feet from the entrance. "Blasted management."

King managed to get onto his horse and ride to his new house, then nothing but darkness.

The punch to his arm became a painful annoyance.

"King."

"God almighty, stop screaming in my ear." He slid his tongue across his fuzzy teeth and swallowed, trying to lubricate his cotton mouth. King glanced around. He was in his bedroom at Courtland Overlook, on top of an unmade bed. *How did I get here?*

"Come on, it's time to go," the dark husky voice insisted.

****

Emma stared at Sam. "What are you wearing?" He stood as tall as Rachel.

"I'm ready." Sam held out his hand, and Rachel handed him a light bulb. "Keep your comments to yourself and turn on the switch."

The parlor grew as bright as the afternoon sun, which had fallen beyond the horizon.

"They're special boots we created, to make me taller, so I could reach higher locations." He smiled, making his eyes disappear.

"Is this the first time you've worn them?" She pivoted. "I'll go to this side, in case you fall off the stilts, and catch you."

"No, it's taken me a couple of times to get used to walking in them." With a feminine sway to his hips, he sidled to a chair, dropped, and removed them.

Emma inhaled. Long said the woman tripped when she came around the corner. Could Sam have been the other "woman" the day faux Jayden was killed? Sam adored Rachel, and he'd want to protect her. If Sam knew Jayden cheated on Rachel, he could have been angry enough to kill him.

"Are we finished here?" Rachel picked up a dress draped over a chair.

"Yes, thank you for your help."

Emma touched the rich brown satin gown. "What are you doing with this dress?"

"It has stains that I can't get out. Unlike someone, I continued to exercise with Raja, so I don't need the empire waistline any longer."

"I continued to get my exercise in the morning, just in another way." She ignored Rachel's prim and proper expression and trotted into the kitchen.

Danny came from the washroom, a white towel wrapped around his waist and a bundle of clothes tucked under his arm. She giggled. "You look and smell nice, Danny. Your face is all bright and shiny."

He glared. "I smell like something Treasure uses to dust the furniture. People will think I've been dustin'." He shoved the possibly bug-ridden clothes into her arms. "Here ya go."

She laughed. "I'll work on the soap and lotion formula. Maybe I should use less lemon balm and more cedarwood."

"Yep." He stiffened his back, continued along the hallway and slammed his bedroom door.

She went upstairs to get a change of clothing, a leather satchel to put the pest-ridden clothes in, and returned to the washroom. After shoving Danny's clothes in the poke, she undressed, carefully putting the special fleur-de-lis made from Henry's vest aside. She stuffed her clothes in the bag and closed the leather satchel. Filling the hip bath with as much hot water as possible, she used lavender scented soap, climbed in, and scrubbed her scalp and skin until it was pink. Finished, she applied lotion to help ease the tenderness. Dressed, her hair brushed and braided, she soaked the pest filled clothes in the wash tub.

To eliminate the boredom of the tedious clothes washing task, she contemplated her suppositions. There were three possible suspects for the murder: Bell the soiled dove, Sam, or Rachel. All three possessed logical reasons to want him dead. The whore because he could have told her their contract was over. Sam protected Rachel. Rachel had been betrayed. Passion was the number one cause of murder, or was it greed?

Bell would help Jayden disguise another man to pose as himself, then he'd put on a brown dress and walk out. She shoved the clean wet clothes through the wringer, walked outside and hung the garments on the clothesline. She plucked a couple of small yellow apples off the tree beside the barn and called Black Bart and Brandy to the fence. Giving each of them an apple, a little bit of sweet talk, and quick rub down of their heads and necks, they soon grew bored and circled the corral.

She wanted to believe the soiled dove was guilty, but she suspected she may have been a witness. Sam. His quick temper would make him number one on the suspect list, no doubt about that, but he wouldn't take a life. Could Rachel have been the killer? She'd voiced her unhappiness and suggested Emma just have sex with Henry and not get married. Her fairytale marriage became a nightmare. Could she have ended everything so violently? What a harsh dose of macabre reality. Both of their ideal worlds had been diminished. Emma refused to let her life and newfound love disappear.

Chapter 26

Emma loosely tied Black Bart's reins to the hitching post. Rachel was on the front porch, rocking the baby. The swollen wood of the chair creaked and moaned creating its own rhythm. She kissed Maggie's sweet baby-scented skin. "Good morning."

"Good morning to you, too. Where are you off to?" Rachel said in a harsh, angry voice, making the gray cast on her face all the more ghoulish.

She glanced toward Henry's house. "Thought I'd take a little ride, let Black Bart get some exercise."

"Danny told me you talked to the man at the saloon yesterday. The one who witnessed the murder." Rachel shouted, making Maggie fuss.

Emma dropped to her knees in front of the rocker; put one hand on Rachel's knee and one on Maggie's back and rubbed soothing smooth circles. "Please tell me what's bothering you. You're not happy. Since we buried Jayden, you come and go into depression."

Treasure stood at the edge of the porch. Emma lifted Maggie Mae and carried her to the unsmiling woman. Rachel didn't say anything. Her face went from angry to weary. Her bow-shaped mouth turned down and tears rolled along her cheeks. Treasure shook her head and carried the baby into the house. Fearing the worst, Emma sat on the bench seat.

"Rachel, it is time to tell the truth. You cannot

carry the weight of the guilt with you any longer." The pain of the knowledge made her heart ache. She clasped her hands together between her breasts. *The poets were truthful, life is ever-changing.*

"I'm sorry." Rachel stammered. "Jayden told me about her before we were married. I thought she was in his past, but she was living in Boulder. I went into Pineview and realized the Bell he frequented was Isabella, his first love. I issued an ultimatum. Either he kept his mistress or me. Since I carried his child, he chose me. At least, I thought he'd chosen me. A few days before you were to arrive, Jayden said he wanted to visit King in Pineview. An inventor of mechanics was going to be in Boulder, so he thought he'd go there as well."

Rachel stood from the rocker and crossed her arms at her stomach. "I knew he was lying. He planned to go to her. Morning sickness made me unavailable to him for the first few months, then I didn't want to engage in the act. I know he tried to restrain the urges. He worked on his inventions and walked the snow-covered grounds for hours. I unlocked the gun cabinet in his library and took a pistol. I put on a brown dress and net hat to hide my features." She wiped the tears off her chin.

"Sam hooked up the carriage for me, and I insisted I could travel alone and would enjoy my own company. I drove the carriage behind King's Court and tied the horse to the post. As I walked past Henry's office, I overheard Miss Cat yelling at Jayden about Bell. I plastered myself against the wall. Jayden stormed out of the office, and I followed him up the stairs." She paused, twisting her hands.

"You heard her doing her job."

"She loved him, no, she was obsessed with him. I opened the door as Jayden was getting undressed. That woman smiled at me, like that evil black cat that lived next door to you." She sat on the rocker. "He didn't know I'd entered the room. Isabella said, 'By the way, I have syphilis, which means you do as well.' His response was, 'How could you do this to me? You know I'm not leaving Rachel.' I drew the gun out of my purse and cocked it. He either heard the sound or noticed the change on his lover's face."

Emma lifted Rachel's hand and held it tight in hers. "Tell, me what happened."

"I shouldn't have let him leave. Would he be alive if I had kept him with me? He reached toward me, but I couldn't let him touch me. I dropped the gun and turned to run out the door. He grabbed my arm, turned me about and pulled me close. Blood squirted all over my dress. He said, 'Rachel, I love you,' and dropped to the floor." She clasped her hands. "He saved my life."

"Bell raised the gun, again. I flew out the door, and down the stairs. I didn't stop gasping for breath until I was home. Later that night, Sam helped me remove the blood. He consoled me, until it was time to leave to get you. Sam left, Jayden's body arrived, and I couldn't let him go. I tried to forget, and you helped me, with the dress making, the antics between you and Henry, and Raja."

Rachel had finished telling her story, relieving her guilt. A horse galloped along the lane, getting closer to the house. Emma handed her a handkerchief and turned to see who was visiting. Sheriff Jones' horse glistened with sweat, as if the poor fellow had been ridden hard. The lawman dismounted and removed his hat, revealing greasy dark gray hair.

"Ladies."

"Sheriff." Rachel twitched in her seat.

"Sheriff Jones." She didn't have respect for the man, and his lack of authority or pride in his job. Did he finally have a lead on the men who attacked her, who were already in custody?

"Mrs. Drake, I'm sorry to bear such bad news," he paused.

Emma leaned against the bench. She couldn't get her stomach muscles to unclench. Henry, something has happened to him. He hadn't responded to her letter, maybe he couldn't.

"A girl from the saloon came forward and said she was an eyewitness. Claims she saw you leaving the room after Jayden Drake was shot. You held a smoking gun. You're under arrest for the murder of your husband."

What? Part of her rejoiced in knowing the news wasn't about Henry. She jumped to a stand. "That's a lie, she wouldn't harm a flea. A prostitute shot Jayden. Maybe the one who claimed to have seen Rachel."

Rachel's face contorted, and her eyes sparkled with rage. "You're not welcome in my home sheriff," she screamed.

"Come along, Mrs. Drake, you'll get a chance to tell your story to the circuit judge next week."

"I need to get my baby," she whispered, defeat so pronounced in her voice she gave the impression she was on her way to the gallows.

"You can't have a baby in the jail," Sheriff Jones blustered.

"She's not guilty. She's tired and scared." She held

onto Rachel's hand. "Do you want to starve a baby, Sheriff Jones?" She spewed the words with enough anger he took a step backward.

He scratched the grease coated gray filaments of hair.

"Why can't we stay here, and Rachel will go to Pineview when the judge arrives?" Emma suggested.

"That's not the way the law works. Stay out of this, Mrs. Courtland." The sheriff spit brown liquid onto the boxwood bushes in front of the porch.

"I need to keep my baby with me," Rachel begged. Her shoulders shook and her hands twisted.

"She has to feed her baby." Emma fisted her hands at her sides.

"No baby," he responded.

"What if Treasure kept Maggie at the hotel and brought her down every couple of hours to nurture? Is that all right with you, Sheriff Jones?" Emma's distain shot through the sarcasm, but he didn't flinch.

"She can't stay overnight. No bawling. No excretion."

"I cannot dictate when my daughter has a bowel movement." Rachel wiped tears from her face.

"We need to get the squalling, dung producing baby, and a change of clothing for her mother," Emma spat.

Treasure waited in the foyer, clearly listening to the conversation.

"You get the baby and items they'll need." Emma loosely braided her hair as they ran upstairs.

Treasure went into the master bedroom, and Emma went into her bedroom, snatched a garter from the dresser and grabbed Henry's pocket knife, then went into Rachel's room.

"Where are you going?" Danny asked, when Emma carried a carpetbag into the hallway.

"Rachel has to go to town for a few days. Treasure's going to take Maggie and stay in a hotel. Do you want to go?"

He scrunched his face. The clever young man knew something was amiss. "I'll go."

At the top of staircase, she stopped and turned toward him. "Do you know where Bell Grind went after she left the saloon?"

"Blair's Mine. Why?"

"I need to find her. Please help Treasure and Rachel as much as possible the next couple of days. Protect them. They're your family too. Okay?"

He shuffled from foot to foot. "Are you going ta do something you're not 'suppose ta?"

"I'm going to help someone I love."

Danny took hold of her arm. "I lost one mother. I don't want to lose another."

She grabbed him and held tight. "I'll be careful, and I'll come back to you."

"Promise?"

She kissed his cheek. "Promise."

He didn't wipe his face like usual.

Sam grumbled as he loaded the carriage with the items needed for the next few days. He reluctantly agreed to stay at the house and take care of the animals. The sheriff tied his horse to the back, the others silently boarded.

Danny kneeled on the coach seat and watched her. She waved, mounted Black Bart, then rode toward Blair's Mine.

"How much farther is it?" Emma urged Black Bart forward. Now she was talking to her horse. Times were gloomy, for sure. She glanced at the mountain range, trying to see the mine and her destination. "The wizen old man at the crossroads told us it's a slice of the mountain that has been cut away and can be seen from miles away."

Squinting into the sun, she pulled her brown leather gloves tighter onto her fingers. "So, carry on my steed."

She glanced toward the cloud encrusted massive amount of rock sprinkled with trees and snow. A waterfall gushed on the left side of the dirt road. A hawk swooped, screeching as its claws snatched a small furry creature.

Sam was innocent. She'd asked him about Rachel's involvement in the shooting. Sam did carry a gun, most men in the west toted a firearm, but he'd never shot anyone. At the time of the shooting, Sam went with Henry's partner to measure land at Crimson Creek. Rachel's story about the prostitute, Bell Grind, had to be true.

If she found Miss Grind, how would she get her to confess? Black Bart cautiously moved around a bend. Bell had left Pineview before Emma arrived, so she wouldn't recognize her as Jayden's half-sister. She could go into the camp as a soiled dove, get close to Bell and encourage her to confess.

"How about Road ta Bliss?" she asked Black Bart. The thin air made her voice sound breathy. She rather liked the new voice; it helped her get into character as a lady of the evening. He shook his head, his mane glistened in the sun.

"We have a name then. There it is." She was at the

base of the mountain admiring the smattering of pine trees growing on the upward slope. A few feet in front of them, a town of canvas tents nestled together on barren ground. Plumes of smoke rose from the center of the hamlet sprinkling the air with wood-scented fog and roasting meat. Her stomach rumbled. She'd left in a hurry, without regard to food and water. Right now, she'd appreciate chewing on the aromatic feast infusing the area.

She slowly meandered into the camp. A wooden sign hung outside of a natural rock gateway, *Blair's Mine*. Three shoeless children ran through the slices of free space between the tents. Around a fire stood two older women wearing gray dresses and raggedy scarves. They stopped their tasks and with dazed stares watched her pass.

An eerie silence coursed through the campsite. Cows, at the back of the town, stopped mooing and the chickens' clucks muted. The scene reminded her of a penny novel. Riders rode through Dodge, and all the people came outside to silently watch the good guy's ride, begging them to continue on but hoping they would stay.

At the end of the main row of tents stood a black-haired woman with painted red cheeks and a bow-shaped mouth. Her bosom drooped in the low-cut dress, once a bright blue color had faded from numerous washings. The frayed hem exposed scuffed brown boots. Fear flicked across her eyes, but her mouth presented an angry frown.

Emma pretended to lose control of her horse, keeping her focus on the woman. "What the Sam hell are ya doing? You cain't move that way."

Laughter chimed throughout the gathered crowd, enjoying the impromptu show.

She tried to maintain her act. Black Bart tossed his head as if taking a bow. The woman snickered and sashayed off to a tent three down.

The miners, noticing the spectacle had ended, returned to their noon meals or to their tents. The children continued to run around the camp. Her horse pranced in place. She'd loosened the bead on her hat strings letting the beaver and felt Stetson to fall and rest on her back.

"Is there sumptin' I can do to help you, Miss?" A man, dressed fully in black from ground up lifted his pale, round, hairless face. "Name's Cal Salisbury, Mayor of Blair's Mine camp."

Why would people elect a mayor for a mining camp? She nodded and waved. "Name's Emma Courtland. I'm looking for a friend. A loved one passed on and left her some money in his will. Wanted to find her and let her know."

He ran a gnarled hand through white sprinkled gray hair. "Who is this woman you're lookin' for?"

She held her hand on top of the pearl handle of her pistol. "She goes by the name of Bell Grind. Also, do you have any lodging for rent? I'll need a place to sleep for one night."

"Charles just died. You can use his tent. I'll show you where it's staked, and then I'll find Bell and ask her if she's interested in talking to you." The mayor led her through the maze of tents.

She remained seated on Black Bart and ambled along. Her breath puffed out in white clouds as she exhaled. Colder in the mountains, she hoped the thin split skirt and lamb's wool jacket would keep her warm.

The mayor stopped in front of a tent, the right flap had been tied back, and except for a cot and a sawhorse the inside was empty. "How did Charles die?" If he died of black plague or flu she wasn't sleeping inside that teepee.

"Fell into a shaft, broke his neck." The mayor turned away.

"How much do I owe you for the rent?" she called out.

"Nothin', as you own the land anyway, Mrs. Courtland."

She swung her glance toward him, but he was out of sight. Henry owned the land and the mine. His brilliant business success continued to surprise her. She led Black Bart to the tree trunk and attached his tether to a branch. He continued to have a wide-eyed look about him, but munched on wheatgrass or buffalo grass, she'd yet been able to identify the plants. She released the saddlebag and bedroll and placed them on the ground. After removing the saddle, she carried all of the items into the tent. A wooden sawhorse took up one corner of the small tent, so she placed the saddle on top.

She hung her hat, by the string, on a metal bar holding the tent erect and busied herself, spreading the blankets out on the cot. It was small, but she didn't think she'd sleep very much. She plopped onto the makeshift bed. What now?

She'd found the place. The mayor would tell Bell Grind to see her. And because money was involved Bell would come, so how should she approach the topic of Jayden? She crossed her legs and kicked her boot forward dislodging a small rock. *Come on, come see me.*

"Hello." The faded blue dress woman she'd seen earlier tucked her head inside the tent. "The mayor said you had an inheritance for me?"

"Yes, please come in."

"Who are you?" She'd thrown on a red shawl and held the material tight in her fist. Her white knuckles appeared pronounced and weathered against the deep crimson of the wrap. Her pocket bulged, so she could be carrying a weapon. The gun that killed Jayden?

She released the strap holding her Colt within the confines. *Start with the truth and see how that works out.* "I'm Emma Courtland, Henry's wife."

"I don't believe you. King would never marry, and he certainly wouldn't fall in love with a prissy miss like you." Bell tossed a black curl over her shoulder.

"Hum, I thought that would work. My real name is Road Ta Bliss, and I was sent by Miss Cat."

"What message did she send?" Bell's close scrutiny made her nervous. As anticipated, Miss Cat was involved with the gang and robberies.

"You've a substantial amount of money, an inheritance," she said. "You just need to return to Pineview, with me, to get the cash."

"How much money?"

"Ten thousand dollars." The lie came fast and sounded believable.

"I can't return to Pineview. I'll be murdered," she croaked out.

"You didn't ask who left you money. Do you know?"

"Of course, Jayden Drake. He loved me." Bell swayed.

303

"Here, sit down." She rushed forward to help the prostitute sit on the cot. "Put your head between your knees and take deep breaths. I've heard you have syphilis. One word to the mayor, and you'll be run out of camp." She knelt in front of the shaking woman. "Bell, tell me what happened the day Jayden was killed."

"I can't." She grabbed the edge of the cot.

"Whether you gave the disease to Jayden or him to you, it doesn't matter. If you stay here, you'll die alone and be robbed when you're unable to get off the cot. If you come back to Pineview, I'll find an asylum, and you'll spend your last days being cared for by professionals."

"I'm scared," she whispered, and her mouth quivered, the mole fluctuated up and down in quick succession. "Jayden led the gang, and they think I have the loot."

Emma sat beside her on the cot. "Tell me where the gang can be located."

"Why should I?" Bell picked up the edge of her wrap.

"It'll be easier for you if you tell someone, and I'm a workin' girl just like you. Who else would understand as well as me?" She patted the woman's thick knee.

"Jayden came to see me, told me about the disease. I knew my life was over. Regardless of how much he said he loved me; he would never leave his wife. I said things I shouldn't have, but anger makes strange bedfellows, and we made love. When he was getting out of bed, a woman walked inside the room. She was wearing a brown silk dress and a black hat with a net pulled over her face to disguise her features. She wasn't like us, Bliss. She threw an identical gown at me and told me to get dressed. She waved a gun. He apologized for the error of his ways. 'What about killing me with the disease?' she said and shot him through the heart." Bell rose from the cot and walked toward the tent opening.

"Why wouldn't she shoot you?" The dead man had half his face missing.

Bell shrugged. "She told me I could never return to Pineview and never tell anyone about her killing Jayden."

"Gather your things. I'll help you. We'll ride to Fort Collins tomorrow, and I'll arrange for your care and transfer of the money. You cannot repeat this story to anyone. They won't believe you."

"Thank you, Bliss." She walked out of the tent.

Bell possessed a good vocabulary and diction, so how did she become a soiled dove? Emma tied the flaps together and moved the sawhorse to block the entrance. She snuggled onto the bed wearing all of her clothes. For protection, she tucked her pistol under the folded blanket acting as a pillow and didn't question if she would be able to shoot another human.

Henry, will you ever forgive me? She wanted the touch of his rough feet on her calves, his sensuous caresses, and his lips making her feel desired. They were meant to be together. She sniffed, then gave in to the river of tears. Maybe he was right. She was impetuous.

Sleep eluded her, especially considering the worry about Rachel. Jayden had created a calamitous event. Could Bell or another woman be furious enough to kill his double and frame Rachel?

Tomorrow, she intended to find the truth. She would take Bell, the tramp, to Pineview and hand her over to the sheriff. Jail for Bell and God willing, Rachel would be released.

"Hi ya Bell, you can't go in thar. The mayor's orders were for me to guard Mrs. Courtland and not let anyone inside." A brassy toned voice penetrated the canvas.

"Bliss?" Bell shouted.

Emma pulled back a tent flap. A six-foot man, brawny arms, and a dirt brown cowboy hat atop of red hair, stared at her. His eyes widened. "Lordy."

"Thank you, sir, for guarding me last night, and please thank the mayor for me. I'll tell Henry how much you all helped, while I was here." She broadcasted a smile. He continued to stare. "Come in, Bell."

Bell clutched one midnight blue velvet bag of items. A jewelry case popped out of the sides and a hair brush extended through the top. Her glance slid to the bed.

"You sound as if you've had some education. What prompted you to become a working gal?"

Bell snorted and her eyes took on a glassy expression. "I once graced the halls of the wealthy and had a dictated background of decorum training. Beaus lined my parents' sidewalk to have a moment of time with me. It didn't matter what token they brought with them; I could not pull myself away from Jayden. We were sweethearts, and he was my first lover. He did his duty when his parents traded him off to Rachel for a sizable dowry."

"You followed him to Colorado?" He begged to

marry Rachel.

"He asked me to come to Colorado. After two years of marriage, he wasn't happy. He needed me, and I needed him." Bell lowered the bag to the floor and sat on the rumpled blankets.

She was probably comfortable on an unmade bed, Emma ungraciously thought. "Could he have had another woman?"

Bell jerked her head up and hissed, "No. He only wanted me."

She wanted to retort, he let you work in a brothel. "Ready to go?"

"Yes." Bell rose from the cot, grabbed her bag and strut from the tent.

Emma carried the rolled blanket, bags, and saddle. After outfitting Black Bart, she settled onto his back and extended a hand. Bell climbed on behind her. Silently, they made their way around the camp until they were at the base of the mountain, where they picked up speed.

"So, you're married to Henry Courtland after all?" Bell asked.

"What's your last name?" She refused to talk about Henry. She'd never share her troubles with a woman who tried to kill her brother and gave a death-sentence-disease to unknowing men.

"I get it, nothing personal. So, they believed Jayden really died. How much did he leave me?" Bell asked.

"You got everything, Bell," Emma whispered. Bell played a part of the double exchange and rejoiced in the outcome. One truth revealed.

"His wife got nothing?"

"No," she gritted between her teeth, "his wife got

nothing from him."

"I know a shortcut, turn along this path." Bell pointed to the right.

"I make a lotion that will help you with those dry callused hands."

"Just ride."

Chapter 27

The grit in King's eyes concentrated on the lower lid as he glanced at his friend. "One more word, Aubrey, and I'll toss you off the next cliff." Front Range Mountain's cooling beauty didn't aid him as a pick tool hammered away at his head.

"Head still feels like a crevice tool is prying at it?" Aubrey laughed. If King could conjure up the energy, the horse would be riderless. "Your house is coming along. Now that you have a bed in the master bedroom you might consider other furniture to go with it."

"Are you seriously talking about decorating, when you should keep both eyes peeled for the Relay Gang?" he groused. "Did you find out the reason your married girlfriend's fingers were in my files?"

"She was searching for a tract of land. Her husband asked her to get close to me and get information." He sighed. "Not my secret affair anymore."

"Sorry, but all for the best. When we get to Blair's Mine, I want to question Bell Grind about Jayden's murder."

"Rumor has it a prostitute ran from the room after the gunshot exploded. Do you think it was Bell who shot Jayden?"

"It's a possibility."

"Do you want to talk about the letter clutched in your hand yesterday?" Aubrey kneed his horse to navigate around a boulder.

"Nothing to talk about." King tugged his hat lower on his forehead.

"You know of course after I pried it out of your hands, I read it. You snore, by the way."

He stopped Maverick in the middle of the path. "You went too far, Carter. You had no right to read my personal letter."

Aubrey halted his brown horse, tipped back his hat, and turned. "It 'pears as if I hit a sore spot. Emma loves you and apologized. Why don't you give her a second chance?"

"You haven't met the conniving woman. How can you back her?"

"You're relaxing toward her a little. The first day, after you received the letter, she was a bitch, and now's she a conniving woman. She seemed sincere in her letter."

"Doesn't matter now. They've returned to Fort Wayne."

He rounded the bend and two men jumped from the boulders. Caught off guard and weighted by the attacker's bulk, King fell to the ground. The raider jumped up and lunged at the bag attached to Maverick's saddle.

King had secured the bag, and a tug wouldn't free it. The bandit climbed onto Maverick. A gunshot pinged off a rock. His faithful steed reared. Both his front legs lifted straight into the air. The man held onto the reins keeping his boots in the stirrups tilted to the side. King took the opportunity to use his Colt to knock the gun from the outlaw's hand, then took hold of the bridle. "Whoa, boy. Easy." Maverick relaxed.

The renegade lifted his boot from the stirrup and kicked. King jumped to the side, then shoved his gun against the man's chest. "Get down."

"Aubrey?"

"Over here," he panted.

"You shot?" King bumped the barrel into the bandit a second time. "Give me a reason to shoot." The blackguard dismounted.

"No." Aubrey limped into the passageway. His horse followed. "The other one got away."

King nodded. "Where's your camp?" Fierceness, seldom leaving his lips, flew as fast as the breeze.

"No tal, los inglese."

King holstered his gun, grabbed the man's lapels and jerked him forward. "I've got a lot of anger in me, because I'm tired of people taking what belongs to me. I'm going to beat you, build a fire, and burn holes into your personal spots." He ground his teeth together, and his pulse vibrated in his right jaw. "Lugar, camp site."

"Si." The man must have realized the thin thread on which he was balanced. "Mountain pass near Blair's Mine." His English suddenly improved. "Small camp near stream, north-west."

"Let's tie him up, put him on the ass of his mule and drag him along. We can throw him in as a bargaining chip." King winced at the increased pounding in his head.

Aubrey grinned. "Okay, boss." He tied the desperado to the back of one of the horses fixed to sage brush erratically growing between two boulders.

King mounted Maverick and glanced north, toward their destination and as luck would have it, Bell Grind. Two for one.

They rode until the dark prevented safe sure steps for the horses. King looked for a clearing with pine trees and boulders to provide a safe cover from three sides. Several minutes later a small fire kept the chill at bay. The Mexican's hands were secured with rope, and his ankles clenched together with his belt. Propped and bound to an Aspen he appeared to be unconscious. King removed a pouch of jerky and uncapped his canteen. He sniffed the beef and sneered. His stomach wouldn't handle the gristle. He drank the water, letting the coolness soothe his dry throat and coat his stomach.

He handed the jerky to Aubrey, who took the offering. Soon, the scent of smoked beef scented the air. King spread the saddle blanket, then a rolled blanket and sprawled onto the hard surface. The last time he'd slept on the ground, he'd been with her, the night after his supposed marriage. He'd let his heart open and fell in love with Emma Cody. She'd played him for a fool.

"King." He slowly peeled his eyelids open and saw a dead man standing in front of him. "I don't want to shoot you, beings you're my brother-in-law, but I will."

"You're supposed to be dead." Yet again, his mouth tasted like sawdust laced with pee. "I can make that happen."

"Yeah, I'm a ghost. You need to get up. My sister has been kidnapped by one of my gang members. We need to rescue her before she's..."

King jumped to a stand and glanced at Aubrey, snoring as if he slept at a luxury hotel. Their hostage remained bound to a tree. "Why should I trust what you say?"

"Considering you love her and all, I thought you were the best man for the job." Drake tilted his cowboy hat and narrowed his hazel eyes—the green and brown exactly like Emma's.

"I plan to take you to the sheriff's office, collect a finder's fee and get some of my payroll money back." His heart raced with the idea she could be in the hands of filthy outlaws. Perhaps he should let Drake take the lead, then hand him and the rest of the gang to the lawman.

"Can't get your money back without me." Drake grinned, like he thought he was funny.

"Emma returned to Fort Wayne with your parents." King ran his fingers over the oak handle of his pistol.

"No, she's been kidnapped." Drake's voice remained firm. "Life and death situation."

Aubrey held a knife to Drake's neck. "Want me to slice him? It'll be easier to take him to the sheriff."

"The longer you take, the more likely she'll be violated." Drake didn't twitch, but his throat bled from the scratch.

King shook his head at Aubrey, who lowered the knife, but stood ready. "I understand why you robbed my payroll, but why lie about Emma?"

"Felt it was part mine. Didn't get all of it." Drake rocked back on his boot heels. "Emma does need rescuing."

"The robberies were for revenge? Because I wouldn't let you become a partner."

"We knew you were a thief before you robbed us." Aubrey gathered his bedroll.

"Really, I just needed the money." Drake holstered his gun, believing King wouldn't be a threat, a misconception on his part.

"Was Emma a part of this from the start?" King's

stomach rebelled at the question, but his mind wanted to know the truth. His heart needed to hear a lie.

"No, she didn't know anything about my activities. You can imagine my surprise when we were going to rob the stagecoach, and I saw my baby sister holding a gun pointed at my head."

"Yes, imagine that." King's heart rate escalated with renewed energy and joy. She wasn't a criminal, just a liar.

"We were always close. Our parents traveled all the time, Emma and I were left alone with the house staff. I basically raised her, and she means more to me than my own life. Get on your horse and let's go save her."

"What did you do, dress one of the robbers in your clothes, shoot him and pass him off as a dead Jayden Drake?"

"Had to. Thought my death would make it easier for Rachel. Did Emma tell you I'm an outlaw?"

Aubrey led the horses closer but stopped. He cocked his head, intent on listening.

"Emma has more honor than you because she didn't tell anyone. As a matter of fact, she sacrificed herself to marry me." He removed the canteen from his saddlebag and doused his face.

"Not true. I saw you together at the Hayworth Rifle Contest. She loves you, not that you'd be my pick as a husband."

Aubrey snorted.

King used his arm to wipe his face. "Nor you as a brother-in-law."

"We really need to go." Drake pivoted. "Diego will slow us down."

"We need to be careful, trusting this one." Aubrey handed Maverick's reins to King.

"Right, both of them are liars. Who knows, maybe she's joined the gang."

Drake threw a fist, landing directly on King's right ear. He'd been lost in his own misery and moroseness for so many days and nights, it was almost a relief to feel pain. He acted like saving her would be a sacrifice, but he needed to see her and talk to her about her letter. That is, if she truly remained in Colorado.

"Don't ever talk about my sister like that. She was protecting someone she loves. She'd do the same for you." He glanced at Aubrey. "Probably not you, though."

"Where is the hideout?" King went to Diego and cut the rope.

"They moved camp when I went to Blair's Mine to see Bell." Drake climbed onto a roan.

"Bell was your informant?" King unfastened the belt on his prisoner's legs.

"I got to pee."

King wrapped a noose around Diego's neck. "You have three feet."

"Bell had contacts and could get the information."

"Paying customers, you mean?" He handed the rope to Aubrey. A moment later King helped Diego onto a horse and tied him to a saddle horn.

"Let's ride." Aubrey galloped, leading the prisoner's horse.

"Until I saw her holding a gun to Emma's kidney, Bell was a friend. We are two hours behind. We need to ride fast."

He rode beside Drake. "After we get Emma, you'll

go willingly to the sheriff, to account for your crimes?"

"Yes. Just help me save her."

****

"We're going upward instead of descending. The town is down the mountain not up." Emma unfastened the strap holding her pistol inside the holster.

Bell sighed. "Seventeen miles. I can tell you're not from this area. You'd know you have to go up before down. It's all winding."

She glanced around, granted all rock formations looked the same to her. Enormous in height, wide enough to hide a team of horses and could literally block sunlight, this sequence of boulders did not look familiar. On the return trip from Fort Collins, Henry kept them close to the edge of the mountain range. If only she could have remained on her honeymoon, none of this would have evolved. For the first time in her life she experienced defeat, having lost the most important battle.

"See the path up ahead, take the left fork."

"Are you certain. It doesn't appear to be a trail that has been frequented?" She glanced to her left, then to the right. A setting sun meant they'd traveled all day. If she had listened to her instincts, they'd be arriving in Pineview. Instead, they were further east, and she didn't have a clue how to get back to safety. The barrel of a gun pressed firm against her back, probably hers...yet another mistake. Blasted day was getting better and better.

Smoke billowed like a twister through the air as she rounded the corner. In front of them, in a clearing, stood a pine log shack. She didn't think the structure qualified as a cabin. One window was crudely cut from the side and a door held onto the face of the box by leather straps. A thin dark-haired man came outside. He was rather handsome with longish locks resting on his broad shoulders. Bell nudged the horse with her knees, which brought them in direct contact. His eyes were as dark as Black Bart's. Emma recognized him, one of the men from the stagecoach hold-up.

At the edge of the cabin stood a giant of a man holding a large wooden handle, stirring contents in a cauldron over an open fire. He wore a wide hat that covered the tips of his ears. He tilted the brim and gazed at her with a vacant blue-eyed stare. Unaffected by the appearance of two women, he continued to slowly push the paddle around in the vat.

"Ladies, are you lost?" The bandit's accent, French with a slight southern twang, rang through the acoustically sound expanse.

Before she could utter a word, Bell held out her blue bag. He automatically took the silk purse and set it on the ground. She extended both arms, and he assisted her down, clutching her to his frontside. His tongue went into her mouth, so far down Bell's throat muscles quickened with rapid movement. Was this man one of her customers?

Emma's nerve endings danced. "I'll be on my way. Good day to you. Bell, come see me when you arrive at Pineview."

A tug to Black Bart's reins, she nudged his sides. French's claw hands grabbed her ankle, hard enough the pressure went through her thin riding boot. A vice-like pain ripped through her leg.

"You do not go away," his loud voice echoed through the sparse trees. The giant stopped stirring the pot, removed the stick, and walked away from the fire.

"My name is Fredrick Ardoin. I'll be your host." He grinned and his handsomeness fell from his face, leaving an evil mask in its wake. Bell giggled and rubbed her hand across his chest, scrunching his off-white flounced shirt.

"I'm of no value to you." The calmness of her voice or her hand sliding along the side of her split skirt alerted him. He shoved Bell aside. Emma extracted the razor-sharp knife attached to her garter. The bandit twisted the knife from her hand.

A rider galloped into the glade, sliding off the back of his horse. Fredrick released her and turned. Emma punched her heels into Black Bart's sides and pulled on the left rein. Feeling the danger, he flew. She kept her head low to his neck, letting him weave in and out of the trees. She lifted up, shifting to the side of the saddle to avoid an overhanging branch. The slab of wood came out of nowhere, then pain and darkness.

Sunlight woke Emma. Something pierced the back of her neck. Bark. She was tied to a tree. The ropes were tight. She couldn't feel her arms and legs. Heat and pain encapsulated her left cheek. She breathed out her mouth and tried to move, but the ropes grew tighter. Although painful, she glanced to her right.

The giant used the board, which in all probability had smashed her face, to stir the pot. The frantic rider rested near the fire and loud snores came from his open mouth. A noise came from within the shack, a grunt, then a groan followed by a bang. The shack shook. She hoped the structure would fall down on their heads.

She rested her right cheek against her shoulder. What an end. She would die without Henry acknowledging that she did love him, true deep-down Romeo and Juliet type loved him.

"Eat!" A deep voice came from beside her.

She opened her eyes. The giant held a plate filled with a large fluffy biscuit and brown gravy. "My hands are tied." She shifted. "Throat...can't swallow. Rope to tight." Her head pounded, similar to an axe hitting wood thumping pain.

"No run?"

Emma held her head steady, refusing to give in to the desire to glance around for Black Bart. She forced her throat to swallow. A painful rub tightened the muscles. "No, won't run."

He set the plate on the ground beside her, withdrew a toothpick knife from the buckskin holder attached to his belt, and cut the rope's tie. Three times he circled the trunk of the tree before the end of the rope fell into his hand. She rolled her neck, then lifted her hands to massage her upper arms. Weak kneed, she dropped to the pine needles covering the earth.

"You run, I kill," he whispered with foul onion scented breath. An evil gleam replaced the vacant look. Two personalities, one large body.

She crossed her arms and nodded. He returned to his fire. She lifted the plate and cautiously broke off a piece of biscuit. Flakes fell onto her jacket, but the tasty bit melted in her mouth. She glanced at Paul Bunyan. His gaze focused on her. She dipped the next bit of bread into the brown, thick paste, proving to be as satisfying as the first bite.

Black Bart snorted. The sound came from behind her. She placed the plate on the ground and stood. "May I use the bushes to relieve myself?"

"I come."

"Fine, don't peek." Emma found bramble bushes opposite where Black Bart was hobbled. She walked deep into the brier, letting the sticky thorns pierce her clothing until she found a long branch reaching out into the deer path. The stem stretched beyond the normal, just the height of the giant's neck. Perfect. She lowered her split skirt, separated the undergarment hole and squat. Nothing. She focused on something other than his breathing. Nothing. "I can't go unless you turn your back."

"No."

"Then we'll be here for a lot longer, Mr..." Her thighs burned from holding them in the same position, and her back ached. She noticed a log nearby, close enough to rest on without alerting her guard. The bark prickled and the moistness was cool on her inner skin, well worth the effort. The foliage kept the limited sun out. Mustiness of the moss and earthy aromas invaded her senses. She contemplated picking up a bit of the cool green earth and holding it against her hot crusty face.

"Name is Peach."

"Okay, Peach." She hummed, waiting.

"You win," he groused and turned his back.

She smiled, urinated, then pulled up her skirt. Excess energy gave her the strength to run like a gazelle. The sprinted jump start would be her only advantage. An outraged Peach yelled, his tones bouncing around the rock faces. Head down, legs pumping, she carried on until she hit a wall of human flesh.

****

The bandit's hands were tied to the saddle horn, his ankles to the stirrups, and his bandana tied around his mouth, shutting off all vocalizations. He wasn't going anywhere. King mentally prepared for a showdown. With nothing to lose, he'd battle until death.

"Smoke, about three miles to the north." Aubrey pointed in said direction.

"Plan?" King tightened his grip on the reins.

Aubrey grinned. "You get shot for proposing such a crazy idea, and I take care of the sweet little widow Courtland. That's what I want from life, money and happiness. Got one, just need the other."

King ground his teeth together. Aubrey attempted to make him see a possible future. He could get killed trying to raid the Relay Gang with limited resources, or he could turn back and get a posse. Then he could go to Fort Wayne and get his wife.

Drake rode beside King. "Let's hobble the horses and scout the set-up of the camp."

"We'll get the Calvary, depending on the number of gang members present." He dismounted and tied Maverick to a branch. His horse snorted, being bound to a tree was insulting. King jerked the desperado's rope. "We'll come back for you and take you to jail."

"Let's go," Drake whispered.

The noxious scent of burning peat bricks drew them to the central location of the campsite. A large ape-like man stirred contents of a black pot over a roaring fire. A woman's shout came from the single building. A dark-haired tall man stomped from the small cabin. Another female, with a horse-hoof-sized bruise on the side of her face lifted a bite of food from a tin plate. The way she moved her hand with slow precise movements struck a chord of familiarity. King glanced at Aubrey and pointed to the right. Aubrey nodded and made a circle motion with his gloved hand.

King crept near the horses. Black Bart held the end position. Damn. Damn. Damn. Drake hadn't lied. The prisoner was Emma. By the bruises marring her face, his exquisite wife had been violated. Fear, anger, nausea roiled through his body. He held the line taut and sliced through the cord hobbling the horses, then wrapped the rope around his hand. Before he could chase them away, a scream ripped through the trees. He tapped the horses' hind ends. Due to the banshee awakening, or his nudge, they galloped into the dark.

King crossed a deer path. A rustling of leaves and sticks stopped him. He circled back and caught her. She punched and raised her knee, aiming for his privates. "Emma, it's me," he whispered.

"Henry." She ran her hands over his chest, then wrapped her arms around his neck. The hard uneven steps and breaking of branches announced her follower. Her red swollen face lifted. Fear glimmered in her eyes.

"Shh, it'll be fine. Come." He led her a few feet to a boulder. They crouched, waiting. He hadn't heard gunshots, but the elephantine stomp got closer. If he could subdue the man without making a ruckus, he could get her to safety. King motioned for her to stay put. She shook her head. He glared at her. Had she learned nothing the entire time they were together or any of the other times she'd been in peril? He narrowed his eyes. She bowed her head and gave a slight nod.

He wrapped the end of a rope around a small boulder, handed her a portion of the cord and pointed to the other side. She nodded. He ran across the short pathway, climbed to the edge of the rock, and pulled the cable around a stone to get leverage and waited. The man drew closer. At the precipice, King pulled the twine tight, catching the man across his lower legs. A great boom sounded as he landed. He knelt beside the man. The giant hit his head on a pointed rock. Blood formed beneath the skin, then he passed out. "Emma, unwrap the rope and bring it to me." She came around the rock and handed him the rope.

"Henry." She glanced into his eyes. He wanted to smooth the worry lines that existed, but not now. There were more gang members.

"We'll be fine, we'll talk later." King knotted the rope around the man's wrist, extended the twine to his legs and secured them. He wouldn't get out of the calf branding position. "Help me get him to the boulder." He pointed to a dug out.

"Peaches."

"What?"

"His name is Peaches."

"Let's roll Peaches under the rock." King used his hand, and Emma kicked the man until he rotated near the rock's edge.

"I need to find Aubrey."

"You're not leaving me here. I'm coming with you." She brushed off her hands and dabbed her cheeks. "Ouch!"

"How many are there?" He scanned the rest of her body, the bruise on her face and neck appeared to be the extent of her injuries. "Damn," he hissed under his breath. He would kill whoever hit her.

With shaking fingers, she tugged pieces of hair, smoothing the strands along the side of her bruised countenance. "A dark French man is the leader, Bell, one other man, and hog-tied Peaches over there. I didn't see any others. Who are they?"

"The Relay Gang, they've been robbing my payroll." He wanted to tuck her near his side and hold her forever, but anger still perpetrated his body. "What are you doing here? Why aren't you in Fort Wayne with Bambridge?"

"Your jealousy is unfounded. I love you. I'll always love only you, and I belong with you." If she hadn't gritted the words out through clenched teeth, the vow would have been easier to swallow and may have softened his attitude.

"Right, Emmet," King growled.

"Hear me out. I realize I've made a mistake. I want to be married to you. I didn't appreciate the way you went about marrying me. Like any other woman alive, I wanted love, romance, and a proposal on bended knee. You've never told me once that you love me. It was evident you had a fear of relationships, maybe because of your parents' history. Why should I believe you were committed to me? Intimacy was the basis for our marriage, and I enjoyed it, but now I want more from you, Henry." The hoarseness of her voice bounced off the stones.

"Stop. You two can do this touching reconciliation later. You'll draw the men with guns to your little alcove, and we'll be sitting ducks. I personally want to live another day." Aubrey tilted his hat back. "Mrs. Courtland, I'm Aubrey Carter, your obstinate husband's partner."

"He's not my husband."

"She's not my wife."

"It's been a while since I've seen a couple more married than you two." He grinned. "Marriage isn't a document, rather a union held together by shared love."

King shot a glance at Emma. She smiled. At least it looked like a smile as her face formed into a red mass on one side. Whoever abused her would die.

"There are three. One is Bell."

"We need her alive. She set Rachel up to take the fall for Jayden's death." She grimaced. "Jayden isn't dead. The man we buried wasn't him. He's robbing stagecoaches."

"I know. He's with us. We'll talk about this later. Now, we'll circle around the camp. Emma will stay with me. They'll be gathering horses, so we'll pick them off like foxes on a hunt."

"Got it. Meet back at our horses unless there's a problem, then shoot twice into the air." Aubrey removed the gun resting low on his right leg and rolled the cylinder around. "Let's go." He took off at a run in a southwest direction.

King held Emma's hand, jogged northeast and stopped where their horses were hobbled. He dropped her hand, extracted the Colt in his left holster, and handed the pistol to her. The clearing was vacant. No sounds came from inside the cabin. One chestnut colored horse munched on grass close to the building. The black pot bubbled, spewing a brown substance over the sides. Birds didn't chirp. No squeaking insects. The wind failed to blow the branches into a scratchy melody. Eerie quiet was a bad sign.

King caught her glance and tilted his head to his left. She nodded. They lightly stepped around a pine tree, past the rancid burned food, and stopped at the rear of the structure. He wiggled his finger indicating he would go around. "Stay." He mouthed.

She frowned but bowed her head. A quick glance right and left, he edged past her around to the front and inside the cabin. Empty. Back outside, he jogged to her. She lifted her eyebrows in question. He shook his head. She pointed to the outhouse. He nodded. Low to the ground, they edged toward the building. They stopped near a large walnut tree, and he motioned for her to remain there. Her glare said more than a frown or nod would have. He snickered and approached the outhouse.

A tug of the leather strap and the door flew open. No one was inside. Damn. Had he lost them? He listened for gunfire, hoping Aubrey caught at least one of them. Nothing. A touch to his shoulder, cold metal bumped against his flesh. He dropped to the ground, rolled, and cocked his Colt. Emma. He unfastened his jaws to convey his displeasure, when she pointed behind the outhouse, which shielded an opening in the side of the mountain. A cave.

"Guard the entrance, I'll see if I can find another way in," he whispered. She bobbed her head. He lightly tucked a strand of hair behind her ear. She turned away, but not before he noticed the glimmer of tears. "When this is over, we need to talk."

He climbed the face of the mountain, finding nature created hand and footholds. At a platform he stopped. Horses snorted and metal hooves clicked against rock. He removed his hat and climbed onto the edge of a boulder. Peering over the rim, he caught sight of Bell climbing onto Black Bart and a thin man holding the reins of a roan horse ready to flee. King eased down the backside of the large boulder and braced his legs in front of the horses. "Get off."

"Bell, you too." He held his gun steady on the outlaw. The man dismounted and edged his hand toward his weapon. King shot close to the gun, without hitting the pistol, but grazed the blackguard's hand.

"Toss it over to the side, and if you have a knife or another gun toss them."

The gun slid, bumping against a rock. Bell remained on Black Bart. Not taking his glance off the Frenchman, he said, "Get down, Bell. It's over."

"King."

He glanced at her.

"They took me hostage. I'm an unwilling victim." She blinked her long black lashes at him, but he wasn't swayed. This whore acquired and shared inside knowledge about his payroll delivery dates and times. Desperate men, needing the softness of a woman, would do anything, say anything to get comforting arms. "I didn't know what to do."

"Right, you're the sacrificial lamb."

Bell sneered in response and focused her stare behind him. Black Bart reared, and she fell onto the rocky ground. The Frenchman dived for his gun, at the same time King shot. The bullet hit the bandit in the gut, and he went face down in the dirt.

Black Bart sprinted along the path. Bell tugged her dress, covering the brown stained under drawers. King pushed the Frenchman onto his back.

Bell moved beside him. Her harsh indrawn breaths echoed in the alcove. "Is he dead?"

"Yes," King answered, looking upward at the rock cliff nearby.

"Your wife told me I had an inheritance from Jayden. Is that true?"

"Doesn't matter, you're going to jail."

"Why would she come all this way to tell me about the money?"

"Because she always helps the people she loves." He lifted the man and threw him on the back of the roan.

She snorted. "Bliss doesn't even know me."

"Don't know Bliss. My wife wasn't helping you, but Rachel." He extended his hand, and she took hold. He hoisted her onto the saddle behind the Frenchman, then walked around to the other side and removed the rope which attached the horse to the hobble-line. King wrapped the twine around her hands and tied her to the saddle horn.

"By giving me money? That's an odd way of showing love to someone." Bell glanced at the bond. "What are you doing, King?"

"Finishing what my wife started, taking you to jail for robbery, kidnapping, and conspiracy to murder." King grabbed the reins and led the horse along the path.

"His wife murdered him," Bell declared.

"The circuit court judge will determine guilt."

She shifted her leg.

"One move, Bell, and I'll shoot you through your cold, diseased heart."

Chapter 28

Emma slid down the rock front, snagging her split skirt on bramble and outreaching stones. She repositioned herself exactly where Henry had left her. She smiled. He called her his wife. They would be together again. She brushed the dust off her skirt and listened for horse hooves. At the thump, thump, thump of iron shoes on a rocky surface, she assumed the position of guard.

"Emma, come out. It's me."

Jayden. Her emotions warred inside her. She wanted to rush forward and embrace him, thankful that he lived. Yet, he'd robbed Henry and other people. He'd put lives at risk. She walked into the light. He might have killed someone. "You faked your death and left Rachel alone to birth your baby." She took another step. "Why?"

"I'm sorry."

"I don't understand why you did all those things."

"So many reasons, I'll explain when you visit me in prison." He grabbed her and rocked her like he had when she was a child. A method of comforting her after she'd taken a spill, or when her feelings had been hurt.

At the crack of a shot Jayden slumped onto her, and they toppled to the ground.

"Emma," Henry shouted.

"Jayden," she screamed.

Gunfire continued to pit the ground around them. Henry drew his pistol and returned fire. She rolled her brother onto his back, an exit bullet hole near his heart gushed blood. Maintaining a flow of crossfire, Henry tugged her to the side of the cabin.

"My brother." She struggled to get footing.

"Shh, I'll get him." He ran along the edge of the clearing.

The roan carrying Bell and the Frenchman took off at a trot. Black Bart found shelter behind a boulder. Henry secured a hold on Jayden and dragged him to the side of the building. Emma removed her jacket and pushed the material between Jayden's shirt and the gaping hole in his chest.

"Is he alive?" Henry reloaded his pistol.

"Shallow breaths." She wiped her eyes, snatched Jayden's revolver and crawled behind Henry. "Go, I'll cover you."

He kept rapid fire directed toward the shadow and ran to a clump of brush, closer to the shooter. Bullets pinged off stone, rock remnants sprayed through the air. Holding both guns, she fired toward the sparked area. The outlaw stood and turned toward her. Henry shot, hitting him in the head. He plummeted over the boulder, flipped and landed face up on the ground.

She bent over Jayden, heaving racking sobs. Henry dropped beside her. "It's over."

She turned and collapsed into his arms.

"Let's go home." Henry tucked a bloody strand of hair behind her ear. She nodded.

He untied Peach's legs and secured him on top of the chestnut horse behind another dead outlaw. Jayden's body went across another horse. A few minutes into their ride, they caught up with Bell trying to dislodge Fredrick.

"It's over, Bell."

"Bliss, King doesn't believe I'm innocent," Bell whined.

"Bliss?"

"My lady-of-the-evening name is Road Ta Bliss," Emma mumbled.

"I hope I didn't hear you right. Come on, let's find Aubrey." Henry wrapped his arm around Emma's waist and tugged the horses' reins.

The circuit judge will be here next week, think he could marry us? She held the words on the edge of her tongue. She'd lectured him not more than an hour ago about love and romance, the idea might be a little overwhelming for him. Instead, she let him hold her and ignored the pain his coat created on her bruised face. She could endure the discomfort.

Aubrey waited beside their horses. "Mine got away. I heard shots from your side. I see you landed a couple." He lifted the head of the Frenchman and let his noggin drop. "Bell, how ya doin'?"

She snarled.

"Bell, you were the gang leader. Are there anymore we need to track down?" Henry asked. Before she could answer, horse hooves thundered on the path. He shoved Emma forward, her nose hit the saddle horn. He covered her with his body and maneuvered Maverick behind an Aspen. The white bark stark against their dark clothing provided a clever cover. He drew his Colt from its holster. Quick thought and action, so fast and he was all hers.

Bell, unscathed, remained sitting on the roan horse

in the middle of the clearing. Aubrey ducked behind his horse.

"It's Black Bart," Emma whispered.

"How do you know?"

"His breathing, he has a bit of a wheeze. I need to read about horses and ailments. I think he'd be a great racehorse if we could control the wheeze." She twisted in the saddle and kissed his lips, wishing they could be alone.

Her faithful steed stopped in front of the tree and neighed. She smiled at Henry, slid from Maverick, and rubbed the side of Black Bart's beautiful equine face. He nuzzled her neck and blew out a grass scented breath. She walked around him and pulled a sugar cube from the bag and handed him the treat.

"Is that Black *Killer* Bart?" Aubrey asked.

King nodded.

Aubrey laughed. "The lady has a way with two and four legged animals."

He glared at his friend. The trip down the mountain proved to be uneventful. They were within a mile of Pineview when darkness enveloped the land, but they kept going. They arrived at the sheriff's office and handed over two dead and two live bandits, plus Bell the leader of the Relay Gang.

Rachel, liberated from the pokey, joined Treasure, Maggie Mae and Danny at the hotel.

"We need to return to the Drakes." He winked at his wife.

Emma nodded, tears choking her. "I know."

At the outskirts of Pineview they collected the horse, carrying Jayden's body, from Aubrey. "Thanks, Aubrey. I'll be in the office tomorrow around nine."

"Yep. Looks like I get to attend your wedding this time." Aubrey laughed.

Emma lifted in her saddle. "Thank you. I appreciate all that you've done for us."

Aubrey nodded and nudged his horse into a gallop.

A mile from the homestead, King guided Maverick closer to her. "I know you were on the rock cliff."

"I heard a shot and didn't want to…I'd as soon as be shot dead instead of losing you."

"Damn, you do know how to take the steam out of my engine. I had a very good mad going, and I wanted to teach you a lesson. Instead…" He pushed her hair behind her ear, revealing her face, wishing he could take the pain away.

"We were meant to be together." She inhaled. "I can't sleep without you."

"I've had a little trouble sleeping myself." He stopped their horses. "I understand your concern about vows and marriage considering what your sister-in-law went through, but I promise you this, Emma Lauren Cody Courtland, there isn't another woman who could ever tempt me the way you do. There isn't another woman who I could possibly love as much as I do you."

"You finally said the words." She kissed him. "Ouch."

"Do you want me to take to you to the doctor?"

Black Bart pranced sideways. "No, thank you, it's just a bruise and will heal in a few days." She pulled a few strands of hair forward.

He halted her hand. "Don't. I don't want your precious face covered."

A moonless night sheltered Rachel's house. "I'm a little apprehensive."

He dismounted and opened the barn door, and she rode inside the slightly illuminated interior. He placed his hands on her waist. She rested her hands on his shoulders, and he lowered her, slowly, to the ground. "I'm sorry, but with warmer weather we need to put your brother underground."

She tilted her head. "We don't have a casket."

"We do, sort of. Sam was making a chest for Danny. It's in the shed."

"King?" Sam's voice came from the open barn door.

"Yes. We must bury Jayden Drake. Will it be okay to use the toy box you're building?"

"Yes. Do you need help?"

King glanced at her. She shook her head. "No, thank you, Sam."

"Thank you. Good night, Sam." She used her sleeve to dab her face. "I might as well get shovels. At least this time we'll be burying the real Jayden Drake."

"Who died trying to save you. At the end, he wanted to confess his transgressions and admit his wrongdoing." He held her close, trying to ease her pain.

Hours later, as dawn was peeking, he and his wife rode toward their home.

She yawned. "We don't have a place to sleep do we?"

"One bed is all that we need."

"Yes. Finally, we'll be able to rest."

They stabled the horses, and then gave them fresh water and extra feed. He held her hand and led her upstairs to the main bedroom. She gasped. "You bought the iron headboard I was admiring in Fort Collins."

"My wife wanted a fancy bed. I was going to give

her a fancy bed." He kissed her forehead. "Love, I'm not a romantic, but I do love you." Taking her hand into his, he bent on one knee.

She smiled and self-consciously drew her hair forward.

"Emma, Emmet, Road Ta Bliss, will you marry me?"

She sighed. "Yes, Henry Courtland, I'll marry you and love you until the end of time."

Chapter 29

Emma wrapped a cotton robe tightly across her chest and tiptoed on bare feet across the terrace outside their bedroom and stood beside Henry. "What are you doing out here?"

"Enjoying the view and a cigar." He tugged her to his left side, draping his arm across her shoulders.

"Your last cigar, forever." She glanced at the gold band, which hadn't left her finger. "Henry, my new honest-to-god husband."

"Yes?"

"Was it really necessary to examine my signature on the marriage license at the private ceremony yesterday?"

"Just wanted to make sure I was marrying Emma Cody this time."

She giggled and wrapped her hand around his arm. "You've created a beautiful home."

"We did together. If we put our minds together, we can create wonderful things." He lifted he hand and kissed it gently on the palm.

"I agree." A baby, she'd love to create his baby.

"What was your favorite bedtime story?"

She chuckled. "As usual, you have an impeccable memory. *The King of the Golden River*, by John Ruskin. It had mountains, the Black brothers, a dwarf, farming in Treasure Valley and promises that were kept."

"You're such a romantic." He kissed her cheek.

"I didn't want to believe in love or marriage until I met you." She rested her head against his shoulder. "Now, I'm a true believer."

Wrapped in his embrace, she glanced over the valley. The full moon speared the plains with its golden haze. The crickets, looking for mates, serenaded all lovers, creatures, and humans. The lone wolf added to the symphony. "Promise me something."

Henry blew out a puff of smoke, making a gray circle in the dark night. "Anything for you, love." He tugged at her waist drawing her closer if that were possible.

"If I die, please do let me go." She wrinkled her nose at the memory of her first day in Pineview.

He chuckled. "Same for me." He extinguished the cigar and tossed the vial stick over the brick edging of the terrace.

Emma sighed. "Rachel got a letter from a lawyer. Jayden put his money in a bank in Denver, guess he didn't trust Morgan Palinurus either. I'm glad Palinurus didn't get Rachel's house. Rotten banker."

Black Bart whinnied and galloped around the corral. Brandy's white coat glistened as she trotted beside him. What was Maverick eating in the other corral, the metal spikes holding the fence together?

Henry kissed the top of her head. "Rachel sent Black Bart's lineage papers, as our official wedding gift. My mother arrives tomorrow to stay for an extended visit."

"What? Your mother? Why didn't you tell me before now? There's so much to do." She pushed against his chest and lifted her nightgown, prepared to run.

He grabbed her arm and swung her back into the nook of his shoulder. "There's nothing to do. We have a guest room. She'll be spending most of her time with her first grandchild."

She snuggled. "Danny has settled in. Do you think he'll call us Mother and Father?"

He chuckled. "He has a mind of his own, I'd anticipate some moniker."

"Well, as the new Mrs. Courtland, I need to make a positive impression. My mother says, 'a first impression is a lasting impression'. I want your mother to like me."

"She will. Who doesn't like you? Come on inside, and I'll help you get that impressive natural brilliant glow."

"Lulu doesn't like me."

"The bar maid?"

"You call the soiled doves, bar maids?"

"Soiled doves?" he snorted.

She twisted from his arms. "Leaving now."

He drew her into an embrace. His cigar scented breath brushed the side of her face. "Lulu doesn't like you because the first time she got close enough to touch me, you pushed an arrow through my cigar and unseated her." He kissed her cheek and nuzzled her ear.

"I did enjoy the splitting of the cigar. Now that I know about the unseating of Lulu, I like the memory. Thank you." She grinned, stood on tiptoes and kissed him, a lush, lip crushing kiss. "Now, about that natural glow."

Her stomach quivered with need and anticipation

of what was to come. "Also, I'm entering a Colt shooting contest next week."

"No, you're not."

"As reigning sharpshooter, I need to keep the honor alive."

"As my wife, you'll not parade around a bunch of randy men who want to shoot something for money."

She stepped back and crossed her arms. "As your wife, I respect your opinion, but the contest is something I want to do, and I believe I'll be successful." She tapped her chin. "I'll enter as Emmet Courtland."

He tilted his head and lifted an eyebrow. "For each shooting contest you enter, I get a box of cigars to smoke at my leisure."

She snorted. "Blackmail, Henry?"

"Negotiation, Emma." His beautiful blue-green eyes glittered.

"The cigars will kill you."

"Not as much as seeing strange men ogle my wife's tight rear encased in men's trousers."

She smiled. His jealousy, still unfounded, was adorable. "This one will be Emmet Cody's retirement entry." She kissed his pursed lips.

He returned the kiss. "What if Courtland-Carter Land Development creates a sharpshooting contest for women only?"

She hugged him, smashing her face into his chest. "I love you, Mr. Courtland."

"And I love you, Mrs. Courtland."

A word about the author...

jj inherited her name and creativity from her grandmother. A love of literature and adventure takes jj to many wondrous places. Storytelling is her passion, an essential part of her world, and she wants to share the magic. Please enjoy pieces of her life through her tales.

@jjkellerauthor
https://romancewithjjkeller.wordpress.com

Thank you for purchasing
this publication of The Wild Rose Press, Inc.
For questions or more information
contact us at
info@thewildrosepress.com.
The Wild Rose Press, Inc.
www.thewildrosepress.com